RYKA AUKI

HE

MELE

A HILO

TOPSIDE
SIGNATURE
NEW YORK

Library of Congress Cataloging-in-Publication Data is available.

ISBN   978-1-62729-008-1 (hardcover)

ISBN   978-1-62729-007-4 (paperback)

ISBN   978-1-62729-009-8 (ebook)

10 9 8 7 6 5 4 3 2 1

Cover design by Michele Rosenthal • michelerosenthal.com

HE MELE A HILO

To my uncle, my grandmothers,
and the Singing Bridge.

ACKNOWLEDGEMENTS

Thank you to Robert Morgan, Archie Ammons, Phyllis Janowitz, and Ken McClane. Thank you to Jean Jenkins, Tom Léger, StormMiguel Florez, and Richard Becker. Thank you to Steph. And thank you to my family, my family, and my family.

"The best thing about fishing is
that you never learn it all."
—Mike Sakamoto

Residents of Hawai'i speak in a dialect called Hawaiian Pidgin English. Use the glossary in the back of the book, and soon you'll feel like a local!

Mahalo!

Chapter 1

HARRY WAS KICKING IT AT THE STORE WHEN HE MET MR. Yates. Actually, he didn't know it was Mr. Yates at first, until he was invited for coffee and found out that yes indeed this man was Mr. Steve Yates, the very high mukka-mukka computer guy who went just buy one huge chunk of Hamakua coastline.

Mr. Yates had come in for buy fishing supplies. He never know much about fishing—he mentioned something about needing cheese for bait—and the girl helping him was more interested in taking care her 2-inch Hello Kitty fingernails than telling him that local fish no like cheese.

Was kind of sad, so Harry decided for help the haole out, at least for starters get him set up with one bamboo pole for catching weke or aholehole or something near Hilo Bay. But then the haole he said he wanted for go night fishing off the cliff in his backyard.

"You? Night fishing? Off one cliff Hamakua side?" Harry blinked. "Sure if you like be one dead stupid haole go right ahead, but then everyone going say, 'Man that was one stupid haole.'"

Haole man looked at his shoes and Harry thought, well of course the stupid haole going to get pissed off—after all he one stupid haole—but suddenly haole man laughed.

"Well, stupid's why I'm here, right?"

It never make sense, and it made even less sense when Mr. Steve Yates invited Harry over to his place on Wednesday for coffee and for talk story about fishing.

One hundred times out of one hundred Harry would have said no, but this haole seemed so strange that he thought whatevers, not much happens on Wednesday. And so he shrugged, and Mr. Yates gave him his card and left.

Once he was gone, Hello Kitty girl looked over and asked Harry if the haole man stay going fishing, why never he buy any fishing stuff? And they both laughed at the stupid haole.

When Harry got home, he was hungry. He went to the fridge, grabbed what he was going cook and was searching for some frozen rice for microwave when the phone rang. Since he was busy, he figured it was Nona. Whom it was.

"Hey Harry, what you stay doing?"

"Cooking."

"Cooking? What?"

"Nothing special."

"So you going fry eggs."

"No!"

"No lie, Harry. If I no cook for you, that's all you'd eat— fried eggs and leftover rice."

"Oh, you think you so smart?"

"Shut up, Harry," Nona said. "And put back the eggs. I go come over with some chicken."

Harry's girlfriend made best chicken he had ever tasted. Maybe was something about the marinade—the ginger or rice wine, or maybe was how she chopped green onions—

or maybe the coating that was so crispy on the outside with just the right creaminess underneath. Auwe! Broke da mouth!

Harry tossed the eggs back in the fridge and scrubbed out the rice cooker. Good for make fresh rice for eat with Nona's yummy chicken! He washed the rice and started the cooker. Since had some time before Nona came over, he looked around for something to do. He could go outside and pull that damned nut grass that kept wrecking his lawn. Or maybe he finally could get those bananas down from the tree before they got too ripe for eat.

Then, he smelled his rice beginning to steam. Of course! He would make rice balls!

* * *

Nona Watanabe was still trying for learn hula. After three years' practice she still couldn't get her feet and hands to match. Actually, nothing about her matched. Her house never match her Chevy never match her blouse never match her shorts. Even her slippers never match, but at least that was intentional—a gift from her rascal nephew Darin in Honolulu. Her favorite color combination was orange, purple, and green, even though her family had no trace of Filipino. Okay, maybe a little Filipino, but no one ever talked about that.

Whenever the halau danced, her kumu, Noelani Choi, put her in the back row. No one ever said it was because she was fat, bad, or ugly—and Noelani was far too sweet to even think something so awful—but Nona knew her place. Just because someone stay one terrible dancer doesn't mean that she's stupid. She also knew that of all the beginning dancers, she had been there the longest, except for Frances Silva, who had been at least eighty years old for as long as Nona knew her, and couldn't always remember the steps.

All she wanted was for blend in with the rest of the halau! How many times Nona felt like crying, not just for herself, but because felt she went ruin another good performance! She never like be one star or get one solo, or even get anyone's attention. She just wanted to match.

Harry said none of this mismatched business mattered. He said orange and purple and green was beautiful, like the island itself. Nona wished that she could believe him. But Harry was a man who could barely fry eggs.

As she watched the oven, Nona tried to hum the song she was already supposed to know for the upcoming show at the Royal Hawaiian Hotel. She faltered, stopped, and started again, as the smell of her perfect chicken began to soak through the kitchen like the silky sunshine on one lazy Saturday afternoon.

* * *

Meanwhile in Pahoa, Kamakawiwoʻole Schulman was neither eating his papaya croissant nor sipping his coconut latte. Instead, he was on the phone, arguing with his brother-in-law.

"Listen, Mel," his brother-in-law said. "What kind of life is that for you over there? Yes, yes, I know you changed your name to Kamasutra or something. Don't pull that Baba Ram Dass crap with me. The point is that your sister and I are worried about your diabetes and that we're not going to be able to check up on you. And remember what the doctor said?"

"Yes, the doctor said lots of things. Thank you and sister so much for worrying, but could it also be that you need me to help finance that apartment complex in Reseda that you are so eager to buy?"

His brother-in-law yelled something awful and hung up.

For Kamakawiwoʻole, or Kam as he would eventually be called, flipping Reseda apartment complexes was the last thing he wanted to think about. If he were worried about any real estate at all, it was the three-room house with the termite-infested porch that he had just rented. But even that was minor compared to the delicious papaya croissant he was finally eating and the thick, fragrant air that was infusing his lungs.

Just a year ago, Mel Schulman was in the Valley, browsing through some used CDs. One of them had a picture of some impossibly large man in a skirt named, of all things, Israel. Israel Kamakawiwoʻole.

Now with Mel being Jewish, this seemed very odd, and more than a little offensive. After all, what's a big pork-eating Hawaiian guy doing with a name like Israel? Even his nickname, "Iz" bothered him.

"Iz? Is what?" he snickered, but the pothead working behind the counter protested.

"Aw, dude, don't be hating, dude. You have got to check out Iz. The dude is awesome, dude."

Despite this incisive review, Kam bought the CD.

And of course he thought it was awful. Sure, the guy had a sweet voice, but the music was painfully simple: I-IV-V progression, major key, toss in a few 7th chords. But then he heard it. IT. That song in his mind that he could almost hum, but couldn't name. A song he had heard before, and here it was again. In Israel.

Kam slapped at a mosquito. He looked out into the lazy fall of green, the mosquitoes, the latte, and even the still-warm phone. He could almost hear harmonies blending as inseparable as the morning and the dew. He heard a mynah bird and something stirred within him, something that needed clear skies and a friendly trade wind. Kam sat there, lost and wondering where his Promised Land might be.

* * *

If anyone had told Noelani Choi that she was lost, she would simply have attributed it to lack of faith. It would be a graceful, lilting reply, familiar as a schoolyard song that is as old as its singers are new.

Noelani's hula was an extension of that faith. Twenty years ago, Noelani's mother brought her to Aunty Kapolinahe Kahakunoe and said, "My daughter loves to dance."

And Noelani danced, almost immediately. Everything she learned—the music, the history, and the language—seemed grow within her, thrive within her, until it was impossible to imagine that she ever had to learn it at all.

As she grew older, it was clear that Noelani was to be gorgeous, blessed with classic Hawaiian features. Deep eyes, proud chin and full lips. Her hair grew long and wavy, cascading over her smooth, nut-brown shoulders. It was only natural that she became Aunty Kahakunoe's pride and joy.

For eighteen years, Noelani loved hula. But then, something began to feel dishonest and wrong. Maybe it started earlier than that, because even back small kid time, even when Noelani enjoyed being the little keiki who danced better than the rest, she recalled how all the girls her age, and even the older ones, were still in the beginner class, trying to learn the most basic moves. She watched them talking together, struggling together, hearing Aunty praise her star student together.

Noelani would try to fit in, maybe try not be so perfect,

sometimes even not practicing or learning the music. And yet, each time, something inside her wouldn't let her fail. Something at the last moment would always save her—a power, a presence almost outside herself, that seemed to blossom in the judge's or the audience's eyes.

Even Aunty was fooled. "'Lani, when I look at you, I know that the future of hula is in the best of hands," she would say.

Yet even back small kid time, was never fair. Most people never have enough leg strength, or flexibility, or rhythm, let alone one intuition of how the moves all fit together. Not everyone could learn the Hawaiian, and even when they did, only Noelani could get the lilt and intonation just right. And kids, they get all jealous li'dat. Noelani knew when she had her birthday party at Lili'uokalani Park, the only reason the others went go is because Aunty made it one halau activity. And although Noelani was hurt, it never hurt that much. And that went hurt her more. Because was true. Friends, shave ice, passion fruit rainbow cake, even Hello Kitty—was nothing to her compared to the dance.

Why? From where had her dancing come? Her parents never even like music. So why? Had to be for one reason, this gift—but from who, why, and was she even worthy?

So finally, Noelani prayed.

Chapter 2

THE TALE OF THE SORRIEST MUSUBIS

Nona arrived at Harry's house with the Tupperware full of chicken. Harry's house was easy to spot. His yard was always preened and sculpted. Craggy rocks and immaculate bonsai trees guarded the front, while fruit trees, orchids and anthuriums made music in the back. Nona thought about her own frumpy kine looking house with the jungle weeds and felt a little ashamed.

"Hey Nona!" Harry ran out and gave her a hug.

Nona was still a little shocked that someone could be so happy to see her.

Nona had known Harry back when he used to drop off his two kids at school before work and picked them up afterwards. Always one smiley kine guy, he would say hello and talk story when he had the chance. About the kids, mostly, how rascal they were, and the next trip the family was taking. Harry was a good storyteller and even though she never actually had tutored his kids, she felt in some ways that she knew his kids better than her own students.

Then his kids left the school and so did he, though of course she really didn't think much about it at the time. Still, something must have made Harry memorable since, when years later, when she read the obituary for his wife, she felt as if she had lost someone she had known, too.

A couple of months after the funeral, Nona ran into Harry at Sack n' Save. He was limping and bent over like one tomato plant needing one pole. He waved and tried to smile, but all he could say was, "Still not used to shopping alone."

"You can shop with me, then," Nona said.

And Harry did.

Over time Harry would call her for go shopping, or maybe for drive over to Leung's for eat saimin, or just talk story about old times or what Harry's kids were up to now on the mainland or how Nona's hula was going.

And then one day he said, "I think you're beautiful," and they realized that they were in love.

Anyway, Nona brought in the chicken and Harry told her since that this was such a nice day, why they no go someplace for a picnic? Nona nodded and the two of them packed their food and a goza mat and drove down to Kolekole Beach.

Just a few miles north of Hilo is Kolekole Beach Park. Kolekole lies at the bottom of a deep, forested gulch. Between the Hamakua surf and the river and the rain, the grass is usually wet, so local people usually eat in the pavilion with the charcoal grill and the rusty mossy roof. But Nona and Harry both preferred to eat beneath the sky, and could usually find one nice place outside.

Today it was a big flat rock by the river, still warm from the day. Harry rolled out the goza mat, Nona opened her

Tupperware, and there were the yummy pieces of chicken that Harry had been thinking about since Nona's phone call.

Then Harry brought out a Tupperware of his own.

"What—eggs?" Nona teased.

"No! Try look, Nona, I made them special!"

Harry opened the Tupperware and Nona tried not to laugh as she beheld what were the sorriest-looking musubi she had ever seen.

All different shapes and sizes; some were vaguely sphere-like, while others were freeform and somewhat harder to describe. Harry had even tried to stuff some with ume, though the pink spots on the outside revealed that the salted plums weren't quite in the middle of the rice.

"Hey, I tried my best—no laugh—I'm only one quarter Japanese, you know!"

But Nona couldn't help it. It was almost as bad as the "crispy potato salad" incident, when Harry never realize that the potatoes had to be boiled first.

Seeing Harry's expression, Nona tried to eat a rice ball without laughing. Still, the rice fell out of her hands.

It wasn't her fault. You see, rice balls aren't really balls. Rice balls, or musubis, or onigiris (on the mainland) are really triangles, and this is important because then you can eat the rice from corner to corner before you get to the middle and the dang ting won't fall apart.

Harry tried to eat one, and of course it fell apart as well.

"Here, give me your hands," Nona instructed.

Harry put his hands out and Nona dumped her tea on them.

"Hey! You trying for burn me?"

"You have to wet your hands first, or the rice will stick."

"Oh." This was news to Harry.

"Now, pick up a musubi."

Harry did so and Nona placed her hands over his.

"You make the triangle like this. Put one hand over the other—no, *sideways*, like this—and squeeze," she said. Then she shifted his grip and guided his hands over the rice. "And squeeze. Again. See?"

"Oh wow! Just li'dat?"

"Just li'dat. Now you try make one yourself."

The two of them sat making musubis on the warm rock at Kolekole Beach Park, as the sun slipped away from a cloud and the green ferns and philodendrons rippled with the rush of the river against the incoming waves. You won't believe me, but afterward, as they ate Harry's formerly sorry musubis and Nona's perfect chicken, even the mosquitoes left them alone.

*   *   *

Mosquitoes are just like people—they get tired of eating the same thing over and over. Notice who always complains about mosquitoes—the tourists and visitors. Mosquitoes don't seem to bother the locals much. In fact, when college students come back Hawai'i for Christmas, and the mosquitoes attack them, all the cousins make fun because it's a sure sign that they've been away too long.

To the mosquitoes, Kamakawiwo'ole was one big exotic Kosher-style buffet line. He had tried everything from OFF! to mosquito punks to Avon's Skin-So-Soft, but the mosquitoes kept coming back for more. In fact, mosquitoes were the reason that he went out to Hilo that morning, because he was fixing his back porch and the Pahoa store was out of OFF! One of the hippies at the coffee shop suggested a macrobiotic diet and meditation as the most karmically pure way to attain an agreement with the little creatures, but Kam simply wanted them dead. So that day, he went to Hilo.

As usual, Hilo was raining, and when Kam drove into the KTA Supermarket parking lot, the weather pretty much matched how he felt inside.

Here he was in paradise, and what? His family had all but disowned him, and though that made no difference to him financially, he had come to Hawai'i to gain something positive, not to lose anything.

But in Pahoa, he hadn't made too many friends. They were willing to talk about, and even to demonstrate which process or philosophy they were studying, but no one was really open about who they were. What about their families, their friends? He scratched at a mosquito bite. It seemed so strange that someone would offer to give him a kukui nut enema, yet wouldn't share where she grew up.

Intimacy

This was not at all what he had imagined, and nothing like the unwordable warmth he got from listening to that Iz guy. He went to the store and bought his OFF! and cold soda. He didn't notice the Japanese lady in the kamaboko aisle asking if him he was feeling okay, or the Filipina check-out girl saying mahalo. Walking back to his car, a truck stopped gently to let him pass, but it didn't register.

He didn't want to return to Pahoa, but he didn't know where else to go. So he took out his phone and sat on a bench. He actually thought about calling his sister, but by God's grace his cell phone battery was dead.

Kam glanced at the community bulletin board on the wall behind him. A lot of people were selling rusty cars. One was advertising a used futon. Another invited everyone to a hula demonstration that was being held at the Royal Hawaiian Hotel.

Kam finished his soda, tossed the can, and pulled the flyer off the wall.

On this flyer was the most beautiful woman that Kam had ever seen.

*   *   *

Harry and Nona, of course, were already there. Nona always wanted to get to the performances a little early, just to make sure she made it on time. As the other women arrived, however, Harry put his hands in his pocket and looked down. Nona had worn the wrong muʻu-muʻu.

Nona looked at the others, then at herself. She had worn the blue muʻu-muʻu with the green trim, while the others had worn the orange and bright red. Nona tried biting her lip, but that didn't make her feel any better. Ignacio Viramontes looked at her with a stink eye, snorted, and went back to talking to Betty Manibog, no doubt about her.

Harry watched Nona start shaking and put his arm around her. "Come, Nona, its still early. Let's go back and get the orange muʻu-muʻu. Come."

Nona lived up the mountain, and there was no way they'd make it back in time. Both of them knew this, but Harry was not going to let Nona stand there and be laughed at by Betty Manibog. And Nona? She just couldn't face her kumu right now. She rubbed her eyes and face with her hands, and the make-up she had spent almost a full hour applying smeared across her face like ohelo jam. Harry pulled off his T-shirt to let her wipe her face and blow her nose. He stroked Nona's hair as they walked past the banyan trees to his car. Then he opened the door for her and closed it gently after.

As they drove off, Nona saw one old Hawaiian lady walking to the performance. For a split second, Nona made eye contact with her before they pulled away. And in that moment, there was peace.

*   *   *

Meanwhile, Kam had just found a shady place on the grass. Generic slack key guitar drifted over the PA as the members of a band were unloading and setting up the heads, cabinets, mikes, assorted stands, cables, more cables, and effects loops.

Kam smiled. No matter how different the music was, no matter where it was played, or the style, or the language, setting up and taking down was the same. Somewhere in the Royal Hawaiian parking lot waited an old van or pick-up truck, much like the one he'd had years ago in Los Angeles, faithfully waiting for its owners to come back after the show, laden with crates, boxes, and cases full of the stuff they used to make the music.

After a few minutes, the slack key ended, and the band cleared the stage. Kam searched for the woman in the flyer. Part of him was already resigned to the possibility that the woman had been simply added to the flyer to garner more interest in the show. Still, the breeze was nice, and it kept those damned mosquitoes away. At the very least, he had a reason to be out of Pahoa.

Then he saw Noelani Choi.

Without any introduction or warning, she picked up the largest gourd Kam had ever seen and slammed it to the stage.

Thoom! Then the rhythm. *Thoom!*

–slap- Thoom thoom-slap-!

Noelani alternately pounded and slapped the ipu as her dancers made their way to the grassy stage. Noelani's voice seemed to be dancing, in front of them, guiding them as surely as if she had taken each one by her hand.

And then, the dancers, in their blue and green muʻu-muʻus, began to sway.

Thoom! –slap- Thoomthoom! -slap-!
Thoom! –slap- Thoomthoom! -slap-!

Here, in the chant, the breath, the dancers, was what Kam had felt before. But again, he couldn't understand it. He looked first at the dancers, then back at the crowd. Some of them were tourists—this was a hotel, after all—but many more of them seemed to be regular folks from Hilo, out enjoying an afternoon—perhaps watching a niece or grandson perform.

What that exactly meant, he didn't know. All he knew was that here, against the blue sky and the Hilo Bay, that part of him was home.

At the set break, Kam wandered to the bathroom and found himself standing next to the band's bass player, a big brown guy with broad shoulders and eyes like a girl's.

He asked if his band were playing the next set.

"Yeah. For the first set the kumu likes to do the old stuff—you know all the chanting li'dat—then we help out with the more contemporary kine stuff."

"It must be real tough setting up your equipment with the rain."

The big guy exhaled.

"You said it, brah—you play in one band, too?

"Not anymore. But I used to play in Hollywood, a long time ago."

"Hey, all right. My name Jonathan, but people call me Jonny-Boy."

Kamakawiwoʻole thought about how he should introduce himself. For some reason, he knew that if he told the guy his new legal name, he would seem like a flake. So he replied, "My name is Kam."

Jonny-Boy shook himself off, zipped, and flushed.

"Gotta go—come visit after we pau!" He washed his hands and left.

Kam thought to himself—pow? Then he remembered. *Pau* was Hawaiian for finished.

✗ sex   <u>And he did.</u>

*   *   *

Soon after Harry and Nona left the parking lot, Harry got a call. Was Steve Yates.

"Hey Harry, remember me? The store? I was wondering if you wanted to come by tonight to—how do you say it—talk story?"

Harry told him that it was not really the best time—he and his girlfriend were feeling a little bit down.

"Yes. I can hear it in your voice. I'm sorry."

"Yeah, you know it goes."

Harry was about to close the phone when Steve said, "Hey! Tell you what. Why don't you bring her, too?"

Harry paused, then shrugged.

"Sure, why not?"

He said this before asking Nona because right now she would say no to anything, especially going to one strange haole's house. Still, nothing he knew could bring her out of this mood, and there was something about Yates that told him that visiting was the right thing to do.

"Hey, Nona, we go visit my friend's house."

She glared. "Who? Ted Kazama? I no like—he always showing us his kukui nuts. Plus he get all those naked lady posters on top his walls." Ted was an auto mechanic.

"No, no, not Ted Kazama—that crazy haole I was talking about. That Steve Yates guy."

"Steve Yates!? How can? I not ready."

"What? You get on one nice muʻu-muʻu, you get makeup in da bag, we get food." Harry stroked Nona's hair. "Look, if junk, we go home!"

The two of them drove up Highway 19, past Hilo, past Ninole, and made a right turn on a road that neither of them had ever noticed before. A couple minutes of driving led them through nothing but jungle and more jungle.

"Eh, you sure this is the right road?" Nona asked.

Harry lolled his head to the side. "Yates said the path is kind of hard to follow. You know how these rich haoles are—always putting their houses where no one can find."

"How you know? You went ever visit one rich haole before?"

"Of course! One time I went George Hamilton's house for deliver one package."

"What? You went see him?"

"No, I went just giveʻem to some guy. Maybe was the butler."

"No lie, Harry. You never visit George Hamilton."

Finally, the jungle cleared and the road became remarkably smooth, ending in a simple loop, at the end of which was a simple house. It looked just like a family house in any part of town. In fact, it looked a little smaller even than some of the homes his friends had Kona side.

"Eh, you sure this the right address?" Nona asked.

But before Harry could say anything, the door opened and yes, it was Steve Yates waving them in.

"Harry, I'm so glad you could visit! And you must be Nona! Welcome! Come in, come in."

The first thing Harry and Nona noticed was that there was a place for them to put their slippers outside the door. Strange—they never know any haoles who took their slippers off before coming into the house.

And then they took a step inside.

Nona squeezed Harry's arm so hard that Harry would have flinched if he hadn't already gone numb. The house— no, the mansion—was huge! High ceilings, big windows, a soft gardenia breeze.

Steve laughed, perhaps because he had seen this reaction before. "My architects worked hard on this one. Let me show you around."

Harry and Nona looked at the paintings on the wall, strange items from all over the world, shelves placed in unexpected places. And yet, there always seemed nearby a clear, empty space, where someone could sit alone and enjoy the quiet. And close by there always seemed to be a window, and out that window was a magnificent view of the ocean, the mountains, or the deep green forest.

Nona elbowed Harry. "So Harry, just like George Hamilton's house, yeah?"

Funny thing, you would think she would have whispered, but what amazed Nona the most was how everything seemed different, yet she was still so comfortable. She would have felt perfectly able to flop on one of the sofas or flip the channels on the TV remote.

On one table there was a picture of Steve with a woman. Although the woman seemed happy, Nona felt a little sorry for her, though she didn't know why.

"That's my wife."

From the way he looked down, and the tone of his voice, Nona should have known not to ask, but once again, something about him made her feel comfortable.

"Where is she now?"

Harry elbowed her. Haoles get divorced, and hey, *what if she stay make?*

Luckily, the answer wasn't so dramatic.

"She's taking a nap right now. She should be up in a bit."

Harry felt the blood run back through his body as Steve led them outside.

A path wove through patches of jungle and clearing, while a river trickled in from the mountains past the house, only to fall off the cliff to the ocean below. Behind the path, they heard what they knew must be a helicopter.

"Hold on for a second," said Steve, as he jogged over to the pilot.

Nona pinched Harry.

"Auwe! What you went do that for?"

"Helicopter! This guy get helicopter!"

"I know, I know. Ow! No pinch me! Eh—that hurts!"

Steve waved them over. "Let's go for a ride!"

The helicopter pilot shook their hands and helped Harry and Nona inside. Steve strapped himself into the copilot's seat and they took off. They flew along the gulches, the valleys, and some waterfalls that were on Yates's land. Then they circled over Hilo town, where they could see the bay, Coconut Island, and the Royal Hawaiian.

Somewhere down there, Noelani and the halau were performing even now. Yes, there it was, two rows of tiny dancers, moving in almost-perfect unison.

Nona thought she'd be upset, yet as they flew all she could think of was the opening scene from *Fantasy Island,* with that "Da Plane! Da Plane!" dwarf Tattoo guy and Ricardo Montalban. And those anthuriums that grow from the tree—what kine anthurium grow from tree?

Steve motioned toward the bay. "Man, you guys are so lucky to live in a place that's so beautiful. Do you ever get tired of all this stuff?"

Harry said nothing, as he peered at places he had smelled and heard, but had never ever seen.

Nona and Harry had no idea of how long they were in the air, but at some point they landed and walked back to the house. Lisa Yates was waiting for them.

She seemed just a little thinner and more tired than in the picture, but she still had the same smile, and from how she touched her husband, Nona knew that he wasn't the problem.

"My wife, Lisa," Steve said.

Lisa had sent someone to bring some malasadas back from Tex Drive-In in Honoka'a. "They're still hot," Lisa said, and nodded to her helper, who served each of them a malasada and a glass of fresh guava juice. As they looked out at the coastline, Steve pulled a remote from somewhere and soon Gabby Pahinui's timeless falsetto filled the house.

"This place is heaven. Simply heaven," Lisa said.

*   *   *

After the show, Kam found the band taking a break before they broke down the stage. Jonny-Boy waved him over and tossed him a beer. "So Kam, what you play?"

"Guitar, some bass."

"You must be good, yeah for play in Hollywood?"

Kam smiled and shrugged. The truth was that Kam had been pretty good. Very good, even. On weekends, he'd sneak out of the Valley, into Hollywood, and work the Sunset Strip handing out flyers for some gigs and playing in others, underage and fierce in six lanes full of leather jackets, Stratocasters, Marshall amps, fishnets and Aqua-Net. Back then, there was so much wonderful music. So many great songs. Now?

All pau.

Jonny-Boy asked if he was visiting or if he lived here, and Kam said well, he moved to Pahoa, but was thinking to move because the people there kind of creeped him out.

Jonny-Boy nodded. "Strange kine place that. Too damn haole. Oh, no offense, brah." Jonny-Boy introduced Kam to the rest of the band: Carl Fernandes the drummer, Saul

Malani on rhythm guitar and Randall Dang on lead, though Randall was leaving for the mainland soon. "We're looking for one replacement, by the way. Maybe you could come to our next rehearsal?"

Noelani interrupted them.

"Thanks yeah, for playing," she said. In Jesus name."

She gathered her things and left without looking at Kam.

Carl shook his head. "That one is crazy. Terrific dancer, but crazy."

Kam asked what he meant.

"You not one crazy kine Christian yeah?"

"No, I'm Jewish."

"Good, good. See, you get your Christians and your Christians. Me, I Christian, but not the crazy kine. Not like her. Everything for Jesus. I mean, that's how it should be, you know, but not so, you know, so crazy."

All shivers, giggles, and wasted motion, Carl was the most jittery drummer Kam had ever seen. But these were new friends, so he smiled and nodded. Plus it wasn't as if Carl wasn't making sense. Kam thought of his sister and brother who, despite being perfectly respectable adults, would completely change the brand of soap or noodles they used if their rabbi told them to. Crazy wasn't just for Christians.

Kam noticed the rest of the band starting to pack their equipment.

"Hey! Do you guys need some help?"

Jonny-Boy smiled and motioned toward a bass cabinet. "Eh, haole—you all right."

* * *

It was strange how time passed at the Yates house. The four of them talked story for what seemed like hours, yet it never seemed to get too late. When it was time for dinner, Nona was honestly ready to eat—even though she knew that eating the malasadas so close to dinner should have spoiled her appetite. Yet her body felt empty, as if the proper amount of time had elapsed before dinner.

Wow, these guys must really be rich if they can afford this kine place, she thought. Was nothing like she imagined. She had pictured lots of Filipina maids fluffing throw pillows and dusting and what not. But this seemed just like a home should seem. There was help on the premises—like the helicopter pilot and Lisa's helper who brought the fresh pitcher of guava juice (oh—and the nice girl who cleaned up the malasada crumbs after they were pau) but they would show up only when needed, quickly do their job, then disappear.

And now, as they were ready to eat, Harry mentioned that they had brought some of Nona's chicken. Lisa smiled, and said that the best chicken she'd ever had was her grandma's fried chicken long ago. Even now, she thought about the chicken, and how she had never been able to find anything remotely like it.

Nona was surprised that these people could have trouble finding anything. Steve Yates laughed at first, but then his expression changed and he looked out the window.

"You wouldn't believe the things we've lost."

He said this absently, as if none of them were there. Lisa ran her hand along his forearm.

"Eh Steve, you okay?" Harry said.

Yates looked back from the window. The dying glow from the dusky sky framed his head in a violet halo, while the warm room lights revealed a softness that was not at all like the face of a mercenary technology giant.

"It's the little things, Harry. The big stuff is easy. We can program a satellite to orbit three planets and vault into space with a computer no more complicated than a vacuum cleaner. But try to program a computer to shush a child to sleep, or walk the dog, or heck, even to tie a pair of shoes so they are just right." He stopped and shook his head.

Just as Harry and Nona began to feel a little awkward, one of the servants asked if he should bring in Nona's chicken. Harry told him was in the cooler and the car door was unlocked.

"You know, Steve," Harry offered, "that's just like Nona's chicken—she can give anyone the recipe, but it never comes out like Nona's."

Harry quickly glanced at Nona.

"Yeah!" said Nona, understanding immediately that Harry wanted to change the subject. "I even gave Eva Matsuoka—oh, you don't know her—but anyway, I gave Eva Matsuoka the chicken recipe, but afterwards she came real mad at me because she said I left out the secret ingredient. Funny, yeah? No more secret ingredient."

"Hmm. That reminds me of my grandmother," Lisa said. "No one could make the chicken exactly like Grandma, even with the same recipe. Maybe the secret ingredient is the spirit of cook."

"Oh...I don't know. Me? I just, you know, throw 'em all together."

"Somehow, I can't believe that."

Harry didn't know about that spirit stuff, but all this talk of chicken was making him hungry. He looked down and saw his cooler. Evidently the butler had retrieved the cooler and set it beside him without Harry noticing.

Lisa asked if they should heat the chicken and Harry said no, let's eat it local style, fresh from the cooler. That nice girl came from somewhere with plastic forks, paper plates and napkins and laid them neatly on the little table by a window. The girl turned to leave, but Nona grasped her arm and gestured to the cooler.

"Please, go take some chicken and musubi. Get plenty for everyone."

The girl smiled, took a bite and closed her eyes.

"Oh wow..."

Steve took a bite and, his entire body lifted, or lilted, as if he were listening to a beautiful piece of music or beholding a great painting. Lisa finished her piece, and reached for another.

"Goodness! You must be a special person indeed."

Steve looked into the cooler and cocked his head to the side. He pointed to some very strangely shaped objects.

"Is that food?"

"Those are my musubi!" Harry grinned and shoved one into his hand. "Here, go try one! Nona is teaching me."

With that bit of reassurance, Steve bit into it tentatively, then smiled, relieved that it was nothing more than seaweed, preserved plum, and salted rice.

"Not bad."

"Eh—next time I can even bring eggs!"

Nona pinched Harry's arm.

* * *

It didn't take Kam long to leave Pahoa. He abandoned the dirty looks, the oily crystals, and his termite house for a place down in Waiakea that Jonny-Boy recommended. Nothing fancy, but clean.

Keep 'em clean. That was what was missing in Pahoa. The clean. No matter where he went in Hilo, unless he was around tourists, he never smelled an unpleasant body odor—even among the workers and everyday folks who sat next to him at the drive-in or the bowling alley cafe. Kam began to be much more self-conscious about his own body odor, often taking showers three or four times a day.

And he did go Jonny-Boy's house for that rehearsal. He didn't even have a guitar. He borrowed one from Randall and began to play.

By the time the roosters started crowing, they guys declared that they had found their new guitarist.

"So Kam, what do you do for one living?"

They were sitting around, drinking beer and watching the sunrise. Sometimes it's good to be a musician.

"Me? I've got some property, some good investments." Laughter filled the room.

"Oh? Rich, eh? We go call you Steve Yates!"

"No no no—not like Steve Yates—I'm doing all right, but I'm not frickin' God!"

"Eh, that's okay. Us guys, we not going pull that class distinction crap on you. No worry, we doing okay, too. I get some good stocks, and Randall—he no need work either."

"Wow. I thought the economy over here was bad."

"It *is* bad—but of us guys, only Saul stay from here. Me, I from Las Vegas, Randall stay from Seattle and Carl—ha! Carl stay from Los Angeles."

More laughter as Jonny-Boy explained that Carl Fernandes used to be Carlos Fernandez, and that somewhere over the Pacific he stopped being Mexican and became half Filipino, half Hawaiian and half Porogee.

"But that doesn't add up!"

"No, it doesn't, but Carl stay real junk at math."

They laughed as Randall tossed Kam another beer.

*   *   *

Noelani sat, rocking gently with the rhythm of a kitchen faucet that had dripped for years, yet had never been fixed.

On her kitchen table was a letter from her old teacher Aunty Kapolinahe Kahakunoe. She was getting old, and wanted Noelani to come back to the halau, if just for a little while, just so she could see her dance. She didn't know what she did to drive 'Lani away, and that whatever it was, she was sorry.

She told 'Lani that of all her dancers, she was the best she had ever taught.

Once again, Noelani prayed, but once again God didn't answer. *Why?* Perhaps He didn't like the hula. Considering the sinful origins behind some of them, that would be quite understandable, right?

Maybe that was why when she danced, she couldn't feel the same joy she felt from even Nona Watanabe—who hadn't come to the performance, which was strange.

It had been another good performance. But what she felt from her halau was becoming much like what she felt in her own dancing. The moves, the expressions, even the love, were there. Yet once the music stopped, there was nothing. No warmth. No afterglow. Just a cold nothing as if some joyful, sinful spirit took over her body for the dance and left when the music stopped—so when the people applauded, she faced them guilty and alone. That was why she had left the halau and Aunty Kahakunoe. It wasn't anger, or hurt. Just cold. Just nothing.

And now, that same feeling had finally seeped into her halau. After the show was over, as she heard her students chattering excitedly amongst themselves, suddenly she asked herself, *who was she to teach?* How could she teach a joy she hadn't felt for years? And now even Jesus had forsaken her. The faucet drips got louder, and louder.

And then for some reason they started to sound like banging on the kitchen door.

"Hello? Hello?"

Someone was outside. Noelani tossed her long hair out of her eyes and with an instinctive lightness walked over to see who it was.

"Hello?" In the garage light, she saw large figure in purple and green and orange.

"Oh Nona! Come inside."

Nona took her slippers off.

"I'm sorry I never make it to the performance, but I wore the blue mu'u-mu'u by mistake."

"Oh Nona, you could have danced anyway!"

Nona shook her head. "I couldn't make the rest of the halau look bad just because I never fit in." Nona's eyes began to water.

"You must think I completely hopeless."

"Nona," Noelani gave her a hug. "I know how hard you work—maybe just concentrate a little more."

Both of them knew that Noelani said this only to make Nona feel better, but it worked anyway, at least a little, and Nona promised that she would practice even harder next time, and Noelani nodded and said how next time it would be a much better show.

Usually, that's how these conversations ended. But this time Nona had something else to tell Noelani—that she had been with Harry to eat at Steve Yates's place.

"Steve Yates? How you know Steve Yates?" Even Noelani knew about how the high mukka-mukka guy just went move to Hilo.

Nona told her that he and Harry were friends and that Steve and Lisa, his wife, were real nice.

If this had come from anyone else in her halau, except Violet or maybe Francis, Nona would have suspected lying, but that wasn't Nona's way.

"I told him about hula and what a wonderful kumu you were."

"Thanks," said Noelani, once again feeling that emptiness.

"Oh! And then he told me to give you something," Nona said, and handed her an envelope.

"Really?" Noelani frowned and opened the envelope. Then she sat down. Not on a chair, but on the floor. For inside the envelope was a note. And that note said:

> Dear Noelani,
>
> I am impressed by your work with your community. Please use this gift to help bring your vision of hula alive. My only request is that you keep this anonymous.
>
> Best Wishes,
> Steve Yates
>
> p.s.— Consider this gift tax-free. My accountant will be in contact to take care of all the details.

With the note was a check for one hundred thousand dollars.

Chapter 3

"KITE STRING?

Why on earth do we need kite string to catch fish?"

Harry turned to Yates. "I guess I better not show you the spark plugs in my garage, either."

Yates shrugged. Harry looked at the cashier and explained was Yates's first time fishing. But she ignored him to speak to the next customer.

"Are all the cashiers on the island this charming?" Steve asked.

"Usually during the summer, when no more school."

Steve nodded as they walked out of the store.

"Okay. Now tell me why we are taking kite string with us? Are we catching flying fish?"

Harry laughed. "That's a good one—I getta tell Nona that."

He was still laughing as he pulled the kite string out of the bag. "I stay thinking. The best kine fishing for your first time out, is for dunk."

"Dunk?"

"Yeah. Dunk. More easy—no funny kine knots, no plastic bait, no need track the line in the dark. Duck soup."

"Duck what?"

"Going be easy."

"Oh."

"Try listen. First we going take one treble hook, and bait 'em with ika."

"Ika?"

"Squid."

"Oh."

"Then, we go up about this much (Harry measured out a length about a foot and a half) and put one loop in the line. We tie a piece of kite string to the loop, and the other end tie some heavy weights. Can use nuts or bolts or what not, but I already get spark plugs in the garage.

"Now, for dunk, you cast the line as far out over the rocks as you can. The weights make the cast go more far so your line can clear the breakers. Then, the line goes 'dunk!' (see—dunking, yeah?) into the water and the weights sink to the bottom. But the bait part floats around. Even if the waves come in, your line stay anchored to the bottom by the weights, yeah?"

"But then you catch a fish, and your line is stuck," Steve protested.

"No, no, no! That's why we use the kite string. You see— when we get one bite, we give the pole one quick jerk." Harry yanked the string and snapped it in two. "The kite string breaks and the main line comes free. See? No more nothing for snag on the rocks!"

Steve considered this and was about to nod his approval when he noticed Harry had already repacked everything and was hopping in the car. Harry had explained the technique not to get his permission, but simply to tell him what they were going to do. There was something refreshing about that—having someone do something because he is right, without any need for a blessing. Strange, but refreshing.

Steve trotted to catch up with his friend.

Harry motioned to him. "Now, all we need for do is find one good place to fish. Should be easy. After all brah, you get so much shoreline to choose from!"

*   *   *

Steve Yates had come here to be with his wife and to get away from his company, his people, and his stockholders. Sure, he still communicated with them, to give his yay or nay on a particular proposal or activity. What they didn't know was that, as often as not, one of his housekeepers was doing all of this for him, speaking through a virtual reality image of Yates that Yates had programmed himself.

Now, this housekeeper had no advanced technical knowledge, nor was she skilled in business. She didn't have to be! Yates hired well, and his people knew how to do their jobs. All they needed was some talking head to tell them yes, their ideas were okay, and if they worked hard at it, they could succeed, and they had genius they had not even realized.

It might seem odd that an expert programmer or project manager or whatever would need this affirmation. After all, isn't that part of being an expert? Yet, reminding his staff that they were competent, capable individuals had been one of the biggest drains on his time. Nowadays, though, he let his housekeeper do the talking for him. At the end of the day, he would check to make sure nothing truly awful was happening. Usually, this took about five minutes, leaving him plenty of time to go fishing.

*   *   *

"Eh Yates—this place all your land?"

Yates wiped his mouth. He and Harry were exploring his coastline to find good fishing spots. They were also eating leftover malasadas, and sugar was getting all over the place.

"Boy," Harry continued."No seem right for someone own this much land, this much ocean."

"Hey, it has to belong to someone."

Harry took another bite of malasada and sat on a rock that overlooked sets of waves crashing against the black and endless green. He was amazed at how much shoreline belonged to Yates. He knew how much land Yates had, but he never know *how* much.

"Wow. No tell the Hawaiians."

"Tell me something, Harry. If you had all this, would you give it *all* back to the Hawaiians? And which Hawaiians? The first one who knocked on your door saying give me the land? The ones from the Marquesas who came a long time ago, or the ones who came later from the Society Islands, and took the land away? No, the Hawaiians weren't all one happy ohana, either."

Harry stopped chewing.

Yates sighed. "Look, it's not that the Hawaiians were bad or good—it's that they were people. They had slavery, dictators, despots—a woman could be executed for eating pork. Whom would you be turning the land over to?"

Harry had grown up here, but hadn't really thought to ask questions like this. Seemed to him that the Hawaiians were always the Hawaiians—their land was taken away by the US, who deposed Queen Lili'uokalani and annexed a sovereign country.

"And what?" asked Yates. "When Kamehameha took over the other islands—did he ask the neighboring chiefs nicely?"

"Where you learn this stuff, Yates?" Harry said, after finally swallowing his food.

"Well, don't you use the Internet?"

Harry grabbed another malasada. They weren't out there to discuss philosophy and Hawaiian sovereignty; they were there to find a good fishing spot. Once they actually *were* fishing—well, that's when they could finish the philosophical stuff.

Was weird, though. Unlike the house and yard, which seemed to have everything perfect, the Yates's shoreline seemed to have only junk places.

"Here," said Yates. "This place looks good. No rocks to snag your line!"

"And no fish, either," Harry said. "Some fish *need* the rocks to feed and hide. Cannot find fish where no more rocks."

And then there were places with rocks, but no waves, and then the waves were too rough, and in one place the cliffs were too sharp, while in another where there were no cliffs at all. It seemed to Harry that the land itself didn't know what it was doing. It was like one aloha-shirt tourist dancing to local music—some inherent understanding of the natural rhythm was missing. All afternoon they looked, but on that first day they still couldn't find a good spot.

Nor did they find one on the second day, or the third.

After the fourth day, Harry and Steve were having lunch. Harry looked at his feet, at an ant that was crawling on a piece of rice he had inadvertently dropped. One ant told another, then another, and soon a whole swarm of ants was carrying the grain of rice across the dirt.

"Steve. Not everything stay on the Internet, you know..."

"What?"

"Like you said before—it's the little things. The little things add up, one on top the other—then they look like big things. So you think you know what's up, by looking at the big stuff. But you don't."

"What do you mean?" Yates asked.

Harry took another sip of soda. "I don't know how else for say this, Steve, but you gotta let the land be."

"What? Me? Let the land be?" Steve tried to laugh, but stopped when he saw Harry was serious.

"This is the *land*. Cannot just tell it what for do. Too many stuffs you don't know. The little things. Let the land be."

Steve took a stick and traced circles into the ground. He felt the scratch of the tip against the gravelly surface, then gouge into the softer earth below. He tried to feel each vibration where the stick slid against a small rock, or leaf, or glided across the mud.

But what was that taste?

Harry had been a good choice, he thought as he tossed the stick away.

＊　＊　＊

THE TALE OF THE EVIL PLATE LUNCH

Once upon a time, there were two plate lunch shops. Actually, once upon a time there were dozens, but one by one they closed down because their owners retired and the kids wanted to either go to the mainland or open car stereo shops or sports memorabilia stores. So now there were only a few, and of these few, there were two.

One of them was Goto's. Goto's had operated for generations without incident, and would have liked to continue to do so, but people started making fun of its name. Not really in one pilau kine way, but when Togos came to town, it was just too easy to make jokes. Shozo Goto, a tough stringy, beef jerky kine man, used to get all bothered by this, and kept a bottle of Maalox in the refrigerator next to the mac salad. When Mr. Goto died, however, his wife and two kids were a little more relaxed about the name, even printing up T-shirts that said, "GOT TO GO TO GOTO'S."

Goto's food was okay. Not great, but you could always get your food quick, even when all the other restaurants and burger stands were crowded. Of course, that implied that not too many people went to Goto's. But since the family owned the property and had nothing better to do, there was a good chance there would always be a Goto's, with a crusty bottle of Maalox still sitting next to the day's fresh mac potato salad.

Where things were really busy was Matsuoka's. Matsuoka's food was known as the bestest, most ono plate lunch on the island. Lots of locals, and even tourists, flooded the shop every day to taste the most authentic local food they could buy. Especially the younger ones, who wondered how the food at Matsuoka's could taste just like Grandma's secret-recipe kau kau.

But that, however, was the dark secret in the plate lunch world. The reason it tasted like Grandma's secret recipe was because it *was*. The entire plate lunch shop community knew that the Matsuokas were *evil*. Charlotte Matsuoka, the store's matriarch, built her plate lunch empire by stealing the best recipes from all over the island. She was ruthless. When she found a recipe she wanted, she would try to peek inside the kitchen, or tell one of her workers to talk to theirs at the bowling alley or while fishing. Most of those guys worked for next to nothing, and hey, if you going buy me one 12-pack Miller, sure, I'll tell you what goes inside the pork tofu...

Sometimes the recipes were more closely guarded, but even that did not stop her. She had been a beautiful woman, and it was well known in the plate lunch community how

Charlotte had ruined more than one marriage by having an affair with the husband, only to dump him when she got the recipe for the rib marinade, daikon kim chee, or tako poke. One time, she even secured a pork adobo recipe from a Filipino family that had been carefully guarded for generations, all the way back to Mindanao. Nine months later, her daughter Eva was born.

People snickered at the dark-skinned baby coming from the Japanese couple. But Mr. Matsuoka said nothing, having long ago submerged his wishes beneath Charlotte's insatiable plate lunch ambition.

In the years that followed, Mr. Matsuoka and then Charlotte passed away, leaving Eva in control of the store. If anything, she was rumored to be even more beautiful and sneaky than her mother, though to her customers and those not in the plate lunch business, she was simply the sweetest, most charming thing. But those who knew the truth were not fooled. They knew that underneath the sweetness was someone born for plate lunch evil. So when Eva joined the Noelani's hula halau, the wisest ladies gripped their purses and gossiped that there must be something there that the plate lunch lady wanted—and it wasn't hula.

And they were right.

During a fundraiser in Honoka'a, Eva had sampled the most wonderful chicken she had ever tasted. It was made by some fat ugly woman named Nona Watanabe. Not a professional. Probably never even know her chicken's potential. Duck soup for get the recipe—just sign up for the beginning hula class, make friends with her, and ask for the recipe straight up. Why, she probably would be honored for have her chicken served at Matsuoka's!

At first, Eva thought she was right. Whenever she would talk to her, Nona would light up with those big dumb cow eyes and talk about how much she loved dancing and the music and her boyfriend Harry, who was no catch himself. It was all Eva could do to try to look interested.

Finally, when she felt that she had made enough progress, she told Nona how much she liked her chicken and how she wished that she could make chicken like that.

"Oh no problem," Nona said, "I can give you the recipe!"

Just like that, Nona took a pen in her chubby hand and scribbled down the ingredients!

"Are you *sure* you didn't miss anything?" Eva asked Nona. Her mother had told her always to ask this question, especially with the amateurs, because so many worked on instinct—often putting a little of this and a little of that in the mix without knowing it.

"It's a wonder how these people can cook anything at all," her mom would mutter.

"No, that's it," Nona said. "Simple, really. I don't know why people make big deal."

Eva smiled and said thank you and that she had to get back home because she was getting tired, which was a lie, of course.

Instead of going home, Eva drove straight to the restaurant and thrust the recipe into her nephew Roland's hand.

"Go make this!"

Roland looked at the recipe, then at her.

"What, you went through all that trouble just for get *this*?"

"What you mean?"

"This recipe is so simple. You sure she never leave anything out?"

"No, no—she said all stay there."

"Okay. I go try'em then."

So Roland made a test batch—another thing Eva's mother said—always test a recipe first. Sometimes people get wise and give you one junk recipe. Not that Eva thought Nona would do that. She had an eye for these things, and Nona was much too open, honest, and simple to lie.

But when the chicken was pau, something was wrong. Was not the same stuff. I mean, was okay, but not the same stuff that Eva remembered.

"See? She went give you one fake recipe. This one, she went fool you."

Why that *bitch!* Eva thought. Okay, so you want to play that way—I'll find a way to get your recipe. You watch.

She took the chicken and threw it in the dumpster.

"Eh—why did you do that? The chicken wasn't *that* bad," Roland said.

Eva shot her nephew the stink eye, and he shut up.

*   *   *

One hundred thousand dollars! She could buy costumes, new muʻu-muʻus, perhaps even expand her practice hall! Noelani's mind began to race and her emptiness was crumpled up like one old soda can. New instruments, lights, a PA system... Jesus had answered her prayers!

And why? Why now? Of course.

He wanted to make hula part of His Plan.

Once, while talking with another Christian at a fellowship, she had heard about villages in Europe that put on Passion Plays that chronicled the death and resurrection of Jesus Christ. And already, every April people came to Hilo from around the world to see the hula at the Merrie Monarch Hula Festival.

Named after Hawaiʻi's last king, Kalakaua, the Merrie Monarch was the pinnacle of hula competitions. It was a grand event, but wouldn't it be much grander if there could be a hula that paid direct homage to Jesus Christ?

Merrie Monarch? Her hula was going to be about the Merriest Monarch of them all!

"HA!"

Noelani pulled out her notepad and began to sketch. She knew the gospel by heart, well, mostly (her hula sometimes got in the way of her Bible study, which was yet another reason to feel guilty about her hula). But with her Bible in hand, she began to chart the chants and choreography for the performance. It would be more than just one song or two; it would be an entire retelling of the Son's life, crucifixion and rebirth! As she scribbled idea after idea, Noelani felt so close to the Lord. She sketched out basic character designs, then began composing the chant and the music. Was going be unreal! She put the notepad down and began dancing in the middle of her living room.

At first, she faithfully traced the steps she had planned out. But slowly each step became a little lighter, a little more joyful than the one before, and soon she was dancing purely with her own feelings, her own intuition.

Oh! How wonderful! She whirled, floated, turned, scarcely able to breathe from all of her excitement. And in her joy, she almost forgot why she had started the dance.

Almost.

All at once, she stopped, disgusted with herself for forgetting Jesus Christ. She fell to her knees and prayed that this sinner would be forgiven, this sinner of a different music, holding herself within her own unworthy embrace.

*   *   *

STUPID HAOLE

"So tell me about Noelani," Kam said. Jonny-Boy was cleaning up after their last jam session. Kam was drunk and everyone else had gone home.

"What? Noelani? Carl's right—she's nuts. But one terrific dancer."

"And beautiful, too."

Jonny-Boy stopped sweeping. Then he started again, but his strokes began to wander. Then he snorted and threw down his broom.

"Hey, wait a minute! I bet you went come to the show just to see Noelani, yeah? What? You like one hula girl for yourself, haole boy?"

Jonny-Boy tried to smile, but there was an edge in his voice that betrayed his feelings about haoles who came to the islands to pick up local women.

Kam's ears turned red.

"No go there, Kam."

But Kam didn't listen. They had all been drinking way too much, and Kam weighed much less than Saul, or even Carl, let alone the big Hawaiian.

No go there? What the hell was he there, for, anyway? He had come to Hawai'i in search of something he still hadn't named, and he still hadn't found it. He hated his family and what he left behind, but at least there was a *who*, a *what*. Here? Nothing. Except times when the sheer beauty of the place took him away, which only made those other times even more empty.

He'd crossed an ocean to find a bunch of weird new-age meth addicts, a Christian hula girl, and a local band whose rhythm guitarist had come from Seattle. Lucky thing he wasn't suicidal, or he would have stepped in front of a truck.

Even so, he almost did the next-best thing. He went yell at Jonny-Boy.

"Who the hell are you to tell me that I can't call someone beautiful? Noelani is a beautiful woman on a beautiful island and what the hell is wrong with that? And if I ask her out, what are you going to do about it? You want to tell me, Mr. Las Vegas? Huh?"

If you ever need for mouth off, remember that it's usually better to mouth off to one big guy. Smaller guys, just a few drinks and they get mean and vicious—like they need for prove something. Big guys though, they take longer for get drunk. Plus, they know already if they throw they can broke your head. So chances are, even if you mouth off, you going be okay. If not, at least you'll be unconscious soon.

And Jonny-Boy had seen his share of mouthing off, so he knew which kine mouthing was bullshit, which was going to lead to blows, and which was just a guy going through bad times. Kam's was definitely the third type. For those guys, was usually best to back down and apologize, which Jonny-Boy did.

"Hey Kam, I never mean to piss you off, brah." He picked up the broom and started sweeping again.

"Yeah, I know. But dammit! I don't know why I'm here! I just know I have to be. Unless I'm just being a stupid haole, right?"

"Eh, no call yourself that."

Kam lurched and grabbed Jonny-Boy's broom.

"No—I'm a stupid haole! Stupid! Me! You know what Kam is short for?"

Jonny-Boy shook his head.

"Kamakawiwoʻole."

Jonny-Boy's mouth dropped open. "You changed your name to Kamakawiwoʻole? Like Iz?"

"Legally."

Jonny-Boy chuckled, and then began to laugh. Kam started busting up, too.

"Boy, you *are* a stupid haole!"

"I know!" Kam laughed at himself till he could hardly breathe, nor keep the tears from running down his haole face. He laughed until the image of his mother dead in a pine box was still and the discordant nasalities of his relatives talking, talking always talking were washed away in the cleansing, forgetful rain.

He laughed until the laughter could no longer sustain itself, until he could no longer sustain it, a last hug, a kiss goodbye, a pretend-to-be-cheerful come again soon. Jonny-Boy noticed Kam going quiet and handed him another beer.

"Suck 'em up, brah."

And somehow, Kam did just that.

As Kam finally slept, Jonny-Boy walked outside with his guitar and sat down and held it as if to play, but for a long time, he just listened to the buzz of the insects and the rain falling on the trees.

Noelani.

*   *   *

SPAM?

The next morning, Kam woke to the sound and smell of brewing coffee. He tried to get up, but a sodden weight in his stomach and a pounding pressure in his skull pushed him back down. Kam melted in the sofa, overwhelmed by the smells of this island, this coastline, this carpet. *Breathe,* he told himself. *Just breathe. If you can keep breathing, everything will be fine. Just keep breathing.*

"Eh, how you feeling?" Jonny-Boy called from the kitchen.

"I've been better," Kam finally said. "What time is it?"

"One-thirty. Good time for breakfast, yeah?"

"I guess so." Kam shrugged. (After all, these *were* musicians.)

"I made Spam and eggs."

"Spam?"

"Yeah, Spam. What, you rather have Vienna sausage?"

"No, it's just that Spam— I mean—it's *Spam*."

"Yeah, yeah, yeah, haole boy, just shut up and eat da Spam! I no going cook Eggo Frozen Waffles just 'cuz I get mainland company."

As Kam dragged himself over to the kitchen, the smells of fried Spam, fried eggs, fried toast, and fried rice jammed their greasy fingers down his throat. He lurched for the door and made it outside just in time. When he was done, he washed himself off and stumbled back into the kitchen, still dripping with water from the garden hose.

"Feel better?"

Kam nodded

"Good. Now eat."

And Jonny-Boy handed Kam his plate.

* * *

Instant Aloha

"Okay, so you know some of Israel's songs, yeah?" asked Saul.

Kam nodded.

"Good, because when we perform, we always getta be ready with one of Iz's songs."

"Why?"

"Try wait. You'll see. How about 'E Ala E?'"

Kam nodded.

In this band, which, by the way, was called Ku'uipo, Saul Malani did most of the singing because his Hawaiian the best by far.

Saul told Kam that he learned Hawaiian from an old kahuna man in Kauai, who spent his boyhood on Niihau. "That's da Forbidden Island, you know. Only full-blood Hawaiians stay there. Once they leave, they no can come back... So when somebody from there stay teach you, get special meaning, yeah?"

Then Carl yelled, "Saul eh, no bullshit—you went just listen to one instructional CD!"

The whole band laughed, in part to humor Carl. But Kam knew that voice came from no CD. Even without the words, Saul's was a voice out of time. Neither old nor young, but simply there, it reminded Kam of Rosh Hashanah and the four blasts of the shofar, which exist not precisely in the past year, nor in the year to come, but somewhere eternally in between.

But Carl was on a roll. "Look, we just Ku'uipo. None of us stay very good, and we never going ever be famous, but we just goofing off for have fun."

Kam noticed Saul and Jonny-Boy bristle, but they quickly recovered. Which was good, because Kam was a little scared of Saul. He was smaller than Jonny-Boy, but the smaller ones, they the ones you need to watch out for. And staring out from under that hat, Saul's eyes seemed to cloud with things that Kam didn't want to know about.

Jonny-Boy looked at Carl and rolled his eyes. "Yeah, yeah... You see Kam—da main thing is that you get, how you folks call 'em? Chutzpah! No worry if you no can talk like Aunty Kahakunoe. Just say 'em like you mean it. Anyways, most people in the crowd, they no understand anyway. You think you the only guy asking, 'What the heck did went say?' at one Brothers Cazimero show?"

Kam remembered how many times at the Roxy he had no idea what his singer was screaming.

"What they after," Saul finally said, "is the music. The

song."

That night, they arrived for their gig at Kalani's—a place that Kam would have never visited to himself. Local place. Think big dark Hawaiians, and little, pissed-off-looking ones. And they were all wondering who the hell was the haole that went come in with the band. As Ku'uipo unloaded their equipment, he could hear the chatter.

"Eh, what happen to Randall? He went quit or what?"

"Dat Saul, he never going take off his hat?"

"Who da haole?"

"Oh! Eh haole, you da new guitar player, haole?"

Kam tried to smile and look relaxed. He didn't know if he succeeded.

The set started pretty well. Kam felt good to be up there with the band. He was very courteous, remembering that he was the new guy and not to hog the stage with guitar solos. They played some older numbers, then some more contemporary Jahwaiian stylings.

Ku'uipo played all the usual stuff, but, sometimes you just don't have it, and this night, Ku'uipo just didn't have it. The audience began to heckle. Especially at Kam. Some people got up to leave. Most of them, though, got drunker and louder. Then, Kam heard it.

"*Focken haole!*"

"Hey, Jonny-Boy," Kam whispered. "They want to kill me." He was sure that any minute someone would throw a bottle.

"No worry, no worry," Jonny-Boy winked. He looked at Carl who looked at Saul.

Saul nodded, and suddenly the music stopped. Saul cleared his throat. Then he put on his most syrupy local voice and said:

"I would like to dedicate da next songs to our dear friend and inspiration, Bruddah Iz, who stay gone, but whose spirit will always be wit us today."

And, as if by magic, the room went silent. Then someone in the audience yelled "Bruddah Iz!" The music started and Saul began singing "E Ala E."

Kam could not believe it. A crowd that had seemed just a few minutes earlier ready to lynch him was now swaying and cheering Ku'uipo's every move.

And when Saul motioned to him to take a solo, the crowd held up their beers and chanted—"Go Haole! Go Haole! Go Haole!"

They ended the set with three Iz songs, and would have kept going if the fire department hadn't shown up to tell the crowd they had to disperse.

As the bar went dark, a weary Ku'uipo loaded their van with their equipment. It was true; Hilo needed more clubs with their own PA systems. On the way out, the manager gave them their cash.

"Good show, you guys. I call you next week," he said.

With smiles, smokes, and a fat roll of bills, Ku'uipo ended up stopping at Ken's Pancakes. It was already three in the morning, so it was the only place that was open, except for Walmart. Usually, Ken's had choke haoles, which meant wasn't cheap, but the food was okay.

"So what is it with Iz, anyway?" Kam stuffed his face with some pancake.

"You tell us," Saul said. "You da guy who went change his name."

"Yeah, I know. But I don't know, the guy had something about him. Not really the music, I mean, it's good music, but—it's something else."

Carl laughed. "I know what you mean. It's like one day Iz just became the symbol of Hawai'i . Anyways, you see that big guy with the long black hair going, 'Ua mau ke e au o ka aina ika pono.' Garans get chills, yeah?

"I tell you one thing, though. All of us bar bands should

get on our knees and thank God every night for Bruddah Iz."

The guy bussing tables turned around and gave the shaka sign and shouted, "Bruddah Iz!"

"See what I mean? Instant aloha, brah—instant aloha."

* * *

Lisa and Steve watched the moonlight trickle through their window. They were thinking of Noelani, hoping that they had done the right thing. They knew she was strong, but sometimes strength is not the answer. They knew she had faith, but sometimes, faith keeps one from love.

Steve reached for a glass of wine and took a small sip, letting the taste soft-shoe over his tongue. Lisa had always told him that there were limits to what even he could do. He knew she was right, as was Harry, who had told him a thing or two about fishing.

Cannot control everything, brah.

Yes, yes, but everything he had came from his action. And now, he was to do nothing?

Lisa shivered. Steve rearranged the blanket to cover her arms, which seemed even thinner in this light.

Still, a promise was a promise.

"I really hope that we find a good fishing spot tomorrow."

Lisa leaned her head on his shoulder and smiled. "Well, you never know."

Steve felt her close her eyes, then opened his own to behold his world. He brushed a strand of hair from her tired, sleeping face.

"But you do."

* * *

Noelani called her halau to an emergency meeting.

"What stay up?" they asked.

"What stay up," Noelani said, "is that Jesus has finally answered my prayers."

"Maybe she went find a boyfriend," whispered Betty Manibog.

"Sssssssssh!" said Violet Macayan.

Noelani pretended not to hear. "This year we are going to do something very special for the Merrie Monarch Festival. We are going to do the life of Jesus Christ in hula!"

Oh my God, she's finally lost it, Eva Matsuoka thought. When you're in the plate lunch business, you develop a sense for what's going to sell and what's going to just sit there in the pot. And this was a real sitter.

But of course others were already shouting.

"We going need new costumes!"

"And leis!"

"Oh this going be so good!"

"Jesus—he would be so proud of you, Noelani!"

Even Frances Silva cheered, though she stumbled and fell and had to be picked up.

Are these people idiots? Eva looked at these people, even that panty Ignacio, wondering if any of them knew what a bad idea this was. One hula with Roman soldiers? Great. And now someone was talking about getting animals for the manger?

"How we going pay for all this?" she finally asked, and amidst all the ruckus, Noelani smiled.

"No worry. The Lord will provide."

Eva had heard enough. Even she had her limits. She'd find another way to get the chicken. She walked out the door, and ran smack into Nona Watanabe, who had already stepped outside.

"Oh Eva! You okay?"

Eva picked herself up, then squinted at Nona. "Nona? I

thought you'd be in there, cheering Noelani along." Eva had always assumed that if Noelani had told Nona to jump off a cliff, she would have done so, gladly.

But Nona didn't even look at her. Instead, Nona stared at the streetlight down the road. She shook her head, rubbed her hands on her legs, and leaned against the wall.

"This is wrong."

"Yeah," Eva said. "What's gotten into that girl—planning all this kine stuff? And no, the Lord does not provide—how she going pay for all this? Selling kulolo?"

"She no need worry about money."

"What you mean? Everything costs—" Then Eva stopped. *Something stay going on here.*

"Not supposed to be this way." Nona stared at the ground. "Not like this. I thought that she would understand, but now it's all wrong."

"Understand? Understand what?"

"The hula. She's supposed to do something for the hula. Just the hula."

"What you mean?" Eva asked again, not just because she was naturally ni'ele, which she was, but because something weird was going on and it involved money.

But of course Nona misunderstood her question, saying something more about how Noelani was supposed to develop the hula for itself, not for religious kine stuff.

"No, Nona, I mean how is she going to pay for all of this? Someone went give her money, yeah?"

But Nona acted as if she didn't hear. Instead she held Eva's arm with her chubby hand. "I'm worried about Noelani."

Eva nodded, but she was already thinking *Nona knows something she's not telling.*

"Is she in trouble? Maybe we can help." Eva tried for play smart.

"No, no. She's fine. Better than fine." Nona sighed. "I guess I going back inside. After all, she's the kumu."

Nona opened the screen door and limped back to the celebration inside. Eva paused for a second, snorted, then rushed to her car.

What Nona was hiding? Oh that Nona—first the chicken, now this! Who'd have thought that she was such a snake?

Eva pulled into her restaurant parking lot and dashed inside. Although Matsuoka's was closed, it was never empty. Roland or her was always inside, chopping vegetables, marinating kalbi ribs, cleaning the floors, filling little Styrofoam cups with lomi salmon or kim chee.

"Roland! Come over here!"

"What?" Roland peeked around, his hands dripping with kim chee juice. "Oh Aunty! Try wait." He quickly washed off his hands, then rushed out from the back of the kitchen, still wiping his hands on a clean white towel.

"What's up, Aunty?"

"I not sure," she said, "but I just had the strangest time at Noelani's. She stay talking about putting on some crazy Christian kine hula show with brand new costumes and lights and what not—and not one word about one fundraiser."

"Christian kine hula show?" Roland paused. "I don't know about that."

"I do! It's one stupid idea! But that's not what I talking about. I was talking to Nona, and from what she said, or didn't say, I bet someone went give that Noelani some money. Big money. Noelani might be crazy, but she knows how much it costs for put on one original production. If she not worried—then someone went give her plenty money."

Roland put his towel down. "Did you read the paper today?"

Eva shook her head. Roland reached into his back pocket

and pulled out the *Hilo Tribune-Herald.* "Check out what's going on at the Hamakua Zoo."

"The Hamakua Zoo? Waste time, the Hamakua Zoo!"

Roland handed her the paper. "Just read 'em, Aunty."

As she read, she nodded slowly, then stroked her chin. Something strange was going on in Hilo. Very strange.

* * *

FOR THE KEIKIS

The Hamakua Rainforest Zoo was always something of—well, cannot say a joke—perhaps a humorous enigma would be the best way to put it. Why? For the most part, it was a zoo without animals.

The zoo itself was a wonderful space, featuring huge sloping hills of emerald grass with paths inlaid in crunchy black cinder. Along one path was a solemn little grove where seven little trees—each for one of the seven Challenger astronauts—were lovingly cared for by the head groundskeeper. There was an auditorium where folks from the Department of Parks and Recreation could hold fingerpainting classes, or the Department of Agriculture could give presentations to schoolchildren about why it was so important not to bring snakes to Hawai'i. There were also little clear terrariums where kids could look at geckoes or chameleons or lizards—no snakes, of course.

The zoo also had its share of birds in chain-link aviaries. Colorful macaws and toucans, weird vultures, as well as native birds like the i'o and nene.

But as far as animals? That was a problem—well, maybe not a problem—but definitely a point of curiosity. Outside of some monkeys, the main animal attraction was a fat, brown, pig-like creature called a tapir. Oh, and there was a giant tortoise, too. But no elephants, giraffes, zebras, or hippos. No rhinos or leopards or chimpanzees. The zoo staff tried to explain that they were representing fauna from a certain ecological niche, but in Hilo most folks thought they knew what a zoo should be, and this was definitely not it. Anyway, *you* try telling your kids that the reason your zoo has no giraffes is because they come from a different biome.

Actually, the zoo did have one marquee animal: a tiger. Outside its enclosure was a beautiful hand-painted poster depicting the various subspecies of tigers and how their jungles were disappearing at an alarming rate. Inside, the habitat was majestic—complete with lush vegetation, an artificial cave, and huge fiberglass rocks for the big cat to take in the morning. Around the habitat was a deep, wide moat to protect spectators should the big cat get the predatory urge to pounce at a particularly tasty-looking child.

Unfortunately, no one had actually seen the tiger. At least none of the visitors. The first question anyone heard after visiting the Hamakua Zoo—well, maybe the second after, "Why did you go over *there?*"—was, "Eh, you went see the tiger?" to which the customary answer was, "No, it must have been sleeping."

The zoo said that the tiger was depressed because it didn't have a mate. They were trying to get a mate, but money was difficult. They had kept trying, though. There was even a nice wooden box in the gift shop where folks could donate a dollar or two in hopes of one day raising enough money to get another tiger.

Last week, the *Hilo Tribune-Herald* revealed, the box was opened and inside was a cashier's check for two million dollars. No one had seen who dropped it in. Accompanying the check was a simple note that read "For animals for the keikis." As the donation was made to a non-profit organization (the Hamakua Zoo didn't even charge admission), the money was tax-free.

The paper interviewed the ecstatic director, who said that although elephants would be too risky to bring to the zoo, perhaps some gorillas and lemurs, and maybe even a red panda would be fine. There was plenty of space, and the money would be more than enough to construct the proper habitats. And the tiger?

"Yes—we'll be getting a tiger, too!" The director paused before continuing. "Look, I'm not religious—but maybe sometimes God provides after all."

"God provides again?" Eva whispered. *"What the heck is going on?"*

* * *

In the days that followed, Eva and Roland read the paper closely, gossiped with customers, and looked around for any other mysterious gifts. Something weird indeed was happening. The Tsunami Museum suddenly was able to finish building an expansion wing. The Performing Arts Center got new LED lighting and put out slick color brochures. Fumi Camacho, a ceramicist who taught at Hilo Community College, announced that someone had anonymously funded her latest project.

All of this would have been interesting anyway to the Matsuokas, since money was always interesting. But then, Roland called Eva to tell her that Goto's had purchased a new refrigerator.

"What? You sure?"

"Yes, Aunty, I saw 'em myself. One brand new refrigerator—stay in the back of the shop."

Eva hung up the phone in disgust. If whoever giving out those gifts were actually funding her competition—not that Goto's was much competition.

Still, with enough money...

It took her less than eleven minutes to get to Goto's. Arnold Goto, the younger son of Shozo Goto, was behind the counter in one of those stupid Goto's T-Shirts. As usual, there were about three people in the restaurant. One of them was Nona's boyfriend, Harry the fisherman, with some man she didn't recognize.

"Hi Eva. Why you stay here? You tired eat your own food?" Arnold was working on a crossword puzzle.

"Arnold Goto! I heard you went get one new fridge," Eva barked.

"Yeah, so what?" Arnold shrugged. "Our old fridge was old."

"Where is it?" Eva walked past Arnold to the back of the kitchen and saw the new refrigerator, a nice stainless steel unit with glass doors.

"Where you went get that?"

"We ordered 'em from one catalog—was on sale."

Eva peered inside at the mac salad, the Maalox, and marinating ribs.

"Eva, is there anything I can help you with?"

"You can tell me who went give you the money for buy this fridge."

"Okay," Arnold sighed. "I tell you."

"I'm waiting."

Arnold Goto put his paper down. He brought his head low and motioned Eva forward to hear.

"We got the money from...the Bank of Hawai'i."

"Bank of Hawai'i!?"

"Yeah, we get one account there. We can take our money out for buy stuff with."

Eva shot Arnold the stink eye. "No play games with me,

Arnold Goto! I going find out who went give you the money and when I do, I going, I going..."

"What, what?" Arnold asked. "You going open one bank account and withdraw some money, too?

"You watch!" Eva swung around and bolted out of the restaurant. "And get rid of that damned bottle Maalox! It's disgusting!"

Arnold looked at Harry and shrugged. "Sorry, eh."

"What was that about?"

Arnold shook his head. "I don't know. I mean we just bought a new refrigerator. We've been needing one for years. You know who she is, yeah?"

"Yeah, the Matsuoka girl."

"That's right. I don't see why this fridge stay bothering her—I mean, those guys—their fridge stay three times the size."

"By the way, this is my friend Steve."

Arnold shook his hand. Harry and Steve got their plate lunches and left to go fishing. Arnold picked up the crossword puzzle and continued working. A few minutes later, Landis Goto, the older brother, came in.

"What's up?"

"Well, Eva Matsuoka came in and yelled at me about the fridge. Then Harry, you know, the fisherman? He came by with I think that was Steve Yates, the rich technology guy."

"Oh yeah. He went move here, yeah?"

"Yeah."

"Cool," Landis said, and reached for the sports section. "You should have asked him for one autographed picture."

Arnold bit his pencil, removed it from his mouth, and filed in another word.

"Yeah, next time."

* * *

"So let me get this straight. Noelani got a shitload of money, is writing a hula version of the life of Christ, and wants us to compose a full score?" Ku'uipo was having another late breakfast at the Hilo Bowl.

"Yeah."

Saul adjusted his hat. "We write. She pays. Sounds good to me."

Jonny-Boy pulled the end of the paper wrapper from his straw, blew, and sent the wrapper spiraling into the air.

Eventually, the waitress came over and asked what you guys like, to which Carl said we like four coffees, four guava juice and four Crazy Omelets.

"Four Crazy Omelets?"

"That's what I said."

The waitress rolled her eyes and went back to the kitchen. Kam could hear the cook grumbling.

"Four Crazy Omelets! Do they know what time it is? Okay. Shoots, whatever." Then some pots and stuff began slamming a little bit harder than they should have.

"You sure we shouldn't have just had the scrambled eggs and Spam?" Kam asked.

Carl grinned.

"No, this Crazy Omelet is real good stuff! You see, get Spam inside, anyway. And corned beef and cabbage and teriyaki chicken and imitation crab meat and some kine fish, I think."

"Any pork?" asked Kam, completely forgetting about the Spam.

"I don't know, maybe get kalua," said Carl. "Any kine stuff get inside. Even get Velveeta cheese, too."

"That Crazy Omelet stay one real crazy omelet."

* * *

THE TALE OF THE CRAZY OMELET

Believe it or not, there was one recipe that Eva Matsuoka wouldn't touch. Not because was junk, like Leung's teriyaki poi. In fact, this recipe was for one of the most popular dishes in Hilo: the Hilo Bowl's Crazy Omelet.

The Crazy Omelet was Samson Miyashiro's nemesis. Samson was the cook at the Hilo Bowling Alley cafe. He was a very good cook, with stints at Chez Kogasaka, the Japanese restaurant by the Naniloa and the Royal Hawaiian, and at Pescavore, an upscale nouvelle cuisine place that catered to the rich Japanese tourists. He was extremely proud of winning the Big Island Poke contest, with an ahi poke made with chili pepper, kosher salt, and 7-Up. In fact, Samson had once been offered a job as a dessert chef at the Bonaventure Hotel in Los Angeles.

But Samson Miyashiro had decided to be a cook instead of a chef. Less money, but less stress and besides, when it came right down to it, he had always wanted to make good tasty food—and for his money, no cooking beat local cooking. So, when his Uncle Raymond bought out the Hilo Bowling Alley cafe and asked him to cook, he was happy to say yes.

What he hadn't counted on was that his Uncle Raymond also fancied himself a cook, and had recipes that he wanted rigidly followed. Samson had never really seen his uncle cook anything. Even steaks on top the charcoal—what could be easier than that? But no, he had his wife grill them. Following his explicit instructions, of course.

The Crazy Omelet had seven ingredients, each requiring its own marinade and unique, distinctive cut. For example, the Spam had to be sliced shoestring style, in long, thin segments. Simply chopping wouldn't do. The celery was to be julienned, then steamed. And the canned mushrooms had to be chopped into cubes. Any deviation would cause his uncle to go into a tirade about how this was his signature dish, and how it put his restaurant on the map.

Samson often mumbled under his breath that it might be better if he just spent a little extra money on some ingredients—at the very least, use Best Foods in the mac salad! Also, what the hell did it matter which way the mushrooms were chopped? They were canned mushrooms, for crying out loud! He was only going to dump the whole mess onto a grill, where any niceties in the cutting would be lost (the shoestrings of Spam were always ripped to shreds)! But Uncle Raymond insisted.

Another problem with the Crazy Omelet was that Uncle Raymond demanded that all of the items be made "fresh" (as if canned mushrooms, Spam, and corned beef could possibly be described as fresh). So to make a Crazy Omelet, Samson had to basically prepare seven dishes first. Which meant that, if Samson followed Uncle Raymond's directives, he would need over 30 minutes to make a Crazy Omelet. Which would be fine if were he still sous-chef at Pescavore, but this was a short order item at a bowling alley!

And when Samson told him how impossible it was to make one Crazy Omelet the way he demanded, Uncle Raymond would tell him that just because he was one big deal chef before, that didn't mean he didn't have a lot to learn about the short-order business.

"You chef guys," he said, as if he knew anything whatsoever about being a chef, "can take all day working on a high-class dinner! You don't know how it is here in the real world."

"Can't we at least use better ingredients?" Samson pleaded.

"It's not the ingredients; it's the love and care we put into the preparation. My mom—your grandma—could feed a family of seven with leftover fried rice and a tomato." Then Uncle Raymond would spout all that stuff about him being a chef who didn't know what it was like to improvise.

Of course, Samson didn't quite know how Uncle Raymond expected him to improvise, being that even his directions for making scrambled eggs were two pages long. So instead, Samson cheated, caching pre-cooked items surreptitiously in nondescript pots and pans. Sometimes he would take the corned beef and cabbage from the corned beef and cabbage pot. (Although they were the same recipe, Uncle Raymond demanded that the corned beef and cabbage destined for Crazy Omelets be kept apart from the corned beef and cabbage meant for the corned beef and cabbage plates.) He also found that a French fry cutter would shred a block of Spam in a second (which also made the fries more ono).

In any case, it was already three in the afternoon and these guys were ordering breakfast when he was already in late lunch mode! And they were ordering four Crazy Omelets!

Out came the precut, pre-sliced, and pre-cubed ingredients. He couldn't find the crab meat, so he got some kamaboko instead. Wham! Wham! Into the mixing bowl they went and from there onto the griddle. Samson looked around.

Good. No Uncle Raymond.

He had gotten away with it one more day.

* * *

"See," said Carl. "I told you this Crazy Omelet was crazy."

Kam nodded, his mouth full. He had never had corned beef and kamaboko in his life—let alone corned beef and kamaboko in an omelet.

Carl burped. "I think this omelet is especially crazy today—usually no more the kamaboko."

"So how's Randall doing?" Kam asked.

Saul laughed. "He's probably riding some bus in Kansas, now." After years of working with middle and high school teams, Randall Dang had left Hawai'i to pursue his dream of becoming the first Asian-American Major League umpire. Right now that crazy buggah was working for some A-level league in Iowa.

Kam looked out toward at the alley. It was full. Had plenty senior citizens, a few younger ones. Even a few haoles. He recognized people from the halau. There was Betty Manibog... And Frances Silva—somehow managing to heave her ball down the lane.

Many of them were wearing league shirts, and groups of lime green, sky blue, and cardinal red splashed through the alley like some impressionist painting. Each of them would bowl, smile or grimace at the outcome, and walk back to the rest of the group giving out high fives. Some bowled fast, some slow. Some bowled a straight ball, while others had nasty hooks. But they were all people he knew from the drugstore, the supermarket—just folks he saw around town.

Kam had heard hula, steel guitar, and kahiko chanting. He had heard children speaking pidgin English and honeycreepers fluttering in the trees. He had heard mosquitoes buzz and fish being auctioned. At night, he slept to the sound of frogs and geckoes and rain falling on the deep green leaves. But today, Kam found that no sound belonged more to Hawai'i than the rainbow cacophony of balls being hurled down hardwood lanes into rows of shiny pins.

Suddenly, Kam's attention was drawn to a figure in a purple print shirt and a long green plaid skirt. Her shoes were red and her ball was orange.

"Whoa! What team is *she* from?" Kam asked

"Who? Nona Watanabe?" They all started laughing.

"That's not for one bowling team—that's just how she dress! Try watch—good fun!"

Kam watched as Nona half strode/half stumbled, as if she were right handed and left footed. As she released the ball, she lurched forward, the backward, taking a quick step back to keep from falling. The ball veered dangerously close to the gutter—not the right side gutter, as with most right-handed bowlers—but the left side—before hooking back to the right and knocking over five or six pins. She ran to her boyfriend Harry and slapped his hand.

"How she do that?" Saul asked. "She throw right-handed, but the ball spin the other way?"

Jonny-Boy shook his head. "Unreal."

Kam noticed Harry and Nona sitting with two folks he didn't know. Then, one of them seemed familiar. *Wait a minute.* He nudged Saul. "Who's that sitting with Nona and Harry?"

Saul shrugged.

Kam thought, I've seen him before, just recently, I think in a magazine—wait a *minute...*

"No, it can't be."

"Cannot be who?" Jonny-Boy asked.

"Never mind," said Kam. "It's nothing."

Saul looked at his watch. "Eh, come on, we getta meet Noelani. She stay paying us, you know."

Carl laughed. "How the hell she get her money?"

Kam looked at the couple sitting next to Nona and Harry. *That must be him! But here? How?*

*   *   *

DANG TING STAY STUCK

"My son and I used to go fishing a lot," Steve said. He

and Harry had their poles, their gear, their buckets, and their bait and were finally at the fishing spot they had found on their fourth day of searching.

"Your son?" Then Harry stopped, because even by Steve's flashlight, he could see he was uncomfortable. "Sorry, never mind."

"No, it's fine. It's just that he goes his own way, nowadays."

"That's kids, yeah?" Harry said. "Sometimes they get hard head. They come back around eventually."

Steve stumbled and Harry steadied him quickly.

"Whoa! Watch your feet. You no like fall here."

They were about a hundred feet over the water, making their way to a black shard of rock that jut into the ocean and curled around forming a natural breakwater. It was low tide, and Harry felt that although it was a full moon, it would be a good time to fish. Steve watched Harry skip from rock to rock. Although it was a moonless night, Harry wasn't using his flashlight, though he made sure that Steve kept his on.

"No shine 'em in the water!" Harry warned. "Otherwise you going scare the fish!"

Slowly they hopped onto the outcropping. When they came to a somewhat level spot, Harry motioned that they set up their gear. After completing up his rig, Harry was about to help Steve when he noticed that Steve had been watching his actions and had set up his own. Just to make sure, Harry checked it out.

"Hey, you catch on quick."

"You have to, in my business."

They baited their hooks with squid and hopped over to the water. Harry helped Steve with the first cast, then found a place a few yards off for himself.

"Okay, now what?"

Harry opened a can of Coca-Cola.

"We wait," he said.

Actually, they did a little more than just wait. They had their plate lunches from Goto's, and some kakimochi. They also had a nice time talking story, though Harry made them keep their voices down so as not to spook the fish.

Harry asked Steve if he and Lisa enjoyed the bowling alley, to which Steve said was real lot of fun. Harry said surprised that both he and Lisa were pretty good bowlers and Steve asked why and Harry was about to tell him when Harry stopped, jerked his line, and started reeling. As planned, the kite string snapped, the line came free, and with one last pull, a fish flipped over the rocks. Was one red menpachi, with huge saucer eyes. Big one—almost a foot long! Harry laughed—quietly—as he pulled the fish off the hook and tossed it in the bucket.

Without reaching for the flashlight, Harry reassembled his rig, tied another couple of spark plugs on, and cast out his line. Steve picked up the conversation, saying that Lisa used to bowl quite a bit when she was in college. She was pretty good, probably would still be, if she were healthy.

There was a long silence.

"I hope she gets better." Although the waves crackled and foamed beneath them, Harry's voice frayed like a line being dragged over rocks.

"Your wife?" Steve asked.

"Yeah. She was one good bowler, too. I mean, your wife probably not the same. She going get better—I mean, you get the best doctors and what not."

The two fished quietly into the night. Despite the quick menpachi strike, neither of them had much luck. Still, Harry couldn't complain. They were beneath the blanket of the moon, the rocking tide, the lullaby of the trade winds.

Steve got up and came back. Then he got up again.

"What's the matter? Just settle down!"

"I'm going to change my rig."

"Why?"

"To make the fish bite."

"You cannot make the fish bite. They bite on their own."

"Well, maybe I can speed up the process." And with that, Steve stumbled out to his line.

With Steve gone, Harry found a big flat rock, and looked at the ocean, skipping moonlight back into the stars. He thought of someone who had left him years ago.

"I still hope you'll get better, you know," he said out loud, hoping that the wind would take his words across an even greater sea. A breaker misted into his face, and he rubbed his eyes with his shirt.

Damned salt. He looked back to see if Steve had heard him, but Steve wasn't there.

"Eh, Steve?"

No answer.

Harry shuffled to his feet and scampered to where Steve had been.

"Steve? Where you?"

"I'm down here, Harry," Steve said, and since his eyes had long since adjusted to the dark, Harry could see Steve was way too close to the surf.

"Hey! Get back here now!"

"I think I caught something, but I can't reel in my line!"

Harry squinted and saw Steve's pole was bending under the strain.

"Never mind," Harry said. "Cut'em. Dang ting stay stuck."

"No—I think I can get it free."

Harry watched Steve struggle. This was serious. The tide was coming up, and in this narrow inlet, the waves had even more power.

"Steve!" He was yelling now. "No be stupid! *Cut da line!*"

"I can get it!" Steve yelled back. "Here it comes!"

"Stupid haole!" Harry scrambled out to fetch Steve was. He was almost there when Steve triumphantly pulled out a fish.

"Gotcha!" he yelled, just before the wave swept him into the sea.

"STEVE!"

Harry took off his shirt and dove in. Since the tide was coming in, he knew at least they would be pushed toward the shore. Still, making it back without being sliced on the rocks wouldn't be easy.

"Relax!" Harry hoped that fear hadn't slipped into his voice. Steve thrashed and grabbed Harry's face, trying to find a place to hold. Harry brushed it away, wrapped one arm around him, and pulled his head back by the hair. He couldn't turn back to the rocks; they were too sharp and slippery. He had to get clear. Keeping Steve's nose and mouth out of the water, Harry began to swim.

Waves grind rocks into sand. It's useless to fight them. Instead, Harry used his energy to stay calm and alert. It was going to be fine. The tide was helping them, so Harry just had wait for the lull between each wave to steer from the rocks to the beach.

As another wave surged past him, Harry realized something was weighing them down. Of course! His leg! Harry twisted his body, arched his back, and with a quick snap, popped it off his stump. His body, no longer burdened by the prosthesis, gradually guided them toward a small beach. With a crash, one last wave tumbled them headfirst onto the coarse, yet welcome sand. Harry coughed out seawater and vomit as he dragged them a little farther, beyond the reach of the tide.

Suddenly, for some reason, Harry couldn't stop thinking about his wife, and that he couldn't wait to see her again, and how he missed her chicken.

But wait, that wasn't her. That was Nona.

How strange not to remember his own wife...

"Harry!" Harry was being shaken by Steve Yates.

"Huh?"

"Oh man, I'm so glad you're okay!"

"Yeah, yeah—what happened?"

"You got us to shore, then you blacked out."

A wave thundered over them.

Steve tried pulling Harry up.

"I going need your help. I no more my leg."

Steve looked down, then back at Harry.

"No worry—it's all right. We go. The tide's rising."

The two men scrambled back to the road. Halfway up, they were met by some of Steve's staff, who carried them the rest of the way.

Lisa and Nona were waiting. For Lisa, seeing Steve entered the house soaking wet was bad enough, but then she saw two of Steve's men carry Harry into the house, and his stump was dripping blood.

She screamed, but Nona calmed her down.

"Don't worry, Lisa. He had that from before. What happened to your leg, Harry?"

Harry coughed and nodded. "I was trying for fight the current, but the dang ting was weighing me down."

Nona started gave Harry a hug. Harry responded weakly, which Nona ascribed to just being exhausted.

She turned to Steve. "What happened?"

"I was being stupid. My line got stuck and I was trying to get it free."

"No, no you supposed to just cut'em!" Nona interrupted.

"I know. Harry tried to tell me. Then the wave came."

Steve's doctor gave Harry the once over (you'll be fine, just be clear next time whether you're going fishing or diving), gave him a pair of crutches (of course they just had a pair of crutches handy) and, once Harry had showered and washed up, Nona and Harry made their way home.

Nona noticed that he hadn't said a word.

"Harry, I brought you some chicken. Harry?"

But Harry said nothing.

"Harry. I so glad you okay. Getta be careful you know." Nona tried again, but Harry still was silent.

The rest of the drive to Harry's place was just as silent and, at his house, when at he fetched his crutches and limped away, he didn't even look back.

"I glad you okay, Harry. If you were gone, I'd be alone."

"Welcome to my world," Harry mumbled.

He walked into his house and shut the door.

Nona sat there a while, as mismatched as always. Sometimes she thought Harry was mismatched, too. But, no, he was just missing something. Someone. Of course that someone wasn't her.

On her way home, Nona never thought about driving her car off the cliff. She just closed her eyes and put her foot on the accelerator. The car hurtled down the road. One second, two... It would be over any time. Three seconds, four... Still, her car was on the road. She opened her eyes and she was still cruising right down the center of her lane.

What happened? She smelled her chicken in the back seat as the rain tapped on her windshield like a mother waking a child from a dream.

* * *

Noelani Choi did not bowl. Not only did she not bowl, she had only been in the bowling alley a few times. She had nothing against bowling; it was just that when she was growing up, hula took most of her time and now that she was a kumu, she was still busy and her students thought of her only as a kumu and a Christian and didn't even think about asking her for go bowling. Actually, Jonny-Boy had thought about asking a few times, but he never got up the nerve.

When Ku'uipo arrived at Noelani's, she greeted them with a big aloha and a smile that was so damned beautiful it made Kam think *Oh my God I think I'm going to die.* After her obligatory prayer, she told them about doing a Passion-Play-type thing in hula.

"But you guys know four hours of chanting can get pretty monotonous." She laughed. "Still, if we can put on one of those big Vegas-kine productions, that would be something, yeah?"

At first Kam wasn't quite listening, caught by the music in her voice. Then it hit him. *This was a terrible idea.*

Even Jonny-Boy curled his brow. "Hmm. Going be tough."

"Nah," said Carl. "Duck soup!" But of course, that was Carl.

Kam and Saul both said nothing, for pretty much the same reasons. The only difference was that Noelani knew Saul, but Kam was a stranger. So, where with Saul, she was able to write off a look of disapproval, she could not ignore Kam.

"What's the matter?" she said sharply. "You get issues?"

Jonny-Boy was going to say something for Kam, but Kam spoke up himself, saying that he thought that she should reconsider what she was doing. He'd seen this sort of thing before, and it never worked.

"What kine ting?" she replied. "Are you even Christian?"

"Of course not. I'm Jewish."

The look on Noelani's face was indescribable. She was confronting her first Jew, her first Pharisee, her first Jesus-killer. "A *Jew?*" she sneered.

"Whoa! Don't go all anti-Semitic on me. Of course I'm Jewish."

There would always be other beautiful girls, but even a lapsed Jew is still a Jew.

"Anti-what?" Noelani said the term as if she had never heard it before, which was true. Although Kam had a hard time believing it at the time, Jews just weren't part of the Hawaiian lexicon. They were distant, mythical, far away.

And Noelani was not only shocked that Kam was Jewish, but that he admitted it. He was even proud of it! Why anyone would publicly admit that he had killed the Son of God?!

"Get out of my house!" she said, her eyes showing every bit of disgust she could muster.

But rather than cowering, as evil was always supposed to do, Kam matched her gaze. Actually, he focused on a slight blemish she had under her lip, the only imperfection he could find on her face. Still, it was enough to anchor him in reality.

"You may be sort of cute on the outside, but inside?" He shook his head, turned, and walked out.

"What was that for?" Carl asked.

"He's a Jew and this is a Christian group."

Saul got up from the sofa and fixed his hat. "I thought that this was a Hawaiian group."

"It is," said Noelani. "But it's Hawaiian and Christian."

"Randall was Buddhist."

"Okay, I guess, Buddhist okay, too."

"And what, Jewish is not?"

"Why you defending that haole, anyway?"

Saul said nothing more. Instead he walked out the door. Carl stuttered, then stumbled after him; Jonny-Boy could hear him trying for talk and not succeeding.

Noelani started crying and leaned on Jonny-Boy, who,

unable to do anything else, put his arm around her and told her everything was going to be okay.

Chapter 4

No Can Dance

The next day, Harry called and Nona didn't pick up the phone. He called again, and again she didn't pick up. The third time, of course was always the charm.

"Hello?"

"Nona, can you come over? I tired eat eggs."

He knew everything was going be okay, just the way it should be, yeah?

"No Harry. I don't think so." Click. Harry stood there with his phone without Nona, and he wasn't even thinking about chicken.

In a way, Nona was relieved that Harry called, but she never feel like talking to him just now. She wondered whom she could talk to, but no more nobody. Eva Matsuoka? Nona wasn't that stupid. Noelani? No.

And Nona had no relatives. Her mom died when she was a baby, and her dad when she was still in high school.

"Hello, Lisa? This is Nona. You busy this afternoon?" She felt stupid the moment she said this, I mean, people like her didn't just call up people like *her*. "Oh, maybe I shouldn't have called, I uh—"

"Oh, of course, please come over!" Lisa blurted, and Nona could feel her smile from the other end of the phone. "Steve is out on business and it gets lonely around here."

When she got to the house, Lisa was in front of a canvas, comparing its half-finished panorama to what she saw out of her window. It was a seascape, but it still wasn't right. *Never mind. I'll continue it later.*

Lisa got up, shivered slightly, and walked over to the door. She opened it just as Nona was about to ring the bell.

"Oh Nona, it's so nice of you to come over!" She gave the big awkward woman an even bigger hug.

Despite their differences, Nona and Lisa had at least one thing in common: neither of them really had any female friends. Lisa had been with Steve for what seemed like forever, and Nona never was part of any crowd, even before she met Harry. As such, neither of them seemed to know how to start talking. So Nona mentioned the painting, and Lisa went on about how it wasn't right. Somehow, the scene wasn't coming to life.

"What do you think, Nona?"

"The colors." Nona let her voice almost die as she said this, because coming from someone as mismatched as she was, Lisa would almost surely think that she was crazy.

But Lisa looked at the canvas and tilted her head.

"Explain?"

"Well...it looks like the plants stay inside too long. If you trying to paint the outside, then why not, you know, paint outside?"

Lisa looked again, slowly, and began to nod. "You're right. You know, I thought I got the colors pretty close."

"I know, but you never going be close enough."

"Nona?"

"Oh Lisa, I'm sorry. I never mean you." She began to cry. "I never mean your painting."

"Shhh. It's okay. What's wrong, Nona? Is it Harry?"

At the sound of his name, Nona started shaking. Her tears sparked in the sunlight as they fell.

"He's been acting, you know, strange. Not just after the fishing trip, but even before. He starts out nice, then he just gets quiet. No can even look at me. And stay getting worse. I know he leaving."

"Oh no, Nona," Lisa protested.

"No, I mean it! And why not? I'm fat, stupid, no can dance, no can wear the right kine colors, the only thing I can do is cook chicken and even that, last night he never like." Nona stopped. Her mouth stayed open, as if to breathe or moan, but neither sound nor breath emerged. Then, she whispered, "Last night, I closed my eyes and drove my car down the highway as fast as I could. I wanted to drive right off the cliff. But even that, I screwed up."

"Oh Nona!" Lisa brushed the hair from her eyes.

Gradually Nona stopped crying. Lisa poured her a glass of guava juice. The smells and color of the juice reminded her of Nona, of rainforests, of being in the sun. She thought of her days spent indoors, trying to paint what was the outside. Nona was right.

"Nona! I think we both could use have a girls' day out!"

"Girls' day out? Where?"

"Um... Shopping?"

Nona shook her head.

"Good," said Lisa. "I don't feel like shopping either. It's just that that's what I thought women did when they went out."

"Only skinny women with plenty money. Oh! I didn't mean that!"

Lisa laughed.

"Point taken. Still...where can we go to get out, to see outside?"

Nona paused.

"Hey—have you been Kilauea?"

*　*　*

"Maybe if you just apologize," Jonny-Boy suggested.

Ku'uipo was back at the bowling alley. Jonny-Boy had figured that two hours was enough time to cool off. All he needed to do was talk some sense into Kam.

But Kam was making sense enough to himself already.

"Reality check, everyone. She should be apologizing to me." Kam didn't even look at Jonny-Boy. He knew he was the newcomer; if they wanted, they could move on with the group and there would be no hard feelings. "Whatever you decide is fine with me. Except I'm not apologizing for anything. Call me if you want." And then he was gone.

Carl fidgeted with a napkin. "Cannot make him work with someone he no like work with. Anyway, life goes on, yeah? Plenty people can play guitar."

"You think so?" Saul leaned back and pushed his hat over his eyes.

Carl and Jonny-Boy said a few more things, actually more than a few, but none of them were particularly important. So Saul didn't listen. Instead, he ordered some gravy fries.

There were only a few cold fries left soaking in the gravy when Saul finally spoke again.

"If Kam no play, I no play either."

What!?

"We need the haole." Saul held his soda in front of him

and watched the bubbles rise around the straw. "Carl, when did we start the group?"

"Ten, no, eleven years ago. Why?"

"Did we *ever* get that kine audience at Kalani's before?"

Carl stopped. Of course Iz was always good for applause, but there really seemed to be something different that night. The music and audience seemed closer and more real.

"Haole boy thinks everybody went cheer for Iz. That's what we told him, yeah? But remember before, how was with Domingo, and then Randall? Was good, but not like this. Not just Iz, you guys. Haole boy special."

Saul ate the last gravy fry.

"And besides, haole boy right."

*   *   *

After he left the alley, Kam got in his car and drove to nowhere in particular. He didn't feel like going to his new apartment. He was out of the band—that much he was sure of—and he probably never would speak to Noelani again. Yet he felt at peace.

He remembered an old, sad tale of a great Jewish teacher who was betrayed, imprisoned, and burned at stake. As the flames consumed his body, he began to laugh. When his shocked tormentors asked him why he was laughing, he declared that all his life he had wondered whether his faith was strong enough to carry him unto death. Now, he finally knew that it was. [*martyr*]

"What greater reason is there for joy?"

And, of course, this was nothing so serious as being burned at stake, and he didn't feel like laughing, but in his peace was the exquisite, invincible joy of successfully passing a test of faith.

Kam bit off some dried cuttlefish that he bought from

KTA, not because it was exotic, but because it was now what he snacked on. The phone rang, and when he answered he knew that whatever decision had been made, his decision had been the right one.

*   *   *

Some people, no matter now hard they try to get good at something, they still cannot get good. Maybe they just don't have talent, or maybe something inside them is not letting them succeed.

What's even stranger is that for some people the opposite is true. No matter how much they try to fail, they still succeed. That was Noelani, who would probably have looked graceful falling into an irrigation ditch.

And even now, as her body convulsed with sadness, had people been there to see, they would have found beauty in her motion. Had they listened to her sobbing, they would have heard music. Had they smelled her tears, they would have smelled like fresh Akaka rain. Blessed, her parents used to say. And for most people, they would think that was enough.

For most people, to have that sort of gift, first of natural grace, then beauty, then to be almost an embodiment of the hula, that would have been enough.

For most people, even a kind word from Aunty Kapolinahe Kahakunoe, who, despite her name was usually far from gentle, would be cause for celebration. To be called the finest dancer she had ever taught—and Aunty made no secret of this—would have been an honor beyond most people's imagination.

But most people were not Noelani.

How hard does a fish have to work to swim? No need work at all, stay in the blood, already. Likewise, was with Noelani and hula. Yeah, she had to work, but the work was to uncover what was already inside, not to find something she never have. And if she were one selfish bitch, would be easy. She could say, "I'm brilliant and they not and that's just the way it stay."

But Noelani never could do that. There were two things that Noelani believed in more than anything in the world. One was that everyone had the capacity to dance the hula. The second was that everyone who desired to dance the hula had the right to dance as well as she. And early on in her art, she realized that there was a huge gap between what she saw and what she knew, or at least thought she knew, just had to be true.

She saw what other people went through to make even modest gains in their art.

Meanwhile, she simply stepped and moved and it was hula. When she opened her mouth to chant, it was as if there was some sort of trick in her throat that made the notes send chills down the spines of the old Hawaiians.

Why did it come so easily for her? There was no logic to this. How she was quickly chosen as the lead dancer in the wahine group despite being only twelve. She saw the envy and resentment from the others in Aunty's halau. Even worse was the awe—some of the fellow dancers looked at her as some sort of dancing spirit, saying how lucky they were that Noelani had come to them to dance and how they could never dream to be anywhere near as good. Noelani would sometimes hear this and come home crying, to her parents who thought that she was just trying to get more attention. Surely, no one could feel bad about being admired! "You lucky, 'Lani! No be ungrateful!"

What they never understood was that by dancing, Noelani had embodied the opposite of what she held dear. The hula should be for everyone. Yet each time Noelani took the stage, her form swayed ever more from the realm of what others deemed possible.

"Of course you can dance like me," she would plead. "You just have to work harder!" Which simply wasn't true.

Many in the halau felt that she was insulting them. It seemed obvious. Of course she would insult them—after all isn't that what anyone would do if she were that good, that beautiful?

Others tried to believe her, and tried to work harder, at least at first. But they could never catch up with her, and they would feel ashamed, not because they hadn't improved, but because they had dared to imagine that they could be as beautiful as Noelani Choi. So instead of resenting Noelani, they resented themselves.

 In the depths of her despair, Noelani discovered Jesus Christ. Not that Jesus Christ acknowledged her. In fact, Noelani felt her prayers to Jesus were words into empty air.

She went to a revival and saw people being overcome by the Holy Spirit. They would be wracked with emotion—crying uncontrollably, laughing, writhing on the floor. But as hard as Noelani tried—the spirit rejected her. But that was a new feeling. She would try praying harder and still no connection. Was this what it was like to feel rejection?

And so, Noelani decided to devote her life to Jesus Christ, to whom all her gifts, her genius, her beauty meant the same thing as they now meant to her. Nothing.

So, when Aunty's halau moved to Oʻahu four years ago, Noelani stayed behind with her Bible and a part-time job teaching hula to children at the Community Center.

And Jesus still had not answered her prayers. Until now.

*　*　*

"Harry!" Steve knocked on the door. "Harry!"

"What what what?" Harry was still making monku because he snapped at Nona, whom he shouldn't have snapped at and now she was mad at him, which she should be.

Stupid stupid stupid.

He had attached his other leg—heavier, but functional, so he limped only a little bit as he answered the door.

"What? What's the matter?"

"Nothing's the matter." Steve had brought over two plate lunches and a large package.

"Matsuoka's?"

"Yeah, I thought I would try them out."

"Well, not to be mean or anything, but I no usually go over there. That Eva—kind of pilau, that lady."

"Yeah, I gathered that, but I had some business to do in the area."

"What's this?" Harry pointed at the package,

"A present. Harry—you saved my life."

Harry laughed. "Me—save *you?* I no think so—you not the type who needs saving. I think maybe you fell into the water to test me or something."

Steve shook his head. "When you said that I should let some things go, well, I let some things go."

"Wait a minute. If you could've been killed out there—why didn't you listen to me? I mean—I thought that you were just sort of fooling around."

Steve bit his lip.

"Damn! Really!?"

"I'll be careful next time."

It was Harry's turn to say nothing.

"Aren't you supposed to say 'Next time—there isn't going to be a next time?'"

"Why should I waste my breath? I know we going back fishing again." Harry finally said. Then he winked. "We in Hawai'i, you know."

Steve looked at Harry's leg. A little blood was seeping

around the top, where it fit into the prosthesis, no doubt because of the abrasions from the fishing accident.

"It's okay. No hurt as bad as when I lost the real one. Work accident. Anyway, that's my million-dollar injury. Insurance is one good thing.

"Besides, how many people can say they get one spare leg at home?" Harry grinned,."Only thing, this old leg cannot go where my other one could. It's heavier. And the plastic going cut on the rocks."

"There are new artificial legs, you know," Steve said. "Smart legs that use nerve impulses to trigger all sorts of motion."

"Yeah I heard of those," Harry said.

Steve grinned. "Not like the ones I'm talking about."

Harry looked at his leg, and then at the package Steve had with him. "You know, Steve, I've been this way for years. This leg is no big deal. So if this is a new leg..."

"Just open the bag."

Harry opened the bag and grinned. It was Harry's leg, the one he had lost at sea.

"Wow! Thanks, eh? How you find 'em?"

"My divers recovered it, then I had it completely cleaned."

Harry reached back and unbuckled his other leg, grimacing as it fell away. He readjusted the stump, then carefully put it into the socket of the new leg.

It ached a little, but nowhere near as badly as he expected. He stopped, then looked at Steve. "Hey—this feels pretty good." He tested his weight, then walked a little more.

"I replaced a couple of the parts with stronger and lighter components. It should be a lot more comfortable. Of course, I still want to get you that new leg. We can have you fitted whenever you...oh, never mind."

Steve let his voice trail as Harry hopped around the house, marveling at the difference just a few ounces and a couple of new parts could make.

GET PLENTY STUFF TO SEE

Lisa and Nona stopped their car and walked outside.

They had come to what was to most desolate place Lisa had ever seen. No plants, no nothing. Just black. The black rock. Not just black the way rich soil gets black, but as pure—unnaturally pure—black as the clouds were white. The black stretch of lava was a mixture of loose glasslike cinder and smoother places where the rock, once molten and flowing like gravy, had congealed into dead and silent stone.

Despite herself, Lisa started to cry.

"Oh no! What's wrong, Lisa? You went hurt yourself?"

"I was just thinking...this must be what the end of the world looks like!"

"Oh Lisa! You got 'em mixed up. This not the end. This the *beginning*. Pele stay all over here, making brand new land." Nona smiled as she mentioned the Volcano Goddess, and for an instant, her eyes seemed to catch fire themselves.

"This is all brand new! One day, between the cracks, going have plants. Pretty soon, going have birds, too. One day, with all the waves, might even be one black sand beach."

As Nona tiptoed toward the lava, Lisa held her breath, hoping that she wouldn't slip on the sharp rocks. But once on the lava, Nona seemed to forget herself and glide across them as if riding on a song. To their left, a plume of steam and smoke rose high into the air from where the fresh lava poured into the ocean. In front of them, an occasional splash peaked over the cliff. Over time, this would all be soil. Rain would fall. A plant would grow. And Nona, all mixed up in color, gliding across the lava shards, was like a single, improbable flower, a brash stunning truth that even here, there was, and would be, life.

Lisa tried to follow, but she wasn't Nona, and for her, the rocks were brittle and very sharp. As she stumbled, Nona hopped over to her and led her back to the car.

"No need walk over the rocks—get plenty stuff to see from here."

She motioned down. "Besides, not all black. Try look. See in between the rocks? The shiny stuff."

Lisa saw little bits of golden string. It looked like seaweed."

"Careful! It's glass! We call that 'Pele's Hair.' It's from the volcano, when the lava flies into the wind."

"Pele?"

"Oh. Pele. Wow... Big question. I know you can read the old Hawaiian stories, and how certain things stay sacred to her. You know, stuff like lehua flowers, ohelo berries. Nowadays, people still making stories about her—how she protect the island, shows up in dreams, sometimes even helps people who stay in trouble."

"And you?"

Nona leaned against the car and sighed. "Too much for me. All I know is, well, you remember what I said about painting outside, when you stay outside? In a way, that's like Pele, too." She pointed across the ocean. "Try look! You see out there?"

Lisa looked, but all she saw was water.

"Over there one more island stay coming up. Even get one name—Lo'ihi. Stay underwater now. They say not going break the surface for over 20,000 years.

"Before I met Harry, sometimes I would spend hours here, just by myself, looking over the waves. I wonder who going live there? Who going call that new island home?"

Lisa, Nona, and the driver leaned against the car,

watching the earth renew. The driver frowned and looked behind him.

"What's wrong?"

"I think someone's watching us," he said.

Lisa smiled and gestured to Nona, who had closed her eyes, perhaps imagining children playing on the future shores of Lo'ihi.

"Don't worry so much. I think we're safe."

The driver nodded and tried to relax. He thought he heard a little girl laughing, or an old woman, and he tried to convince himself it was a bird, though there were no birds overhead.

Lisa took a deep breath in this new place. Here, just a few feet away, were places where no one, no human or animal, had ever walked, where no seed had ever landed, no roots had ever taken hold.

* * *

Kam answered his phone. It was Carl.

"Kam, we need you to stay with us," he said.

"Cool," said Kam.

"But—"

Kam sighed. There was always a "but."

"Yeah?"

"But we like you to try work things out with Noelani."

"I said I'm not apologizing!"

"No Kam! Wait! Nobody need to apologize to nobody if you guys no like. We just like you work 'em out between yourselves. We went call Noelani, too. Please."

Kam said nothing.

"Look, Kam, if no can, no can," Carl hesitated. "You still going be in the band. But you no think that at least you should try?"

A younger Kam wouldn't have listened.

But a younger Kam wouldn't have moved to Hawai'i, either.

"Sure. Why not?"

Carl laughed his high-pitched laugh and Kam could hear him yammer to the rest of the group, "He said yes, going be okay! See I told you guys, yeah? What did I say? Going be just—"

"Okay okay!" Kam tried to shut Carl up. "Now what?"

"You know, go meet with her. She stay waiting at her place. Go over and—"

"No."

"Huh? B-but you just said you'd talk to her."

"Why should I go over to her? Tell her to meet me at Kapiolani Park this afternoon—you know, in the pavilion?"

"Yeah, okay. I tell her. But what if she get's mad?"

Kam hung up.

*　*　*

Kam bought a couple of sodas, a copy of the newspaper, some sushi from Goto's, then drove to the park. As an afterthought, he pulled his guitar from the trunk. Kam wasn't sure if Noelani was even going show, so he figured that he might as well entertain himself.

It was one of those afternoons where the sky is a little cloudy—overcast, even—but the sun is shining just above the clouds. Hilo is on the wet side of the Big Island, so plants grow like crazy in the rich black soil. In light like that, all the green from the plants seems to dance across the land.

There was no one under the pavilion, so Kam found himself a nice picnic table and, resting his feet on the bench, sat on top. He looked out at the ohi'a trees, seeing huge cymbidium orchids and philodendrons climbing up their trunks. His mother once tried to raise a cymbidium in LA, but it was never wet enough. He thought he might call her one day. Maybe sooner than he thought.

A bird flew under the pavilion, and he smelled a light veil of rain misting upon the jade green grass. He pulled his guitar from the case and started making up a song to the rain.

Kapiolani Park was placed right where the river met the ocean, so the water was at times fresh, salt, or in between, so at various places along the park route one could see different types of bird and fish. Lots of kids went there to feed the ducks. Today, some kolohe ones were feeding the ducks bread spiked with chili pepper sauce.

Oh oh, here comes their tutu! Kam watched her give one of them a good smack across the okole. More stuff to put in the song. He smiled, gulped some soda, and grabbed a piece of ahi sushi. He dunked it in the shoyu, shoved it in his mouth, and licked his fingers clean. Then picked up his guitar and resumed playing.

Hmmm... Saul's voice would be perfect.

He just bought the guitar. Most of the musicians he saw were playing steel guitars, but Kam felt that the gentle sound of the nylon perfectly matched what he felt from the place. Kam had missed playing, more than he cared to admit. He had been one of those rare L.A. guitar players who, rather than to get laid or famous, had actually taken up the guitar to play the guitar.

It was just something he did and did well, though maybe like one faithful girlfriend who would always be there, maybe he took the guitar too much for granted, because one day he put it down, said "I need to make some money," went to business school and that was that.

Until, of course, he got on a plane to Hawai'i, in search of something he couldn't even name.

Suddenly, Kam noticed a small kid looking at him.

Skinny boy, about eight, with brown hair, brown skin, and big brown eyes and a mouth that was open. He stopped playing.

"Hey kid. How you doing?"

The kid looked a little scared and made to dash away.

"No no! Come back here!" Kam laughed. "You play too?"

The boy nodded.

"Here," Kam handed him the guitar. "No worry—you're not going to break it."

The boy tried to stretch his fingers across the fretboard.

"This is a classical guitar. The neck might be a little wide."

The boy nodded and started playing—slowly, and with a lot of mistakes—an old Hawai'i song. Still, it was only two chords, and Kam recognized it immediately.

"You're learning Hi'ilawe?"

"Do you know Hi'ilawe?" the boy asked, and he was not asking, "Eh, how one haole know Hi'ilawe?" but simply, "Wow, do you know that song?"

And for Kam, who had been trying to justify his existence to everyone—who had been feeling so left out, so separated—this was the first time he felt like he was actually a part of the landscape. And it simply felt good.

"A little." Kam shrugged and reached for the guitar. "Here, let me show you. Okay. You usually play this one in slack key, but you can do it with standard tuning, too. You're learning it in standard, right?"

The boy nodded.

"Good. Learn the standard way, then you'll appreciate slack key even more.

"Now, this song only has two chords in it: G and A7."

He played the chords back and forth a few times, mechanically. "Sounds kind of boring after a while, right? So you've got to play it with a lot of feeling."

And suddenly it became music, and the easy, yet painfully mournful beauty of the classic song once again serenaded

Kapiolani Park, where it had no doubt been played at parties and family gatherings for generations.

"Don't snap the strings like you're fighting them. Pull them and set them free. You see?" Then Kam began to sing...

Kamaka ka ikena ia Hiʻilawe
I ka papa lohi mai aʻo Maukele

Pakele mai au i ka nui manu
Hauwalaʻau nei puni Waipiʻo

Aʻole no wau e loaʻa mai
A he uhiwai au no ke kuahiwi

Kam stopped. "I forgot what comes next. Do you speak Hawaiian?"

The boy shook his head.

"Good. Me neither!" Both of them laughed. "If my friend Saul were here, oh he'd be singing this like you've never heard. But never mind. No need for words. Just the song. All you need is the song."

Kam started playing again. The boy listened.

"Hey! Boy! There you are! I was looking all over for you!" The boy's father looked over at Kam. "He was bothering you?"

Kam shrugged, "No, no. We were just trading guitar secrets."

The man nodded. "Yeah, this one." He mussed the kid's hair. "We go home, boy."

The boy looked at Kam. Kam winked.

"Now, go play!"

Kam chuckled to himself, turned, and saw Noelani. Still beautiful as ever. But —

—but... Noelani had been watching Kam for the past ten minutes as he taught the boy. Listening to him talk to the boy, and then talk about the song....

Noelani had almost not come to the park. She was still angry with Kam for presuming to say that her inspiration might be a bad idea. How dare he?!

Also, judging by the way he acted, he probably had one crush on her, which was repulsive anyway. She was *not* into haoles—too clumsy, too noisy. Always talking about themselves, too. But Carl had asked her to just try work things out, and well, he was so earnest about it, for Carl. And inside, she knew Kam was the best she had heard. So she said sure, why not.

"Kam."

"Noelani."

"Nice Hiʻilawe."

Now, Noelani said this not just because she meant it. Growing up as a beautiful exotic woman, she developed a "haole test."

Here's how it worked. Noelani would compliment a haole guy. The haole guy would first say, "Oh, that's nothing," then go off for an extended period talking about himself and how wonderful he was, his job and his skills and his blah blah blah.

Some would do it directly, some would do it almost covertly, while seeming sensitive and caring. In they end, however, it was failure all the same.

But Kam didn't talk. Instead he nodded from somewhere far away.

"Come in from the rain. You're getting all wet."

So she did.

"Want a piece of sushi?"

"No, I already went eat."

"I was almost hoping you wouldn't come by."

"I almost never."

Noelani looked at the stream, not sure of how much was freshwater and how much was salt.

Chapter 5

"HARRY AND I ARE PLANNING OUR NEXT FISHING TRIP. If you don't mind."

Lisa sipped her tea.

"And if I minded, could I stop you?"

"Yes, you could."

There were some rules even Steve Yates had to follow. Even for Lisa. Especially with Lisa. The first time she got sick, she nearly died, but Steve said no. Sometimes helps to be high mukka-mukka. So it was the second and third time and after. Finally, Lisa told Steve enough. She wanted to leave this world as naturally as she came in. She was tired. And, for all his power, Steve knew she was right.

Lisa put her teacup down.

"Oh, that Nona. She's amazing! You should have seen her, Steve, skipping over the lava like it was a dance floor. So beautiful, against the black and the blue, blue skies...so beautiful."

"Harry was talking about his wife," Steve said.

And Lisa finally understood why Harry was acting so

strangely to Nona.

Sometimes being too faithful can break more than one's heart. To love so much, so long, after someone is gone, and never coming back.

You could lose yourself, in your faith, as time passes you, as months and years slip past saints, shooting stars and ancient trees.

Time passes. How much more, Steve wouldn't say. That was his prerogative. He had been acting very concerned towards her the past few years, so she knew the time was probably coming soon. It was okay.

She had outlived so many friends. For once, perhaps it would be nice not to be the one to say goodbye.

Pele

There was a knock on the door. Lisa looked at Steve who, *Pele* puzzled, looked back at her.

"I wasn't expecting anyone. Were you?"

Lisa shook her head.

Lisa heard the butler speaking with what sounded somewhat like an old lady.

"Oh what a nice house," the voice said. "Can I look inside?"

The butler said something, but the voice and its owner pushed past him into the living room.

"Oh—don't worry—I just came by to see my old place. Yes, yes."

"I just wanted for stop by and say hello." The voice belonged to an old Hawaiian lady with in an old style high-necked mu'u-mu'u. Her laugh was like birthday candles, and her smile caused something inside Lisa to melt.

"This area used to be my home. Right after I moved from Kohala. All this place. Oh, was so nice. But you folks stay make this place nice, too."

"The two of us put a lot of work into it, but it's mostly Steve's doing."

Lisa looked around for Steve, but he had disappeared from the room.

The old woman handed Lisa a brown paper bag. Inside it was a mason jar, and inside that was what looked a bit like cranberry preserves, only the red was deeper and wiser. "Here—I like you have this. Ohelo jam! Real homemade kine. Cannot buy this in the stores, you know."

"Thank you," said Lisa. The old woman winked, and for a split second, Lisa saw fire dancing in her eyes.

"Oh! I so happy have one nice young couple living over here," the woman walked out, smelled the air outside. "Maybe bumbye you can spend some time for talk story with this old lady. I love stories, you know"

"I would like that very much, ma'am," Lisa said.

"Child, this is Hawaii—just call me Aunty."

"Thank you, Aunty. Please come by any time."

The old woman winked.

"Aloha."

"Aloha," Lisa said as the old lady closed the door. Soon, Steve came back into the room and Lisa showed him the ohelo jam.

"Where did you get that?"

"That nice old lady gave it to me."

"Nice old lady?"

"The one who was just here."

"Here?"

Steve walked over to the door, opened it and frowned.

"I don't see anyone."

"You're kidding, right? She left not more than a minute ago."

Steve shook his head. Strange. He was used to knowing who was coming and going from his land.

Lisa opened the jar. The jam smelled sweet, fresh, like her drive with Nona. Not fresh like the ocean, no.

It was the freshness of the volcano.

"Are you sure you should eat that?"

"Don't be silly!" The stuck her pinky in the jar and tasted. It was as if the music and sunsets and fire of a thousand years had been somehow blended with four cups cane sugar and a pouch of Certo fruit pectin.

"Steve, you've *got* to try this."

Lisa dabbed jam on Steve's tongue. Steve paused, then shook his head. He tasted nothing. Not good or bad. Just nothing.

"Really?"

Steve went back to the door. "Did she say who she was?"

"Just that she had lived here on this land before. What's wrong?"

"Nothing, nothing..."

Steve had done extensive research on this land, the way only Steve Yates could do, and he knew there were no records of anyone having lived on it before.

*   *   *

Nona finally picked up the phone. Harry said let's go mall, but Nona said she'd rather just walk around the park. Maybe even the beach.

Oh, that Lisa was so nice, Nona thought. And so sad to be that sick. Nona had eyes. She could see how Steve looked after her when they went out. Maybe cancer or something. Whatever it was, was bad.

Harry's wife had died of cancer. Harry hadn't talked much about it, but his wife was always in his mind. Many times Nona felt maybe she should say something, but it never felt right. And that wasn't her way. Her way was to go out somewhere, maybe the park, maybe the beach, where Harry might talk to her, maybe not out loud, but in other ways.

Had Harry known this, he would have laughed because it was so much like fishing—being patient, the finding the right spot, then waiting quietly. Instead, he looked at the ocean and thought of his time in the water—where he had not looked forward to joining his wife, but instead had struggled so hard to stay with Nona.

death

It never occurred to him that he might cling so hard to life. He was to be reunited with his wife. But then, not spending another day with Nona Watanabe? Not going shopping at Longs, or watching her throw that crooked ball down the alley? Not smelling her cooking while he was outside pulling weeds, or eating mountain apples at Coconut Island?

He missed his wife, but he wasn't ready to go just yet. Not now.

"What the hell you going do?" He asked out loud, but not really out loud. He turned to Nona and just looked at her.

*　*　*

Hula practice that week was much more upbeat. Noelani had designed new outfits— headdresses and shirts of coarse linen, much like what might have been worn in the Middle East, while the bottoms remained reminiscent of ancient Hawaiian clothing. "Lucky those guys had hot weather too," Noelani joked.

One of the big problems for the production was that Jesus and his Apostles were men, while her halau had mostly women. Noelani didn't want to ask the other halau for male dancers because she didn't want to let them know her plan.

She held up a malo, then looked at Kuʻuipo.

"Uh, no way I going wear one diaper," said Carl.

"They're *malos*, and you'd look so cute!"

Suddenly, Bernadine Torres pointes at Kam, "Hey, Kam can be Jesus! He looks just like him!"

Everyone nodded "Yeah, Kam can be Jesus!"

"I am *not* going to be Jesus. I'm Jewish."

"So was Jesus," said Carl, hoping this would divert attention away from his having to wear a diaper.

"Noelani?"

Noelani laughed. "No worry, you no going play Jesus. You no could even dance the part." Noelani giggled, turned, and it was a musical thing that left Kam speechless. "Anyway, if Kam stay Jesus, who going play the music?"

The halau nodded. Made sense.

"Then who going play Jesus?" someone asked.

"I think Ervin would make one wonderful Jesus," Noelani said.

"What—Ervin Shimabukuro? One Okinawan Jesus?" Bernadine Torres whined. "Who ever heard of one Okinawan Jesus?"

Arlene Aragaki stood up. "So what kine Jesus you like, Bernadine—Porrogee?"

"Eh—at least us guys Christian!"

"What about Ignacio?" Nona ventured.

"Yeah, what about me? I the best dancer here. You get something against one Filipino Jesus?"

"No, matter if Filipino or not," Frances Silva stood up and the old woman pointed a finger at Ignacio. "But Jesus shouldn't be mahu."

The room fell silent.

"Mahu?" Kam whispered to Jonny-Boy.

"Gay," Jonny-Boy answered.

"Oh shit," Kam shook his head. He thought of Noelani's

reaction to his being Jewish. He was reminded that, as beautiful as this place was, he was still on an island.

"*Why not?* You tink Jesus nevah went save us too?" yelled Ignacio.

"Jesus Christ was *not* mahu," insisted Frances.

"Well he wasn't Okinawan, either," Bernadine quipped.

"Quiet, quiet!" Noelani clapped her hands to get their attention. "We stay getting nowhere. I said Ervin Shimabukuro going be Jesus, even if he Okinawan."

"What you mean by 'even'?" snorted Arlene, but Noelani pretended she didn't hear and continued, saying Ervin going be fine. Ervin squinted, shrugged a decidedly non-Jesus-like shrug and waved meekly.

Ignacio pouted. "I the best dancer here. If I no can be Jesus, well maybe I quit, then."

"Go then!" said Frances.

Noelani threw up her hands for help that never came.

*   *   *

"Noelani, this is *not* going to work."

Kam and Noelani had decided to remain after the practice to sort more stuff out. They had a good talk in the park, as evidenced by Kam's being at the practice in the first place, but there was still more to talk about.

"Noelani. Can you honestly look me the eye and tell me we can pull this off?"

"With Jesus, anything stay possible." She said this with as much conviction as she could gather, but to Kam's ear, it seemed a little too mechanical.

"You don't believe that."

"You wouldn't understand what I believe."

"Really?"

Noelani started putting away the equipment from the

practice. Goodness, her students could be such slobs sometimes! She started humming to herself.

Then Kam picked up his guitar.

"No even *try* follow, haole."

Noelani thought about the other times other musicians had tried to follow her music. Uniform disasters. They would ride roughshod over the music, or pay too much attention to the notes, or rush the timing...

Musicians and their instruments, *waste time!*

But then suddenly Noelani felt a song rise around her. It was as if what she were about to sing was being played even as she thought of it. And, since the song was all around her, without thinking, she began to dance.

Kam made that guitar cry. It cried, with every lonely night after hula, wishing to fit in with the other dancers, peering past even the vision of Aunty Kahakunoe. Because he understood. That beauty without reason or purpose was a barren, lifeless wasteland.

The moon had shifted, the tide had come in, and after all those years of feeling alone, there was a song. Suddenly, she stopped.

Jonny-Boy had all this time been peeking in the window. He covered his eyes knowing, just knowing, that Noelani and Kam were about to kiss. But their faces never turned.

* * *

That night, Kam had a strange dream. He was at the beach fishing—it seemed like Kolekole Park. Steve Yates, that multibillionaire guy—or at least someone who looked a lot like him—walked across the water to him.

"Catch anything?"

Kam shook his head.

"Be careful—the waves here can get pretty wicked. I should know."

Steve stepped ashore and sat next to him.

"Weird place, isn't this?"

"Yeah," agreed Kam, surprised that he would treat Yates so casually.

"I've been watching you, Mel—I mean Kam. You've been out here quite a bit. What are you fishing for?"

Kam nodded, though he wasn't a fisherman. Then he remembered that this was a dream and the fishing part probably had some deeper meaning.

"Just one fish. One special fish. Is that too much to ask?"

"You know, fishing doesn't always work out that way."

"Mmm-hmm." Kam nodded, not really wanting to be bothered. The sun was already going down, and he was hungry.

"Nice sunset, isn't it?" Steve said this in a way that made Kam look around. It was more than nice—it was spectacular, as if the wind had caught fire, burning with the smell of fruit trees. "Sometimes," Steve continued, "just going fishing is reason enough to go. A dear friend told me that."

Steve got up and walked back out over the water. The sun was setting over the ocean—which Kam thought was strange, because Hilo was on the east side of the island. Still, in a dream, anything is possible, yeah?

"Boy, the sun gets bright sometimes," he said.

"You know, Kam, night fishing can be pretty entertaining, too."

Kam winked.

"No, I didn't mean it that way. Oh well, what can I expect?"

Then he was gone.

Chapter 6

Eva Matsuoka had a choice: to forget the chicken and go back to Matsuoka's, or to return to Noelani's halau and risk making an ass of herself with Noelani's stupid Christian hula. She paced behind the counter, going over her options. Meanwhile, Roland was trying to switch the service trays from breakfast to lunch.

"Ah, come on, Aunty! We no need that chicken!" And in a way, Roland was right. After all, they had so much good stuff already.

But Eva knew that that was not the way to stay the best. Her mother Charlotte had never stopped looking for the best recipes. Sometimes, not even to use them—just to know that if they had to, Matsuoka's could make 'em.

"Never stop looking, Eva. Never stop looking," she would say, and Eva would say "I promise, Mommy," and then her mom would put down her ladle and hold her like the most precious secret ingredient, ever.

She had to get that recipe. And not just because was the

best damned chicken she had ever tasted! Somewhere, somehow, this became personal.

She had underestimated Nona Watanabe. This woman was not as stupid as she looked! Eva still could not believe that she had fallen for one of the oldest tricks in the book. She had accepted a fake recipe?

Eva could see her mother shaking her head right now.

"Oh Aunty, we doing okay. We already so busy, no can keep up with orders! We even went hire Kayla!" He gestured to Kayla Tajima, the new server, who was busy wrapping napkins, chopsticks and forks with rubber bands.

But Eva knew a classic recipe can happen at any time. Like Spam musubi! Who on earth could have predicted that? In order for stay ahead, you had to understand this. Always look for the latest thing, and do whatever you can to get the recipe. That's all you need. That, and money, of course.

Which brought her to her other fear. Someone in Hilo was giving out money. Construction on the new giraffe habitat was going on right now at the Hamakua Zoo. Kalani's just received a new PA system (one of her workers had told her). To top it all off, what if someone had given Goto's enough money to buy a new fridge?

This was bad. Real bad. Eva knew that someone giving a little money here, a little there, could disturb the balance of Hilo. It didn't take much. A nice fridge might attract a slightly better cook, some word of mouth. Might inspire Landis guys to clean up a little bit—get rid of that damned Maalox bottle. And then they'd have more customers...

Eva Matsuoka knew that food wasn't everything in the food business. Sure, cannot have junk tasting food, but most of what keeps people coming back is word of mouth.

"You really think that most people know the difference

between our tako poke and the tako poke at KTA?" She turned to Kayla.

"Ours tastes more better!" Kayla said.

Eva nodded and smiled. The girl had promise.

"Of course. To you and me. But most people, they only know that something is good because everyone around them is telling 'em that. If the place get good *reputation*."

"Listen, Kayla. Maybe five percent of our customers know what is good and what is junk. The rest of them? They look for food that's cheap, or get big portions, or whether the place stay clean, or even if the waitress is cute."

Kayla blushed.

Eva continued, "We not spending all this time getting recipes for the ninety-five percent. Those guys would eat Hamburger Helper. We trying for impress the five percent who know what they want, who know the best. Then they tell their friends, and that's how we get our reputation."

Kayla nodded.

"But since plenty things can make one reputation, a little extra money can endanger all we worked for."

What Eva wasn't quite sure of was why the money was being given. And she wanted to find out. And where to go if she wanted to find out?

Nona Watanabe.

"Damn that woman!" Eva slammed both hands on the counter.

Kayla flinched. Roland almost spilled a whole container of nishime.

"Hey, watch it, Aunty!"

But Eva knew. She knew that she had to go back to the halau. She had to beat that Nona Watanabe!

* * *

Strange Kine Funny Tings

As Harry got to know Steve, while going holo-holo around town li'dat, he noticed a few strange kine funny tings about him. Which of course in some ways never surprise him, because whenever you meet someone new you notice strange kine funny tings, yeah? No lie!

Anyways, some of the strange kine funny tings—this buggah sometimes would pass for local. No, not like one haole trying for talk pidgin and get one tan—maybe after watching some Frank DeLima videos or something. No, Steve Yates would dress like one tourist, speak as mainland as ever, but people would talk to him just like he was a local.

Harry would shake his head, "Shoots, seems like you stay in disguise or something."

"No, it's just me. I am what I am. But, you know it's not as if we all don't wear some sort of disguise—even when we don't know it."

Then Harry would give Steve a beer, laugh at what he said, and say, no, you still haole.

Another strange kine funny ting was that even when people went find out who this guy was, most people never know *who* he *was*. Even if they knew he was not from around here, even if they knew he just went buy one huge place Hamakua side, most people never know he was Steve Yates the computer guy. One time at the computer store, Steve's face was on one magazine by the cash register. But Harry saw Yates go in and buy some kine electronic junks or another and the clerk never even double take!

And Harry would have been thinking about all of this stuff. He would have been thinking about how Steve had found his leg so easily—he knew those waters, and no one ever finds stuff down there.

He'd be thinking about how Yates knew so much about the town and the island, giving money all over to all these to these people and places. And how something about his friendship with the guy seemed almost meant to be, as if he was destined for be at the store the very minute Steve was there.

So many strange kine funny tings to ponder, yeah?

But Harry was thinking about one other strange kine funny ting even closer to his heart. He was thinking about Nona.

He would be with Nona, maybe eating saimin, or going out for buy Advil and new rubber slippers, having the best time, and being so happy for who she was and how they were. How he looked forward to their next movie, or dinner, or next Christmas beach, or just having a home together. Then, something inside him would shut off and just like that he would go dark, like one empty house with no more lights.

He never could help it, and he never know why. Or maybe, as Steve might say, of course he knew; he just didn't want to.

*　*　*

Jonny-Boy and Saul were setting up at Kalani's. Kam and Carl never show up yet, but that was okay because Kalani's had one new PA system. And from Carvin on top of that.

Ku'uipo and the other bands had asked for a new PA for years, but Kalani's kept saying how running one business stay hard—no can waste money on extra kine stuff. This pissed them off because Kalani's had 3 pool tables, four brand new electronic dart boards, one bar bowling machine, and two of those three mechanical finger grabbing things filled with stuffed animals.

But now Kalani's had one PA.

Junior, the manager, looked up from his cash register and shrugged.

"Shoots, last month someone came in and went give us some money. I was going use 'em for buy one more stuffed animal machine, but he said no, was for the bands. So they no need bring their own PA. So okay, then, we went buy one and put 'em in."

"You mean someone went just give you guys money?"

"Yeah—amazing, yeah? I think was one Chinese guy."

Jonny-Boy's eye's looked like they were going to pop out of their sockets. "One *pake* went give money?"

"No, just kidding," Junior smiled. I mean was strange, but not impossible. Then, he paused. "At least I no think he was pake."

"Okay, then what was he?"

Junior paused. "Shoots, must have been haole. But maybe... Oh, I don't know! Was just one guy—I mean, I can picture him in my mind. Strange, yeah? I usually get one good eye for faces. You need one in this business." Junior walked back into the office.

Jonny-Boy looked at Saul. "Eh, you think this the same guy who went give Noelani the money?"

Saul shrugged. "Why you no ask Noelani?"

Jonny-Boy downed his beer. "Nah... Noelani probably stay with that damned haole. They stay together all the time nowadays."

As if on cue, someone walked into the bar. Jonny-Boy closed his eyes and finished his beer. He never even need for look—was Noelani. With Kam. How many times Jonny-Boy had asked Noelani to Kalani's see them play? How many times she went say no?

And now? Was his idea that Kam should join the band. He remembered their first jam session. They had gotten drunk together. He had cooked him breakfast.

Those two needed each other, he realized. Sure, Jonny-Boy played bass, but get one big difference between playing the notes and really being good. Just like with dancing—when you saw Noelani, it was more than just the years of practice, or the beautiful form. Something about her dancing just made part of you weep. Whether from being happy or sad, it was like you filled with so much music you felt you going burst. And, as Saul said, Kam had that something, too.

In the end, cannot get in the way of things that were meant to be. The haole and Noelani. Noelani and the haole.

Sure. But how come always getta end like that?

Kam examined the new Carvin PA system. "Hey Jonny-Boy! What's up with the PA?" Jonny-Boy said nothing, so Saul told him what Junior said.

Jonny-Boy tried not to think about Noelani or Kam or that new PA. He clutched his bass and imagined a sound rumbling deep beneath the surf and sea, locked like the rhythm and the tides to a cycle that cannot be broken, cannot be denied.

* * *

Because there truly was something different when Kam played guitar. At first, Jonny-Boy and Carl worried that Kam might make Kuʻuipo sound a little too Mainland, but somehow haole boy made them seem more local, more Hawaiʻi. The crowd at Kalani's was noticing, too.

At first, Kuʻuipo was just another bar band—you know, da kine for chew toothpicks and shoot pool to. But more and more, people would be there to listen. To them. And they'd bring friends or dates. They would sway to the slow songs and dance to the fast ones. But whatever they were doing—they were there to see Kuʻuipo.

And then, one evening Lois Cabral, the host of "Local Eye" on local NPR station KWBY Hilo, came by Kalani's to see what all the fuss was about.

Now, these guys had been playing for years, but this was something new. People dream of coming to Hawai'i, but for those already there, dreams die as easy as the next of-course-it's-perfect day. One by one, the members of Ku'uipo had tried to convince themselves they were mainly in it for fun. Oh, and the chicks. They would listen to the radio and pick their favorite songs. Then they would jam. Was one good life. Good fun.

Even their name was sort of one joke—they went figure if they called themselves Ku'uipo, which was Hawaiian for "sweetheart," they would never have to market themselves—there was already so much jewelry and what not with "Ku'uipo" on top that it was like having free publicity.

So after the show, when Lois Cabral rushed up to them gushing praise and asking, "How did you get your name?" they were completely unprepared. Her tone was so honest that no could say, "Was just one joke."

So Carl went make up something about how the band all loved the music they played almost like one lover felt for his sweetheart—Ku'uipo—get it? Saul almost spit his beer and Jonny-Boy coughed to stifle a laugh. Lois's nose twitched slightly, but then she smiled sweetly and turned to Kam.

"Your guitar is incredible. Where have you been hiding all these years?" And Kam stuttered that he had only been here a short time—was from Los Angeles.

"Amazing." Lois shook her head and asked how he was able to feel the local music so deeply.

"Who, Kam?" Carl laughed, "That buggah, he went go so native he went change his name to Kamakawiwo'ole."

Kam felt the blood drain from his face. Saul stepped on Carl's foot. But the damage was done. The joke was over.

Except instead of laughing, Lois nodded.

"You changed your name to Kamakawiwoʻole? To honor Iz?"

"Yeah." Kam could only tell the truth now.

"No wonder you play like one native. The spirit stay inside you."

Kam looked at Lois for signs of bull, but Lois was being dead honest.

"It's not me; it's the music," Kam tried to explain, but Lois just stared at him and said, "That's what Iz would say, too. By the way, you guys get one CD?"

They shook their heads.

"You stay working on one, though, yeah?"

"Uh, not really," Jonny-Boy stammered.

"That's a crime, you guys." Lois Cabral gave them her card. "You guys get one card?"

They never, so Carl went write his phone number on one napkin.

"I go call you guys. I going try get you on the air."

"Yeah, right, whatever," Saul said, but the rest of them noticed that he said it only when Lois was safely out of earshot.

∗   ∗   ∗

On Coconut Island

Just off the shore of the Royal Hawaiian Hotel lies Moku 'Ola, also known as Coconut Island. There's a legend saying it is a piece of Maui caught in a demigod's fishhook, but the locals prize it more for its spacious picnic pavilion. Also, there's a cool diving platform where the kids gather after school. You get to Coconut Island by walking on a bridge—

it's short bridge, but a nice walk. Samson Miyashiro decided to go there after work, to clear his head after another day with Uncle Raymond. He took out a couple Spam musubi and found a clean, flat rock for sit on.

"Eh Samson!"

Samson turned around at the familiar voice. "Oh Uncle Harry! Howzit?" Harry was sort of Samson's uncle—actually Harry and Uncle Raymond were cousins once removed.

"Oh, just poking around. What about you? Your uncle stay working you hard?"

"Un*real.*" Samson shook his head.

"Yeah, I know," Harry said. "Even from small kid time that Raymond had to have things his way."

"Where's Aunty Nona?"

One small kid was on the platform, but looked like she never like jump.

Harry grimaced as he thought about Nona—they still were sort of fighting, yeah?

"She stay hula practice."

Some of the other kids were yelling at the small kid, "Go jump! Go jump!" And she would make like she would, but then would back off.

Samson threw a rock in the bay. "Wow, she always practicing, yeah?"

One older girl climbed to the top of the platform—looked like was the little girl's big sister or something.

"Yeah. Their kumu stay working on one big new hula production. Practice, practice, practice."

Like one good sister, the big girl went tell the other small kids for leave her sister alone.

Samson laughed. "You mean that Jesus hula?"

The other kids were all sad now, and the little girl was laughing at them from behind her sister's back.

"Oh wow, how you know?" Harry asked.

"People stay talking about it. I not offending or anything by laughing, eh?"

Suddenly, the big girl turned, and with a quick push, knocked her little sister off the platform and in to the glassy blue-green sea. Samson cringed.

"What you mean? If funny you should laugh," said Harry.

But the little girl came up giggling, and Harry and Samson understood then that this was a game that had been played many times before. In fact, Harry and Samson had played it themselves, many years ago.

"I know, I know. But you know, people they talk about what everyone stay doing. And Noelani's Christian hula—people stay talking plenty. Only thing..."

"Yeah?"

"Yesterday at the alley, two Filipino guys almost went throw blows, I think."

"What you mean?"

"I mean, one guy was saying that wow 'ass one stupid idea, and the other one said no call Jesus stupid. And you know how that goes."

"Yeah."

Harry sighed, wondering what Steve Yates was up to, even now.

* * *

What Steve Yates was up to, as he sat on an upturned plastic bucket in his garage, was getting the sand out of his favorite reel. Lisa came out and brushed his shoulder.

"Hey big guy! Whatcha up to?"

Steve didn't even look up.

"Check out this new dress I got today in town."

Steve picked his nose and went back to the reel.

"Nice day, isn't it?"

Steve grunted.

"Steve. *Steve!*"

"Huh?" Steve looked up.

"I *said,* 'Nice day, isn't it?'"

"Yeah, it is. And—hey, that's a nice dress. When did you get it?"

"God!" Lisa snapped. "Nothing gets past you, huh? Oh, and you have sand on your nose!"

She whipped around and stormed inside. Steve watched her, startled. She hadn't been that angry in a long time. She hadn't been that angry in a long time because she was too sick to *be* that angry.

Wait a minute.

Steve dropped his fishing gear, now completely cleaned, dried, and reassembled.

"Lisa?"

He was running now.

"*Lisa!*"

* * *

What the doctors told him, of course he already knew.

Lisa was getting better. *But this was not possible.* Steve knew more than anyone that everyone has a destiny. It was his to lose Lisa. Lisa's condition was hopeless.

Lisa had said, "Look, I'm a human being and human beings die. You have to understand that."

But though he understood virtually everything, he could never understand that. In fact, he thought that perhaps that was the lesson he would take away from this wonderful, beautiful love. Yet, to think that his love for Lisa existed merely to teach him a lesson was repugnant.

So this improvement bothered him, and yet he felt guilty to be bothered.

He would watch her getting thinner, more drawn out,

more tired. And she had wanted to go to Hawai'i. He had to laugh. Of all the things he had done, all the places he had visited—and she had wanted to go to Hawai'i. In all the time they had spent together he had known that, yet 'till now, he had never thought to bring her there. Now at the end of her life, it had the feeling of an epitaph:

"She had wanted to go to Hawai'i."

But now, she was recovering. How?

Suddenly there was a flash, then a clap of thunder, and he stared at the torrents that suddenly tumbled from the sky. Steve was accustomed to being in control, but now he was realizing there was something else out there to whom this rain, this sun, this place might follow. And, for all he was, upon this land he might be tethered to that something else, as well.

* * *

Not much later, the rain let up, and not long after that Harry came by with his gear.

The two of them didn't talk. Instead they nodded and hiked down to the same general place where they had been before. To Steve the place seemed a little different, but Harry seemed to remember each turn and rock. Steve commented on this, and Harry said he might not be the smartest guy in the world, but once he'd been down a trail he usually committed it to heart.

They put their stuff down and sat to eat. Harry opened up his Tupperware. "Nona's chicken," he said. They took in the flavor and aroma of the chicken, the crunchy, delicate skin.

And Steve was crying, and Harry knew what Steve was asking.

"I would say everything will be fine, but I'd be lying."

Steve looked over, not bothering to wipe his eyes.

"Your lungs will feel ripped out. Your legs and arms will go numb. You'll wake up every morning and have no idea what to do, what to think, where to go. You won't wish you were dead, because you wouldn't know the difference anyway. And it doesn't get better. Not even with your own kids."

Steve took another piece of chicken. He wanted to say it wasn't fair, but of course he knew better.

"What about you? You still feel that way?"
"Yeah. All the time."
"Even with Nona?"
"No, of course not with Nona. But, yeah, all the time."
"That's not right, Harry."
"No such thing. You should know that. You, of anyone."

* * *

OKAY, ONE MORE TIME...

"Okay okay—we going try this one more time." The dancers in the community center groaned as Noelani circled them and bit her fist.

Ervin Shimabukuro was not doing well as Jesus. Noelani had pictured the figure as a stately, dignified vision in white linen and maile. But Ervin was only five three—shorter than some of the women—and was built like a professional wrestler, with hairy legs and arms. Which was all well and good for kahiko hula, but in this costume he looked like a gorilla in a toga.

And on top of that, since he felt unworthy to play Christ, he danced like he was on eggshells, as if the slightest misstep would mean lightning bolts from Heaven.

After lots of bitching by Ignacio, Noelani decided to let him try the role.

As the chanting began, Eva, who had returned to the halau, stood there with her jaw open. As bad as Ervin was, at least he didn't wiggle his okole.

"You dancing like one panty," shuddered Frances Silva.

They tried a couple of the other kane dancers, but each one was worse than the last. Kealii Cabral had tattoos up his leg that showed whenever he kicked.

"Cannot have tattoos," said Noelani. "Maybe can wear tights."

"But the tattoos are authentic Hawaiian tattoos," he argued. "I *got* them because of hula—I no going cover 'em up."

"But the Son of God never have tattoos."

"He never dance the hula either," Eva snorted. Before Noelani could respond, others in the group nodded their assent.

"Maybe we no need put Jesus inside the show," Nona ventured.

"Yeah, maybe no need Jesus!"

"Quiet! QUIET!" Noelani yelled, and everyone shut up because Noelani never ever yelled. "Everybody LISTEN! We cannot give up. We cannot let Jesus down. You folks think about that! Practice pau today!"

"Noelani." Violet Macayan tried to calm her down, but was no use.

"I said go HOME! Practice pau!"

*　*　*

"No sir, kamaboko is extra," Eva scooped some corned beef and cabbage onto a plate and smiled sweetly to the next customer.

Eva Matsuoka had figured what was going on. In the

plate lunch business, one gets a lot of information from people waiting for their food.

"Hey Roland! Need more long rice!"

Roland went back to the kitchen, where Kayla was already scooping the transparent noodles at just the right time into a clean stainless steel serving tray

And one story was appearing over and over—some high-mukka-mukka guy had moved into Hilo and was giving out his money.

"Would you like one large or extra large fruit punch with that?" Eva winked and wrapped a rubber band around the container to keep it tight.

And, that high mukka-mukka guy was *Steve Yates*.

"I'm sorry sir, was that kalua pork or pork luau?"

She could not get over it. The most powerful businessman in the world was here. In *Hilo*.

*   *   *

"No! Still not right. We need space for the animals!"

"Animals!?"

"Yes, the ox and lamb."

"Why we doing a Christmas show, anyway?"

"It's not one Christmas show. It's one Jesus show."

"How the hell you going do a manger scene and not have people think it's a Christmas show?"

Kam and Noelani were working together for another night at her place.

Kam had never worked with anyone like this before. His bandmates—past and present—really didn't write anything original. Kuʻuipo would jam for a while Carl or Jonny-Boy would howl one throwaway line like, "Girl, without you I cannot go on!"

But with Noelani, there was an understanding of the

music that challenged even his ability to convey. And when he transformed and brought in his own motifs—she felt them and tried to use the best of them as well.

As for Noelani, she knew that Kam was not too crazy about the subject matter—he still wasn't— but what he came up with was amazing.

And he argued with her. No one ever did that before. *Christ figure* Aunty Kahakunoe didn't have to. No one else would dare.

"Well, when you put it that way..."

"Okay, then. Tell me. What exactly do you want to say?"

Noelani thought, then started speaking, of Jesus, of salvation, of how hula breathed life into her heart. Of what hula was. Like ocean. Like volcano. Like rain and wind.

She didn't bother to classify, she just went with it, hoping—no—demanding—that Kam keep up and keep track.

But then Kam stopped.

"Noelani. Noelani!"

"What? What?"

"Noelani, you're talking about creation."

The room spun under her. Of course! Noelani sat on the floor, then laid down with her hair all outstretched. The Creation— Noelani laughed. She thought about the animals and the new costumes and the arena she wanted to rent out and the angels and the Okinawan Jesus.

"How could I have been so stupid?"

Even with the money from the Yates folks...there was no way she could do that. Was all wrong—was setting her up to look stupid. And for all the wrong reasons!

She sat up. The Creation. Yes, the Old Testament— Adam's fall. The trick was not showing how Jesus was born, but *why*.

"So, who going be Adam and Eve," asked Kam. "Or if you

use Ervin and Ignacio, maybe Adam and Steve?" He laughed.

But no, suddenly Noelani knew. She wouldn't use all those weird props and stuff. No multimedia extravaganza with the Okinawan Jesus. Only need the dance. Only the dance.

"No going need Adam or Eve or the Snake or nothing. Just hula. Let me try make something up. Try watch and follow!" She said this not as a challenge, but finally, as an invitation.

But Kam shook his head.

"What now?"

"Try listen," he asked softly. "Let me play this for you. Please? Just this one time. Try follow me." And he played her the song he had started at Kapiolani Park in the rain.

It was well into the morning when they stopped, and that was only because they both decided that sleep would be the best way they could keep moving. Kam left Noelani's place at about 6 in the morning. Noelani laughed at what people would say if the neighbors saw him leaving, but both of them felt so tired and happy with their progress that they said the hell with it.

And of course, no one saw Kam wave goodbye, anyway.

Chapter 7

By the way, did you know how good Nona's chicken was?

Well, sometimes, even Harry would forget! Sometimes he'd go a few days or so and he would think hey, maybe the stuff at so-and-so's is just as good, too. Or he would be telling people about her chicken and—you know how everyone knows a good cook—they would bring up someone else's lau lau or long rice and he would think, yeah, maybe Nona's chicken is just like that.

But then, he would taste 'em again.

Hard to believe that someone could forget something so good, but Eva Matsuoka would not have been surprised in the least. Eva knew people, and she knew food.

Some foods were like most music—popular for a while, then the fad would die down. All this ling hing popcorn and mango and now even malasadas—big sellers, but most of it going be pau after a few years.

Then get place that serve haolefied Hawaiian fusion, or cuisine, or whatever. People read in one shiny magazine it's good food, but really, how many just stop reading and taste? Just like some of these new Hawaiian groups with their pretty eyes and tattoos and long hair and native speech with the precise glottal stops—everything seems right, but something is missing. And once again, the no one going remember.

Eva knew what the missing ingredient was. What Nona's chicken had.

Was truth.

Take Gabby Pahinui. People, they can listen to one song by Gabby and be moved to tears, yet afterward not be able to hum even a few lines. But years later, when they hear it again, right away all the tears and memories come back.

Was truth. A thousand years from now, people would still be enjoying Gabby's Hiʻilawe.

And, if Eva could have her way, they would be enjoying Nona Watanabe's chicken, too.

* * *

After a few more sessions, it was finally time for the rest of the halau to see what Noelani and Kam had completed. Noelani and Kam were a little nervous, which was strange, since they were both so used to performing. Of course, this was just a performance for her halau, but they were taking them into unknown territory, and they both knew it.

One of the real tragedies of being one kumu is that you have to think of yourself as one kumu. When you teaching, you stay focused outward, on your students, making sure they step the right way, they pronounce the words correctly, they smile—all while trying to listen to the music or the chants and staying within the beat.

Which is one good thing—but you're not performing. So the students start seeing you as one teacher and forget that you a dancer, just like them. You're expected to always get the answers, the corrections. So, when you finally present yourself as one dancer, you no like make mistakes.

Was probably one good reason why many kumu stopped dancing and stayed behind the ipu. If you waver, or if they no like your dance—how you going face them as a kumu?

But Noelani felt that she had to show them why this performance meant so much to her, why it could work—how it would look when it worked. Although her halau respected her, she knew too well that they did not see what she was seeing. Nothing she said would make them open their eyes. There was only one way Noelani could do that—by dancing herself.

Noelani dressed in a kahiko outfit, with leaves, flowers, and maile. Kam dressed in a white outfit with a single simple plumeria lei. As the halau assembled, even Eva had to admit that the costumes, although seemingly incongruous, made a bold, exquisite visual statement. Sort of like seafood salad next to rice with umeboshi garnish.

The rest of Ku'uipo came in to sit down. Kam noticed a strange look on Jonny-Boy's face as he saw Noelani—and not like a brother's. Stupid of him to miss it before. He had gotten so wrapped up in the music that he hadn't noticed the big guy's feelings for Noelani. But later—no time for that now.

Noelani came out first and said that this was the prologue of the show. She wanted to show them the essence of what they were all going to do. This was different from any hula they had done before.

Noelani stretched her one arm upward, the other across her body. Most people did this with the arm pointing forward, but Noelani modified it to better point out Heaven. Yet she arched and leaned so that her hair fell like a supple river across her back, And instead of looking up, she looked down, as Eve first beholding her reflection in the newborn waters of the world. Then her arms swayed slowly like branches and her fingers fluttered quickly, like the leaves on the branches on the Tree of Life, in the breeze, in the breath of the Creator.

She planted her back foot in the ground and with the other tapped out the four directions of the compass; it was as if she were showing the struggle between exploring the temptations of the world and keeping grounded in one's spiritual center.

Then, Kam started with his guitar, using a slide to rest upon a melody so hypnotic, so enticing, that it seemed Noelani could not help but dance. Once again a difference. They were doing the prologue of the piece—they were doing Genesis—and that was kahiko if anything was. Yet, Kam composed a pure auana piece. The words weren't finished, but Kam had something special in mind. But even as it was, it was so pretty that Noelani insisted they should share it.

She began to sway her hips, breathe, slowly shift her back foot... And as the music intensified, she brought her hands down with the music, the audience, the knowledge of good and evil.

But Noelani was not portraying a weak Eve character. Whatever Kam would play, she would develop into a thing of beauty. Then Kam might change the melody—another test, another trial, and Noelani would change the steps, bringing in other ideas, other memories. Then, suddenly, she would turn it on itself, so this time Kam would have to answer.

Eva heard herself exhale. It was like watching music, opera, prayer, an arrangement of flowers—her mother in the kitchen, over the always-fiery stove, humming to the beat of a saucepan and wooden spoon.

Nona no could even think—could only see and hear.

And feel. The maile and the plumeria. The sound of the guitar and the swish of feet on the floor. Although nothing was amplified, the sound filled the room almost to bursting.

Noelani looked out into her halau and and scanned their faces—but most of them weren't happy or sad—they were just watching.

The music stopped and Noelani finished in the same pose in which she had started—looking downward, hands pointed at Heaven. And Nona thought for that night there was no other place like that halau in the whole entire world.

But when audience clapped Kam knew immediately that something was wrong.

You see, get plenty kine clapping. Get da kine that just overflows from the bursting—when an audience get what it expects, only more so—you know, when you see one legendary performer put on a terrific show. That's the best.

Then get da kine surprised kine clapping—it starts out slow because everyone is so surprised. But then they realize the show stay pau, and they clap more loud. Actually, that's pretty good too.

But finally, get da kine—when they clap, they sound weak and uncomfortable. That's when they clapping to be polite. And that was what Kam was hearing now.

And Noelani noticed, too—though Kam could see from her face that she wasn't used to it.

Then Ignacio cleared his throat and said, well, some of the moves are nice, but I don't think the judges will like the mixture of kahiko and auana. Beverly Gomes wondered whether the moves were correct or not—some didn't seem to be hula—and the music—well, it was okay, but shouldn't it be chanting? Betty Manibog nodded. Nice song, for one haole, but really, we need something more flashy, yeah?

Noelani had never heard this sort of talk before; Kam was sure of it. Though she smiled and said that with practice we can make this work, he knew that she was being raging inside.

Some people seemed to get it. That old woman, what was her name—Frances?—still had not opened her eyes. Nona Watanabe was blowing her nose into a tissue.

But wasn't going to be enough. Kam knew that this new hula would be hard enough under any circumstances. But if the halau did not believe in the project, it was dead.

After practice, people left quickly. A few people, Frances and Nona being among them, gave a hug and said it was wonderful. But most of the halau twittered amongst themselves. Kam watched them go.

"We going talk about his soon," he said. "You know was beautiful, yeah?"

"Yeah, I know," said Noelani in a way that made Kam feel a little better about leaving her alone.

And so he did.

*   *   *

DIFFERENT STEPS

Nona was confused. It was the most beautiful performance she had ever witnessed, wasn't it?

"Sure, some of the music was new, and the steps different, but so what? Was beautiful! Isn't that the point, Harry?"

"Sometimes people don't know what is good and what is junk."

Nona sighed and plopped down on the sofa like a multicolored eggplant.

Harry went to the fridge. "You like fruit punch? How many ice cubes you like?"

"Three 'nuff!"

Nona smiled absently as she heard four cubes plink in

her glass.

"No listen to Ignacio and Betty guys. They make pilau to you anyway, yeah? Like I went say, no worry about what people think. Trust your own heart, yeah?"

And then Harry thought about himself, and how he thought about Nona. Was he was the same way? He hadn't thought of it that way before...

Nona saw Harry trail off and wondered if he was about to go into another one of his spells. So she changed the subject, hoping to avoid a fight.

"How's your leg, Harry? I forgot to ask you."

"Oh it's fine, fine..." He squatted and stood back up. "See?"

Nona smiled, happy that she had shaken Harry out of his funk.

"That Steve Yates. Boy, he unreal."

"Yeah, I noticed." Nona knew that now that Harry was pau talking about her hula. Sometimes it would make her mad when he forgot about her, but today, she was feeling so useless anyway, she figured she deserved it.

Besides, Harry still missed his wife.

Nona could never replace her. Never. How can? They had been married, had one family! Nona remembered that Harry's wife was quiet and stayed in the car. But Harry always seemed to make time to chat with Nona after school talking about where they were going for Christmas, the baseball games, and of course all the fishing.

Oh, Nona would listen, and something inside her would wish she could have those things. But even back then was getting late for kids already, and most men wouldn't even want to be seen with her, let alone get married.

And now this very same man, the man she loved, was taken, and there was no way she could compete with one memory.

Sometimes Harry would tell Nona about one time that he and his wife had together and Nona had to say, "No Harry. That was you and me."

To which Harry would either laugh or get angry or stop talking—and Nona could never be sure which one it would be.

Nona was sorry that Harry's wife died, but in a way, Nona felt that wahine was lucky. At least someone had loved her full time. At least when she saw him she knew he was looking at her and not past her to someone who had come before.

*   *   *

LET THE RAIN COME

Noelani listened to the screen door shut and looked around. It was over. Pau. When one kumu loses the confidence of the halau, no sense continue.

But damn! It had been good. So much work Kam and Saul went put into 'em. Boy, that Kam picked up fast the language—almost like he was born to 'em! And yet the halau never like 'em. She shook her head. Ignacio's comments—and Beverly's—not only what they said, but she knew that they spoke for the whole halau—or most of them, at least. Alone in her studio, Noelani didn't know whether to cry out loud or silently. So she let go and what came out was something quite unexpected.

She picked up an ipu and smashed it against the lime-green cinderblock wall.

She knew what people thought of her—that she was some sort of Jesus freak. And maybe she was, and maybe this started only as a way to glorify Jesus. But tonight this became something more. Tonight, this became personal.

Because she finally knew why. Why was this so easy for her.

She had always felt undeserving of the praise. That somehow, she was unworthy. Why did it seem so easy for her? Why? Suddenly, she knew.

It wasn't that she was unworthy! Wasn't one lie! It seemed so easy because, frankly, it *was* so easy.

Not the dancing part, the body training, the leg strength part. No—not any part of the training and the learning. That's not what she meant. Hard work is hard work.

But after someone learns all the movements, the nuances, the intonations of the language and the dance— what then? Aunty Kahakunoe had danced hula for all of her 87 years and what? *Getta preserve the tradition, getta remember the legacy of the hula and the islands. Getta dance for our ancestors.* Noelani laughed again.

"What about now?" she said out loud. She picked up one 'uli 'uli and twirled it by the feathers. The island is still creating itself—why are we, the children of the island not creating ourselves? What is hula, anyway? A group of prescribed conventions?

Ignacio was right—she knew how the judges would judge her work. Judges and awards—*was that it?* There had to be more!

She picked up another gourd and ran outside into the night. She smelled the air, felt the warm rain on her face and the red mud between her toes. She held the gourd over her head, and stared into the sky. The rain fell into her eyes, but she didn't blink. She didn't cry. Slowly, a smile peeked across her face, and then laughter as the rain grew stronger, the drops tapping the gourd more powerfully, yet more delicately than any human hand.

She was tired of the same old odes to the island, the calls to Pele. Not because she was tired of Pele, but because the calls themselves had become tired. She was tired of choreographing the same dance steps over and over and the nit-picking of the hula judges—about whether this flower was right for this performance...

Hawai'i was not always the same chords, the same steps. Look real closely; everything in Hawai'i changes. Big Island grows, Kauai shrinks. Plants and animals go extinct and evolve. Japanese come, then the Filipinos... And the rich haoles...

If Hawai'i changes and the hula embodies Hawai'i, then—hula changes, too. These are tomorrow's ancient times, tomorrow's Golden Age. We are conquerors and colonizers. Warriors, and dancers. Noelani laughed and cried and thought and spoke and the words, though one listening might have heard Hawaiian, or English—or, for that matter, Chinese, Korean, Portuguese, Japanese or Filipino—the meaning and the music would have made tears, almost inexplicably, come to their eyes—the music, the dance:

"Let new rain come! Let my feet sprout roots and may leaves spring from my arms. In the morning I shall feed off the sunlight and give shade to the children in the hot afternoon. Let new rain come and fill me with life!"

*   *   *

Lisa opened the door to see it was Harry. Harry immediately noticed that she was looking better.

"So Steve went find another doctor!"

Lisa shook her head. "I'm just feeling better. The doctors say nothing has changed, but look!" She pirouetted. "I haven't been able to do that in months!"

Harry smiled, despite himself. "I'm so happy for both of you. Steve must be one happy buggah."

Lisa curled her brow. "Well..." Then she looked at Harry. "But you're not here to see Steve."

"How you know that? No, never mind. You get that kine vision like Steve, too."

"No, no. Steve's the vision guy. I'm just a gal from New Jersey. But I figured you'd visit. Nona and I talk, you know."

"Yeah yeah yeah. That's why I came."

So they started talking and was one typical kine conversation at first. Harry was still understanding why Nona was upset, and though that was sort of okay—boy-girl misunderstanding has been going on since the beginning of time—what bothered him even more was that he knew he acted strange sometimes, but he didn't know why. He wasn't used to not knowing himself. But of course, he hadn't really been himself since his wife passed away.

This leg thing bothered him, too. It was getting better—as better as one amputation can get. In fact, he hadn't even thought about his leg when he jumped in to save Steve that first time they went fishing. As he grew used to not having his leg it became even less and less of a big deal.

Except for a couple kine things. He and Nona were getting closer and that meant well—uh, they might get married or something one day and that meant maybe they might—I mean—well they would be married and—they would get—you know—intimate.

Lisa's eye's widened. "I thought you'd already been together. Uh—I mean, I'd assumed."

Both of them turned beet red.

"No no. We both kind of—you know—old fashioned. Taking 'em slow. I mean, get time, yeah?"

Lisa thought about Nona and their conversations. "I'm not sure Nona feels the same way."

Harry ran his hands through his hair. "I know, I know... You know, for one long time, I never feel nothing about this leg until just after I went get 'em back from Steve."

"You think he messed it up?"

"You kidding? Feels better than ever. Anyway Steve doesn't mess things up, right?"

Lisa rolled her eyes. "You wouldn't believe."

Harry remembered Steve and his coastline.

"Yeah—I guess so. But no—I mean, lately I been thinking about the leg. How Nona might act after, you know, we get married."

"Harry, you know that's stupid."

Harry thought about it. "You're right," he conceded. "But the other reason is even stupider. I was thinking..."

He paused.

"Yes?"

Forgiveness "I lost my wife before the accident, you know. When I see her in heaven—you think she would forgive me?"

*　*　*

"Steve. When I'm gone, don't worry about me."

"Huh? But you're doing well."

"Oh Steve, this is nice, but you know that I'm dying. Maybe the air, or the smells, or the malasadas are giving me some energy, but I'm dying."

It was like a layer of clouds had blocked the stars. "And I can't help, can I?"

Lisa shook her head. "You've done enough. After all, *love* part of being in love is the loss, right?"

Steve thought of how confident he had been. Yet for all of his existence, for all he was, had he ever *been* in love before? He had often asked himself why people acted the way they did—and so often the answer was "they fell in love."

Steve could not predict how these people would act, these lovers. And it bothered him. He had not chosen Lisa to fall in love with. He had chosen someone else, actually, but when he allowed love to guide him, it guided him to Lisa.

And, Lisa resisted. But he persisted, and she began to understand that somehow, impossibly, he really had fallen in love.

She had asked him, "Are you sure you want this? You have no idea of what you're about to get into."

"Don't you know who I am?" he had asked.

Of course, she did. And of course, she was right.

* * *

Ku'uipo was working out the parts to Kam's new song when the phone rang. Carl as usual was the first to stop the music and run to the phone. The rest of the group could hear Carl's high-pitched chirping cough-giggles.

"Yes yes yes!"

"What what what?" asked Jonny-Boy.

"It's that Lois Cabral! She like put us on da radio!"

"When?" asked Kam.

"In two hours—turns out her interview with the crepe place went cancel."

"WHAT!?"

"The crepe place, you know the place stay make the crepes?"

"We know what is one crepe, lolo," Jonny-Boy said. "It's that pancake thing with the sugar, yeah?"

"Yeah, yeah but these crepes really ono. Get papaya inside." *3 stages*

"Oh wow! Papaya crepes! Get guava, too?"

"Yeah! And get mango and mountain apple and—"

Kam cleared his throat. "Um, guys? The interview?"

"Oh yeah," said Jonny-Boy.

"So what we going wear?" asked Carl.

"Stupid!" said Saul. "'Dis RADIO."

And they all tried for laugh, but everyone was nervous. And when they walked into the studio, even though Lois Cabral smiled and joked and gave them paper cups of ice-cold guava juice, she noticed they were fidgeting and their hands were shaking.

"Guys, don't worry—everything's going to be fine. You're all doing me a big favor for coming in on such short notice. Just be comfortable—I'll take care of the rest. I going ask a few questions, and then maybe you can play a couple songs, okay?"

So they did one quick sound check, and put on their headphones, the red light went on and they were "Live, in studio, with Lois Cabral and Local Eye from Hilo, Hawai'i!"

The interview part went pretty well, except Carl went freeze up, Saul kept answering questions with a shrug or a nod, Jonny-Boy kept stuttering, and Kam—well—let's just say he was still sounding like a haole.

But Lois was true to her word, smoothing over their rough edges and somehow making sense of the interview— even when Jonny-Boy started comparing Ku'uipo to poke aku.

"Thanks again to Ku'uipo for coming to the studio— they'll be playing a couple songs right after this important commercial message from our sponsors. This is Lois Cabral and you're listening to Local Eye on KWXY Hilo."

The red light went off and Saul turned to Jonny-Boy, "Poke aku? What kine nonsense that?"

"Well, at least I stay *saying* something!"

Lois laughed. "Guys, guys! You're doing great! So what are you going to play for us?"

"We figured 'E ala E,' and maybe 'In Dis Life.'" They were both Iz songs.

Lois frowned. "I was hoping to hear one of your original songs."

"Aww, how we going follow one song from Bruddah Iz?"

Carl began to stammer, "We really no more too much. Maybe we go play the 'Rubbah Slippah Shuffle?'"

"Shut up Carl," said Saul. "We can play what we stay working on. The new song Kam wrote for Noelani."

Jonny-Boy cringed at the idea of Kam writing a song for Noelani, even if they said was only for the hula. Would be only a matter of time before they—oh well, nevah mind—it was their best song.

"Kam?" asked Saul.

"I'm good. You okay with the words?"

"Shoots, brah. Duck soup."

So after the pledge break stuff was pau, Ku'uipo went play "E Ala E."

Then, Saul started chanting. Not Iz's song. But Kam's song. Ku'uipo's song. And bass started, then the drums, and finally, the guitar.

After the song was pau, and the interview was pau, Kam asked Lois, "So how you think it went?"

Lois smiled. "I not going be surprised if people already stay calling in—may we have your permission to play this recording later?"

"Of course," Jonny-Boy said, and everyone gave a thumbs-up.

Afterward Ku'uipo decided to go to the bowling alley. They sat down, and noticed some of the people were looking at them, and whispering. Saul took off his hat to make sure a bird never kukae on it. Jonny-Boy and Carl smelled themselves.

Suddenly a young girl came up to Jonny-Boy and said, "Are you guys Ku'uipo?" and he said yeah.

She looked back over her shoulder at her friends who motioned frantically. Then she was shaking as she produced a shiny Hello Kitty notebook.

"Can... Can I have your autograph?"

Jonny-Boy grasped the pen, which felt tingly and alien in his hand. Each of the band signed after him.

"Thank you—um—I really liked your song!" She ran back, giggling, to her friends.

Suddenly another girl came up with a notepad and Jonny-Boy reached for her pen. She pulled it away. "What you stay think? You going write down your order yourself?"

"Oh, sorry!" Jonny-Boy blushed.

"We like order four Crazy Omelets," Carl said. Samson cringed. The waitress rolled her eyes.

*   *   *

THE TALE OF THE POPOLO

Harry and Steve sat like two damned fools after their latest fishing trip, which had, like the others, been pretty lousy. This time, Harry dropped the lantern in the water early in the evening, and they though they tried heroically to continue, without the lantern, in the new moon, they couldn't see a thing. The lines kept getting snagged and if you ever tried tying a hook on your line when was pitch black, you know how frustrated they were.

So they gave up, and decided that they should build a small fire and finish eating the food they had brought. Neither of them smoked, though, so neither of them had a lighter.

"Shoots, Steve—you no can snap your fingers or something and make some fire?"

Steve said nothing, so Harry shut up. He wasn't quite sure about Steve. He was certainly more than one high mukka-mukka haole, but sometimes he didn't seem too savvy. So he did what he often did—except with Nona—and said what was on his mind.

"Hey Steve, you more than one high mukka-mukka haole, but sometimes you don't seem too savvy."

"Oh yeah, if you think you're so smart, why are you sitting out here with me then, huh?"

"You know how us locals are—always keeping you haoles out of trouble."

Steve laughed and laughed.

"What's so funny? Hah?"

"You would never make it on the mainland, Harry."

"What do you mean?"

"I mean you wouldn't survive. You've been calling me and Lisa haoles all this time."

"But I never mean it as one insult—"

"What makes you think we're haole?"

"Huh?"

"What makes you think we're haole?"

"Huh?"

"*I'm not haole!* Neither is Lisa!"

"Huh?"

"I'm a black man, you idiot."

"Huh? *Popolo?*"

"If there were any moon in the sky, you could see that!" Harry could hear Steve grumble. "Only in the islands—only in the islands..."

Harry thought about it—I mean—he had assumed, he thought—I mean the guy was so high mukka-mukka and in computers and for crying out loud—he might even be God on earth—not that popolos can't be...

"You not playing with my mind, Yates?"

"Nope," Steve shook his head and threw a stone in the water.

"Hey—you going scare the fish!"

"What fish?!"

Steve threw another stone into the waves.

* * *

"Hey Nona, did you know that Steve folks popolo?"

"Huh?"

"So, you never know, either?"

"What you mean? Now you stay mention it, I wondered why you kept calling them haole."

"You never think they were haole?"

"I wasn't really looking."

"Weird, yeah?"

"They real nice people. You shouldn't be prejudiced."

"Prejudiced? I not prejudiced. Is it prejudiced to say they popolo? They are—you know—popolo."

"Harry, sometimes I wonder why I put up with you!" Nona cried, which shocked Harry, because that was the first time she had ever said anything like that.

"Nona?"

"Never mind!"

Nona had never been the same to him since the accident with Steve. He knew it was something about his wife, that he should talk to her about it. But was like something inside of him still wouldn't let go.

* * *

Four Crazy Omelets pau and Samson was feeling pretty good until out of the corner of his eyes he saw his Uncle Raymond.

"What did you just do?" He walked to the griddle. *"What did you just do?"*

"Look, Uncle, they went order four of these at once—"

"Of course they did!" shouted Raymond. "The Crazy

Omelet is worth ordering again and again! It's one experience, Samson, a masterpiece of coffee shop cooking."

Samson had finally had enough. "Uncle, it's chop-suey-stuff-with-eggs."

He scooped the omelets onto plates and added rice, tsukemono and mac potato salad and rang for the waitress, who took them out.

"How could you do this to me, Samson? I trusted you with my customers, my recipes. You're a chef—I thought you at least knew how to julienne vegetables!"

Samson slammed his spatula. "Crazy Omelet, Crazy Omelet—I know why you call it one Crazy Omelet—it's because YOU crazy! Who the hell cares whether the corned beef is supposed to be for the Crazy Omelet or the corned beef plate—huh?"

"You never went mix the two corned beefs up?" Uncle Raymond was in shock.

"What? You no could tell?"

What's it matter if you can't tell?   (164)

* * *

Dream...

For some reason, Noelani was cutting bananas in a garden. She didn't understand why she was cutting bananas—it was simply what she was doing. Suddenly, she realized that she was being watched. She looked up and instinctively raised her machete...

"Noelani, put that down, will you? It's just me."

"Steve Yates?"

"Yeah, Steve Yates—and I'm not haole, okay?"

"Huh?"

"Oh, never mind. So how goes the bananas?"

"Humbug. All this sap gets on everything... Hey, this is a dream, yeah?"

Steve nodded.

Noelani looked at the banana oozing sap in her hand. "Oh damn. It's one of those Sigmund Freud dreams, yeah?"

"No, no," Steve laughed. "Sometimes a banana is just a banana."

"Good, 'cuz I no more time for that kine nonsense. Get one show to do. In fact, your show."

Steve nodded. "I know all about it. Your halau was pretty tough on you, wasn't it?"

"You said it."

Noelani kept cutting the green bananas off the stalk.

"Hey, can I have one of those?" Steve asked. "I'm a little munchy."

"One of these? They would make you sick."

"Why? Aren't they bananas?"

"Yeah, but they're not ready yet."

"But you just picked them."

"Just because I picked them no mean they ready. Getta wait a little more for them to get ripe."

"You sure?"

"Yeah I sure—I've been picking bananas all my life," said Noelani, which was true because this was a dream.

"Oh."

"You getta have patience," she laughed. "No worry, these good bananas. Just wait 'till they come ripe—you'll see."

Noelani kept cutting.

"Well, I better be going then," Steve said.

"Uh-huh. Sorry, yeah?"

"No problem. I have all sorts of patience when I know something good is on its way. Patience a wonderful virtue, isn't it?"

Noelani looked up to see Steve blow away into the wind. She looked at the banana in her hand, and thought she heard it turning ever-so-slowly sweet.

* * *

God

Harry was in the bathtub. Was one of his things he always did. Even before his accident, he never liked to take showers. He just couldn't relax standing up. He figured that, hey, he was standing up all day at work. He might as well take a bath and get some relaxation, yeah?

The nurses and physical therapists said after amputation the hardest adjustments often weren't the big things like walking or even bowling, but the little things, like having to be extra careful in the shower.

Harry figured would be so much easier for people if they just got off their feet once in a while. Shoots, if you used to not standing all the time, then when you cannot stand anymore you already comfortable with the idea.

Harry smiled and thought of Buckminster Fuller. That crazy haole—and really a haole, too. Putting up all those domes around the country. Pretty neat stuff, but just too intense. He used to say that "God is not a noun. God is a verb." As if activity were more than the main reason for existence—as if it were existence, itself.

That was the main reason he remembered Buckminster Fuller, that and his funny name. Harry had never met a verb. Never spoken with a verb. But it seemed like he had met and spoken with God before, and not just recently. When he lost his wife, he spoke with God all the time, and God didn't seem like a verb. When he was outside in the yard, doing nothing but pulling some nut grass, it seemed like God was nearby. Certainly, his wife had done enough during her life. It would seem unfair for her to spend the rest of her life as part of a verb.

In fact, it was those times when he was perfectly still, when there was a smell or a sound that held him for what seemed like a small piece of forever, when Harry could best feel God's presence. He was a deeply religious man, although probably no one in town would have guessed it, and certainly none of the various ministers or priests, who never saw him in church or temple.

But that seemed fine to him. He had never seen a minister out fishing, or a priest lying under a tree. He had never seen a bonsan strolling along his way at Prince Kuhio Shopping center, or biting into a hot malasada from Honoka'a.

Objectification And that was real strange, yeah?

Now though, it seemed like things were moving faster. Ever since Steve Yates showed up—though it really wasn't his fault—all Yates had wanted was go fishing. And help a few people. Which wasn't such a bad idea, especially when you were either literally or figuratively God on earth.

But wow, when you that powerful, anything you do can make big waves. And big waves, when you stay on one island? Things going start moving, yeah?

The usually peaceful director of the usually peaceful Hamakua Zoo was in a decidedly non-peaceful argument with a group of board members who wanted to bring in a variety of animals to the children of Hawai'i. Some even wanted to bring in snakes!

The director's position was that many of these animals were banned by the government as being potentially catastrophic to Hawaii's delicate ecosystem.

But then, some of the Hawaiian sovereignty groups took issue, saying the US government had no right to tell them what animals they could bring in. "It was the haoles who brought in those hostile species and now they want us to stop? Our children stay at one educational disadvantage if they cannot see all kine animals!

"Besides, what can snakes do that you haoles never do already?"

One religious group even joined in, saying that if their kids couldn't see snakes, then how would they recognize Satan? And also, since God had placed the snake with Adam and Eve, it was not right for humans to live anywhere where there were no snakes.

The director had moved to resign, but the Hawai'i Department of Agriculture stopped this, saying that the director had to remain because no one else was qualified to manage the Hamakua Zoo's present resources, let alone the resources to come.

Which of course set off the local groups even more, saying if the Hamakua Zoo had mostly indigenous fauna and we stay indigenous, then do we need one haole to tell us how for manage our own kine stuff?"

Harry closed his eyes. The phone started ringing, but he said to heck with 'em. He knew wasn't Nona—she hadn't called in a while, and he never want one subscription to the damned *Honolulu Advertiser*, anyway.

The answering machine picked up. Was Steve. "Hey, I found a great spot this afternoon. Let's go fishing! I know we'll get something there."

Harry slid down into the tub and let the water splosh over his head. Deeply religious man → Suicidal

*   *   *

Lois was right. People loved Ku'uipo's song.

In fact, Lois had so many requests, soon she made "In Da Beginning" Local Eye's official theme. Was good for Ku'uipo—in fact they were now playing at the Royal Hawaiian as headliners, and even there was talk of going to O'ahu.

But Kam was feeling guilty. He had told Noelani right after the show what they had done, and she seemed to be okay with the idea, but he felt that without her, the music was not complete. The success of the song only made it worse.

Because the song was a collaboration. He would provide the music stuff and Noelani Choi would provide the art, the Hawaiian spirit (and some music, too, of course).

Because even after playing with Kuʻuipo, even after being applauded by local crowds, even after getting drunk with them, he still felt like he was missing something about Hawaiʻi.

"Thou shalt have no other gods before me," his god had commanded, though the impossibility of the commandment seemed beyond even his comprehension. So many gods out there, and in so many different forms, from the usual gods with their statues and temples and everything to a cell phone ringing or a Nike logo or an idea about the nature of color.

For Kam? All irrelevant save his question that something was missing inside of him. He had learned and discovered and befriended so many people here, yet he still hadn't figured out why he couldn't just be. And this was his new world, sometimes black and desolate, then full of wet sunshine, sweet and floral scents dripping through the air like syrup.

He got in his truck—he had bought an old Toyota pickup—and drove away.

* * *

Saul Malani alone had noticed that Kam had left all bothered after the call from Lois Cabral. Carl had been too busy talking about what this or that might mean—the same nonsense he always did. Jonny-Boy? That lolo had been in a funk since Noelani and Kam had met, but that was real stupid for two reasons.

First, because there was nothing romantic going on between Kam and Noelani. No way. Saul had seen the way they worked together. They needed each other more as artists than they ever would as lovers and both of them were, thank God, smart enough to know it.

Second, and more stupid was that Jonny-Boy never have the alas for tell Noelani how he felt. Waste time! What did he think she was going do—magically come up to him and declare her love? For one big guy, that Jonny-Boy could be real gutless. So there he was, monku-ing around when he should be celebrating.

Saul laid back in his chair and put his hat over his eyes. He thought of a woman, in the rain, and all in green.

Chapter 8

Uncle Raymond was the only local food shop owner on the island who did not give a damn about Eva Matsuoka, except that she was pretty cute and he wouldn't mind giving her a sample of his blood sausage, heh heh. Never mind that Matsuoka's was the most notorious restaurant on the Big Island—perhaps throughout the entire outer islands. Never mind that these recipes represented the best of generations of island cooks—Matsuoka's was *still* using other people's recipes.

What was the purpose of putting your name on a place if the recipes weren't yours? Why bother?

Even Eva's best recipes went come from other people. But Uncle Raymond could point to any food in his shop and say, "This is mine. Everything here stay my way because I *make* it my way." The Spam marinade was never varied from his instruction. The tonkatsu was fried at exactly the temperature he ordered. He even demanded that his rice be weighed before cooking.

Sure, sure, other people could make tonkatsu and Spam, but *his* was always uniquely the same. You could count on it.

* * *

AN UNINTERESTING ORDINARY DAY

It was an uninteresting ordinary day. A young Raymond Miyashiro was on Maui in one rent-a-car looking for one place for eat. He thought maybe he should go Nazo's—you know for the oxtail saimin, but shoots, wouldn't you know it, Nazo's was closed. Tasty Crust was one option, but he never like drive Wailuku...

"Oh, heck with it, I just like go eat one Big Mac," he thought.

And on his way to McDonald's, Raymond Miyashiro wept.

No, it wasn't one stupid tourist driver, or even one bug in his eye. It was inspiration!

McDonald's! He had visited the Mainland and found McDonald's Big Macs tasted exactly the same as they did in the Hilo McDonald's. When he went to Japan, he found that the Big Mac tasted the same there. And in Kahului, he took his first bite. Yes! Exactly the same! *Exactly.*

Of course it was a hamburger—everyone had hamburgers! But this was more. This was one Big Mac. One *Big Mac.* Something everyone knew. Everywhere. From Europe to Asia to Alaska, it was more than a hamburger. It was in the specifics—the specifics made it special. And because it was special, the man who made the Big Mac had conquered the world—a whole world eating his food.

This was immortality. This was his calling.

And even though people were looking at him funny kine, he couldn't help but hold his Big Mac and laugh.

Was so easy! So clear! All he needed to do was get some recipes and change the ingredients around a little bit here and a little more there. He would make them his own creations, then make sure the recipes never varied in the slightest. With a little tweaking, he figured somewhere would surely be his Big Mac. Never mind, of course, that this wasn't an original idea—the Big Mac was a *burger* and his would be *local food*. His recipe. His calling.

He was more than a cook. In fact, why prejudice his mind with mundane practicalities? He was Raymond Miyashiro! He would create an indelible cuisine, an everlasting mark, to show that yes, Raymond Miyashiro had *lived*.

Eventually, he bought out the Filipino family who decided to move back to Manila (something about the man sleeping around) and set up shop. At first, business was slow, and then it remain slow for a while. After a few more years, though, it remained unchanged.

Raymond read some more, cooked some more, and threw some food away. He altered his recipes every month, which cost him yet more of his customers. But he didn't care; they were still tied to the concept of food as something they already knew. Besides, who went make the law saying no can mix mango with corned beef, anyway?

Still immortality was hard, lonely work. And one fateful Thursday morning, in a moment of frustration, Raymond Miyashiro dumped all of the junk he had in his kitchen into one big omelet and served it to his breakfast customers.

And they said, "Hey! I've never had one omelet like this— crazy, but good!"

The Crazy Omelet was born! Luckily, even in his moment of frustration, Raymond had meticulously transcribed his every ingredient and procedure. Now he could make the Crazy Omelet exactly the same Crazy every time!

Better yet, as he began attracting customers, he would hire workers to make it! But he would train them diligently! Only when they understood that no deviation was permitted were they allowed to cook the Crazy Omelet.

"Think about it. Would you like your Big Mac to taste different every time you ordered it?"

To which, of course, they said, "Shoots, I guess not."

And that was that.

*　*　*

Eva had spent weeks trying to figure out how to get a sample of Nona's chicken. Then one day after hula, she just gave up.

"Nona, can you make me some chicken?"

"Sure! I bring some over tomorrow afternoon."

Eva couldn't believe it!

At first she thought might be one trick, but the smell from the next day's Tupperware was so intoxicating she knew that this must be the one!

Eva rushed back to the restaurant and handed a piece to Roland.

"Try this!"

He took a bite.

"Okay, Roland, what you think get inside the chicken?"

He took another bite.

"Roland?"

Roland said nothing.

"*Roland!*"

"I don't know. I don't know. I mean—I don't know."

Eva took a bite and the taste just sat her down. *My God, what a recipe!*

Douglas Kubo, a homeless drunk who lived along Mamo

Street and aimlessly wandered Hilo town, lurched inside the restaurant.

"I like that one," he mumbled.

"No, not for sale!" Eva gave him the stink-eye, and he stumbled back outside. She turned to Roland.

"Roland! You the one went brag you can take apart any recipe, once you had one taste. There's your one taste. So no give me any grief. Make this recipe!"

"Aunty... I sorry. Cannot."

Eva sighed "I know, I know," she conceded. "Cannot help. We need the recipe." She put her hand on Roland's shoulder.

Then she reached for another piece of chicken.

*   *   *

"I am resigning from the community center."

Noelani said this right after she assembled her halau. Some people gasped, some people said, "Nonono!"

But most of them said nothing. Because most folks had joined the halau after they went see stuff like the Merrie Monarch on TV, and thought, Yeah, I like do that, too. I like be on TV. I like get up in front of one stadium full people and dance and have everyone say how good I am. I like be one winner.

And they felt cheated because Noelani was not interested in that. As they saw it, Noelani must have been in some fight with her old halau, the current champions, probably because she was too Christian and making funny kine new dances. Even though looked interesting, it was never going win competitions.

Then, they looked at Ignacio, how he chanted, played three instruments. How he seemed to have the right attitude to win. Ignacio was the senior member of the halau; he had actually taught on Maui before moving to Big Island.

And he was already weighing offers to teach in Pahoa. Betty Manibog showed all her big teeth and winked at Ignacio, trying to be sly, but in plain view of everyone.

Noelani cried a little inside as she saw her halau. Surely they were thinking how they stay finally with one kumu who could win prizes li'dat. She saw them, looked at Ignacio, and something inside her wanted to break. But as usual, she did the beautiful, graceful thing, taking one deep breath, gently clearing her throat and wishing Ignacio well.

Then she added, "But I still doing my project with Kam and Ku'uipo. If anyone like follow, I would be honored to work with you. But you have to trust me."

Noelani gave her best smile, turned toward the door, and walked away.

Nona followed immediately. And Frances Silva. And Violet Macayan. Eva shrugged and joined them. Finally, bringing up the rear, was Ervin, the reluctant Okinawan Jesus. Noelani looked at him like *you sure?* And he shrugged and shuffled like, *No, not really, but I like follow you, anyway.*

And Noelani looked at the five people behind her. *Well, at least I no need find one big space for practice...*

And so they left the community center and the door had not even closed before Ignacio's voice shouted, "Okay everyone, enough wasting time! Let's get started!"

* * *

THE OLD LADY Pele

Lisa answered the door. It was the old Hawaiian lady. She was dressed in a wonderful red and white mu'u-mu'u and for some reason Lisa noticed how friendly the wrinkles around her eyes seemed to be—they made her think of music, of singing, of her long-departed grandma still dancing in her dreams.

"Hi! How you?"

"Oh, I'm fine, Aunty, and how are you?"

"Oh, so much stuff going on nowadays. Busy busy busy! But not too busy to visit such a nice young couple."

Lisa giggled.

She winked at Lisa. "You looking much better from last time I came. Good to see."

"Oh thank you, Aunty. And I really do feel much better. Still, my health is day-to-day."

"Child, *everything* is day-to-day."

Lisa thanked the lady for the ohelo jam and when the old lady smiled, the crinkles around her eyes had smiles of their own.

"So, you folks having good time Hawai'i?"

Lisa nodded. "Steve's out with Harry again looking for a new place to fish."

"Oh, those two—they funny!"

"Can I get you something to drink—some juice? Water?"

"Oh, I don't drink water," she said abruptly, then smiled again. "Stay such a nice day. Try see."

Lisa hadn't been outside all day. She and the old lady walked in the back yard, taking in the fresh air and talking story. What they talked about, she wasn't sure. But she was aware of the smells around them, the feel of the breeze, the patter of rain on the roof. Eventually, the old lady looked at the sky.

"Oh! Aunty has to get going. Take care!"

Lisa gave her a hug, then lingered just a bit longer outside.

When she came back indoors, she saw another bottle of the homemade ohelo jam upon the kitchen table, sweet, and vibrant, and new.

*   *   *

RIPPED

Nona Watanabe cracked her fat knuckles, grabbed the butcher bag from the refrigerator, and sighed. The only thing she knew how to do was to cook chicken. Still, she dreamed of dancing the hula.

Nona had followed Noelani for the most simple reason. Noelani's dance was beautiful. Sure, Ignacio would teach the rest of the halau all those moves that did well at the Merrie Monarch, but for the first time in her life, Nona understood that no matter how you like be part of something, sometimes you have to leave.

She wondered if it was also going be true with her and Harry. Yes, Harry would be nice to her, but she felt that she was getting leftover love—and although that seemed far better than what could have without him, it didn't make her feel beautiful.

Nona cut a fat pale thigh with the bumpy chicken skin all over it. Funny, yeah, how something so ugly could turn into something so wonderfully tasty? If you put one cut up raw chicken in the middle of the kitchen table, everyone's appetite would come spoiled. But once you got that golden brown—oh the jaws drop open and the saliva starts coming out.

Nona sighed. She would always be an uncooked chicken. She mixed her huli huli sauce with the flour, and added some chopped onions, some Korean chili powder and some aji no moto. Into the mixture, she placed the chicken pieces. Had to marinate for a while—she never measured the time.

So she was about to leave the kitchen for one walk when the telephone rang. She hoped it wasn't Harry—she never like talk to him. She was still mad at him, but if they talked, she knew she would end up telling him how much she loved him, how she couldn't live without him and so on and no, she never like do that at all.

But then again, it might be Lisa or Noelani.

So she picked up the phone, and it wasn't any of them. It was her nephew Darin. Darin was from Honolulu, and she never could figure him out. He was born and raised in Hawai'i, but the guy couldn't swim. But he could ice skate, though. And snow board. And play squash, though she didn't even know what the sport was. Anyway, she took his word for it.

His family on his father's side had come up with one real ono recipe for soda crackers and from the recipe made one whole bunch of money. Shoots, you can even buy the crackers mainland, and not just at Marukai. So they sent Darin to all kine private schools—even Punahou—but every time he seemed to get bored and then pau.

But he was the only child, so they tried to put the best spin on it, saying he was going be one entrepreneur. Right now, Darin was running a carpet cleaning company or something like that. He had gone to some seminar in Las Vegas and his family set him up with the business license, the van, the equipment, and everything. Nona even invested a little bit of her savings into the business, not so much to make money, but because he asked, and when he asked, you just wanted to help him, 'cuz he was just that way.

"So how's the carpet business coming?" Nona asked.

"Oh, that? Aunty, that all pau. Was junk. The real money is being one personal trainer."

"Personal trainah?"

"Yeah, personal trainer—the clients pay you to tell them for exercise. You show them how and help them and with nutrition and technique and whatever."

"What? You no need special kine classes for that?"

"Oh—not too much—the main thing you need is

connections. Oh yeah, and one good body. That's the tough part. I taking protein powder, creatine, branched-chain amino acids—you should see me Aunty! I stay ripped!"

Nona wasn't quite sure what ripped meant, but she assumed from the tone of his voice that it was something good. It sounded sore. She hoped it wasn't sore.

"So, no more carpet business?"

"Nah! I sold the business to buy supplements and some training videos. You know—sets and reps and lats and glutes—muscle confusion."

Nona frowned. It seemed that more than Darin's muscles were confused.

"No worry, Aunty! You still stay my business partner—only in one new and better business. I stay so excited!"

"Well, that's good." And Nona meant it. Was good to hear one happy voice. Probably that was the reason why Darin was always her favorite nephew, even if everyone else thought he was the family good-for-nothing.

"Oh, Aunty—how you?"

"I okay." She lied a little, but figured that Darin wouldn't notice and he didn't.

"Oh, that's great! I was calling to tell you that I going be visiting for one competition in Hilo."

"Competition?" What kine competition?"

"Bodybuilding competition. I going enter the novice division. My training partners say I making great progress. And good for the business if you stay ripped."

Nona nodded and noted that ripped must be a very good thing to be.

"So, when you coming? You going stay over here?"

"In a couple of weeks. No worry, I going stay with some friends."

"Well, you can always stay over here."

"Really?"

"Of course. Go come, go come."

"Well, my friends might be disappointed, but it's always good to stay with family, yeah?"

Nona knew that Darin didn't really have any place for stay, but he didn't want to come right out and impose. Was one funny thing about Darin—for all his talk, the guy was honest. Lots of people said he was perfect for be one sneaky salesman, but what they never realize was that Darin had never told one lie in his life. At least not an important one.

*   *   *

Nona hung up the phone and drove to the bowling alley to meet Frances and Violet. When she got there, they had already gotten a lane, had their shoes on and were talking some kine good story. When Nona asked about what, they said Noelani and Kam.

Nona shook her head, "Really? I no think get anything there."

Neither did Frances. "Noelani not going stay with one haole. Not to be politically incorrect or anything—did I use that right—politically incorrect? My granddaughter was saying something about what was not politically correct that was going on her school. Stay causing trouble. She's one teacher, you know."

Frances was old and part Porogee and so she would start talking double-time without warning, and then swerve off the subject besides. But if you waited, she'd eventually come back to what she was talking about first place.

"See, can tell when someone going go out with one haole. My granddaughter Bernice—"

She stopped to nudge Violet that she stay up next, then continued, "Bernice all through school date only haole—oh this blonde head, that blonde head! But I knew. I told her mother no worry—she going settle down and marry one local guy. Turns out she found George (Samuelson, who, despite his name, was three-quarter Hawaiian).

"But my other granddaughter Gertrude—for sure she going marry one haole. Probably going leave the island, too. How I know? Get feeling, yeah? I just get one feeling. You know the haole type. And Noelani not the haole type."

Frances shouted her last point over crashing pins as Violet picked up the spare.

They cheered and Frances got up for her turn.

"Good, because poor thing yeah, that Jonny-Boy."

"I know, yeah? Poor thing!"

Everyone knew that he had one big crush on Noelani.

"Why doesn't Noelani do something? For sure she knows that Jonny-Boy in love with her?" asked Nona.

Violet laughed. "Noelani? Girl, Noelani no more time for look for one man! She so used to being with her hula— she going need someone for step out and go after her."

Violet nudged her shoulder.

"Hey Nona, you stay up!"

Nona approached the lane in her mismatched shoes, which, despite their look, weren't rental shoes, and let the ball go, and since she wasn't as bad a bowler as she thought she was, her purple ball careened into the pins, tumbling all of them down.

And as her girlfriends cheered, it occurred to her that even though she had been dancing hula for quite some time, up to now her dream had been to simply disappear. She had always been too fat, too pale, too junk. All she had wished for was to blend in unseen with ensemble's beautiful matching costumes, music, and movements.

But then, she saw Noelani dancing alone.

As far as Nona remembered, that night was the first time she had really seen Noelani perform. Not as a patient kumu, but as a true dancer. And was so beautiful, so unexpected.

How could one single dancer so completely fill one's senses with movement, poise, and song?

In a way, Noelani was just as alone as she was. But, oh! How she danced! And now, instead of wishing to blend in, a very small voice inside Nona asked, "How can I dance like that? How can I be that beautiful?"

And as she asked this, her thoughts of Harry became less frantic. Yes, she loved him, but she felt that maybe it was time for her to dance her own hula and see if Harry would take up chase.

* * *

For Eva, the chase was no question. She had to get Nona's chicken recipe. Nona's chicken was *it*.

She looked at the huge stack of boxes of fried tempura and cone sushi that would be gone by 9:00 a.m. as warehouse workers, and office workers and teachers and bus drivers and city maintenance workers all came by to get their lunch.

Not by accident, either. You see, the food business stay tricky. Always have to smile and be in one good mood, even if you stay having one rough day. One person talking stink and all of a sudden everybody go across the street instead. So talk story, but not too much, especially if get people waiting. No can take nothing for granted, yeah?

But the most important thing was the food. Had to be ono. Real ono.

When Eva was younger, and still even nowadays, she traveled. All over the place. Not just go Vegas blow money like those stupid Goto brothers. No way! Eva went to big cities like Chicago and New York and even toured Europe. Twice!

Why? For eat! For taste the best food she could find! Not just the fancy kine places, but the down-the-street places where the real food was served. And you know what? After all her travels, she realized that nowhere had food like Hawai'i. Local food was not just ono, was the most ono of onos.

And her food was. And would always be. Had to be. Like Nona's chicken recipe.

She had tasted that chicken with her expert taste buds and could not break that recipe down. Even Roland could not figure 'em out.

And all her attempts to get at Nona's recipe directly weren't working. As she paced behind the counter, Eva could almost feel her mother Charlotte glaring over her shoulder and raising her wooden spoon.

Waitaminnit.

"Roland!"

"What, Aunty?"

"You not feeling well. You stay coming sick."

"What? Aunty, I feel fine! I—"

"NonoNO!"

"What?"

"You going be sick. Tomorrow. And Thursday I going have one big party to cater."

"But Aunty, you no more party."

"Shh! Listen! So I stay in one emergency, yeah? Then I going ask Nona Watanabe for come Wednesday and help me out in da kitchen. Then I can watch her make da chicken right here! No chance for mess 'em up!"

"Wow, Aunty, you think Nona going be that stupid for come in here and show you her recipe?"

Eva smiled.

"Garans ballbarans, Roland."

* * *

"Oh Eva, I sorry—your nephew going be okay?" Nona was out of the shower, wrapped up in a large, lime green beach towel.

"Oh, of course I go help. Big party? Okay, okay. I go be there. Oh, poor ting that Roland!"

"Yeah yeah. Okay. Maybe I can make my—yeah, I can make my chicken. Eva, you get big kitchen, yeah? GOOD! Okay, then—Wednesday? Okay. Can. Yeah yeah, of course. Trywaittrywaitrywait! Tell your nephew drink plenty fluids, okay? Juice! Juice good! Okay, bye!"

Nona hung up the phone. *Poor thing that Roland! He must really be sick. Eva never ask for help before.*

Nona pondered what she should bring. Even though people said that Eva was sneaky and pilau, she knew that Eva was really one good person inside. All she needed was friends. And now she was asking for friends! Nona was so happy to help. But was going be hard work! Roland and Eva, they were professionals, and she was only a small-time cook.

So Nona picked up the phone and started dialing.

Meanwhile, Eva was giddy. "We got her! We going get da *real* recipe dis time Roland, for *sure!*"

"How you figure, Aunty?"

"She went ask if we get one big kitchen, Roland!" Eva twirled, unknowingly doing so just as Noelani had taught her. "Right after she said she was going make chicken, she asked if we get one big kitchen!"

Roland scratched his head.

"Roland, how lolo can you be? You saw the recipe Nona went give you, yeah?"

Roland nodded.

"That recipe, you could make 'em on top one small countertop. Why would she need one big kitchen for one simple recipe?"

Roland paused. A smile slowly appeared on his face.

"Oh yeah, Aunty. You *right!* She must get one different recipe!"

*   *   *

That Wednesday, Eva answered a knock on the door and there was Nona.

And Violet. And Frances. And...

"This is Lisa Yates. She like help, too."

Eva stood there saying nothing as the women began to scurry about the kitchen.

"I told them you needed help, that Roland stay sick. We all agreed you needed plenty help 'cuz that Roland one hard worker." Nona hugged Eva.

"Oh...thanks..." Eva felt a little faint.

"Oh Eva, don't mention it. I tell you, you get plenty friends who like help you out. Watch out, Frances!" she said, as the old lady tottered past her with one Tupperware full homemade takuan.

Eva sat down, her mouth wide open, as these people began preparing food in her big kitchen.

"How many people?" Violet asked.

"People?"

"Yeah, for the catering."

"Uh, 75." She made up a number.

"75? And you and Roland was going handle all by yourself?"

She nodded, of course. I mean, didn't they always handle everything by themselves? Except for a couple helpers, it was always that way.

Violet frowned. "Really? Oh my goodness."

Why did Violet frown? What was so bad about working alone?

Then everyone began cooking, and Eva pushed these

thoughts from her mind. *Just watch Nona make her chicken.* Never mind the other people. *Just watch Nona.*

But as she watched Nona, she realized that Nona was boiling potatoes. Then cutting vegetables. Then slicing fish?

"Nona, isn't your chicken going take a while for prepare?"

"Oh yes. But no worry," Nona smiled. But Eva was getting nervous. Two hours into the night and Nona hadn't even touched a piece of chicken.

Another hour passed. "What about the chicken, Nona?" Eva tried not to let panic seep into her voice.

Nona smiled, "No worry, Eva. Lisa, she get 'em."

"*What!?*"

Eva had been watching Nona so hard she never notice the skinny girl just now putting two large buckets of chicken—soaking in marinade—into her refrigerator.

"All pau, Nona! Did I say that right?" Lisa asked.

Nona smiled and nodded. Nona noticed the shocked on Eva's face. "No worry, Eva, I showed her exactly what to do. Now all you need for do is bake 'em tomorrow morning like I went write down."

The evening was a blur of cooking and cutting and boiling and laughter, though none of it was Eva's, who for some reason was just sitting there with her mouth open and not even blinking.

"Poor ting," Violet thought, "That girl seems so shocked—like she never knew how friends help each other out. Poor ting, yeah?"

* * *

"DAMMIT GUTFUNNIT!"

Eva stormed in her kitchen, long after the women had gone home. Was real late, and for Hilo that means real dark, except for Kalani's, Walmart, and Ken's Pancakes.

And of course the restaurant kitchens. Even now, the Goto brothers were frying a fresh batch of tempura while an earlier batch cooled on racks. Samson Miyashiro was helping his uncle slice cabbage for the tsukemono, and nishime vegetables were all in their white plastic buckets, waiting to be combined with the chicken marinade.

"Now I know she never outsmart me this time—but why? How come cannot get this one stinking recipe?"

"Aunty, you just like dat Coyote guy." *Looney Toons*

"Hah? What kine nonsense you talking Roland?"

"You know Aunty that Roadrunner Coyote guy. You know the one always stay falling off the cliff li'dat. Then da bird go 'Beep-Beep!' and run away?"

Eva gave Roland the stink eye.

The two of them looked around at all the food the ladies made. Everything was neatly wrapped and packaged in bowls, in Tupperwares, in serving trays...

"Wow Aunty—they went do all this for you?"

"Huh?"

"Those ladies—they went do *all* this?" Roland waved around at the kitchen and all the food. And Eva looked around and for the first time noticed that the kitchen was choke okazu.

Her jaw dropped. So much food no can even begin to describe. And the pots and pans were all washed and put away.

"Aunty—try look the stockroom!"

"What? Oh *no!*" Eva ran back. "All this food—I bet they went cook up all our supplies and—"

Eva stopped. Nothing was touched. Not even the shoyu. Not even the vinegar and sugar and chili pepper. Not even the cabbage or bean sprouts or kamaboko.

The women had come and gone and filled her kitchen with all kine kau kau. And they never use one thing—not one thing—from her kitchen. And the food smelled soooo ono. Not that Matsuoka's wasn't ono, it was just that these smells were full of...

Aloha.

"Wow—even get Maui-style fried soup with the square noodles—I never have that in the longest time!"

Everything was ready, except the chicken, which was marinating.

"Only 'ting—how sad, yeah? The chicken," Eva gestured to the two buckets in the refrigerator. "I hope it's not too bad."

Roland frowned. "I think going be okay, Aunty. If no come out, we can always throw 'em in da fried rice or make chicken salad."

"You right Roland," Eva looked at all the food again.

"You right."

*   *   *

HOW CAN THIS *BE?*

Friendship

Early the next morning, Eva put the chicken in the oven, still wondering why everyone would cook for her. Why did they go out of their way like that? Even stay bringing their own ingredients?

Then, as the chicken baked, she slowly became aware of something. Something impossible. This smell was coming from the oven—a smell she could not believe. A mouth-watering, unearthly smell. A smell that could make one's the head dizzy and the stomach growl, no matter how full it was.

Cannot... She went to the oven and almost pulled open, but stopped just in time. Absolutely rule #1—no open the chicken while cooking. Otherwise sure for come tough!

Roland dashed into the kitchen.

"Aunty, I can smell that from the parking lot! What is that?"

And then, was time. She pulled the chicken out from the oven that Lisa had prepared. Eva called Roland, and the two of them burned their mouths on the still-hot pieces.

How could this *be?*

Was impossible.

Was Nona Watanabe's chicken. *Was Nona Watanabe's chicken!*

"Aunty, you sure she never make 'em?"

Eva shook her head—she never even touch the chicken! Of all the recipes she had ever tasted, this was the *one* recipe she knew she had to have, but it was also the one she could not get.

"Wow—then she must have given the recipe to that nice popolo girl."

But there was no time to talk. Was only breakfast, but already people were lining up to buy food.

They said, "Wow, different kine kau kau today!"

Or, "Oh, Roland, I heard you were sick—feeling better? Good!"

But mostly, "Wow! *Some ono* this chicken!"

People were coming back for seconds and thirds. People bought extra for take to the other people in the office, or home to the family.

And then, "Aunty—someone just called for one last-minute catering order!"

"What?"

"Aunty—for 75 people."

"Roland! Call Kayla. Tell her we need her for come in early! And tell her for bring the station wagon!"

"I already called, Aunty!"

People were lining up outside—that's how word of

Fishes &
Loaves

mouth works. And was so weird, Eva thought—but somehow no matter how much kau kau she sold that day, had more.

"How much food they went *cook?*" Kayla asked, as she rushed to the station wagon with a huge catering tray of Chinese chicken salad.

"I don't know," Eva said, passing out another chicken plate.

And somehow the tray of chicken never empty at all, not until the end of the day, when Eva, Roland, and Kayla were left with two pieces chicken each.

* * *

THE TALE OF THE WEED PULLER

Harry looked at his yard. The nut grass was somehow creeping all over his St. Augustine. Damned nut grass. You see, nut grass get these real deep roots, and if you leave even a little bit of the root in the ground, the buggah can grow right back. Harry didn't ask much out of life, but one of them was coming home to a neatly manicured lawn. If not for that damned nut grass!

Harry's cell phone rang, but it wasn't Nona.

"Hey Harry. It's Steve."

"No, not fishing today—I stay busy in the yard," Harry said.

"Oh, okay. I'll come over."

Harry hung up the phone. Strange that this Steve Yates had so much time.

Steve came by because he wanted to talk about Lisa.

"I don't get it."

"What don't you get?"

"Lisa is getting better."

"So?" After the helicopters and the coastline, Harry wasn't quite sure of Steve. Maybe just snaps his fingers and all pau, right?

"She's real sick, Harry. And she's so tired. She's lived a long life, you know."

Steve said this in a way that made Harry wonder how many times Steve had snapped his fingers.

"And she told me that this time was enough," Steve continued. "But now, she's getting better—and I'm not doing a damned thing. I would sure like to know why." *Steve— Control*

Harry tossed Steve a screwdriver. "Here. Help me out."

"What?"

"Nut grass. Try look. Worst kine weed you ever imagined. The stuff get real deep roots—almost like bamboo underneath."

Steve picked up the screwdriver and started on a large patch of weeds to his left. He thought he was getting the hang of it, when he heard Harry yell NO! NO! Harry looked sick."

"Steve that's not weeds! That's St. Augustine grass! I *paid* for that!"

"St. Augustine?" Steve laughed. St. Augustine had never been much of a gardener, either.

"What? You never weed before?" *weeds*

Steve shook his head. He had done many things, but weeding a yard wasn't one of them. He usually let things sort of weed out themselves.

"Here." Harry waved him down.

"You getta push the screwdriver in like so, then rock'em back and forth gently for get the whole root out."

Steve examined at the weed that Harry dug up. For the life of him, he couldn't tell the difference between the nut grass and the St. Augustine.

"No," Harry said, "Try look. If you look carefully, you can

see that they slightly different color, and the nut grass blades are slightly wider."

"If they look almost the same, why do you care?"

"You going help or not? Now watch me and try follow."

(handwritten in margin: 135 Why care?)

"You know, Harry," Steve said as they worked, "if the blade were forked, it would grip the weed better. And with a bend in the shaft, you could get better leverage."

Harry stopped and looked up. "They make them already. They're called weed pullers."

"Well, why don't you get some weed pullers?"

"Why? Get screwdrivers. 'Nuff."

Steve watched Harry, nodded and continued to weed. After a while, he didn't need a weed puller, either.

*   *   *

The next day, Steve went into town to buy supplies for their next fishing trip. But on the way back, he felt a little hungry. So he shrugged and decided to go to Goto's.

As usual, no one was there—just Arnold Goto reading the *Tribune-Herald*.

"So what you like eat today, Mr. Yates?"

"Oh, one musubi, three pieces of Spam and some shoyu chicken."

"No more chicken—sold out," Arnold said without looking up from the paper. A fly landed on his arm, stayed for a while, then went back outside.

"How about the ginger beef?"

Arnold got up, grabbed his tongs, and stopped. He put his tongs down and scratched his head.

"I was going to get around to ask you. Can you give us one picture for put on top our wall? We like put pictures on the wall of all the famous kine people who come to Goto's and eat our ono (and cheap) kau kau."

Steve looked at the walls. They were empty, except for one fisherman's calendar from three years ago that showed high and low tide and phases of the moon. Oh, and one old plastic ahi.

Arnold shrugged. "Well—no one famous has come inside here before you," Arnold said. "But my brother went to the Mainland and said in the restaurants they put famous people pictures on top the walls."

"Well, I usually don't like putting my picture up—"

"No no, never mind—if you no like be bothered, 'ass okay with us. Shoots, must be real humbug, yeah? Everyone stay *annoyed* recognizing you and asking you for stuff." He grabbed his tongs again and put the food on one paper plate. Another cool thing about Goto's was their plate lunches still came in paper plates and rubber bands, rather than those Styrofoam clamshell things.

Steve laughed. "You know, most people don't even recognize me."

Arnold put another paper plate on top the first, then strung a rubber band around both.

"For real?"

"For real. In fact you're the only guy who recognized me the first time you saw me. You must be into computers."

Arnold put Steve's plate lunch in a brown paper bag, along with napkins, one pair chopsticks, and a foil packet shoyu. Steve watched Arnold, amazed at how each *this* movement seemed to take just a little longer than necessary, *whole* but not long enough to be irritating. Arnold folded the bag *book* carefully, stopped and looked at the popolo.

"Me? No, I no even like my computer. But I know who you are."

"Hmm?"

"You do any kine stuff. I see your name all the time in the newspaper—you stay helping out this group and that group—didn't you give 100 million dollars to that homeless organization? And before that 500 million for the AIDS foundation?"

Steve nodded. "Yeah. I guess I did. So that's how you know me?"

"Yeah. But no worry—I no going tell anyone that you stay giving all that money to the zoo like that."

Steve's jaw dropped. "How did you know?"

Arnold creased the folds he had made and laughed. "Oh! Who else going do that? Get other kine mukka-mukka people here, but most of them no mix with us local people. But you—you stay fishing, bowling alley, watching hula—shoots—I even seen you inside the Ben Franklin—so must be you giving out the money."

blending

Arnold took Steve's five-dollar bill and leaned over the counter. "You know that Eva Matsuoka, right?"

Steve nodded.

"Remember how she came in here, looking at our new refrigerator? She thought you went buy 'em for us! Can you believe that?"

Arnold shook his head and gave Steve one dollar and eighteen cents change.

"Eva Matsuoka. That's one smart lady, that—you should know. Poor thing, too. And her parents—da real ones—fates intertwined by lust, greed, and pork adobo...

"But no worry! She no going tell anyone, either. She keeps her secrets."

Arnold handed Steve his lunch and looked longingly at Steve's fishing supplies. "So you going fishing again? With Harry? Wow... I wish I could go fishing with him, too."

"Not tonight. Anyway, to be honest we just haven't had any luck."

"Really?" Arnold asked in a strange tone.

"Yeah, really. Nothing. Maybe I chose the wrong guy to show me how to fish."

But Arnold was smiling a strange, faraway smile. "That sneaky buggah... I wonder what he stay up to?"

"What do you mean? Harry hasn't caught anything either. He's—"

Arnold laughed and slapped the counter.

"What—Harry?! He used to make his money fishing— that's how good he is. On the spot kine! He would ask you, 'Hey what kine fish you like? How much you want?' And he go catch 'em. *That day!* Only guy I know who can do that. That Harry! If you no catch nothing, trust me, stay 'cuz he no like you catch nothing."

Harry fishing [handwritten margin note]

It was a long, long time before Steve Yates opened his plate lunch.

*   *   *

TRY FOLLOW

Noelani and her troupe of dancers gathered under a coconut grove in Kapiolani Park.

Frances, Nona, Eva, Violet, Ervin... All their questions, Noelani put to the side. Instead, Noelani put her finger to her lips, then asked if they ever noticed the sound of the little stream that ran through the mossy jade hillocks.

"No, cannot," Frances offered. "That stream no make noise."

Noelani took a long deep breath, "Sometimes we get too bogged down in the noise of stuff for notice the dance."

"I just like you think about it for a while—silence, and what hula is supposed to look like when the music not there. When no one stay watching you.

"You getta remember that before the music starts, before anyone ever sees you onstage, only get you and silence. And after the show is all pau, that's all you going have left."

True for birth, life, + death [handwritten margin note]

Noelani saw that everyone was looking confused. Especially Ervin.

"No worry! I no going ask you for dance to the silence or nothing—at least not yet! For now, your heads stay full of so many rules for dance the hula. Getta hold your hands certain way, move your legs, you getta smile, move this way or that.

"But before all of this, remember the silence—the song of a quiet stream just like this one."

Noelani started walking, and each of them followed her, careful not to block the silence that they were trying to hear. For about half an hour, they followed Noelani, in silence, over gravel, over tree stumps, asphalt, and rocks. Noelani went slowly, so that even Frances could follow, and chose her path carefully, so that even Nona could be step lightly.

Finally, Noelani stopped, turned, and laughed.

The shock of her laughter broke through Nona's ears, and only later did she understand that Noelani's laugh was actually a soft chuckle, meant to cushion the impact of her voice when she finally spoke and told them practice was pau.

For the next two weeks, that was all they did—find a place and walk in silence. Sometimes it was in a park, sometimes it was at the beach, or by the river, or in the green fern forests Kulani side. Sometimes was hot, sometimes had rain, or wind. Hilo is that way, yeah? And eventually, never even need the outside for be quiet, for each of them learned to summon their silence from within.

And her students followed, without music, the presence of their own bodies.

This was the way Noelani danced. Not the only way, maybe not even the best way, but Noelani's way. All she needed was a mirror and an empty floor and even the mirror was too much. She would practice the movements thousands of times, marveling at how each one could just belong to her body. She would watch her feel her fingers bend, her back gently sway, her weight shift from the balls of her feet to her heels—all without music—just the body, moving as it would.

That was the first and most important insight she could ever give to the dancers:

Oh! How good it feels to move!

Nona didn't quite know why these walks were so important, but she trusted Noelani. She knew that she could never be as graceful as her kumu, though she was getting better. Or was she? Her body felt different. But how?

And, if someone had been watching, she would have noticed that each of them, in their own way, were moving more and more as their natures desired.

At the end of the two weeks, Noelani gave each of the five dancers an envelope.

"We going start dancing to music next time. Up to now, moving has been just for yourself. Once get music, we going be giving—to the viewers, to the musicians, to God."

With great effort, Eva managed not to roll her eyes. "Think of the chicken," she told herself. "The *chicken*."

"So take your envelopes and understand what it is to give." She motioned them to open the envelopes.

Inside each was twenty thousand dollars in cash.

"Now—I ask you give to people you think would need it."

Nona gasped. Violet and Frances smiled.

Eva trembled. This was going be harder than she thought.

Chapter 9

GIBBERISH

"No! CANNOT BUY A NEW *nothing* WITH THE MONEY!" EVA stormed back and forth while Roland filled the little Styrofoam cups full of lomi salmon. In her hand, she held twenty thousand dollars.

"But Aunty! Can buy one new sign, one new cooking range, some new lights..."

"Noelani Choi went say give 'em to one charity or needy person li'dat."

"And since when you listen to Noelani Choi?"

Eva snorted. "Not Noelani. It's that Nona Watanabe. If she find out I went swindle the money, we can kiss that chicken recipe goodbye."

Roland looked over at his Aunty, all bunched up like one old paper towel.

"Oh Aunty. No recipe is worth all this hassle."

Eva glared. "*Look at me!* How can you say that?"

Roland sighed.

"You right, Aunty." And he went back to filling the cups with lomi salmon.

Roland knew what she was thinking, and she knew he knew. Her mom. The adobo. Her.

"Damn." Eva put the envelope in her purse. She got in her car and drove to the Hilo convalescent home. ~~hospital~~

*   *   *

"Now this gift getta be totally completely anonymous, okay?"

The Filipina nurse nodded. Then she opened the envelope and gasped.

Eva read her thoughts.

"No, no! It's okay! Not criminal kine money. Just one anonymous donation for make the patients' lives more happy."

"Okay, but try wait, yeah, so tell I can tell the supervisor."

Eva nodded. The nurse rushed off, and in her rush, she stumbled into a large potted ficus. She glanced back at Eva, turned a corner, and clattered away.

Eva looked around her shuddered. Was the Alzheimer's wing.

One lady was cleaning a one-inch strip along the hallway with a toothbrush and paper towel.

"Oh, she does this every day," the orderly said.

Eva waved, and the old lady waved back, smiled, and went back to her cleaning. Another one was apparently bedridden or restrained. She gestured to Eva.

"My son. He always comes to visit me. Can you ask the Japanee nurse if he called?"

But when Eva asked the nurse, she shook her head and said that the lady's only son had died in the Korean War.

Eva noticed that the ward held mostly ladies. Where were

the men? Probably dead, yeah? Most old couples, the men were usually older than the women by ten, twenty years easy. Or they smoked. Or the never take care themselves. Eva was disgusted. How can they leave their wives like this? How can?

"Charlotte Matsuoka!"

Eva jerked at the sound of her mother's name. It came from a Chinese lady in a wheelchair staring in a mirror, adjusting her shawl. Her wispy hair had been dyed jet black, maybe a couple of months ago; the stubborn white roots already grown about a half-inch.

Eva approached. "You know Charlotte Matsuoka?"

"That's my fish roll, not Charlotte Matsuoka's! She went take 'em. Charlotte Matsuoka! That damned Charlotte Matsuoka!"

"She's like that all the time," the Japanese nurse said. Eva nodded, then she felt herself flush, as she recognized the nurse as one of her customers. Surely she knew that Eva was Charlotte Matsuoka's daughter...

The Chinese lady held herself tight and rocked back and forth.

"My fish roll. The surimi rolled inside the lup cheong and fried in the tempura batter. Thass my recipe that! Charlotte Matsuoka! She went steal my fish roll! She stay making money off my fish roll!" The old lady groaned and pulled at her scarf.

Eva felt sick. She knew that fish roll, and had actually stopped selling it years ago because it wasn't moving. Now, all that this woman could remember was losing a recipe that wasn't even being used. The Chinese lady suddenly grabbed her arm Eva almost screamed because she was sure that the old lady recognized her as Charlotte's daughter, but then the lady coughed and smiled.

"I tell you though one secret," she whispered. "'Cuz you honest."

Eva blinked. No one had ever accused her of being honest before.

"That Charlotte Matsuoka! She never get the whole recipe." She fumbled inside her coat and handed her a crumpled piece of paper. It smelled like mothballs.

"I give you, 'cuz you one nice girl. The secret ingredient." Eva hesitated, but the Chinese lady pushed it into her hand. "I give you. Not that damned Charlotte Matsuoka."

She nodded and let Eva go. "Charlotte Matsuoka." The Chinese lady started rocking again. "Damn that Charlotte Matsuoka!"

Eva left the building before the Filipina nurse returned. Eva had no doubt the money would be used, but she just had to leave.

Without a word, she rushed to her car and started the engine. Then, almost despite herself, she glanced at the paper for the secret ingredient the old Chinese lady had given her.

Ten minutes later, the engine was still running, but the car hadn't moved.

On the paper was gibberish. Nothing but gibberish. *Secret ingredient*

*　*　*

Nona Watanabe gave her money to the school library where she had worked for most of her life. Harry insisted on going with her because dangerous carry that much cash around. Nona said no worry, but Harry insisted, which made Nona happy.

She felt so good. Was just nice to know that the money was going to one group of people who would use 'em for something good—computers, maybe even some books.

Nona noticed a new group of classrooms at what used

to be the far end of campus. Not that getting new stuff was surprising—even Hilo changes once in a while—but goodness, had it been that long since they went away?

"Hi Miss Watanabe!" Was Pikake Griffin, who used to be a student aide at the library and was now a third-grade teacher fresh out of UH Manoa.

"Pikake! How you doing? The kids behaving themselves?"

The tall blonde laughed and shook her head. "These kids—they driving me nuts!"

"Oh, you were like that before!"

"No, not me!" Pikake said with mock indignation.

Then the bell rang. "Oh no—I going be late for class!" She stumbled, giggled, and ran to her room.

"Watch out Pikake girl!"

"Okay, Miss Watanabe!"

Nona sighed and smiled. Some things never change. As she turned toward the library, she looked for Harry, but Harry had disappeared.

Harry walked along the school grounds. This was where he and Nona went meet. He turned a corner past an old bench that used to be new and remembered how he sat there, telling Nona about his family's fishing trip to Kawaihae. His family. His wife.

Harry looked around at the place. Was really that long ago?

Harry sat down and took out his wife's photo from his wallet—first time he did that in a while. He had pictures of his wife in his house, but his wallet picture was real special, from the time they went to the mainland.

Disneyland.

"Was really that long ago?" Salt water and time had turned the whole picture reddish and faded.

And the school bell shook him to the present, and he looked up at the bright and colorful kids schooling all about him. He carefully folded the picture back in his wallet and waited for Nona. The nut grass was always growing, and no amount of weeding would ever clear his yard for good.

Finally, Nona returned. Actually, she never really like come out of the library. She was talking with some of her old friends and they asked her if she and Harry had wedding plans and she had to say no, but they understood and were being so nice, when out the window, she had noticed Harry looking into his wallet.

It would be easy for settle for what Harry offered— companionship, a good person to go shopping with, to talk to. And was not as if there were people waiting in line for go out with her.

But she still could not bring herself to say it was okay and not be sad. Just like she knew she would never be able to be beautiful with the hula, but she would keep going to practice, humming a melody caught between gratitude and tears.

*   *   *

Ku'uipo got a letter from Ku'uipo. And another letter from Ku'uipo. And another. All in all, five other Hawai'i bands by the name of Ku'uipo had heard of Ku'uipo and their song "In Da Beginning."

Lois called. Since her show was playing their music, she had been getting these notes, as well.

"Don't worry, you guys. As far as I can tell, no band has released anything commercially. Let me send them a note. If they cause trouble, we can find lawyers. For now, remember that every show you play strengthens your claim to your name."

"Lawyers?" Jonny-Boy sighed. They had actually known

about two other Kuʻuipos before they started their band. Shit, they had even went to visit the one on Kauai once to play on the same night as one joke—turned out that they were pretty good guys. They figured what the hell—the name was so da kine, that everyone could share, yeah?

But now, since they were getting famous—really—was hard to believe, but was true—the other bands never like it.

"Oh man—lawyers. I hate lawyers," Carl started chattering.

Saul closed his eyes. "Shut up, Carl. When was the last time you went deal wit one lawyer?"

Jonny-Boy looked out the window northward, to the other islands.

"The other Kuʻuipos—they get as much right for use the name as us—I mean stay just one name."

"I know, but if we back off, the other bands might push more," said Kam. "If only one band can be Kuʻuipo, then it needs to be us."

"Is that what you think, haole!?"

Everyone froze. Jonny-Boy's tone was not playful.

"Okay Jonny-Boy, why you stay pissed off now?" asked Saul.

"It's all his fault! The haole!" Jonny-Boy pointed at Kam. "If he never write that damned song, we would never have to go with one haole!"

"What you mean 'go with' one haole?" Carl shrugged. "We not going on tour."

"He's not talking about the music," said Saul.

"What you mean?" said Jonny-Boy.

"No bullshit. This get nothing to do with Kuʻuipo. You stay thinking about that wahine. Noelani and Kam stay friends and you no like it!"

"Go to hell, Saul!"

"For what—for tell the truth? You like hear more? You gutless."

"I said go to hell, Malani! Of course you stay backing him. You always like kiss-ass to the haoles, anyway!"

Carl and Kam froze.

Saul reached into his wallet, pulled out a twenty, and tossed it on the table.

"I not hungry right now. And neither are you, so we going outside right now." Saul got up and walked a few steps. He turned back to Jonny-Boy, who still had not moved.

"Now."

Jonny-Boy slammed two fists on the table and followed. Lucky was the bowling alley and not too many people heard. Carl looked at Kam.

"Should we follow them? I mean, unless they like be alone."

Kam said nothing, took the check, and walked to the register.

Once outside, Jonny-Boy said, "I sorry, Saul, but—"

And that was as far as he got before Saul hit him. Jonny-Boy staggered backwards, and Saul hit him again.

"Gutless!" Saul said. "You stay in love with somebody right in front you, and you no can even tell her."

Jonny-Boy screamed as he rushed at Saul. Jonny-Boy was bigger, but it was no contest, as Saul sidestepped and rammed his knee into Jonny-Boy's midsection. The impact slammed both of them to the ground. Saul got up and dusted off. But Jonny-Boy didn't even move.

Carl looked over at Saul, but Saul said. "No, he's okay. He knows I right."

He walked over to Jonny-Boy's prone body and kicked him onto his back. He was crying.

"But *Kam*." Jonny-Boy whined.

"This not about Kam, stupid. If you lose Noelani Choi,

stay no one's fault but your own. <u>You get the one you love</u> right in front of you. *<u>You don't know how lucky you are!</u>"*

Saul bent over, picked up his hat, and limped away.

"What did he mean by that?" Carl whispered.

"Shut up," Kam replied.

*   *   *

No Shame?

When Darin Watanabe came over to Nona's place, first thing Nona noticed was that he was not really that big.

Darin had been telling her all the supplements he had been taking and gains he had been making, so Nona thought she was going see muscles, but Darin was still the same old Darin.

"If you going be one muscleman, Darin, you should have muscles, yeah?

"Nah! Aunty, that's because I'm natural! With all the supplements that are around nowadays, no need for the go on the juice."

"What—drinking juice can make you grow big muscles? Okay, what kine juice the best? Guava juice? Papaya juice?"

"No, no Aunty! Not any kind juice. The *juice!* You know—steroids."

"Steroid? No take drugs, Darin!"

"No worry, Aunty. To be one personal trainer, you need for be healthy because you going give nutritional and supplemental advice, yeah? Anyway, the steroids too expensive and I no like needles."

"Okay. But if you go take steroids, I going tell your father!"

Darin laughed. "Here! I just got these," he said proudly,

holding up a skimpy pair of bikini bottoms. "The latest professional posing trunks. Not bad, yeah?"

Nona turned red. "You going wear those? No more shame?"

"Oh Aunty, it's one athletic competition—no can be shame. What about the hula guys running around in their malos?"

Actually, Nona thought that was a little too much information too, but had never said anything out of respect for Noelani.

"By the way, how's the hula going?"

Nona sighed. "Darin, that's one long story."

"I get time."

＊　＊　＊

Frances Silva gave her twenty thousand dollars to the cemetery where her family had been buried for generations. Was on Maui, where she grew up before moved to the Big Island to live with her son and his family.

The old cemetery was bordering a beach, and though the hotel next to the beach was not allowed to build over the cemetery, that didn't stop the developers from putting a parking lot right next to the cemetery boundary. And on the other side of the cemetery was the ocean, so you can imagine all the vacationers walking back and forth over the cemetery plots to get from their cars to the beach. Beer bottles and suntan lotion and Big Mac wrappers littered the grounds. One old Japanese man would come by to sweep the place from time to time, but was too big a job for one person.

So Frances decided to send the money to the county for maybe hire some kids after school for help keep the cemetery clean. Wasn't exactly charity—she was gaining something, too. But you know, everyone buried there needed a little respect, yeah?

So that's where she sent the money. And that night, she had one of the nicest sleeps she could remember.

*   *   *

For the longest time, Ervin Shimabukuro sat there with the money wondering what the heck he was going with 'em.

Give it to someone who might need it?

Right...

Ervin was the type of guy people wanted to be friends with, but only if he was buying dinner. Was kind of sad, but he figured that was just his lot in life—go work, pay for friends. Come home. Eat. If no one looking, go hula practice...

To his family, Ervin's dancing hula was already bad enough. His father thought he was one mahu. To him, Ervin should take up one more respectable sport, like golf. Ervin's mother would have given him some support—after all, she loved to watch hula—but she thought he was a little too chubby and clumsy to be dancing hula and who ever heard of one Okinawan hula dancer anyway?

But he kept going. First he had gone because he thought he might find a girl who might like him. Then, he found that when he danced he didn't hurt so much.

You know how sometimes you make like you going meet your friends for go hang out, but instead you drive by yourself all the way to Kamuela because you feel yourself trying to scream against the night? And no matter how you hard you try, how hard you push, there is nothing to hear but the darkness, your shame, and the road?

But when he was dancing...it all was better. Especially

when Noelani was leading the class. Not just because she was beautiful. Well, lots because she was beautiful, but also because... Oh, because she was beautiful.

And that she always smiled at him the same as she smiled at everyone else. They even talked story once in a while! And when she showed a dance, he tried extra hard, and the trying made him better.

So, now, when he tried to decide who to give the money to, all he could think of was Noelani.

Only, Noelani didn't want the money.

So now what? No matter how he tried, he wasn't able to think of one group, one person who needed the money.

He looked at the envelope, and thought of all the good it could do someone if only he could decide. And he still couldn't decide! How pathetic could someone be? Tell him what to do and he maybe could follow, but to think on his own? How can? He was too stupid. Too weak.

Besides, his parents! If they found out he went just give the money away because his hula teacher went say so? Pau.

So, Ervin Shimabukuro called his friends.

"Hey," they said, "we could use the money—lots of good we can do with 'em. That's what your koomoo meant anyway, right?" And since Ervin had no better idea, some money went to online poker, some went to eBay, some went to smokes, lots went to beer, some went to the mall.

And when the money was gone, not even Kamuela was far enough for Ervin to drive.

* * *

Violet Macayan gave her money to the Church, because that is where charity should go. Of all Noelani's dancers, she was the one who spoke the least, reacted the least, complained the least, and expected the least.

Expect what? She was happy. Violet liked her first name, and loved her last name because it reminded her of her husband every time she wrote it on a thank you card, a letter, or even a check at the supermarket. She had three surviving children and thought each of them had turned out just fine. One of her children had died in childhood, but life is something for God to both take and give away. No can help sometimes, and besides, her daughter was with God, anyway.

She had come with Noelani because she would rather dance with Noelani than Ignacio. That was it. The competition part of the hula that Ignacio was so full of second-guessing the judges, the other halau, the musicians. Waste time, yeah? Besides, Noelani was one better dancer than Ignacio and had her heart with Jesus, even if she did seem a little pupule sometimes. At least was fun—and now that she was able to give such a sum of money to the church, made Violet feel like she was doing something useful, too.

* * *

Noelani never did ask any of her dancers where the money went. She said it was really none of her business. She just wanted them to feel what it was like to give something to people who no more.

"Look you guys, when we dancing, that's all it should be—giving. Not everyone has taken time to learn the mele, or to dance, or string wonderful leis. So we do it for them. Everything we do up there is giving. We giving music, dance, a smile—makes difference, you know.

"So when we practice from now on, think about giving. Think about how you felt when you gave that money. Think of the people you helped. Think of the aloha you were able to bring."

Nona, Frances, and Violet danced peacefully. Heck, even Eva, at least a little bit. But Ervin looked like he was weighed down with thirty pieces of silver. _Judas_

Noelani noticed this, of course. At break time she asked him, "Hey, Ervin, you okay?"

Ervin looked at his beautiful kumu and thought of how he went waste all the money, but the father inside of him caught in his throat and bent his neck to the ground.

Noelani put her hand on his shoulder. "It must have been difficult, yeah? I know for some causes $20,000 isn't enough, but the main thing is we try, yeah?"

Noelani never even suspected that he had spent the money with his friends. It wasn't in her nature, not even a little bit, and this only made Ervin feel worse.

* * *

Harry and Steve were fishing again when Steve said, "Boy, Harry, I don't see how the Hawaiians ever survived if fishing was this hard."

Harry laughed, "Well, maybe they were just better fishermen than we are."

"So tell me, Harry, how good a fisherman are you?"

Harry laughed and looked at the empty bucket. "I guess not too good."

"That's not what I heard."

It was weird that Harry could hear him speak so quietly over the waves.

"Harry is the best fisherman on the island."

Steve said it not as question, but a statement.

Harry sighed and closed his eyes and reeled in his line.

On it was one big papio. Must have been fifteen pounds—
and was night time and then!

"I figured I couldn't fool you too long," he said.

Steve looked at Harry, and Harry's face was so honest
that even though Steve was angry, he couldn't act on it.
Instead, he simply asked, "Why? Why did you lie to me?"

"I tell you after."

"After what?"

"After you bring in that fish."

Sure enough, the pole had been shaking in Steve's hands.
He gave it a quick jerk to sever the kite string and reeled
in a very nice-sized menpachi. Harry laughed and despite
himself, Steve began laughing, too.

Harry and Steve took their respective fish off of their
respective hooks and chuckled some more and drank their
sodas. Harry thought maybe he was off the hook (no pun
intended) when Steve grunted, "Okay, so how did you do
that?"

"Do what?"

"Don't play dumb, Harry. All this time I wanted to catch
a fish, and all this time I couldn't. Now how did you do
that?"

"You didn't say you wanted to catch fish."

"What do you mean, I didn't want to catch fish?"

"You said you wanted to go fishing. Part of fishing is
knowing that sometimes you whitewash. If every time you
come home with something—might as well just go get fish
from KTA."

Steve sat there, stunned.

"The guy from Goto's said that's how you used to fish.
You'd always bring fish in."

"Yeah, that's sort of why I stopped. That and my leg. Well,
not really my leg. Good excuse, though. 'Cuz wasn't fair,
yeah?"

"So you kept me—*me*—from catching any fish. How? I usually get my way, you know."

Harry chuckled. "Is that what you think?"

Steve flared, "Don't screw with me, Harry."

"And who stay screwing with who?"

Steve thought he knew what Harry was going to say, you know, the usual stuff about sickness and war. But Harry did what he usually did, which was to stay close to home.

"Try look the Hamakua Zoo. You went to give them money for buy animals for the keikis. Now the zoo is closed."

And it was. The zoo director had resigned in protest; his staff had resigned, too, and none of the activists had any training in keeping the animals. So some folks from Honolulu had to be shipped in to take care of the monkeys, the nene and the tapir and even the tiger (one would guess) until homes could be found for them.

Steve was about to say something, but then Harry brought up the artist who used the money to move to Manhattan, leaving the school ceramics program without a teacher and Kalani's, which because of its new sound system, brought in louder and rowdier bands until was shut down by the police and lost its business license.

"So, you wasted my time."

"Yeah. No choice. I mean you haoles come over here and stir things up. Yeah, yeah, I know you not one haole, but sometimes you no act much different."

"Hey!" Steve protested. That hurt!

"No, really! You come over here, you say you going relax, but then you start changing stuff. You give money to people, you build things. You help zoos and charities all so fast... You no listen first. You just jump in.

"Even with fishing! The first thing you wanted for do was go fishing off the cliff at night! Stupid lolo! You no even understand the place and you like go da kine dangerous places. Besides, if you went catch fish that first night and the nights afterward—what? You would have plenty fish, but would you have been fishing? I no think so.

"There's more to fishing than catching the fish. Like getting the equipment ready. Like waiting for the moon to be right. Like driving out to the right spot, like walking down the cliff with the tackle box, the lantern and the plastic bucket with the brown paper bag with the plate lunch inside.

This whole book

"And even if no more fish, we can pick opihi from the rock, or maybe bring home some wild watercress from upstream. We can talk story or no talk story. Listen to the waves. That kine stuff. And you learned all that, right? So no. I no think I wasted your time."

"So. Are you trying to tell me that all the help I've been doing is like my fishing—too direct, with not enough listening?"

"No. I'm saying have another soda. Stay ice cold. And get two more piece Vienna sausage. You like one?"

A conclusion is not always necessary.

* * *

Lisa was feeling better, so much so that she wanted to go watch Nona's hula practice. With Harry and her husband going fishing all the time, and Nona hard at work learning Noelani's hula, Lisa had been feeling a little bit left out of things—except for an occasional welcome visit from the old Hawaiian woman.

Lisa spent most of her time walking around the house and now, more often, the surrounding yard. Steve's staff kept an eye on her in case something should happen. A doctor was nearby at all times. He lived in a guest house on the property and his only job was to make sure that Lisa had the best of care. He helped the local families in his spare time, and they thought he was a fine doctor. But his main duty was to help Lisa.

"Heck," said Steve. "We have personal secretaries—why not a personal doctor?"

Whatever. Anyway, none of this felt suffocating to Lisa—she knew these folks weren't there to keep tabs on her, as if Steve wouldn't know of anything she did, anyway. In fact, usually, she enjoyed the company. But she was feeling stir-crazy, so when Nona said, "Hey, I'm going to hula practice! You like come?" she said, "Sounds like fun!"

"Meet us outside?"

"Uh-sure!"

Nona went say meet outside because she was also bringing Darin. No sense let Darin poke around the Yates house, yeah? Her nephew, although basically a good guy, could be a pest, especially where money was concerned.

"I stay one bodybuilder," Darin told Lisa before she could ask. "Mostly amateur stuff. My real job is one personal trainer. Hey, you seem a little skinny! Maybe you should think of some resistance training."

"Darin! Lisa is not feeling too well," Nona hissed.

But Darin had already reached into his gym bag and pulled out a glossy catalog of nutritional supplements. "Try look! Now for you, maybe start with some protein powder, maybe some good calcium supplements for build the bones. That's especially important now that you're beginning to age."

"*Darin!*"

"Oh, sorry!"

Lisa laughed. "No problem. How old do you think I am?"

Darin looked at her and stammered, "Maybe about thirty-eight—but a young thirty-eight. Popolo people age better, you know..."

Nona gripped the steering wheel and whispered a prayer under her breath.

Darin started to chatter something about doctors, but Nona pulled into Noelani's driveway before he could finish.

"Noelani, this is my nephew Darin. He staying with me for a month."

Noelani looked at him closely. "Do you dance the hula?"

"Oh yeah, yeah. Plenty! You play 'em, I dance 'em," said Darin and Nona looked at him funny, 'cuz she knew he nevah.

"Really?" Noelani pressed her iPod and some of Ku'uipo's music came over the speakers.

"Can you improvise?"

"Improvise?"

"Make something up," Nona explained.

"Shoots, no problem," said Darin, because that was the one thing that he was good at—make stuff up. And now he was dancing for this beautiful lady and hey, maybe get chance, so he started combining the two weeks of grade-school hula he remembered with a little of his posing routine, showing off his biceps and deltoids and abs and all those other muscles he had been loading up on creatine for.

Lisa tried not to laugh. Nona buried her head in her hands. Noelani looked puzzled, then pained, then turned off the music.

"Thanks Darin, please stop. No! Really, *stop.*"

Darin smiled. This kine stuff never bother him, because he was that way. On the drive home, Darin asked his aunty why Noelani went ask him for dance in the first place.

"Oh, Noelani, even though the show not about Jesus, she still want someone for dance the kane solo. One warrior kine role."

"What about that buff guy?"

"Buff guy?"

"Yeah, that Okinawa guy."

"Who—Ervin?"

"Yeah, yeah—him! Boy, if I had genetics like that... Shoots, you see his quads?"

"Ervin? Quads?"

Nona noted that "quads" must be a good thing, too.

* * *

"So, let's go fishing."

"Not today. I'm tired. Besides, get too much nut grass in the yard."

"You know, I could take care of that."

"And where would that get you?"

"Fishing."

"Really?"

Steve always had the hardest time talking to folks who talked back to him. At the same time, he just couldn't help liking some of them. Like Harry. Although he was still was angry at Harry for fooling him about the fishing, he had to give Harry credit and even laugh—after all, fooling Steve Yates was not the easiest thing to do.

"Hey Steve, instead of going fishing, we go Hamakua Zoo."

"The zoo is closed today."

"Oh and stuff like that going stop you? You'll find a way to take care of it."

At the zoo, the tapir was lying in his muddy water, looking very relaxed. Even the tortoise looked mildly happy. At least as happy as a tortoise can be. But the iʻo was ruffled and muddy, and the turkey vulture rested on the ground instead of its usual perch.

Outside the zoo, protesters chanted at the gates, holding signs with biblical verses and pictures of giraffes and elephants playing with keikis.

Inside, a staff of Honolulu people uniforms and clipboards fidgeted about with worried looks, for both the animals and themselves. They rushed past them almost as if—well, exactly as if—Harry and Steve were invisible.

Harry decided not to bring it up.

Instead, he focused on Steve and the animals and at how one simple gift had caused so much humbug.

Could God ever make a stone so heavy that he couldn't lift it? Was the childhood question to which the answer was yes. But then he couldn't lift it. To which the answer was of course he could. But it's too heavy for him to lift. Uh-huh. And?

Of course now, Steve felt that the stone was sitting squarely between his shoulders. He had only wanted to give some animals for the keikis and now no one could even see the animals that were here. What a rockhead.

"I only wanted to help. That's what I do."

"Maybe you should try for do something else. At least sometimes."

Harry looked at the powerful Steve Yates, so unsure of himself. Then he patted Steve's back.

"I know can you do it, brah."

"Why? Because I'm high mukka-mukka?"

"No. Because you one good guy."

Steve looked at Harry, thought of Hawai'i, thought of Lisa, and bowed his head.

"Thank you, Harry."

"Maybe you should just start over."

"Maybe, yeah?"

* * *

As Steve and Harry walked out of the zoo, kids rushed in, and with them, the adults, looking wearily ahead to another afternoon with the same old tapir, the nene, and the inevitable questions about the elusive tiger. The zoo director smiled at the two men as they exited, asking if they wouldn't mind giving some small change kokua for get the tiger a new mate. Steve hesitated momentarily, then looked at Harry, who laughed and put in a buck in the collection box.

And so did Steve.

*   *   *

Kamakawiwoʻole Schulman couldn't sleep. Not because of the heat or the humidity or the mosquitoes. What kept him awake was a letter his sister and brother-in-law had sent about Yom Kippur. With a photograph. Strange. He in a black suit and hat and she—she was covering her hair?

He had gotten inklings of this before. Letters and emails about how his sister had met these wonderful people, the Feldmans, and went to their first seder in years and years. How friendly they were, how welcoming. Even his brother-in-law mentioned in a phone call that the Feldmans seemed even more like family than family.

Later on, his sister had written—between the usual accusations that he was abandoning the family—of her koshering her kitchen, and how difficult it would be to give up Boar's Head cold cuts. But she knew it would be okay.

They had never struck him as Chabad types. Still, there they were. His sister, covering her hair. I guess her shaytel was at the dry cleaners or something. He started laughing at his own joke and began crying even more. He had almost forgotten how much he loved his family.

Not many too people you could talk to about this in

Hawai'i. Here, they ate Spam, Crazy Omelets, octopus poke, and Portuguese blood sausage.

And it all was ono, and he knew it, so when he was trying to tell Saul about Jewish dietary laws, even he sounded unconvinced.

"So, the Jewish people, they not haole?"

"Well, some would agree, and some would disagree. But, yeah, they haole."

"But they no can eat haole food?"

"It's hard to explain, but certain animals, like pigs and shellfish, can't be eaten at all. Other kinds, like cows and sheep, have to be killed and prepared in certain ways. Oh, and if you eat meat, you have to wait a couple hours or so before you can eat dairy products. So no cheeseburgers."

"But you guys believe in the Bible like the Christians?"

"We're Jews. Big difference. The Christians think we killed Jesus, which, actually, we did, I guess."

"But you believe in God, yeah? As for the Christians, Jesus had to die, otherwise, he couldn't rise again, for save the Christians?"

"I no understand why they stay hating you. Seems like they should be grateful."

Kam nodded. He had gotten those same disbelieving comments from other people he mentioned this to. And then there was Noelani's shock, that first meeting not so long ago.

Was it possible that his people—supposedly chosen—could have so little relevance? He had always taken it for granted, that for better or worse, the Jews were somehow important.

Were they? And did it really matter? His sister's family looked happy.

And Kam? He had his music. And Spam.

"Hey Kam! Long time no see."

Kam looked up and saw Steve Yates, hauling a rolling ice chest behind him.

"Hey Steve."

"Mind if I sit down?"

"Sure, go for it."

Steve plopped on the sand and opened the chest. It contained some Coronas and limes on ice. Steve shrugged. "I know it's not exactly the Hawaiian thing to do, but, sometimes nothing beats a Corona with a twist of lime."

The two of them sat there listening to the waves. "What the hell am I doing here?" Kam asked out loud.

"I was going to ask the same thing." Steve chuckled, then yawned and stretched his arms.

"Oh yeah? What's your story?"

"Well, I've been going fishing for the past two months with my friend Harry. You wouldn't believe it—no luck at all. Today I find out that he's been taking us places where there aren't any fish—on purpose. He said I had to learn some lesson or something. So now we can catch fish all the time, except when we don't. And that's okay, too. On top of that, my wife, Lisa is somehow recovering from an illness and I don't know why. Besides, who needs giraffes anyway, right?"

Kam nodded. "Yep. I understand."

Steve drained his bottle and started another. "You do?"

"Yeah. I came here looking for Hawai'i. I found termites, a band, a beautiful hula instructor, and I'm now getting major airplay throughout the island. And my sister became an Orthodox Jew, to boot. Gee, I hope my bass player doesn't kick my ass."

He half-chuckled, slapped at a mosquito, and opened another beer."

"This is one strange place."

"Yeah."

Steve looked at Kam's photos. "Your sister and brother-in-law."

Kam nodded, then realized that Steve wasn't asking a question.

"Ahh. Chabad."

Steve tossed his bottle into the ocean, but it made no splash.

"You Jewish?"

"Sometimes."

"Oh." The beer had loosened Kam up a little, and he thought, *Yeah, that's the answer that I thought he'd say, if he is who I think he is. Besides, why am I talking to Steve Yates anyway, unless this is a dream.*

dream

"So Steve, tell me are we the Chosen People or not?"

"Sure, if it makes you happy."

"No, don't give me that! I want a straight answer. Are we the Chosen People or not?"

"Let me tell you something a dear friend told me. Sometimes there's more to going fishing than catching fish."

"Huh?"

"Look around you, Kam. The sun is up, the day is clear, the sky is blue and it smells like some packed you a real ono picnic lunch. Whether or not you're chosen, does it matter?"

"No NO! You're not getting off that easy!" Kam opened another beer. "Of course it matters. Look at all the people who've been killed by Jew haters. Families, entire communities devastated, all because of this Chosen People bullshit! Look!" He held up the picture. "Look at what happens even when no one's trying to hurt us! Of course it matters!"

Steve sighed and sucked on a lime. "Atrocities? Genocide? Impressionable relatives joining sects with anachronistic dress codes? I'm sorry, Kam, but that happens everywhere, whether people are Chosen or not. Even on this island. Even with the Hawaiians."

"The Hawaiians? They're about the farthest folks from the Jews I've ever seen."

"Oh really?"

Kam tossed his beer bottle into the ocean. No splash either. Kam watched as Steve grabbed yet another beer and lime. How many bottles did he fit in that little ice chest, anyway?

"Anyway, why should I listen to you? You don't look so happy yourself!"

With that, Steve turned, and Kam stopped, completely lost in the sadness in Steve Yates's eyes.

*   *   *

Noelani was having a particularly nice day because her favorite shampoo was on sale, and after four months, her hula was almost pau. Kam was coming by early; the other band members were on their way. Noelani's day was going so well, in fact, that she forgot to pray, even when she opened the envelope from her old halau.

And she barely felt the spirit of God come into her and save her sanity when she read that her kumu, Aunty Kapolinahe Kahakunoe had died of a cerebral hemorrhage.

When someone like Aunty Kahukunoe dies, you don't really feel sad. You don't really feel.

You sit there, on the floor, or a chair if you're lucky, wondering when you're going to wake up. Actually, not when, but if. Because it's so weird, so improbable that any time, for sometimes months or years afterward, you are still waiting for an end to the sleep.

Kam found her there, after knocking on the door a few times and finding the screen unlocked.

Kam found her there, Noelani, on the floor, rocking back and forth, back and forth.

He didn't have to read what still trembled in Noelani's hand. Kam knew Noelani's kumu had passed on. He had come to know Noelani that well. So it was understanding and trust, when she reached out and held him, because she needed to hold something that would not betray her.

And Kam didn't even notice her beautiful face, the arc of her body, her watery, transparent eyes. He didn't notice the pikake in her hair, the soft warm breeze coming from the sea, or the screen door opening. He didn't notice the footsteps enter the hallway, even though they came from as big a guy as Jonny-Boy. All he noticed was Noelani, her silence, and her dance.

Jonny-Boy entered the room to Kam and Noelani embracing on the floor. He felt his nerves pull tight in his chest and gut. The big guy turned around and left as quietly on the outside as his rage howled within.

Blind the buggah was, because as soon as Carl showed up, he saw Kam and Noelani and the letter and that she was crying.

"What's wrong?"

"Noelani's kumu died. No practice today."

Carl nodded, but Noelani sniffled and shook her head.

"*No.* Now even more important to practice."

Noelani got up, steady, and her eyes were as sharp and smoky as Pele's tears.

*   *   *

If you asked Uncle Raymond about music, he would probably say that music is food for the soul. That being said, anyone who knew how Uncle Raymond treated food would cringe at the thought of ever hearing him sing.

The alley had closed for the night, but Raymond was being asked by Ro-Ann Madeiras, the bowling alley's owner, to rename the Crazy Omelet the Kuʻuipo Omelette (note the extra "te" at the end) in honor of Hilo's most famous musical group. Sure for bring in extra business, she said, because even though Kuʻuipo was being low key about their hangout, people were starting to come to the bowling alley cafe just because they might catch a glimpse and get an autograph of the band.

Raymond couldn't argue that business was picking up like never before, but he imagined it was because of his new tsukemono recipe. Or maybe his li hing malasadas— what an idea that was!

"No, no, you've got to be crazy," sneered Ro-Ann. "No one orders those malasadas and try look, no one is eating the tsukemono, either! Why? Because *junk*, that's why!"

Raymond wobbled and placed one hand on the smooth cool counter.

"Maybe if I change the recipe a little, bring in some heaters for the malasadas...."

"Uncle!" Samson came out of the kitchen because he heard the racket. Lucky the alley was already closed—he saw Ro-Ann yelling over Raymond, now curled on a chair, his head in his hands.

"What did you say to him!?" Samson demanded. She may be the boss, but Uncle Raymond was family.

"I told him that his tsukemono was junk and his li hing malasadas was junk and that we should name the Crazy Omelet for Kuʻuipo and change the spelling of Omelet to Omelette for be more classy."

"Cannot change the name of the Crazy Omelet!" Raymond pleaded. "That's my signature dish. Every ingredient that stay in there, I put in for one reason. You tell her, Samson."

The owner gestured toward Samson.

"What? Him? He think you crazy, too!"

Samson looked at his uncle and for the first time saw how thin he was. And he knew that deep inside, his Uncle knew that the only reason more people were coming into the place was to maybe see Ku'uipo.

And even though business was the best it had been ever been— must be terrible, yeah, when get nothing to do with you.

So what if Uncle Raymond yelled all the time about the smallest little things, even da kine that never make any difference? So what if he used cut-rate ingredients in some of the weirdest ways (like using sugar water to stretch the Sprite syrup)?

Uncle Raymond sat there, as thin as light escaping through the closed kitchen door into the now-dark alley.

"We cannot change the name. The Crazy Omelet stay famous." Samson finally said. "Besides. Ku'uipo comes here for order the Crazy Omelet. If we change the name, then how they going order what they stay come here for?"

Uncle Raymond nodded frantically, as if Samson had made perfect sense.

"What? You must be crazy, too!"

"Maybe, but at least I crazy with family."

"Maybe you folks should be crazy somewhere else!"

Suddenly, Uncle Raymond slammed the table.

"OKAY! We going compromise."

"Uncle! No!"

"That's okay Samson. Ro-Ann get one point."

Ro-Ann smiled triumphantly.

"So I going change the name of the Crazy Omelet to the Crazy Omelette for be more classy."

Ro-Ann rolled her eyes and stormed away.

"Thank you, Samson," Raymond said.

"No problem, Uncle. We family, yeah?"

Of course, Samson would never tell Ro-Ann Madeiras that he was even more irritated with the Crazy Omelet(te) and Uncle Raymond's crazy recipes than she would ever be.

Still, Samson couldn't help but smile.

* * *

Ku'uipo waited for Jonny-Boy to come to practice, but he wasn't nowhere to be found. One hour passed. Then another. Finally, Saul said, eh maybe we should all take a break.

"You think so?"

"Yeah! Hey, we never have one break in a long time."

"You like go holo-holo?" Carl asked.

"Nah—I just going stay here for a while."

Kam shrugged, not surprised.

"What about you Kam?" chirped Carl.

"Shoots, why not?"

And they left Saul at the beach.

* * *

Saul wasn't particularly interested in going out, or anywhere, for that matter. It had been too long since he had so much empty time at the beach. Hilo Bay most times had somebody fishing or paddling canoe, or camping and talking story.

The fishing part was strange, because Hilo Bay basically had no fish. Saul used to wonder why folks fished there—not much success, but he eventually decided that for some people, the only thing that's important is wetting the line, just like the kine people who buy guitars, whack the strings, but never learn to play.

And the air is perfect, Saul thought, as he dozed off.

Steve Yates walked across the water, to Saul. "Hey, Saul, how you doing?"

Saul stirred slightly, but kept sleeping. This puzzled Steve, so he repeated himself a little louder.

"Hey Saul, how you doing?"

Still nothing, just peaceful snoring.

Steve put his hand in his pocket and walked back out over the water.

"Well how about that? Usually, people wake up for me."

Chapter 10

But Saul was already waking up for someone else.

Saul was only twelve, visiting his family on the Big Island. Honolulu boy, used to hanging out at Ala Moana or Pearlridge, eating at Likelike Drive-In. His older brother and sisters would complain about Kaikoʻo Mall and the lack of night life in Hilo—back then never have the Prince Kuhio Center yet, let alone the Walmart—so they took off to Kona, leaving him with his parents and Aunty and Uncle.

People who look at Hawaiʻi on the map, they see everything so close together, and think you know, Hawaiʻi is only one place. But every island is different.

But Saul noticed the differences, that even the saimin and malasadas were different. He noticed that the smells on the Big Island were a lot clearer than the smells on Oʻahu. He could smell orchids, then fish. The ocean at high tide. Someone cooking rice. Not all mixed up all hustle and bustle like Honolulu—and he didn't smell car exhaust at all.

Then, he smelled something so faint that he couldn't ignore it.

"It's the wind blowing off the volcano," his Aunty said.

"The volcano? Can we see?"

His aunty and uncle shrugged and so they went off to see Pele.

The color of Big Island dirt is different from Oʻahu. I mean, Oʻahu dirt looks like dirt—almost like Mainland stuff—umber, brown, the product of plants and grasses dying, then dried out in the sun, maybe with some kukae like that—but the stuff is dirt.

On the Big Island, though, what covers the ground is different. Alive. Red and fertile—like upcountry Maui dirt, but even more deep. Or rainforest black, full of beetles and mulch. Or crunchy with cinders and lava, 'cuz the island still young—in fact some of it is still even now waiting under the earth for be born.

And as they went up to volcano, Saul saw the landscape get even more different. He smelled another smell—sulfur—from the vents that were still steamed from the earth. He looked inside, thought he saw moss growing, but was not moss—was crystals—like frozen rotten eggs—and his uncle pulled him back, saying no get too close—the steam can kill you. And he listened, but still couldn't turn away.

It was getting late and they were getting hungry, so they stopped at the Visitor Center to go shishi, then the grownups started talking about where to eat.

Saul was usually a good kid, and did what he was told, but he had never seen anything like vents before.

When he got back to them, was already a little darker, and he had to lean a little to see the crystals. Suddenly there was a pop, and a plume of steam erupted from below.

Suddenly, someone grabbed his hair and jerked his head away from the fumes.

"Watch out!"

Saul turned—and saw one girl, about his age.

"What's your name this time?"

"Saul—Saul Malani." he said. And he wondered why she had said "this time," and why her voice made him feel ancient and like a baby all at one time.

"Well, Saul Malani, that stuff is *pilikia*." She laughed and she was just like a local girl, except her eyes were green.

"I know—but I wanted to look around." As he looked at her and, for the first time, he knew what beauty was.

"You are so pretty!" he said before thinking.

She laughed. "You always say that! Would you like some ohelo berries?"

"Are they good?"

"Of course!"

Saul nodded. He tasted a berry, and fell in love.

She laughed when he reached for another.

"Cannot take all, otherwise Pele going notice."

"I was only going take one more."

"I know—ssshh." She gave him two. They were sweet and tart on his tongue and he would never forget their taste. "Just don't tell her, okay? She can get real mad!" And she put her finger to his lips.

She asked Saul if he liked Big Island and he said it was so different from Honolulu, but he enjoyed it. And she said you can come live here one day. And he nodded.

Because that was what you did when you answered your true love.

"*Saul!*" Was his uncle.

"You better go now, Saul Malani," the girl said, and Saul turned around and back and noticed, just before he went back, that realized that he smelled the rain, that the last rays of sun reflected green off her hair...

"Eh, Saul where you went?" The big Hawaiian was worried the way big Hawaiians can get worried, you know, all gruff like that on the outside, but you can tell inside they just full of concern. And Saul was going tell him, except he couldn't. He tried to tell him, but the words were not there. As they drove away, he could see the girl, even had the taste of the ohelo berry still in his mouth, but he couldn't tell anyone why.

Not that it really bothered him, though everyone was a little sad because they had gone all the way up the mountain and ohelo berries were out of season.

"Known" Biblically?

Saul had known lots of girls and women since that time, but whenever things started getting serious, he remembered that girl on the mountain. The memory never faded the way memories usually do, and when it was quiet and still and the smell of the earth and roar of the ocean was all that was in his head, he could taste those three ohelo berries and hear her song.

"Rich = having the one you love

In fact that was why he came back to the Big Island. Not for a job or an opportunity. Saul wasn't rich like the other guys—next to him, even Jonny-Boy was rich—but he never care.

There were two things, two loves in his life. He wanted to play music close to his heart, and he wanted to see that girl once again.

And now, he wondered if they might be the same thing after all.

* * *

For Nona Watanabe, however, the love in the music was not the same sort of love Harry that would give her. Or not, especially when he had glanced into his wallet or his heart and saw his wife.

She was getting tired of half loving, of half belonging, of

hearing Harry talk about his wife like she was perfect. She was tired of nodding while biting her tongue, because she had remembered Harry's wife, and she was nice, but certainly no angel.

And no, she couldn't dance hula.

Sometimes good, sometimes, bad...how the hell I know? Every day you stay guilty about your wife is one more day I no belong.

But not belonging isn't always the worst thing, right? Sure, she never match nothing. But not because she was colorblind. Not because she never understand that purple and orange and green can clash.

No! Was not a mistake! She *liked* purple and orange and green. But whenever she wanted something, was always off. No match.

Not fair! She thought she should pray, but she never even know to who. Sometimes she went Buddhist church sometimes Christian. Sometimes she go see the kahuna or odaisan. ~~Japanese Buddhist~~

wiseman (Hawaiian)

Even that never match!

Was so hard, with Noelani asking them to "live hula," and having a good day at practice, only to come home and Harry no even like talk. But when she was busy, he expected her to drop everything, just because he like go out. And for what? Listen to him talk about his wife?

So when Harry called last night to say he "didn't feel like going to the beach because, you know..." she finally snapped.

"YOU LIKE BE WITH YOUR WIFE SO MUCH, GO DEN!"

Harry didn't answer.

"'Ass right. You so sad you not wit her. Sorry she make, but I stay living and I tired wait for you. You like be with her? Go den! GO!"

And Nona hung up.

Harry sat there, in his yard, watching the nut grass seem to grow before his eyes. The phone rang and it was Steve Yates.

"Hey, why don't I come by and maybe we can go get some plate lunches and go to the beach!"

"No—you know Steve, I think I like be alone tonight. Maybe I going fishing."

"Tonight? I'll get ready!"

"No. Just myself."

"Harry? You don't sound so good. Maybe I can come with you."

"No, I get something for do."

Then Harry hung up. Would be just him and the fishing pole. Was getting dark and on the way he noticed that the batteries in his flashlight were weak, but whatever. He had to think, to sort things out...the nut grass, the chicken...his wife...Nona...Steve...

All this time he had been just trying to go with the flow, you know—smile and say everything was going be okay. But somehow things had sped up—from the time when Nona went wear the wrong color mu'u-mu'u and Steve Yates went ask him for go fishing. And Steve went do that stupid move and fall in the water—why wasn't he thinking about his wife, yeah?

And all the time, just trying to smile and go with the flow...

But now Nona went yell at him—he never quite know what for do. Aren't you supposed to be faithful to your wife? Isn't that what forever means?

Even his leg itched like a whisper or a ghost. He thought about scratching something he could not even place—that maybe wasn't even there.

"Why don't you go anyway—keep an eye on him?"

Steve rested his head on Lisa's shoulder.

"He wants to be alone."

* * *

Eva was going to every practice, just like Nona, doing those silly Noelani visualization and breathing exercises. Like last week, before they started dancing—Noelani asked them to imagine a flower arrangement, and if they could smell the scent of the different flowers.

"Of course," Eva said.

"You sure, Eva?" asked Frances.

"Of course! When you working on okazu, you getta smell all the different ingredients in all of the foods like that, to make sure that they all stay being prepared right. Main dish, salad, rice, two sides, drink."

Suddenly, Violet spun Eva around.

"Hey! What you doing?"

"We go test you!"

Frances put a blindfold on Eva. Then, Noelani brought out a flower arrangement.

"OK, Eva, what get?" she asked.

Eva stopped fidgeting. She straightened her back, tilted her head, and smelled carefully.

"Get gardenia, get pikake, get Vanda orchid and oh, and get anthurium."

"Anthurium?" Frances asked. The entire room was stunned because anthurium has no scent. Noelani had put it in the arrangement to stump her. "How you can smell anthurium?"

Eva took off the blindfold and laughed. "Oh come on, we on the *Big Island!* What flower arrangement no more anthurium?"

Noelani had to stifle a smile.

"I thought we had you."

"Look, Noelani—you went spend all your life for the hula, right? I've spent all my life for plate lunch. When you spend all your life for one thing, you get one understanding. I bet if you came to my place for cook, you'd catch on pretty fast, too."

Friendship Noelani had never felt such kinship with someone as she did in that one moment.

*   *   *

While everyone was waiting, Jonny-Boy was thinking as usual about Noelani, though he would not admit it even to himself. Instead, he ordered some chicken from Blane's Drive-In. The rest of the band didn't go there often so this is where he went when he wanted to be alone.

And that was about it, at least all that he expected. It was raining, and the mud seeped over his rubber slippers, making a murky squish when he walked. Had some outdoor tables at Blane's, but one section near the front was particularly empty because the awning stopped right at the parking lot, so even the slightest breeze brought the rain on top your head. Was gray and wet and the empty.

And that's where he sat. Not that he gave a damn. The chicken was warm and the soda was cold and the mac potato salad was somewhere in between. Was good. Was quiet and nothing surprising. Kind of like plate lunch—but even with plate lunch always had someone talking about how this one was better than that one and that whole Eva Matsuoka stink.

This was just chicken—not awesome, but pretty good. It tasted like pretty good chicken and the soda was cold, not bad bubbly sweet, and the mac potato salad was nothing special, but okay.

Somehow the big guy identified with this. Especially the mac salad. He poked it with his fork and took a strangely small bite for such a big guy. He let the taste and texture melt over his tongue—the mayonnaise, the salt, the macaroni, maybe just a little too soft. Had butter, too, and under it all was the barest hint of crab. The creaminess of the mayo played with the rough feel of potato on the roof of his mouth.

No one ever paid much attention to mac salad—it was just a side dish. But without mac salad, plate lunch wouldn't be plate lunch. No ways. Something would be missing—no matter how good the tempura was, or the katsu, or even the chicken.

Something has to be there, between the main kau kau, to make everything one true meal...

Jonny-Boy took another bite of the salad, then some chicken. Then some more salad. Then a bite of tempura. He smiled. Was ono.

* * *

Nona had never snapped at anyone like that, not even the kids at school when she was working.

She still was mad at Harry. Still, if she never make up with Harry, she realized she would never be able to cook her chicken without thinking of him, and what good would that be? Besides, not fair to just yell at him no warning.

So she called him up to say maybe they could go to the beach tomorrow night, then not getting any answer, then thinking maybe he was mad, then driving to his house, then finding his car was gone, then calling Steve and having Steve sound real weird and Lisa choking up on the phone.

She got in her car and drove, and for some reason ended up on a road she had never taken, and that's where she found Harry's car, over the side.

Police cars and a fire truck and an ambulance came by a lot sooner than they usually did. Steve Yates got out of one of the cars, almost like Jack Lord in Hawai'i Five-O. Lisa Yates rushed over to Nona, who hadn't moved from where she first saw Harry's car, the cell phone still held tightly in her hand.

Then a helicopter descended to lift Harry the fisherman away.

*   *   *

"I don't know why you're still alive," Steve had said.

"What do you mean, you don't know?" Lisa had replied.

"I don't know. You should have gone by now." He walked over to the sofa and tripped on the carpet. "Always thought my feet were too big."

He tried to smile, and failed.

Lisa's eyes widened, as Steve rarely failed at anything. Or had he? Since being on Hawai'i, she had never seen him so unsure, or felt in love with him so much. Or felt so needed.

"Why not save him, Steve?"

"He didn't ask for my help."

Lisa took a deep breath. "But Steve—so what?"

Steve chuckled at the irony, then closed his eyes.

The sculptor who had moved to New York mysteriously found that she had left too much of herself in Hawai'i and sheepishly asked to return. The PA system at Kalani's broke, leaving the bands to grumble about carrying their gear all over again. Even the new building at the Tsunami Museum began to spring leaks, and was in danger of falling down had the local community not raised enough money to pay someone to fix it.

In fact, the only one undamaged by his gift was Noelani Choi, the first one he and Lisa gave money to, who in turn gave to her students, who in turn gave it away.

"Steve?"

"Shit." Steve sniffled and tried to rub the red out of his eyes, but failed at that, too. He's going to die, and the last thing he told me was he did not want me with him. I can't, because he's my friend."

"Oh Steve! Don't you understand? Because he's your friend, you *can*."

* * *

In the hospital room, Steve was examining Harry's artificial leg—twisted, torn, and smashed as the rest of him.

"Maybe the leg slipped off and that's why Harry went lose control?" Nona asked.

"Maybe. We're looking in to that." Steve replied. Steve didn't have the heart to tell her how he had improved Harry's leg. If the prosthesis had detached, Harry must have meant to take it off himself."

"Dammit, Harry!" Steve muttered.

Suddenly, Harry said something.

"You think I stupid enough to kill myself? I was trying for scratch'em and damned thing went just came off. What kine junks you went give me, anyway?"

Ever wonder why God had to say Let There Be Light? Why not just think'em, yeah? Maybe cause was safer that way. It would be confusing, yeah if every time you thought of something the damned thing came true...

And Steve had been doing a lot of thinking.

"What?" Steve thought and realized that Harry was still *inside* *Steve's* *head* comatose. Nona was still holding Harry, but then Harry was telling him, "Hey—never mind, Steve—I just kidding." → *non-object*

And now, Harry and Steve were walking on the rocks

holding all of their fishing stuff. Steve said, "Harry you're not here. You're in a coma on a hospital bed in Honolulu."

"If I stay in bed, how come I just went stub my toe on that last rock?"

"Oh, come on, Harry."

"You going tell me this is one dream?"

"No, you are in the middle of a coma. You went for a drive and your car crashed over the side of the road."

"Yeah Steve, that's funny. It's one beautiful day! Let's go for one walk."

*   *   *

Nona would not stop stroking Harry's hair. She looked at every wrinkle in Harry's face, every black hair, every white hair, and everything in between.

Then Harry's heart stopped beating, the machine went beeeeeeep and Nona screamed, "No, no, no, cannot be *cannot be!*"

Steve was frozen—unsure if he was sitting next in the hospital or with Lisa or at a board meeting or walking with a dead man.

What is real? When Lisa is listening to you tell her stories, when Harry is listening to you try to explain life, when the board of directors is listening to you saying that everything is looking pretty damned good?

When everyone is listening to you, and everything you say can move the weight of the world? What is real?

Nona's tears. They were real.

"Why do I put myself through this?" Steve would say a long time from now, far into the future, when Loʻihi broke the surface and all of this was coral shore. And he would remember the sounds of Nona crying—not because they

[handwritten margin note:] Reality

were any louder than anything, not because they were louder at all.

But because they were closer. Because he heard them as if they were a part of himself. A part of his flesh and bone. A part that ate plate lunches and special recipe chicken. A part that walked around Ben Franklin Arts and Crafts looking at frames and round Styrofoam balls.

A part that couldn't tell nut grass from St. Augustine.

And that was his answer, at least for now and for as long as now would ever last.

He reached down and held Nona's hand and, with her, prayed.

Whom he prayed to, he didn't quite know, and he felt a little silly doing it, but then again, did that make him any different than anyone else? He had heard so many of these prayers—some of joy, some of desperation, some in high voices, some whispered out of the corners of one's eyes.

It was a clear night, and his thoughts were so unlike the silent flight of his angels, as they would surely were surrounding him now, though he couldn't hear them over his thoughts, the blades of a helicopter clumsily stabbing empty air.

Chapter 11

To Close Their Eyes Behind the Rain

Jonny-Boy felt a hand on his back. He looked up at Kamakawiwoʻole Schulman. He looked right into the haole's eyes. He hadn't done that in quite some time.

He could tell the haole was shaking, because he was. Because it was a pretty stupid thing for the haole to have approached him, being that he was real pissed off and could have broke Kam's face easy if he wanted.

But he never. Why he never swing? As easy as would be, he just never.

So Kam sat down, and why bother, yeah? Going be one of those stories, he just knew it, where the haole guy going be real reasonable and take away the beautiful native girl. Or he going say that he going help him, that he going teach the savage brown boy how for be one self-actualized human being. You know—be open to your feelings kine bullshit.

Haoles. Always thinking they know something. And even when they know something, they make it seem like it's everything. If no make sense to you, then you either one haole or stay in love with one haole. And even then...

Jonny-Boy chewed a chili pepper.

"How you knew I was here?" Jonny-Boy said, and was immediately pissed off that he had said anything.

"I saw your truck in the parking lot."

Smart-ass haole.

Rain ↓

Now it might seem a strange time to talk about the rain in Hilo, with Jonny-Boy and Kam about to fight, but sometimes it rains when you no expect, and the rain is pouring and all the little rivulets that come off the mountain one drip at a time—they grow big and strong and look like rivers that they were there the whole time.

But get more than water to the rain. Get smell, for one thing. The rain falling on the warm ground and the heat and the moisture take with it the smell of whatever stay on the ground—the moss, the guava, orchids, asphalt, the trash bin around the back.

And the sounds, quiet at first, but if you listen real careful, you can hear the difference between the sound of rain falling on the road, in the trees, on the ocean, or on the grass. And everything stay growing; you can almost see the plants swelling, the rocks turning soft and green.

You can lose yourself in rains like that, wandering with nothing on your mind but a home you never knew you left.

And something inside Jonny-Boy got lost, too, on one afternoon outside at Blane's Drive-In in one heavy Hilo rain.

He took one sip soda.

"You know, haole, I never ask for anything special in my whole life. Just be one of the guys, you know, no make waves, like that. It's one good way for live. Good fun for play bass—you just whack the right notes in the right time and you make everyone sound more better. No need be in the spotlight. But afterwards, when everyone stay saying how good everything was and they stay talking about the singing or the guitar or even the sound man, you kick back and smile 'cuz you know part of that sound, way down at the bottom, that part came from you.

"I might not be too special, haole. Not like Noelani—or you, for that matter."

"You one fantastic player, Jonny-Boy."

"No make li'dat. You know what I mean."

Kam said nothing, because he did.

"That's okay brah, really. Get one place for folks like me. One day I going tell Noelani I love her. Going be okay. I know it. Because even the fire needs to rest once in a while, and even the stars must close their eyes behind the rain."

*   *   *

DREAMS, GOOD AND BAD...

Nona was thinking, even as she was losing Harry, about the hula, and how she would not be able to dance with him looking from the audience ever again.

Every stumble, every off-beat, every stepping on Frances Silva's mu'u-mu'u—she would find Harry in the audience and see him there with that twinkly smile on his face.

No embarrassment, just a smile—okay, sometimes a little kolohe— but always everything's fine, even when she was crying on the way home and he turned off the radio and just listened to her.

And she realized that there was more to their relationship than her chicken. Oh, she had known this all along, but there was a difference between knowing something and really knowing it.

Sometimes, when you praying about one thing, you find

yourself praying for something else. Sometimes when you asking for one thing, you receive another.

Such a strange gift, though, to know inside that Harry not going pull out of this, and only then, to know for sure that he stay in love with you. _wife? Pele?_

And through the tears, Nona began humming a song to Harry, a song from Ku'uipo—a song that was just written, but was as old as love itself.

Harry's jaw dropped. In front of him lay one simple plantation-style house, clean, and neat. In front, had the perfect lawn, twice the size of the one he had back home. And the banana trees in the back—the leaves were broad, rich, and green. In the red dirt had peanuts growing, and onions. The Manoa lettuce never have bugs, and the fruits and squash never get bee stings. No more fruit flies—on the ground never have nothing for pick up—not one single rotten papaya or breadfruit. And the garage had three big sacks full peanuts cleaned and ready for sell.

"Hey, not bad this place," Harry muttered.

Harry wandered back to the big front yard. "No nut grass! Can you _believe_ it? One big yard like this and no more one blade of nut grass!"

"Harry, you know this place is not real, you know. Not for you."

Harry turned. "Oh Steve, I was wondering when you was going show up!"

"Really? I'm impressed." Steve said.

"Oh, come on, brah! Try look this place. This place stay all over you. Everything perfect. Just like when we went fishing first time, remember?"

"Yeah, I remember. Except without fish."

Harry winked. "But this place, I bet get plenty fish. I

think I going try soak bait. You like come, too? Guarantee we going catch plenty."

Steve squinted. "Why? You know you don't belong here."

"I figure we stay on vacation. I going relax a little while. Nice place this. I get lots to think about, anyway. Lots to see." Steve watched Harry limp around the yard. "Try look over there! The papayas smell so ono!"

Then Harry heard laughter and froze.

It was a laughter that he hadn't heard in years.

"H-HONEY! You ALIVE!"

Harry lurched toward her, as fast as he could, artificial leg and all. But try as he might, he could not get any closer. Then, he saw her smile, but not at him. Was someone else—another man holding one full bucket fish.

"Who da hell that?"

Then he stopped.

Because it was not another man. Was him. Harry. With two legs. And they were happy. But as he watched them, he felt empty. I mean, that was him. But he was here. But he was with his wife. But he wasn't.

Steve put his hand on Harry's shoulder. "You see? Everything is fine. She's happy. And she's with you, forever."

And Harry nodded, then thought he heard someone calling him back. He thought of mismatched colors and bowling alleys, and hula and shark-bait skin. And the chicken, and that he hadn't fried eggs in so long.

"Let's go," said Harry.

"You sure?"

"Yeah. For reals."

Harry's eyes fluttered. He yawned. Nona looked at Steve, then at Harry. Then, because Harry was Harry, he gave one big smile.

"Whassamatta you guys?"

*   *   *

...AND JUST WEIRD

"...a bowl of clam chowder? Clam chowder? *What?*"

Eva Matsuoka thought she had seen it all. But now this was it. Lunchtime came and Matsuoka's was empty. How can be? Folks were lining up around the corner at Goto's.

"Roland! Go over there and find out what they stay eating!"

Roland went out and came back one hour later—still never get any more customers—before he came back.

"Sorry, eh, Aunty, but the line stay so long, went take me this long to get da soup."

"Soup? They stay waiting this long for soup?"

Roland nodded.

"What kine soup? Fish soup?"

"No."

"Miso soup?"

"No."

"Tripe soup?"

"No."

"Porogee bean soup?"

"No."

"Well gutfunnit, what *kine soup it stay?*"

Roland scratched his head. "Clam chowder, Aunty."

"*What?* Clam chowder? *In Hawai'i?* Give me that!" Eva took the Styrofoam container from Roland, looked inside—and saw New England style clam chowder. She jabbed her finger in the chowder and tasted it.

"They stay waiting in line for *this?*"

"Arnold Goto went tell me they went run out of Portuguese bean soup so he went Costco for buy more ingredients, but the Campbell's Clam Chowder was on sale so he said shoots why not and people started coming for buy'em. He stay go through three cases already!"

"*What?* You mean he stay selling clam chowder right out of the can?"

"Yeah—that's what he said."

"I don't believe it!" Eva thought of all the recipes she and her mother had painfully acquired, beautiful, they were. And no one was even eating them! "Clam chowder not even local! And this stuff stay from one can. Why they stay buying 'em?"

Roland shook his head. "I don't know, Aunty—I don't know..."

Clam chowder, clam chowder, clam chowder... Eva could see it now, people eating clam chowder instead of saimin, or nishime. At family gatherings, at picnics, at parties. Clam chowder! How can? And straight from one frickin' Campbell's Soup can! Eva ran outside, to someone spooning clam chowder from one Styrofoam container.

"Hey you! Yeah you! Manong wit da clam chowdah! Why you stay eating that?"

The uncomfortable-looking Filipino guy said, "I wen wait in line tree hours."

"Why—*Why?*"

"'Cuz the line was long, asswhy."

"No you stupid lolo! Why did you order da damned chowder?"

The man went scratch his head. "I don't know—everybody went say was ono asswhy."

"And what?"

"What you mean, what?"

"Stay ono?"

"Huh?"

"Da clam chowder! Da clam chowder stay ono or what?"

He frowned. "Must be. You know how long I had to wait in line for this chowder?"

Eva looked at the stupid guy and this red red rage went

through her. She picked up a chair and smashed him WWE Wrestlemania style right on top the head. The guy stumbled, spilling the Campbell's Clam Chowder all over the street.

"You stupid, stupid stupid!" She slammed his head again. "Stupid, stupid *stupid!*"

Roland came out. "Aunty, what you doing?" And her hands went cold when she saw that he was eating the clam chowder, as well.

She looked at him in disbelief. "Not you, too?"

"But Aunty, everyone else stay eating 'em, and..."

Eva threw the chair at him and screamed—

And the scream woke her up. She sniffed the air for the scent of clam chowder, but there wasn't any. It was quiet outside, and over at the kitchen, she could hear Roland chopping vegetables.

It was the best sound she had ever heard.

* * *

That morning, Roland came in to see his aunty waiting for him with car keys in her hand.

"Aunty?"

"We going talk to that haole girl!"

"Uh, she not haole."

"I know I know—not important anyway!" Eva fumed. "I already stay wasting too much time with that stupid Nona Watanabe. Somehow she went give that haole the recipe."

"Popolo."

"Whatevers."

"So?" asked Roland.

"So? *So?*" Eva started pacing. "That woman is *Lisa Yates.* Her husband is the richest man on the planet. All she need for do is snap her fingers and poof she can have one whole chain of restaurants selling that chicken!"

"Oh wow, Aunty! I never think of that!" Memories of the chicken made Roland's mouth water even now.

"Get in the car, Roland!"

"Huh?"

"Get in the car! We going visit those high mukka-mukkas right now!" Eva slammed her door and pointed the car up the coast. What Eva was going to do she didn't know—she'd think of something. But this was too much. She didn't care how much money or power these folks had.

Already past Hilo and Hamakua, they saw how what was once canefields had gone from mac nuts to papayas to now eucalyptus trees—

All this trouble, Eva thought, just because they don't know what the land stay for—for grow ono kine stuffs for cook and serve with rice and mac potato salad. Or for fill with people who were hungry.

If you don't know what you for, she thought, you lost. You pau. Eva remembered her mother laboring at the okazu-ya. Yeah she went get other people's recipes—but only because they never guard 'em close enough. Just like Nona Watanabe—they never understand the value of what they had. For one case of beer, you going give me your secret cha shu sauce? The one your family went keep for generations? *What the hell you stay thinking?*

Shoots, if you that stupid, well—what can I do?

Anyways, Eva thought—better that Matsuoka's get the recipe anyway—at least one local place. Someone going steal the recipe, anyways—folks like Sam Choy—and garans they going change 'em.

Eva had never changed a recipe in her entire life, and as far as she knew, neither had her mother. Each of them had this faith and appreciation of local cooking, that it was somehow natural and of the land, and that if you thought too much about changing this thing or that thing, it made it less real, less satisfying.

And this chicken was like that. Even more.

Eva had followed Nona down the highway that one night, and knew, just knew, that she could find the road that led to the Yates house. Of course, I can find 'em. Of course.

And she drove left, then right, two exits past Papaaloa, where she had been before, turn makai, towards the ocean, down through the jungle—she could smell the chicken, she knew she could and she was almost there, another wind, another. Roland didn't even ask her if this was the right way, because he knew it seemed familiar, too.

Then, there was a break in the cavalcade of green fern and philodendron, and when they hit the pavement, there was a big bump, and when they looked up...

They were in a parking lot. The K-Mart parking lot.

Eva Matsuoka looked at her nephew. He was shaking.

They were at K-Mart. But Hilo no longer *had* a K-Mart. And the sun was on the wrong side of the island.

Which meant they had somehow been transported to...

"Cannot be!" Eva rubbed her eyes.

They had somehow been transported to *Kona*.

Steve looked out his window and chuckled.

"What are you laughing about?" asked Lisa.

Steve exhaled at the expanse of ocean, the expanse of lava, and the expanse of green...

"You know, I really miss those Blue Light Specials," he said. K-mart Deals

Chapter 12

It came to Lisa Yates unexpectedly, as she was sitting outside on her veranda—a nice word, that, veranda—listening to the recordings of some old Hawaiian music that the old lady brought her one day with some—what was that, ulu?

Breadfruit—it was a delicious thing with a little honey and nutmeg.

With an iced tea and the music, Lisa closed her eyes. Then she realized that she would rather have them open. And a brush of sunlight swept along the coast, as refreshing the wind itself. Echoing of the black rocks, deep ferns and forests, of rainbows porpoising off the crashing waves, the playful day danced with all the goodness of a mother's kiss on newborn skin.

Wasn't it a few short months ago that she had come here to die?

It had been years, years, and more years. Seasons

changing. Friends changing. She would watch each individual leaf on each maple tree, give some of them names, relish their springtime green, then watch them change. From yellow to red. Then brown. Then dead.

When there was no joy at the leaves that replaced them, Lisa knew it was her time to fall from the tree. She had asked Steve—no—*made* Steve—promise not to try changing her mind. A time to sow, a time to reap, a time to cast away stones, a time—well, you get the idea. Time to die · Biblical

Or so she had thought. Until when? The ohelo jelly? The malasadas? Nona Watanabe dancing on the lava? The amazing chicken?

This was more than mere paradise. And now, it was raining again, and in the softness she could have sworn she heard babies crying, plants bursting leaves, fish shimmering just below the surface. There was something eternal here, beyond creation or judgment, that would always be here, never taken away. You could lose yourself here, to this place.

And she thought that one day it might be nice to take up the hula.

Or, maybe something even more delicious.

*   *   *

Harry was making remarkable progress. Five days later, his wounds were healing so well that the doctors shrugged and said time to go home—here's some Tylenol and some gauze.

Nona said something stink about stupid HMOs—Harry was almost killed, you stupid—but Harry cut her off, saying he was fine and he wanted to go home and check his yard.

"I think he took care of it." Nona glanced at Steve.

"Uh..."

"Nona, let's go." He gave Steve the stink eye, grabbed his Tylenol and his gauze, and was back home within the hour.

Was still light when he got there.

No wonder Steve had looked funny. Had lots of weeds in the yard. Real lots.

*   *   *

Ku'uipo.

Up 'till now, Saul Malani would have agreed with Carl. It was a fun name, no need take 'em too seriously, yeah? But now, he wasn't sure. This new music stay reminding him of something he never know was missing. And it all led back to her.

Walking along Kino'ole Street, Saul drifted past the same old 7-Eleven and the Longs Drug Store. He had walked this way countless times, but now Saul could almost feel the ground swerve and swell with the millennia and the rain. If he listened, he could just make out the chatter of the island reaching southward. He felt like a schoolgirl who drank too many cappuccinos 'cuz was so sweet she never know had caffeine inside.

"In Da Beginning." At first he thought that his job was for follow Noelani and Kam—you know, like Jonny-Boy and Carl. But no, he was more than that. Kam and Noelani had given the song their music and movement. But Saul had given it his voice.

His voice. His tale, and the tale of the girl he had met for the first time all those years ago by the volcano. Or he had thought, but now, a music that had been with him all those years began to gather from a place he had long forgotten. He had never felt that way before. But of course he had.

The air, the sea, the wind, the way rainwater flew off the Chevrolet that sped past him right now—everything seemed growing, yet timeless, yet new. Why the island was telling him this, he didn't know. Why he understood the language, he knew even less.

The wind went mess up his hat, so he stopped to fix it before continuing on his way.

* * *

Noelani got one letter in the mail inviting her halau to prepare for the upcoming Merrie Monarch. She wrote back saying she never have one competition halau now, and that they should forward all correspondence to Ignacio Perez.

She got another letter, but she didn't open it. And she went outside and watched another sunset. *end of her old hula way*

* * *

Harry's yard looked like it had been neglected for months. Weeds and weeds and weeds. Some of his planters were *crown* broken, and the ground was dust. Not just nut grass, but sleeping grass, with the thorns. The banana trees looked like they never get water, either, and that was strange, because had plenty rain.

"Oh...no. How can be? How long was I out?"

"Only two weeks, Harry."

Harry yanked out his phone.

"Steve! Youcomedownheredisminnit!"

When Steve got there, he found Harry sitting in the dust, scratching a scab with a piece of broken planter.

"Whoa—what happened to your yard?"

"What you mean what happened to my yard? You should know what happened to my yard! Stay only two weeks! Who else going do this? But how come? Da lawn nevah do nothing to you! How come? You still mad about the fishing? I thought you went understand!"

weeding

"I do. Harry I didn't have anything to do with this."

"*Harry!*" Harry and Steve whirled as a banana tree withered and fell.

"Gutfunnit!" Harry stumbled to his garage and grabbed his screwdriver. He pushed past Steve, past Nona, and started weeding, even in the dust. Even as the weeds seemed to grow twice as fast as Harry could pull them out.

Steve and Nona watched Harry frantically plunge the screwdriver into the dirt. As he worked he mumbled about how hard he was working to keep the yard neat and that all he wanted was one clean yard and who the hell went mess up his yard.

Steve tried to help, but Harry said, "NO! I going weed this garden and I going buy one new banana tree as soon as I get my disability check, and—"

Harry coughed and spat up dirt.

"Harry! You not healthy yet, you know. The doctor said you no can exert yourself li'dat."

"Like what, Nona? All I wanted was one clean yard, right? One banana tree, right? *Right?*"

Harry heaved like he was about to throw up..

"Harry!"

"DAMMIT!"

The old screwdriver snapped in his hands, slicing his finger.

He fell on the ground, face sideways in the dirt, clutching his hand, as weeds grew around him.

Steve was already rushing to Harry and calling for his helicopter to make one emergency trip to the hospital.

But something stopped him. A small, strong thing.

Nona placed her hand on his arm.

"Let me take care of my Harry," was all she said.

Nona didn't care if Steve argued. Of course, she knew

Steve would want to handle everything. But this was her Harry. The only Harry she had.

"Harry, come we go my house," she said, and it was not a question.

She helped him up and guided him over to her car.

When she got him home, she sat him on the sofa and examined his wounds. She took care of his hand right away. But he was dirty all over, and she was scared the dirt would get into the cuts and give him one infection. Which of course meant she had to bathe him.

Nona left him on the sofa and went to fill the bathtub. She had worked as a volunteer nurse's helper at the hospital, so she had seen one naked man before. Same thing, she tried to tell herself, but her shortness of breath betrayed her knowledge that no, this was not the same thing.

When the tub full, she walked over to Harry, took a deep breath, and removed his shirt and pants. She wondered what to remove next, his boxers or his leg. She decided to remove the leg first, reaching around the back, undoing the two straps and gently nudging the prosthesis off the stump. Had one scab, still from the earlier accident with Steve.

She decided that maybe would be easier to leave his boxers on, so she said, "Hey Harry, time for go furo!"

Somehow, that got through to Harry, who was still pretty much one sobbing mess. She held Harry underneath his arms and helped him to the edge of the tub. But on the way, Nona noticed that Harry had one mean scrape on his hip, and that blood was oozing through his boxers. So she took a deep breath and eased them off.

As he entered the tub, she tried not to look at him, tried to make the water soap up quick, but she couldn't help for look a little, and a feeling she had not had in a long time stirred. Not the sexual kine—well, maybe a little bit—but more like one <u>kolohe</u> kine feeling, like one small kid gets when she stay making mischief and she knows the teacher no going find out.

[margin note: Mischievous]

She smiled a little, then started washing him, his arms, his head, the wounds along his back.

"Auwe! That hurts, Nona!"

"No can help," she said. "Going come infected otherwise."

Then she reached lower and she washed down there.

Harry froze, "No, no I can handle!"

Nona was scared, too, but she told herself Harry still stay injured, getta help him, so she shushed him and moved down to his thighs, his stump, then his calf and foot.

After pau, she rinsed him off and brought him his leg.

What about my clothes?"

"They stay dirty. I going wash them."

"Huh?"

"You can put on one robe meantime." Nona had some laundry of her own to do, but decided to wash his clothes separately. She thought about how she had touched Harry, how he seemed to have responded.

Naah, how can? Harry stay injured and even then he not really interested in me that way.

Nona looked at a pile of clothes that looked like one Filipino-Porogee rummage sale, all mixed up kine colors—in all the large sizes—from Walmart and Ross Dress for Less. One big, fat pile of dirty laundry. *Yeah, who da hell would be?*

Nona dumped Harry's clothes in the washer and came out of the garage to see Harry flopping around in one lime green bathrobe. Suddenly, it hit her that she had one naked man in her living room except for one bathrobe, just like on TV, except that instead of looking manly and sexy, Harry looked like one giant bean.

[margin note: real life - funny]

Harry looked up. "What you stay laughing at?"

"You look like one giant bean."

"Well, dis bathrobe stay real big, yeah?"

"*Harry!*"

"Oh, sorry!"

"Nevah mind," Nona giggled. "Your clothes going be pau after dinner. I go start cooking."

Harry started to nod, but then stopped.

"No—Nona, not now."

"What, you not hungry?"

"Yes—I mean no. I mean... We can talk story for a while?"

"Yeah. Sure, Harry." She went to the fridge and brought out two cans guava juice and they sat down on the sofa.

"You okay?"

Harry ran his hands through his hair and said nothing. But Nona knew he had a lot on his mind, so she never try fill the silence, instead letting Harry fill it on his own.

Finally, "How can? The place ruined. No more nothing. I no ask for much—my yard, my lawn, my banana tree, right?"

"You right, Harry."

"Now, I no more nothing. Nothing..."

But then, Nona thought of hula and that one Hawaiian lady who looked at her at the Royal Hawaiian that awful day of the mismatched dress.

"You get me, Harry."

"Huh?"

"You get me."

Harry started shaking, and that dirty laundry wanted to make Nona get up and cry and run or do something, but it was as if her own music was giving her strength.

And Harry closed his eyes tightly, the way men do when they are trying not to cry but cannot help.

"I can only love one woman."

"Only get one woman here, Harry."

"I know. I know," he whispered. "Nona?"

"Yes, Harry?"

"Nona..." He started crying now, and Nona hugged him, and, for the first time in all those years, he hugged her back. They kissed, and she could feel his heartbeat flush against her skin.

"I sorry, I so sorry," Harry said and Nona said, "no need, no need."

Was a long time they held each other, feeling tears wash between them like rain after the long drought. Was more than that—was like one flood, unstoppable, now that it had finally begun. Then another kiss, then hands and bodies moving where they had never been before...

Nona looked up at Harry, draped all in green and thought of those times small kid time, when school was pau and the rain was pau and she walked into the forest and sun dappled through the green green ferns and just off the leaves, the light would come through and make one rainbow so small it went fit inside the palm of her hand.

Sex? no sex? "Maybe we should move to the bed," Harry whispered.

"No," Nona said. "Let's stay right here."

In the morning, they went back to Harry's house. Harry looked a little disappointed.

"I almost went expect this place to be all fixed up," he said.

"That's okay," Nona said. She put her arm around Harry. "We going fix this place up together, you watch."

Harry kicked a dry patch of weeds and exhaled.

"You think so?"

"For sure, Harry. For sure."

Somewhere, an old Hawaiian lady closed her eyes and smiled. *Pele*

*   *   *

One guy who was not smiling was Ervin Shimabukuro, one-time would-be Okinawan Jesus, now really guilty guy. He would have talked to his friends, if he still had some, but they were da kine friends who would take his money and spend 'em all, then feel perfectly fine blaming him for having one rotten time and telling him no bother call until he get more money.

Which is exactly what they did.

And of course, Ervin no could go to Noelani. What would he say? That he went let all that money go to waste? Twenty thousand frickin' dollars down the tubes, just li'dat?

He was in his room. Thirty-four years old and still living with his parents. His father sat in his big chair with one beer on one side, one cigarette in the mouth and the Honolulu Advertiser sports page in front his face. Every time Ervin went out, he would shake his head, which Ervin knew meant, "Where da hell did I go wrong?"

And his mom would look at him and try for smile when she was not cooking food for one crowd that would never come over. Always too much food, and the freezer was all stuffed with leftovers that his screaming father would throw out every month or so in one of his beer tantrums, saying, "I tired see all this shit in da icebox!"

No more kids, no more grandkids, no friends—not even church kine friends. One day Ervin's sister went leave Hawai'i with one Laotian man and moved to Minneapolis. Mom would pray and pray, but nevah help, and his father went yell at her no go church no more. Waste time pray! One day he went throw one beer bottle at her, and after that Mom just stayed home.

Ervin thought would be good for kill himself, but he knew he no more guts. Once he went hold one knife to his throat and said he was going cut himself and his father went laugh and say go then, you waste time anyway. And Ervin knew he was right and put the knife away.

He was going cry, but he never even had the guts for do that. And his mom was making another dozen musubi, 'cuz you nevah know who might drop in....

Ervin knew he looked like one typical hairy Okinawan, all wiry arms and bowlegs and square jaw. Just like his father, only the skin was not so beat up by motor oil and rust and canefield sun.

Just like his father. Except his father used to be one good bowler and played shortstop in the Buddhahead leagues. If he was a little taller, he could have played wit da haoles. At least that's what he would yell at the TV after his second beer.

But Ervin? Useless. His father would yell that, too.

Once, Ervin thought maybe would be best to move Oʻahu and find one job at one office or something. He went pass three computer classes at Hilo Community College and felt he was pretty good at using Microsoft Windows. But of course he couldn't—he no more guts, yeah, for move to the big city? Still, he would go Hilo town when he felt depressed for look at the computers li'dat.

And today, when he went looking around at the store, he noticed Steve Yates, the guy from the magazine, right there in the store, talking to the clerk, who unbelievably did not seem to notice the resemblance between the guy talking to him and the man smiling on the cover of the magazine next to the cash register.

In fact, folks were just going about their business, and Ervin thought *how can?* For some reason he knew he was not mistaken. So he tried to sneak closer to him, for listen to him. Maybe he could even touch him—maybe if he could touch him, just touch him, some greatness would rub off on him, or at least he could tell people that at one time in his life, that one mediocre loser had touched the great Steve Yates.

And then he tripped on the carpet and plowed into Steve Yates, sending them both to the floor.

"Hey! You stupid lolo!" the clerk yelled.

"Sorry, mistah! That creep always coming here, sneaking around, no buy nothing. That's it! Get out you! And no come back!"

Ervin struggled and staggered out the door.

"Hey! Wait a minute!"

Ervin heard Steve Yates call after him. *He wants to sue me! I just know it!* Ervin started to run. He never have money and the way that lawyers are, they would go after his parents and then they'd have no more house... *Oh Ervin! How stupid can you be?*

"*Ervin Susumu Shimabukuro!*"

Ervin froze. The most important man that he had ever met (sort of) had just called him by name.

"Come back here."

"Y-yes, sir."

"Don't look so scared. I'm not going to bite." Steve put his hand on Ervin's shoulder. Ervin had an overwhelming urge to kneel.

"No, don't do that. It's a little over the top, you know."

"P-please don't sue me!"

"Now why would I do that?"

"Because you're Steve Yates! You can do whatever you want," Ervin said, and a little wonder crept into his voice.

"Really?"

Ervin nodded.

"Well, I was trying to get that sales guy to give me a good deal on that smart phone and he wouldn't budge."

"Didn't you tell him who you were?"

"He wouldn't have believed me."

"How can?"

Steve laughed, and suddenly, everything stopped. Everything. The people, the cars, the mynah birds. the traffic lights.

"Ervin, didn't you notice that out of all the people in the store, you were the only one who recognized me?"

"I thought maybe I was crazy. Or maybe they were?"

"No, you're okay, Ervin. And so are they. But sometimes the eye only sees what the mind expects. Open your mind, maybe you can see more possibilities. Come to think of it, if more people knew that, I'd have a lot more vacation time.

"Anyway, whatever I want isn't always important. Look around. What do you see?"

Ervin look past Steve and saw everything. People not just frozen where they were, but what they were looking at... where they were going...what they were smiling, or crying, or angry with. And in all these creatures, he saw...truth?

So much truth! Truth. But what is truth?

"Well, that's actually two questions, isn't it?"

"Huh?"

"One you can answer. One you can't."

"Huh?"

"Like right now. Aren't you hungry?"

And Ervin looked around. They were at Goto's.

"You like the pork ribs, right?"

Ervin nodded.

"There you go," said Steve, as if he had made a significant point.

They got their food and walked some more. They walked all the way from Kilauea Street, by the bank and the newsstand, all the way down the Kamehameha Highway past the Royal Hawaiian and over the bridge to Coconut Island.

And the whole time, as he watched all that was around him and listened to Steve, it never dawned on him that this was an awfully long way to walk, and that by now he should be having blisters or sore feet or something.

Instead, he was thinking that he had just eaten tempura and pork ribs and mac potato salad with the great Steve Yates, who had canceled God-knows-what to continue talking with him.

*   *   *

One thing Kam really missed about LA—besides having stores open past 10 p.m. that weren't Walmart—was having a variety of different music to listen to. Local groups played local music, which wasn't so bad, except they all seemed to feature the same chords and harmonies. Even the lyrics seemed as if they were cut and pasted from song to song. It reminded him of what he heard from middle-class blues musicians in the San Fernando coffeehouses back home.

But even at the most insipid, frappé-infused suburban blues café, he could always just leave to hear something else down the road. Here, there was really nothing else down the road.

The whole time he had come to Hawai'i, he had come looking for something he was missing. As if there were a missing piece of himself he had to find. And each time he had discovered what he thought was a piece of himself, it had turned out to be a part of what he wasn't, instead.

What was even more befuddling was that the less he found out about himself, the less concerned he was with the question. Just a few months ago, he would have been completely freaked out if he felt that Hawai'i possibly might not hold what he was looking for. Now, he wasn't even sure if it was that big a deal.

At least life was giving him moments. Like that time right after the "drought" (yeah, like in Hilo if no rain for two weeks it's a drought) when the sun got the asphalt so hot that when the afternoon rains finally came, steam veiled across Kino'ole street up and down, like a lacy fog, but hot and oily and flowery all the same time.

Or the time when he got hardheaded and decided he would try his hand at fishing, but instead sat there on the edge of the bay, watching how the light made the ocean seem almost like molten glass. He spent an entire afternoon there, unable to fish, to move, or even to exhale.

He asked Jonny-Boy once if he ever got tired of this, as they watched a rainbow flutter in the mist coming off the trees and Jonny-Boy shook his head and said no, I never do.

*   *   *

Ervin didn't know how to talk to strangers, or so he thought, but as he talked to Yates, he felt himself speak about his mom, his father, his friends, or lack of them. Like when Susan Machado told him that he was a creep—wow—Ervin had never said that to anyone...

But Steve laughed. "Yeah, lots of people thought I was creepy, too. It happens."

"I'll bet."

"But of course, Ervin," Steve continued without offense, "it's not your success that changes other people. Success transforms you. You carry yourself differently—and people can't help but react to that."

Ervin still couldn't believe that Steve Yates remembered his name.

"So tell me," Steve said, almost offhandedly. "What are you carrying right now?"

The question took Ervin off-guard, and before he knew it, he said, "I hate myself."

And once he said that, he couldn't stop.

"I hate who I am, who I was, I hate the way I look," and Ervin thought *I am such an ass*, as he started crying right in front of Steve Yates. "I'm hopeless. If I had just had a little more backbone I could jump in front of one car or something. Now what—how I going face Noelani?"

"Oh, don't worry about the twenty grand," said Steve.

"How you know that?!"

But Steve just continued. "It's pretty hard to just give money away, anyway. Believe me, I know. Walk with me," said Steve, and they were at the zoo, looking at the lack of animals.

"Why are we here?" asked Ervin, deciding that he might as well accept where he was.

"I don't know," Steve said, though he clearly did. "How are your folks? You know, it's pretty kind of you to stay with them."

"Kind? I don't think so. They wish they could get rid of me," Ervin mumbled.

He turned, but Steve was next to the tapir, who was lying on its side as if dead, but for his nostrils flaring open and shut with disinterested regularity. It reminded Ervin of his mom listening to him talk about hula practice.

"You would be amazed how people act when you're helping them. Especially the stubborn ones. They complain, argue, ignore... and all the time they're deathly afraid that you might leave them."

"You think so?"

"I know so, Ervin. Just like I know you."

And Ervin felt his neck and upper back change, straighten. *Maybe his life wasn't a waste.* Maybe just by being, he could serve some purpose, have some value. He didn't have to be weak. He could be strong, as well.

Then Ervin thought of Noelani Choi.

"I suppose you had better tell her what you did, Ervin."

Ervin turned red, and like he did when he drank beer.

"Yeah."

Ervin got up and dusted off his okole. He knew he was insane to be breaking off one conversation with Steve Yates, since he had never even met the guy until now, but somehow, something in the conversation made him feel that it was the right thing to do and that somehow, if he did this he would probably see Steve Yates again.

When he looked up, Steve was gone. Ervin had almost expected himself to be magically transported back to town. No such luck, though. Eleven miles. Oh well. Was a good day for walking.

*   *   *

"Man," said Harry much later on, "you went just let Ervin walk like that? You something, you know that?"

"Forgiveness shouldn't be too easy."

"Oh yeah? This from the guy who just went go li'dat for put the zoo back to how it was?"

Steve picked up a small rock and threw it into the bay. He smiled.

"Touché. Now give me another piece of chicken."

Chapter 13

AND ERVIN HADN'T WALKED DOWN THE HIGHWAY MORE than a hundred yards or so when he heard one car honk.

"Hey Ervin, what you doing?" came a voice more graceful than he had any right to hear.

"Noelani?"

"Get inside. Why you stay walking out on the highway like that?"

*   *   *

It's hard to explain, but sometimes time beats down on the soul like the sun, fading the hues of each moment, each heartbeat... It's as is you're seeing life through a dusty window, with gloves on your hands and a clothespin on your nose.

You know the apple pie is there, and it's just out of the oven, and, if you are asked directly, yes, of course it smells good. You know it does. But that's the problem—it's all what you already know. There's no craving, no hunger. The mouth doesn't water the same way, the fingers don't start wagging like a puppydog tail.

It's as if all the flavor has gone away.

This is how Lisa was, how she thought she was always going to feel, until she felt nothing more. But now?

It was funny how it feels—to be able to smell again. To be able to want to smell, to hear music when the stereo isn't even on. To smell, before thinking, and to look and see the rainbows that surround every form and feature that catches the eye.

It *is* time to breathe, to do more than breathe—to inhale. To linger on tradewind air, feel the its motion permeate the lungs, the arms, legs, fingers, and toes, and then even farther outward, as if one is breathing both in and out of the body.

To be alive. It's not such a big deal, and yet it's everything in the world. It's all one can taste. All one can touch. All one can see, and now—it was like it would never, ever, ever be all.

All. That was the problem, wasn't it? She had been fooled by all, by all the big things Steve Yates had done.

Because all isn't big. It's got nothing to do with big. It's having ohelo jam on a Saloon Pilot cracker, listening to nothing in particular, watching just another philodendron bursting through the hood of a rusted old truck in the neighbor's back yard.

Even at the mosquito that sucked a teeny bit of blood her leg, she felt nothing but joy. She was being alive. Thank you. Thank you. Thank you. She spoke to no one in particular. Maybe to the land, maybe not. Her pain wasn't gone—it was simply irrelevant. Just another aspect of another precious and intricate day.

And Steve. For the first time, she had seen him puzzled,

as if something were out of his control. But that didn't matter. Later tonight, he would just ask how, why, and seem completely surprised, and that would make her fall in love with him even more deeply.

He'd brush her hair and smell apple pie. He'd wipe a tear from her eyes—or was it his own? He'd stare deeply into the moon and say, thank you. Thank you. Thank you. And it would be as if the ocean were speaking, and the sky, and the stars beyond.

And she would peer into the moonlight, to see the outline of another island in the sea, full of fruits and plants and animals and music that waited to be explored.

Lisa looked around, wondering what to do next. She had no chance. A loud, uncontrollable laughter greeted the heavens and earth, the forest and the sea.

*　*　*

Steve was walking along the road, eating a Macadamia nut ice cream he bought from the Mauna Loa Nut factory. He thought he heard laughter, but when he turned around, no one was there. Which, of course to him, meant nothing.

"You can come out now," he said, and an old Hawaiian woman dressed in a beautiful red mu'u-mu'u walked out and smiled.

"Hello, Steve Yates."

"You."

"Of course it's me, silly! Who did you think it was?" The woman laughed and Steve could hear the joyous sound of fire lighting a cold dark night.

"What do you want?" Steve asked.

"*Nothing*, silly!" the old woman said.

"Everyone wants something."

"Lighten up, you! Why you always so li'dat?"

"Like what?"

"You know! Business, business. Always getta be doing something. Relax already! After all, you stay in Hawai'i."

Steve said nothing as the smells of the place suddenly became immediate. The air became poetry, the earth a song that he finally tasted, and heard. The old woman couldn't be doing this to him. Or could she?

The old woman nodded. "You and your wife such a nice young couple. But so sad, you guys. Poor ting."

"I'm not that young."

"Oh, *I know who you are*," the lady continued. And for a second her eyes were lava itself. "I could get real mad for everything your people went do to this place. But wasn't you, yeah?"

Steve thought about this, and smiled in a sad way. "No, it wasn't. You wouldn't know."

"No, I don't think I would," the old woman agreed. "Still, I know one thing."

"And that thing is?"

"Sometimes, Everyone needs a miracle." And as she said this, he suddenly tasted the wonderful tangy sweetness of ohelo. The soft glowing scent of ohi'a wrapped around him like a warm familiar blanket or a story being read by candlelight.

Steve blinked and she was gone, except for her voice. And it smelled like fire.

"Even You."

*   *   *

Kam stared out and thought, *You know what—I don't understand what the hell I'm doing here.*

Saul took another beer. "I bet you stay wondering what the hell you stay doing here."

"What—are you some kind of psychic?"

"Nahhh, just a musician. And your friend."

Kam blinked and exhaled.

"My song."

"What"

"I came here looking for my song. I still haven't found it."

The two of them sat silently for a long time. Then Saul sighed.

"Maybe you get 'em, already."

"What you mean?" Kam asked, in the truest pidgin he had ever spoken.

"You! You say you looking for one song, but you stay giving everyone this amazing music. That music must come from somewhere, yeah?"

Kam thought of his time since coming to Hawai'i, first with nothing, then meeting Jonny-Boy, and Noelani, and Ku'uipo. The little boy in the park.

"Hey, by the way, what's your real name?"

Kam shook a little, but not really sure why.

Identity

"Mel."

"Mel? Short for Melvin?"

"No, just Mel. I don't know why. I used to tell folks my parents were so poor that they couldn't afford another syllable."

Saul started laughing, and it was children and cousins and uncles and grandma sharing dried squid, teriyaki sticks and musubi with ice-cold fruit punch.

"What's so funny?"

"You! You so funny. You call yourself Kamakawiwo'ole to be more Hawaiian, but you already get one good Hawaiian name!"

"What?"

"Don't you know your name in Hawaiian?"

"No."

"Mele."

"So?"

"Mele, you stupid lolo. Mele!"

"Mele?"

"Yeah, lolo. Mele. MELE! It means 'song.'"

* * *

Sometimes the answer stay all around you—so much so that you stay inside it—and you the last one to find it. Other times it's right in front you, but in the hardest place to look.

Ervin looked at Noelani.

"I no think I can dance for you anymore."

"What? Why you say that?"

"The money."

There. He said it.

"What?" Noelani asked, not comprehending.

And now Ervin had to explain. But had to, yeah? Just... just had to. So he took a deep breath and thought of Steve Yates.

"The money. The money you gave me. I was supposed to give it to charity. But I gave it to my friends and they went gamble 'em away. I was weak, and screwed up real bad. I sorry, Noelani."

Noelani wasn't sure what to do. For a second she thought she was going to cry. Then she wanted to yell. Then turn away. But when Noelani looked into Ervin's eyes, she saw something that wasn't there before.

"I understand if you throw me out. If you no forgive me. But Kumu, please believe when I tell you..." He started to cry. "Nothing makes me happier in the world than when I dance...

"Please let me dance!" he cried out suddenly, from the bottom of his soul.

Finally. Was it strength? Commitment? No. It was truth. She knew it had been inside Ervin, but buried, the song of the self who had never known he was there.

And a voice, sounding like, if anything, her old kumu, whispered to her. *Forgive him, child. Was meant to be.*

To find truth. What was that worth? Twenty thousand dollars? Twenty million? $ and truth

Noelani sighed. Then she smiled. "I forgive you. I've made some mistakes, too."

It was the last thing Ervin expected to hear. He put his head down and started sobbing. "Sorry, sorry... I cannot help. I never going forget this, Noelani. I never going let you down again."

She drove up to his house. "Now get some rest before practice, okay?"

And, as Noelani drove off, Ervin yelled after her, "I going make you proud. I promise!"

When he went into the house, his father didn't even look up. His mother said, "Get plenty food in the fridge. Go eat 'em. Otherwise I going throw 'em away."

Ervin looked at the food, thought of the performance, then thought of him.

"No thank you, I stay training now for dance."

"No talk to your mother that way," his father mumbled. "Eat!"

But Ervin went to his room and closed the door.   triumph?

*   *   *

Nona Watanabe was too white. Yeah, too white. No can help. Just too white. She knew it. No matter how hard she would try for do the hula, she would always be too white.

Harry said, "Nona, no be like that. You look fine."

"Fine? Fine? I tell you what is fine. Try look all the kanakas dancing the hula. *That* is fine!"

"No can help. You Japanee."

She glared at him. "You no understand! Easy for you—look you—you all mixed up. Me, I only get Japanee blood!"

"I no can believe this. Nona. *Nona!* The hula is one dance, not one paternity test. Anyone can do 'em—even the haoles."

Nona knew he was right, she supposed, at least on some level. But she would practice the hula with the others every day, and was always obvious that she was the one who stood out. Even when the muʻu-muʻus went match, still, she was the one with the whitest skin.

"Harry—what one Japanese girl like me going do?"

"Try dance obon?" Harry joked.

Nona gave him the stink eye. "No make A, Harry!"

"Nona, I not da one making A. What you—who cares how white you stay? Skin not important!"

"You no understand!" Nona stormed away.

Nona grumbled all the way home. Without thinking, she reached into her fridge and pulled out chicken parts. "If only I could somehow match—just one time, gutfunnit." She paused for a moment, thinking that "gutfunnit" sounded funny coming off her mouth, but dang it, why not?

She laid the chicken parts in the breading to rest, then started humming the wonderful, wonderful new music that Kuʻuipo had been creating for their hula. Simply beautiful, and when Saul folks started singing 'em sent, it chilled her body like it was one big giant spine.

You see, sometimes—no, most times—when you dance, you no even understand what the whole thing going look like. You focus on your part. Only the kumu knows what the dang thing going end up looking like. But this was different. This was going be *special*.

Nona lay the pieces on a foiled cookie sheet and put them in the oven.

But Nona was terrified that she was going screw 'em up, somehow. How? Just by not matching.

Her skin was just too white! Hula was one Hawaiian dance—how can be Hawaiian? Her long hair she could wrap up in ribbons for make wavy, but nothing could disguise her skin.

How can be Hawaiian with skin like this? I just like Noelani's hula be perfect. Maybe more better I no dance.

Long time ago, when she was crying after Jose Bulosan went call her Fat Nona, her father went tell her if she smile on the outside, then the smile sure thing going work its way inside. And she smiled and was hard at first. But slowly it felt better.

But sometimes smiling was just too hard.

"Aunty! AUNTY!"

Nona looked up, coughing. Her chicken was burning and Darin was opening the windows.

"Aunty, you okay?"

Nona never quite know what to say—it took a few seconds for her to realize that she had burned the chicken.

"Aunty, you okay?"

"Yeah—"

Darin pulled out the oven rack and beheld the delicately flavored pieces of charcoal.

"I no think so, Aunty. What's wrong?"

So Nona told him.

"Hmm..." Darin said, slowly. Then he snapped his fingers and winked. "I think I can help you!"

Darin left, and a few minutes later he came out with a cardboard box.

"You know how da kine bodybuilders always getta be tanned, yeah?"

"No."

"Oh. Well, they getta be tanned. And some of them get real white skin. So instead of one natural tan, they put special kine cream on top their skin for tan 'em."

"What? Dye?"

"No no, not dye. Specially formulated skin pigments." He shuffled around the box pulling out plastic bottles and magazines and bubble wrap.

"Sounds like dye." Nona raised an eyebrow.

"No no! Works real good—the professionals all use 'em. Comes in one tube—just like this!"

"Really?" Nona frowned, as she examined the tube. "You tried 'em?"

"Me? No, I no need. I already get tan."

Nona closed her eyes and shook her head.

"Oh, sorry Aunty..."

*   *   *

Across the Rocks

Harry and Steve were fishing again. It was new moon, very dark, and the two of them had their buckets and line and flashlights and walked down the rocks to one of their favorite places. Harry led, but didn't bother looking back. Steve had become quite good at climbing across the rocks.

They found a good spot and assembled their rigs. Not much was said, or needed to be. A million things were going through each of their minds. Harry was wondering about his wife and Nona, and how it felt to let go of a surface memory for something deeper. He loved Nona, but somehow he felt it was finally okay.

In another time, Steve might have proffered some

wisdom of his own, about how it is to love and then love again. Or perhaps he would have come to Harry in a dream and let him figure out its significance.

But instead, Harry just walked out to the point, flung his line across the waves and listened to the cloudless sky.

Steve was wondering about Lisa and the old woman, and Harry might have talked to him, too.

But Steve sat there, his line in the water, listening to the universe breathe.

It's that way when you fish, letting the time slip like water through fingers, not tasting the water, but experiencing it in other ways. A fish bites, is reeled in, then nothing. Then a false strike, then nothing. Then another fish. Random events. You can do everything you can to increase your chances of catching the fish, but there's no way to predict when, where, or if a fish will actually bite.

The only thing that's certain is that you don't catch fish unless you cast the line.

Nona had asked Harry once if fish wanted to hide from other fish, then why were they so colorful? And Harry, being Harry, knew the answer.

"You see, under the water, the light not the same. In fact, you know the menpachi? Stay all red, yeah?" And Nona said of course, cause was true.

And Harry said, "Under the water this fish looks gray. No can see 'em. The weke, the hinalea, all da kine colorful fish—under the water they all mostly gray."

Nona thought about it. "Poor thing, yeah?"

"Poor thing? Why?"

"Poor thing that they have such beautiful colors, but no can even tell."

At the time, Harry had chuckled. But now he realized

that he had never paused to think of fish that were never caught, only to be devoured by other memories, or covered with crabs and snails.

Such a fish can't understand the joy it can bring to a family, a meal, a cause to give thanks, a celebration. It can't understand that the alternative is to die submerged and alone.

But a human being—well, that's love , yeah And besides, by the grace of God, by a strange quirk in the universe, when a human allows itself to be caught by love, it gets the best seat and the coldest beer at the big luau in da sky.

Steve reeled his line in, inspected his bait, and cast his line back into the sea. It disappeared almost immediately into the night, and though he could have easily determined where it was, he didn't bother, confident in gravity and the arc of his swing.

*　*　*

Noelani thought about all that kine bullshit junk she had been working on. All that thought about the grand hula with the life of Jesus and all that kine da kine. She thought about those lessons she was trying to pass on to her dancers, of silence and following silence, and the music.

The music had held her hostage for as long as she could remember. Even in her silences, it enveloped her, permeated her, would not let her rest, would make her arms sway and her feet step. Oh, was from her training, her kumu, her halau, people would say. But no. Wasn't even close.

Even without the halau or her kumu. Even without the competitions. Even without the hula itself, Noelani knew the music in her head would live. It was a music that had been there before the first Polynesians came to these islands, before these islands themselves broke the surface.

She had thought that the music was Jesus, and she

thought that in the church she had heard echoes of these same melodies lilting salvation from the choir. But when she tried to blend and harmonize her music with what she heard, there was only discord. Only loss.

Was not Jesus after all, yeah? But then, what?

She heard it first, a most beautiful voice singing deep and soulful. She looked for its source, and in the pavilion, she saw.

She saw Frances, Nona, and Violet going over the dance steps they had been working on. Even though she had told them they weren't going be at the Merrie Monarch, it didn't matter—they were practicing. The deep voice belonged to Saul, as he was playing ukulele and accompanying their practice. They didn't see her, and she sat down on the grass, watching them in the distance.

Frances stopped, forgetting, and the other two laughed, and they started over. Saul shook his head and by the way his shoulders moved, Noelani could tell he was laughing, as well.

As Noelani watched them, she cried tears like she never had before. They just wouldn't stop; they just streamed over her, full of sadness and joy. And a voice appeared in her head, sounding like an old old woman, yeah, sounded crazy, but was almost like Aunty Kahakunoe, but even wiser, with more kolohe in her voice, but more aina, too.

Probably just dreaming, yeah, the way sometimes you jumble things up in your mind then it comes out like voices, only since they came from you it's only you talking to yourself the whole time, yeah?

Anyway, whatevers. What mattered is that the voice opened to her and what it said:

Who are you, child, to question me? Who created the cosmos. The ocean, the wind that blows across the ocean. Who created

*the gravity that raises and lowers the tide. To whom the largest
whale and the smallest opae are all the same.*

Who are you child, to question me?

Noelani Choi had not known that she even was
questioning—only that she wanted to know the source of
the music in her head. That was really the only question
she wanted to know.

Who are you child, to question me? The voice came, more
insistent, this time. All the fear and shame in Noelani was
about to gather and she was about to say *I am nothing, I
am nothing.*

But then, Saul's voice and guitar lilted over the green. It
resonated with the song within her, like the river sounds
through a window screen on a warm autumn night, that
continue even as one's breathing moves in and out with
the deceptive meter of dreams.

It was a song that burrowed into the beams and eves of
her being. Noelani had never heard this before. Yet it
sounded like her, like everything she not only wanted to
be, but *had* to be. Like all the moments that can change
one's life, if only one is able to hear the song, the invitation
to dance.

She didn't run away, or cry, or leave Oʻahu. It was no
longer time to run, but to open the choreography within
her. And she faced the voice and said, "This is who I am."

And she gestured, and she evoked black lava at volcano,
a splash of color in an otherwise dead expanse, whirling
beneath a perfect, featureless sky.

"The dance, the dance, the dance.... I have always been
this dance. My fingers are its fingers. My feet are its feet.
Where it travels, I travel." And she turned, and the forest
sprang beneath her feet. When she raised her arms, the

scent of pikake washed over the air. When she smiled, her hair beguiled the rain clouds then set them free.

"This is who I am, tutu. And I ask you now."

Why do you need why?

She wasn't sure if she was asking or answering. Yet the need to know the source of the dance and the music suddenly dissolved. Yes, there would be days when Noelani would wonder, and they would be difficult days. And inside, she would always know that parts of her would always be with her, even when they chose to remain unseen.

Chapter 14

Get fishermen and get fishermen. Oh yeah, and get fishermen, too.

You see, get fishermen who just like go to say they go fishing. They get the right poles, the right spinners, the right lines. They bring the beer and the flashlights and what not. And they talk about this bait and this place and that rig and all that stuff so that people who don't know fishing think that they real good fishermen.

And that's really what they like. They like people think they good, and good for them.

Then get da kine fishermen who just like get the fish. That's it, these guys. They just go do their business and fill the buckets full. Sometimes these guys fish with dynamite or use bleach for get tako. They no care about the water or nothing. They no like talk about what they do, where to go or nothing. No like give away secrets, these guys. All they like do is take, even when no more. But whatever they get, never going be enough.

And the other kine fishermen?

They da kine that can fish the ocean for generations, yet always still going get fish in the sea. Da kine that catch 'em not by the pound for sell, but for the good times and stories they can tell, with one Tupperware full chicken or Styrofoam plate lunches, one soda sitting next to them on the rocks...

They da kine who know where the fish are, during what phase of the moon they going come out, whether the tide stay high or low or in between. What the air smells like, how thick it feels between one's fingers and on the tongue.

But more than that, they know the fish themselves, beyond pounds and inches, they know what the fish is—to the smaller fish it devours, as well as to the larger fish beyond. They know what it means to a proud father coming home with one heavy plastic bucket dangling from one bamboo pole to that rascal hanabata kid.

They know the laughter of birthday parties when get plenty sashimi and ahi poke to go with the poi. The taste of dried aku washed down with one cold bottle MGD.

And they da kine who know that the fish color is brightest when it courses through the water, and that it quickly fades as the fish gasps and quivers the last life from its gills. Sad, yeah?

But from sadness come good times, too.

You know da kine.

*   *   *

When Harry met Nona that night, he was stumbling and fumbling a bit more than normal. Nona thought maybe his leg was bothering him.

But no. He had one strange look in his eyes. Like he was about to throw up, only more nervous. Nona thought about her first dog and the feeling in her stomach when she watched it struggle with arthritis after 12 years. And then one day her dad said no can help. And they buried the dog the next day.

That's how went Harry look.

"Harry you okay?"

"Yeah yeah yeah. Just..." And he went fumble some more. "Nona... We been real close yeah, over the years, yeah?"

"Uh, yes Harry."

"And..." Harry started shaking a little and Nona wondered what the heck was going on. A stupid thought went through her head, but left before she was even aware of it, though she would play that thought in her head over and over for the rest of her days.

"Nona," Harry said and stumbled to a knee.

"Oh! Harry, you okay? Here I can help you up!"

"No no, I mean yeah yeah, I okay. I mean wait wait! I mean, Nona!

"Nona."

Nona stopped, and Harry looked into her eyes. And somehow, amidst all the fumbling, he had retrieved a little box and opened it in front of her.

"Nona, will you marry me?"

Nona froze. The band was two interlocking fish, one silver, one gold. There was a center diamond, surrounded by one emerald, one amethyst, and one bright orange fire opal.

She felt herself floating while she was looking at the ring, looking at Harry, feeling her head nod and her mouth form yes, even though her voice wasn't there. And Harry slid the ring, gently, on her finger.

From the look on her face, Harry knew it was perfect. He smiled to himself. Sometimes having Steve around was one good thing.

She felt the ring and started shaking uncontrollably. Harry got up and pulled her to him.

"I sorry," he whispered. "I sorry went take so long. I promise we going have the best years we ever had, Nona. You and me. Just you and me."

"Promise?"

"Promise."

"Promise?"

"Promise."

"Promise?"

"Promise..."

Steve Yates was driving to his house on the Hamakua coast, smiling and trying to keep the tears from blurring his vision. This kind of thing still got to him, and probably always would.

* * *

Meanwhile, at the bowling alley, Ku'uipo was all there, except Saul, who never come yet.

"So, you think I should change my name back to Mel?" Kam asked.

"Shoots, why not? It's your name, right?" Jonny-Boy replied. "But maybe keep using Kam on stage."

"Huh? Why?"

Jonny-Boy laughed. "Because, haole, no one going ever believe your real name is Mele."

* * *

Noelani dancing alone, not in one physical space, but in the halau she kept within her wherever she traveled.

Dreaming, listening, not merely with the ears, but with the hands and feet.

To the stories, the mele, the oli, to where meaning was not necessary and beyond, to where it was not adequate to contain the meanings. Even salvation...

Even salvation, even the image of Jesus bleeding fire across the crucifix, that wood, the wood of the earth, bathed in the blood of a savior, nourished by the wounds, yet the very substance, the very structure into which the iron nails were hammered.

Personification

Yet the wood never felt the wounds, and it stood there, unfeeling, even as the source of its new life yielded beneath a crown of thorns. Standing there, not even perceiving whether its lover was alive or dead.

Not even that story, not even salvation was adequate to contain the dance.

For she had known how those very same people who had come to the islands to pass word of her savior had also been far worse Pharisees to the people they found. No need to go into details. That because of them, most of the hula she learned had not been the rich tradition of the ancients, but simply what had survived the centuries of persecution, misunderstanding, and scorn. Most of the hula did not make it to us, her kumu had explained. We must hold what has survived close to our hearts.

But even this closeness missed something.

She thought of the Hamakua Zoo, these birds and animals—this one going extinct, and that one stay endangered. Kept in glass compartments or wire mesh cages. Guaranteed for life never to be forgotten—at least by the folks who weren't searching for the tiger.

But what kine life is it, yeah? The i'o no can fly; even the tapir cannot move around. What kine life is that? Stuck in one cage, with one bunch of zoologists making observations from time to time. No can grow, no can discover new things and places. Always stuck on display.

No, the tradition alone could not contain the dance.

"So what next?" Noelani asked. "We not going Merrie Monarch." She faced her halau and shrugged. "We no fit any of the categories, yeah?"

The rest of the halau nodded. They knew that Ignacio had been right, way back then, that the judges would probably not approve of what they were doing.

"Sorry, you guys." And suddenly, Noelani had no idea of how to continue. She had just wanted give her group the dance. That was it. And now? Now that her dancers understood, the next step was to take the dance where it needed to go. Back, out to the people. But how?

"If only could show our work," sighed Nona. "But how can? They only interested in proper hula."

"*Bullshit!*" said a voice in the corner, and everyone turned, startled to hear Frances creaking like one folding metal chair. "Proper hula? I tired of proper hula. You think what we stay dancing is what the Hawaiians were dancing? We say kahiko, but so many of the dances were wiped out, just like the people who loved them. The stuff you see now is *renewed hula* memories of memories of what used to be. We say auana, but how is bringing in new stuff different from what the kanakas did when they first came to these islands? Proper hula? I say it's right there." *philosophy*

Nona never even think of that kine stuff before. She looked at that wonderful mixed-up ring that Harry had just given her and she wasn't sure if she was crying because she was sad for Noelani and the dance, or happy to be part of something new and wonderful.

Eva knew that this was important, but one look at Noelani

and she knew it was time. Had to serve the food now, before it got cold. She cleared her throat.

"Okay! But what can we do *now?*"

Then Ervin had one idea. And was worth more than twenty thousand dollars.

"Shoots, why no have one performance and webcast 'em?"

"What?"

"You know, put on top da Internet. 'Cuz Nona—Nona your friends—yeah? Maybe they can help."

And, just like that, Noelani asked Nona who asked Lisa and Steve who talked back to Noelani and was settled that they were going to construct a stage for a live performance and web cast of Noelani's hula.

"Oh, this will be so much fun," said Lisa.

And, just like that, everything was set to happen, one night, Steve Yates's place.

* * *

The Yates place was alive with construction. Pounding, digging, big trucks with metal bars. All over the island, people were talking about the ho'olaulea at the Yates place. Friends told friends and they told other friends. Lois Cabral announced on the radio that Ku'uipo was playing, and Noelani Choi was going dance. Everyone, it seemed, was excited. Everyone except Harry.

When Steve drove by to talk story about Noelani's show, Harry was in his front yard, pulling nut grass as usual.

"At least this time you had the sense to hire local labor and not just snap your fingers," Harry said. Then he looked up. "Shoots, Steve, you never learn *nothing* from before?"

And Steve sighed, "I understand. But this time it wasn't my idea. At least not completely."

"It was mine, as well," Lisa said, coming out from the cars. Harry scratched his head.

"Harry, let's take a walk," said Lisa, and they left Steve to call some company for handle electrical wiring and lighting.

"You know we came by to check on you."

"I'm fine. I'm fine. You guys? Not so sure."

"I know you're worried. But it's different this time. We're just taking after you."

"How so?"

"Well, if you could help out a friend, or family, wouldn't you?"

"Yeah, but before—"

"Harry," Lisa interrupted. "That was different. Before we were trying to help strangers." And all the warmth that the island had given her seemed to pour from her eyes, not like radiance, but something so youthful that it had to be older than time. "This time we're helping friends. More than friends. Family." Communion

Harry scratched his head, and finally, he smiled. "Well, if you put it li'dat." He set his screwdriver down and sighed. "You guys ate lunch yet?"

Steve put his hand over the phone. "Harry, I'm offended! Do you think we would eat lunch before we came to see you? Where you like go? Goto's? Matsuokas? KTA? Crazy Omelette?"

"You know, what I would really like is one Big Mac."

*　*　*

Which meant three less customers for Samson to deal with, which was fine by him. He had never been so busy, and not just because of the Crazy Omelette. Somehow, word had gotten out about Uncle Raymond's li hing malasadas, and suddenly, everyone had to have one.

Not just from Hilo, either. Recently, some guys went

come in for taste the malasadas and asking all kine questions about what went go inside. Not tourists, but no one Samson had seen before.

"I knew it! I knew it!" Raymond almost skipped into the alley. He had just delivered two-dozen li hing malasadas to the fire station. "Dat Ro-Ann Madeiras went say who da hell like eat li hing malasadas? Everyone da hell like eat li hing malasadas!"

"Eh Darin, you go fill da orders for a while. I like tell my uncle something."

"Sure boss," the new guy replied.

"Hey, Uncle? You went see all da new faces come in here recently?"

"Yeah. They talk local, but they driving rental cars."

"I know! Well, they stay asking any kine stuff about the li hing malasadas. I tink they from Honolulu. If we not careful, some buggahs from Oʻahu going claim they went invent da dang tings."

Raymond laughed.

"Let them."

Samson dropped his spoon.

"Huh?"

"Samson, I know other people like steal ʻem. Let them try. Garans ballbarans, no going even come close! How can? Not even Matsuoka's can steal my recipes!"

Samson thought about this and nodded slowly.

"You right, Uncle! Nobody can think of recipes like you."

"And not just that, Samson."

"What you mean, Uncle?"

Raymond Miyashiro patted his nephew on the back.

"Nobody can cook my recipes like you."

Samson Miyashiro was speechless.

"Now try come! I going show my next creation!" His uncle

went to the refrigerator and pulled out one stainless steel bowl.

Samson looked. Had fish. Had inamona. Had... Portuguese sausage and eggs? A horrible thought came to him. *Cannot be...*

But it was. And, just li'dat, Uncle Raymond had that crazy look in his eye. "Going be the next big thing! *Breakfast poke!*"

* * *

It was a strange afternoon, strange because Saul Malani was singing a song to himself that he forgot he knew. The rain was coming down real steady and the wind was banging one branch against his window. He got up, brushed teeth, washed face, put on some shorts and his hat and hopped in his car.

Saul drove down the road, the one that went down and away from the main highway. He drove down, then made the quick turn to Kolekole Park. Never mind the mosquitoes, they never bother him nothing. Was almost like a scene out of time; as he walked out to the beach he felt somehow like he was meeting someone, though he knew no one, and no one knew where he was going.

With the sure footsteps of someone who knew the place, he skipped across the rocks, out a bit farther than maybe he should have been. But never mind. Sometimes that's where you supposed to go, yeah?

Was still raining, a warm rain, and there was one guy, one county worker, cleaning up the place, looking at Saul real funny, because locals usually don't do stupid things like sit on one rock in the middle of rough water looking at the ocean in one big rain. But the county man figured better not say nothing, because nowadays, any kine weirdoes coming around.

"Saul Malani!" His body knew before he did. It was her.

He might have been crying, though it could just been the rain.

"How you, Saul?"

Saul turned, and beheld the same girl he had seen so many years ago, now all grown up and beautiful. Her mu'umu'u was green, as were her eyes. Part of him tried to understand and make sense of it, but was only a small part, and just like that, it trickled away.

"Where were you?"

"I was going ask you the same thing."

"I waited so long for you," someone said, but it wasn't clear who said it.

"When I first saw you, I thought you unreal. I thought you was one ghost. Or even Pele."

"Well. I'm *not* a ghost." She winked and twirled. "Besides, Pele already had her chance." And with that odd comment came the same playful laugh that he heard, echoing through Volcano, the same one that he had kept so close to his soul.

"You waited all this time?"

"Even then. As even now."

"What's your name?" asked the part of Saul who should have known, as well as the part who thought he might still be dreaming.

"Later, later. Right now, just call me...Ku'uipo."

"So when I going see you again?" Saul asked, and she laughed that same little girl laugh he had heard so long ago.

"Not yet, but soon, my love. Just like in the legends, and the chants, remember?"

"Remember? What do you mean?"

She held him, and the world spun motionless.

"No! Don't go!"

She touched her finger to his lips. "Not now, beloved. But soon. And I'll be watching. Waiting. And always, as I always have, I will be listening to your song."

"Who are you? Who am I?"

"Just a little longer... You will remember soon. We are creatures of legend, you and I. You'll know. And when you sing, the story you sing will be ours."

The county man looked at the two of them dancing on that rock in the middle of the powerful waves which should have swept them away, but somehow left them alone. He had no idea how the wahine got there. He finished up and got out of there as fast as he could, spooky kine chicken skin up and down his spine.

*   *   *

Not long after, Noelani found the road going in to the Yates house—funny she never knew had one road there before—and went down the path. On either side had some of Yates's guys clearing out the road, making 'em a little more nice and wide. Then she came to the turnaround that Nona went tell her about. Nona and Steve and Lisa were waiting.

"Noelani, try see try see!" Nona said, and they went around the back of one beautiful stage with lights and everything.

"So, Noelani, will this be okay?" Lisa asked.

Noelani gasped. Had seats for maybe 2000 people, and cameramen and lighting guys were busy setting everything up for the webcast.

"Why are you folks doing this? You already gave so much."

Steve grinned. "Which you decided not to take, remember"

"Noelani, as always, we just want you to dance," Lisa said.

Chapter 15

WITH SHOW ONLY A MONTH AWAY, NONA WAS MORE AND more convinced she stay too white for dance the hula. And to Harry, she was making less and less sense. Finally, Harry called Noelani Choi.

"Eh, you know Nona, she stay real nervous about this performance."

"Oh, she always nervous—but going be okay; she practicing real hard. Oh, tell her wear da purple and orange mu'u-mu'u this time, okay?"

"Okay, purple and orange—got 'em. But not just that, Noelani. This time different. She stay worried about something else. Stupid kine stuff, really."

"Really?"

"Yeah, she worried that she too white for dance the hula."

"*What?*"

"She worried that she too white for dance the hula. She say white skin stick out too much. Silly, yeah?"

Noelani said nothing.

"I mean, silly, yeah, she stay worrying, yeah?" Harry ventured again.

"Oh yeah, right right. That real silly!"
"So I can tell her no worry, den?"
"Yeah, tell her that from me."
"Thank you thank you! Okay, bye."

*   *   *

Oh my goodness, Noelani thought. *What have I been blind to? What have I been part of?*

Some people thought that since hula was Hawaiian, then Hawaiian kine people should be the ones dancing. That's why all the dancers grow their hair real long and then they wrap 'em all up so when they unwrap 'em come all curly wavy. [looking the part]

And some halau tell their more white skin students 'eh maybe should get one tan, even in one joke kine way. So they look more better in line. But usually, they no need tell, because people can figure 'em out.

And though Noelani never was one to say anything, she had always assumed that this was the right way for present things, that the students knew what would be best.

But what is Hawaiian? Where you stay born? The color of your skin, your hair? Your blood? Would be easy, yeah? Maybe if you eat opihi or kulolo?

But what is Hawaiian?

Suddenly, everything she had held dear about the Hawaiian ancestors and the Hawaiian past were like dreams. Each assumption, each image she approached would come apart and disappear. Old people. Old stories. Tales of outrigger canoes and chewing 'awa. She would touch them, and they'd dissolve.

Would have been easier if she were less concerned with hula. Would have been easier if she could just say hey no

matter, yeah, everyone who thinks they are Hawaiian—
that's good enough.

But she knew history of the dance, how it had almost
been stamped out. How it had been changed, forgotten,
misrepresented—all by people who had considered
themselves more than or better than Hawaiian.

Would have been easier if she were less concerned with
everyone else, like one secessionist, to say no, if you don't
have the blood, the lineage, forget it. Oh, you can learn
some fun kine dances, but the true stuff, the deep stuff,
well, no. Why don't you learn your German folks dances or
something?

But too many hula died out not because they were
exterminated, but because the people who knew them could
not find someone with the right heritage who was willing
or able to learn.

It wasn't always about blood or culture. It could be.
Sometimes, the spirit gets passed on to someone born from
the aina. But sometimes, it passes to someone without one
speck of Hawaiian. And then what? You cannot just say no.

No matter what, Noelani decided, the dance is the dance.

*   *   *

But all this, even the words of her kumu, the words from
her Harry, Nona never heard. Instead, she heard Darin and
Darin gave her one tube of green lotion. "This da stuff
bodybuilders use for get one tan." And Nona took 'em and
Darin said, "Be careful. *No use too much.*"

And when Noelani called to ask her if everything was
okay, Nona just said, "Yes, no worry, Noelani, I okay. Oh,
you know that Harry, he always stay worried about me."

And she never show Harry nothing. She knew he would just say, "No be silly, you already Hawaiian enough, and besides. You beautiful just like you are." But he was just that nice a guy, and would never understand anyway.

*   *   *

Meantime, Noelani had Kuʻuipo and her halau working around the clock. Noelani's practices were like nothing the halau had ever experienced. Not just more difficult, but demanding. Instead of each of them learning their part, Noelani had them learning everything, even the solos. It was to give everyone a feeling of belonging, Noelani had said, and even thought Nona had no idea what she meant, she went along with it, even if she was a little confused.

Still, Ervin and Nona especially were getting real nervous because they were scared that they would screw up.

"Don't worry," said Frances and Violet. "Take your time. This dance is different." And they were right. Was not competition athletic kine hula. That wasn't the point. Somehow Noelani had crafted a dance that had nothing to do with that kine stuff. Was real beautiful. That was it.

Or was it? Because the way it played on the body was like the way you feel in the morning when you first roll out of bed and decide to take one big gigantic stretch. That was the kine way Frances felt about this hula. Hurts at first, but then when the hurt pau, you feel like everything stay the way it should be, and all that other time you weren't really moving right.

That was the way with this hula.

And more than that, thought Violet Macayan. You see, when Noelani went start planning the life of Jesus in hula, Violet thought might be fun. Besides, nothing better than Jesus.

But now she saw in Noelani something wonderful. You

see, with Violet, Jesus was all about joy—not the jump up and make big noise kine, but the deep warm kine that smells just like Mom's house just before dinner. And that kine joy was always missing from Noelani. Noelani's relationship with Jesus—it never gave her peace.

And despite her better judgment, Violet had found herself asking, "Why should Noelani suffer like that?"

"Oh, I know that the Lord's way isn't always easy," she said to Father Luzon. "But not always supposed to be so much, you know, so much torture. You should see that girl. And that poor Jonny-Boy—he only like make her happy, but she no listen to nobody. 'Only Jesus,' she says."

And Father Luzon, who was actually fifteen years younger than Violet, would say something about the Lord's way sometimes being mysterious and everyone is better for accepting Christ, no matter what it seems like and what not, and Violet would say thank you and cross herself and that would be that.

But she knew that that was simply what he had to say. And then back to Noelani. Poor thing, because it wasn't as if she was *never* happy. In fact, she was happy quite often, even if she never recognize when.

When? When she was dancing, of course! When she was dancing, forgetting about all that hula heritage and Jesus talk and just dancing. *Happiness transcends history + dogma*

The joy on her face made Violet so happy, that even if Noelani was no going mention Jesus, it really didn't matter, because Jesus would be there anyway, and so would Violet.

And so if you had met Violet at church and asked her what the heck the hula was about, she would shrug and say "I don't know, but going be real wonderful. Try go come!"

Truth transcends words—it's an experience

* * *

In fact, that's what all of them said, even Nona. Even

[handwritten margin note, left side:] Dissatisfaction with Christianity (Catholicism)

[handwritten margin note, left side:] Beauty

Ervin. Heck, even Eva Matsuoka put up signs in her restaurant, and not just because Steve had asked her to cater the event.

She had been making kalbi ribs when Kayla ran into the stockroom, "Ms. Matsuoka, one popolo man he like talk to you.

"Popolo man?"

"Eva, is that you?"

Steve Yates walked into the kitchen.

"I'm sorry sir, you no can come back here!"

"That's okay, Kayla," said Eva. "He's okay. You go back out front."

Kayla nodded and left.

"Eva, we'd like you to cater the food for the hula show."

"Why not ask KTA or Goto's?"

"Why did you say that?" Steve frowned.

Eva lowered her head and took a deep breath, "Because I know you guys no like me." Eva looked up and her lower lip quivered, like it did when her mother would scream at her father. "I know who you are, Yates. Why you stay here, I don't know. But I know who you are. You no like me." *Who is he?*

"Why?"

"Look at that Noelani, dancing li'dat," Eva sniffled. "Everyone saying ooh how beautiful—so wonderful, yeah? *Fulfilling* To do what you stay born for do. "Except if you stay born *Destiny* for what? Sneak around for steal people's recipes?" She thought to that old lady at the nursing home, which wasn't really that hard, because it had never left her mind.

"Look at me. Look at me, Steve Yates! My mother—had—me because she needed that pork adobo recipe," Eva started shaking. "That's why...that's why I was born, yeah?"

Steve didn't have to nod.

"You don't know how that feels! To be born because of

one adobo recipe! Sometimes I sell the adobo and someone gives me the kine eye like they know and—hoooooo!" She wiped her eyes. "Some hard to serve 'em!"

"But I do—yeah? Have to, yeah?" Eva sat down on a chair she kept around but hardly ever used.

"Sometimes, you just no feel like fight anymore. So, no. I no like cater this party of yours. I no like you guys laugh anymore. I no like you guys exchanging your recipes behind my back, or coming over to cook for me without using any of my ingredients—I don't know why you guys did that, but I know you stay laughing at me.

"Go ask someone you like! Go ask Goto's or KTA!" She started sobbing again. "Just go."

"What about Ray Miyashiro at the Hilo Bowl?" Steve ventured.

"Not Raymond!" Eva started. "Crazy chop-suey omelets, ling hing malasadas? No sense, that one. If not for his nephew that place make-die-dead. Now what—*breakfast poke?*"

"Eva?"

"What?"

"Eva." Steve winked. "His breakfast poke is still supposed to be a secret."

Yates started laughing.

"No, no laugh at me already!" But she started laughing herself. Couldn't help. When you born for find out recipes, what else you supposed to do? She laughed until tears streamed down her face, until she could barely breathe.

"You right. I no care if it's all one joke," Eva said. "I still care about my okazu. I still care about okazu. Even if I have to drive back from Kona. Even if the old ladies talk stink about my mother behind my back.

"I still care. I still going serve my pork adobo. I still going mix the Papa'aloa bay leaves with the garlic and the sugar cane vinegar. I still going ask myself if it was all worth it—even if stopped expecting one answer long time ago...

"So—yeah, Steve, okay. I cater your party. And everyone can talk about how my mother stole this or that. Just like they always do. Let them. I show them. I show you, too."

Then, she started crying again, and when Roland came to the kitchen, he saw his aunty crying alone. Roland stood there for a while, not sure of what to do. Then he got the scrub brush and cleanser and bleach and gave the restaurant toilet the best cleaning that he could.

* * *

A HILO SONG

Bowling, fishing, working two, three jobs. Going Walmart in the middle of the night for get cat toys. Jade philodendrons growing out of the rusty chassis of an old Chevy truck.

Finding who get the best musubi. The best chow fun. Diving off the old lighthouse off Coconut Island.

Driving a Plymouth Satellite across the humming bridge. And always listening to the rain, while the haze from the volcano makes the rising sun go purple against the sky.

Not the things Kamakawiwoʻole Schulman imagined he would find when he came over here. But there they were, in his heart, as the mosquitoes buzzed past him indifferently.

He had come to find himself. He thought there was something else here, something that was missing, something of cosmic significance. Sort of the way people who come from the Promised Land might do. Looking for one cosmic kine solution to their problems.

He had started lighting Shabbos candles in his room on Friday sunsets. He didn't know why, he just started. And they weren't quite Shabbos candles, either—actually Buddhist candles from the dry goods store.

First time he did it, he never know why. But he needed to be out there, surrounded by things not cosmic. Pushing aside one bag of kakimochi to make room for these two little candles, and a plastic lighter. But he lit them, saying a little bracha to himself. Just because.

Just because it seemed like the right thing to do. Sometimes when everyone you knew or loved or thought mattered to you is across the ocean, scattered across a multitude of continents, generations, and philosophies.

And you? You leave everything behind. Start with nothing. And nothing, at first is what you get.

Those times, you think everything is lost, gone. Except not. You realize that you still have yourself. You didn't even bring your guitar. Yet your music came with you.

And the new people you meet, and stuff you see. And it's okay. Better than okay. You just sit there, taking it all in.

And you discover that you are a song.

It would make you feel like lighting some candles, yeah?

*　*　*

After their most difficult practice yet, Noelani made an announcement.

"You folks all know the parts, right?"

They looked at each other—well, yes, after they had been working so hard.

"I have sketched out the performance, and there's no practical way for me to do all of the solos. Any volunteers?"

Silence.

Then Eva said, "Ervin and Nona."

"What?" both of them said, but Violet and Frances agreed.

"Oh, what a wonderful choice!"

"Why?" asked Nona.

"Because the hula means more to you folks than anyone," Eva said.

"No way! I mean—"

"Shut up, Ervin!" Eva snapped, the way she did with Roland when he was being urusai. "I see you dancing. You too, Nona. You guys should be the ones for dance solo."

"Is that okay, Nona?" Noelani asked.

"I don't know if I can do it, I mean I not the best dancer—in fact I no even blend in with everyone. Maybe—"

"Oh Nona," Noelani said. "No worry about blending in. If you blend in too much, no one can see you, anyway."

Nona stopped. She had never thought of it that way before.

"And you, Ervin?"

Ervin, who had never wanted to be Jesus, felt part of himself bursting. A part of him that was so happy, so alive. So much so, that it managed to quiet the nightmare of his father staring from his living room chair.

So much so, that he nodded.

"Good! Then it's decided. Shall we begin?"

And they did.

Eva stuck around after practice was pau. She looked at Noelani with a strange respect.

"Noelani Choi," she pointed at her. "I thought I was sneaky. But you, you the best."

"What you mean, Eva?"

"No play stupid with me, Noelani!" Eva smiled. "You meant for give the solos away from the beginning. But you knew if you said that at the start, we would all be too nervous to learn."

Noelani laughed. "How you went figure?"

"Oh, why you went teach us the solos? You—saying was good for learn all parts of the dances. That was important for us for know the solos so we would appreciate the ensemble—all that kine stuff! Just enough to make us believe, but you knew all along you were going let us dance 'em. You one sneaky girl, Noelani. I glad you no more restaurant." Then she winked and left.

And you'd make a pretty spooky kumu yourself, thought Noelani.

* * *

Nona couldn't believe it. She went go home, unable to stop talking.

"Solo? How I going dance solo? But Noelani said I can do it. And Eva—can believe Eva? That girl!"

Harry pulled two mugs of hot water from the microwave and added the chocolate. He set the two mugs on the coffee table, then got a bag of boiled peanuts from the fridge.

"Solo! Harry, I going dance solo! I have to practice, Harry. That Eva, can you believe her?"

Harry smiled, as the rain outside played a steel-roof roof lullaby.

Meantime, Ervin went to his house, all full of music, just like Nona. But one look inside his house, and it all fell away.

There his parents were, Dad reading newspaper and Mom was asleep on the sofa, a half-crocheted potholder bunched on her lap. He walked in softly so as not to disturb them, but his dad grunted slightly—just enough to let Ervin know that yes he HAD disturbed him, but the disturbance wasn't worth him looking up from the paper.

Ervin went to his room and took a deep breath. He pulled out his dinner—an energy bar and a protein shake. He looked at his weights—then at his arms.

He checked his email and with its usual spam. And then he noticed a note. It was from Steve Yates! He hesitated, took a breath, and opened the message.

Hey Ervin,

I heard you're going to be doing one of the solos for the He Mele a Hilo show. Congratulations! I look forward to seeing you dance.

Best,
Steve Yates

PS—Remember. Two questions. One you can answer. One you can't. :)

And Ervin, who hadn't even been sure that Yates remembered him—smiled and practiced his moves to the music in his head. Then he took out his weights, more out of duty, of determination, not realizing that his arms were filling with the endless power of the sea.

* * *

Ervin's father wanted Spam and eggs. Usually his wife would go shopping, but she was sick, so he went Sack 'N Save get sale on eggs.

"Try go buy two dozen. Oh yeah, and try get some toilet paper, too," his wife said.

Why he went marry that woman?

Ervin's dad went Sack 'N Save, grumbling to himself because he had wanted eggs and now he was going miss the news. And plus had traffic outside. And he had just gotten comfortable in his chair and grumble grumble.

So he got one squeaky cart with one crooked wheel and picked up a couple dozen eggs and some toilet paper and might as well get some natto. And now he had to wait in line, because of course was going have one big line.

"Eh, Gozo!"

Divine Providence

Ervin's father turned and saw one guy he never recognize at first. He grunted.

"Gozo? It's me, Ciles."

"Ciles? From the mill? Eh, Ciles, how you?" Then he looked at Ciles and saw not good at all. The buggah had plastic tubing up his nose and was dragging one oxygen tank behind him.

"Not too good, Gozo. The doctors said pretty soon, pau. Too much smokes, yeah?"

"Oh hell, Ciles, I nevah know."

"Paper or plastic?" asked the salesgirl.

"I know. Always the smokes, yeah? So how you?"

"Paper or plastic?"

"Oh, paper, sorry, yeah?"

The salesgirl with the long painted nails grunted.

The two of them walked out and found an empty bench outside Leung's Chop Suey.

"So, how you?" Ciles repeated.

Ervin's father's usual response to the question was to complain, but Gozo couldn't do that to Ciles. At the sugar mill, Ciles had been like a big brother. And now he was so skinny and frail. And old.

"Everything okay, Ciles. Fine."

"Bullshit. What's bothering you now, Gozo?" Gozo had never been able to hide anything from the Ciles.

"Oh, just... My stupid kid!" Was too stupid to mention that he was pissed off for getting eggs, so he went knee-jerk to his stupid son Ervin.

"Ervin? What, he not dancing hula?"

"Yeah—funny kine."

"Why, how you figgah?"

"Oh, that boy. Waste time that buggah. Him, he dance around, or stay on that stupid computer. No more friends, no nothing. The buggah stay thirty years old and he still stay living at home. When I was that age I had one house, one wife, stay working at the mill."

"Eh, no make li'dat. The mill stay closed—" Ciles started coughing.

"You okay, Ciles?"

"Yeah, yeah... No get old, Gozo. Waste time get old."

"Too late," Gozo said.

"What you mean, too late. You still young yet!" And they laughed, gently, so not to get Ciles coughing again.

"How your boys?" Gozo ventured. "Those kids were real smart yeah?" He had always admired the Molina boys. One went Princeton, one went Stanford.

Ciles smiled. "Branson, he stay living in Manhattan now, and Jarald stay in France.

"They no call, though. Sometimes I try call them. But, they always so busy. Last year, I never even get one Christmas card."

Gozo shook his head. "They must be busy."

But Ciles never need say what they were both thinking. You see, sometimes, you stay talking about your kids being good for nothing, wishing that they would go make something from their lives, be genius kine kids, the straight-A kine. But those kids, they get their own heartaches. Especially if you live on one outer island in the middle of the Pacific.

The smart ones always seem to leave for more opportunity. And the smarter they are, the farther away they seem to go. Off to schools on the West Coast, the East Coast, or even beyond. They learn how big the world outside the islands are. They learn how small their world used to be.

Lots of times they no like ever look back. They see their bowlegged no-get-teeth parents who spent their lives working with their hands. They come ashamed. So they hide 'em. Bury 'em. Try never to go back, or look back. Just spend of their lives trying to catch up for some lack of growing up in one house where they watched TV, played hanafuda and watched sumo, rather than going to art galleries, the opera and reading Faulkner.

"Two sons, two families, no can send one Christmas card between them? I mean, not to complain. Pretty soon I going be with my wife, then pau, yeah?"

Gozo never say nothing.

"Lucky you get one kid who appreciates the old kine ways. Your boy stay dance with Noelani Choi, yeah?"

"Yeah."

"Shoots, you know, when I was younger, I tried for dance, too."

"What? You!?"

"Oh yeah, I tried—but boy, you know how tough the training, yeah? Your boy probably told you." And Gozo nodded. Of course, Ervin had told him.

It was just that he had never listened.

"If your boy stay dancing with her, he must be something special, Gozo. By the way, what time the show start?"

Gozo Shimabukuro stumbled.

"What, you don't know? You going find out yeah? And let me know?"

"Why? You going?"

"Shoots, brah! Even if my lungs stay broke, of course I coming. After all, Gozo—that's your *boy!*"

That evening, as Gozo sat in front of the TV, he turned to his wife and said, maybe we should go, yeah? And his wife, nodded, continuing with her crocheting, trying to be silent, to hold in her joy, and she almost succeeding.

*　*　*

Noelani was helping Frances bend properly at the wrist

when Lisa Yates called to remind her about the upcoming tech rehearsal. With Steve, things usually went okay, but not always, yeah?

"Of course, Lisa, what's the schedule?" Noelani asked.

Steve like meet with all the kumu, to run over what you are doing."

"All the kumu?"

"Well, with this wonderful stage, we decided that we could have a whole night of it. First we asked Ignacio from the community center if he would join us, and he said yes. Then we asked Halau o' Kahakunoe to come from O'ahu, and they agreed, as well! Imagine! Your old halau!"

Lisa said a couple of things Noelani didn't hear, then hung up.

Because Noelani didn't have to imagine. "Kahakunoe's coming," Noelani said to her class. Then she stared out the window, into the night.

Since she had left O'ahu she hadn't spoken to them, and they probably still saw her as running away, even snubbing her old teacher. And she *knew* one reason they had agreed to come to the celebration was that they wanted to see that crazy Noelani and how far she could fall.

Which of course resonated with her *other* ex-halau, at the community center, and she had heard through the grapevine that Ignacio had been talking real stink about her, saying that the wahine went crazy, cracked, that she no could take the pressure of being one kumu.

But dammit, she hadn't fallen. No, she hadn't.

Had she?

Eva looked at Noelani. She was the kumu and if she cracked, then all pau. But before she could say anything,

Violet walked over and put her hand on Noelani's arm. "Noelani, we stay with you all the way."

Noelani began to shake.

really old

Frances grabbed Noelani's arm. "Noelani! Girl! Look at me. You look at me right now. *'Lani!*"

The young girl looked up at her elder.

"That's right, 'Lani. I remember you small kid time. I remember Kapolinahe small kid time. I remember Kapolinahe's mother small kid time."

She turned to the rest of the halau. "I've been trying for dance so many years. I can remember names and people, but the dance? I forget everything! I was hopeless."

"No, no," said Violet.

"No! You let me finish! How many years I try? I no remember nothing. Until her!" She pointed at Noelani. "Somehow this girl, this one, this music and this dance. Noelani. This girl, the best kumu I know.

"'Lani, I know the other halau stay talking stink about you. They think we all crazy. But I remember when parents would stop their kids from learning hula—when missionaries would try stop them. But the kumu would teach, even when never had way, because they couldn't let their dance die out with them. You need to continue, 'Lani. For them."

Noelani took a deep breath, then she nodded and hugged Frances. "Thank you, tutu," Noelani whispered.

Frances turned and saw Nona and Ervin. Their mouths had been open like two-day-old fish since they realized that they would be doing their solos in front of the Merrie Monarch champions.

"What you guys doing?" Frances barked. "We still get one more hour practice! And close your mouth! Going catch flies."

* * *

On Friday, Ignacio Viramontes drove down the winding path to the Yates house. He snorted as he thought of Noelani kissing up to some stupid rich mainlanders. Crazy or not, Ignacio had to admit the bitch knew who to blow for money. Still, this whole hula performance seemed strange. There was no venue here. He wouldn't have even given the invitation a second thought, except that Yates had money, and maybe he could get these guys to support him, rather than Noelani.

Suddenly, the road turned and Ignacio saw the rainforest break into the most beautiful outdoor theater he had ever seen. The stage was luminous as technicians tested the various lights. Overhead, projections and LCD screens that would provide close-up views for the audience, who were to sit in rows of seats that fanned and feathered into the green hills. Some dancers were out marking the stage— from Halau o' Kahakunoe, Ignacio guessed, since he saw a tour bus parked next to the stage. And there was Noelani, talking to the lighting crew. Bitch.

Ignacio licked his freshly whitened teeth.

Game on.

Noelani waved back at Millicent Kapolinahe Ponui. It had been years since she had seen her. Even Noelani felt a bit intimidated to see the power of her former halau, but then she smiled to see that Steve Yates's stage amazed even the dancers of Halau o' Kahakunoe.

At least their reaction was honest. When Ignacio Viramontes arrived a few minutes later, Noelani noticed him hide his initial shock behind his trademark disinterested smirk. Still, Noelani held her herself together. It wasn't easy, but she did. After all, performance is performance. And when the kumu met with Steve, Noelani greeted Ignacio without letting him see how she felt inside.

The meeting was more than a friendly greeting. Even if this wasn't a scored competition, Noelani noticed Ignacio probing, chafing, looking for an edge. Millicent was far too secure to do such a thing, but Noelani knew that under the sweet exterior was a will of iron. Ignacio said he was prepared to do one kahiko and one auana number. As did Millicent.

Noelani looked at Steve and the other kumu.

"We're only going to do one number."

Ignacio snorted. "After all this time, you only had enough time to prepare one number?"

Even for Ignacio, this was rude. But before Noelani could recover, Millicent shouted. "What you mean by that? Who you to talk like that to Noelani Choi?"

"Look folks, we're just here to have a good time."

The kumu glared at him with eyes that would have burned Pele herself.

"I mean—uh," said Steve, deciding to clarify rather than retreat." When I say a good time, I mean a time that is good. A time that is positive. I brought everyone here to do something good for the island and my neighbors."

"The stage is beautiful," Millicent said, gracefully changing the subject. "And the hotel rooms are wonderful. We're really grateful for your patronage."

"Thanks—we try."

"And we're webcasting this event all over the world?" asked Ignacio.

"Just call it a pet project," Yates said.

Millicent turned to Noelani.

"So Noelani, you're only doing one number?"

Noelani nodded. "But it's a bit longer than a normal routine. More like a story."

"Sounds wonderful... We're really looking forward to seeing it."

"Yes we are," mumbled Ignacio.

*   *   *

After the meeting, Noelani and Millicent went for a walk.

"I never know you were coming," said Noelani.

"I sent you a letter, but you never write back," Millicent said.

Noelani remembered the letter she never opened.

"The halau missed you, Noelani. Aunty never got over you, you know. She really wanted to see you, one last time."

"How did she go?"

"She went well. In her sleep, they found her, with one sketch pad of another dance by her side."

*   *   *

Ku'uipo heard about the new developments from Lois Cabral, who dropped by in person to say that since the Merrie Monarch winners and the boys from Kahala were coming that this was turning out to be a major island event.

Of course Ku'uipo knew all about Kahala. Who hadn't? They had been playing Honolulu for quite some time. They had won more Hoku awards than Kam had mosquito bites, and had played often in Vegas, as well as at music festivals around the world. Their last album was one big hit on Akamai records.

And that's when Carl lost it. "Oh, no! We cannot. We not in their league."

"So, you say we should just back out on Noelani?" Jonny-Boy asked.

Kam felt his ears get warm, and the room started to spin because he couldn't believe what he just heard.

"Look guys, who we stay fooling? I mean they da real thing. Us guys, come on? Kuʻuipo? It's all a joke right?"

"What the hell is wrong with you?" asked Jonny-Boy. "How you can even say that?"

"I was just saying—look, we not in their league! The radio was good fun, the music good fun. The free drinks and chicks. But this... I cannot. I not saying we going look stupid in front the whole island, but what if we do? I know, Noelani... Maybe you folks can find one replacement for me. After all, the music is not—"

"Good idea," said Saul.

"What!?"

"Go. We can find another drummer. I not going on stage with someone who stay scared."

Carl looked around nervously. "Jonny-Boy! This haole making trouble, right? I mean, try look at him and Noelani."

But Jonny-Boy didn't bite. "Go to hell, Carl."

"But you said we stay just in this for fun!"

"We see the people stay smiling and singing our music! That's fun! Seeing people liking our songs, not just Iz or Kaliʻi or even Gabby's songs. But our songs. Kuʻuipo's songs."

Jonny-Boy looked over at Kam.

"Right?"

"Yeah," Kam said, startled that Jonny-Boy had defended him.

"I thought we were family! Ohana!" Carl walked, then ran out the door.

Jonny-Boy turned to Lois, who hadn't moved this whole time. "Sorry about that."

Lois stared at the remaining members of Kuʻuipo. *Not in Kahala's league?* Did they, even now, know how good they were?

"Looks like you need a drummer," she finally said. "I think I can find you a good one." And Lois pulled out her phone.

* * *

Okay, Carl had been in Kuʻuipo having fun, and then Kam the haole came in, and now he stay out?

At least that what Carl was thinking, would think, and would tell everyone for the rest of his life, long after he put his drums away for good, and started spending his afternoons on the bench just outside Prince Kuhio Mall telling anyone who would listen that him, yeah, him, was one founding member of Kuʻuipo and that he was railroaded out of the band by Mele Schulman, that stupid haole. That they turned their back on him and forgot ohana.

And that was all he saw and would ever see.

But in that moment Saul and Jonny-Boy told Carl to leave, they realized that respecting ohana was exactly *why* they had to play without fear. Kuʻuipo had music that might bring people some aloha, or maybe a space where they could create their own.

"You see," as Saul would say later, "we stay surrounded by ohana. Some of them no even know it. And if were went stay just in da islands, we would have never have met them. Ohana?" He would smile.

"Get ohana all around the world."

"Looks like I got your drummer!" Lois Cabral said.

As a radio host, Lois knew dozens of musicians, and

Carlos Garcia was one of the best. And Carlos was already a fan. Carlos, see, was doing session work in Oʻahu and had heard Kuʻuipo on Lois's Internet show, and had asked if they needed a drummer. And just like that, Carlos was on an Aloha Airlines 737 sipping fruit punch from a plastic foil-sealed cup.

"From Carlos to Carl back to Carlos," Lois laughed, a little nervously, but as soon as Saul and Jonny-Boy and Kam met Carlos at the airport and said, "Thanks ʻeh for coming so soon," she knew they were going to be fine.

Carlos who, despite his name, wasn't Filipino or Porogee at all, but one popolo from the Dominican Republic, gave a them hugs and said, "Don't thank me, man. Your music moves me."

"Carlos, you hungry?" asked Jonny-Boy.

"Yeah, as a matter of fact. Do you guys have a Zippy's over here?"

"Zippy's?" The band laughed. "Is that what they've been feeding you in Honolulu? Come on—you ever have a Crazy Omelette?"

*   *   *

A couple days of omelettes, plate lunches and practice, and Carlos was on the horn to his people out in Miami. "We've got this killer group called—how do you pronounce that? Koo—oo—eee-poe? Anyway, my God, you have to hear these guys. I'm gonna ask them to come out and play back home."

As for his playing, Saul and Jonny-Boy and even Kam had never been pushed that hard by a drummer before, someone open to every possibility they threw out, while adding more of his own. He picked up one of Noelani's ipus and worked it like a conga, but without sacrificing any of the characteristic sound of the gourd.

Jonny-Boy shook his head. "Wow, I wish that he could be playing with us all the time."

"Yeah, but let's just focus on the show," said Kam.

"Which, if you can believe it, is this Friday."

*   *   *

"You no change, you know that?"

Saul turned around and saw a woman dressed in red. To most people, she was an old lady, but Saul saw her with dark hair, perfect skin, and fiery, fiery eyes.

"I know you," he said, because he did.

She looked at him and it for a second, it seemed as if she were about to cry. "I am glad."

Then, as if by instinct or memory, Saul stumbled backward and fell. He scrambled back to his feet and pulled off his hat, waving it in front of him as if to ward off a wall of flame.

"NO!"

The woman watched him, and spread her hands. They were empty.

"I know, I know. But that was a long time ago. And now you belong to her. Now, and forever."

"But I don't even know her name."

"Really?! Oh that girl! Always making trouble!" The woman shook her head. And then she told him.

"And you. Do you know who you are?"

And finally, he did.

Chapter 16

IT WAS FRIDAY MORNING. NONA WAS GETTING READY. SHE thought of Noelani and Harry. She thought of the wonderful hula she would be performing on the stage in front of so many people, as well as the Merrie Monarch Champions. And for just a moment, she believed. In her purple and green and orange, Nona Watanabe believed that despite her too big feet and flat cow face, despite her mismatched colors, she was going be okay.

She believed it so much that she thought that wouldn't it be nice if she could just be a little bit darker?

So she reached into her medicine cabinet and pulled out that skin stuff that Darin went give her. She put a little on her palm. Smelled funny kine, but she rubbed a little on her forearm.

Nothing happened at first, but slowly a soft golden glow was apparent on her skin. Encouraged, she put a light coat on her arms and legs and a very light coat on her face.

The stuff wasn't like any kine makeup she had used before; it made her skin tingle, which was sort of freaky.

But when she looked in the mirror, she jumped up and down and screamed.

It worked! She looked at the tube in her hand and shrugged.

"A little more hurt wouldn't hurt, right?"

*　*　*

Meanwhile, a line of cars wound up and down the Hamakua coast. And for some reason, although the highway was never meant to hold so many people, there were no traffic problems.

The cars began parking at the Yates place. "Funny—we never noticed this road before," the people said, and the parking area looked kind of small, except that everybody found one space easy. And when they walked down to the stage, had plenty seats, even though there was no way so many people could have fit in such a small area.

miracle

*　*　*

"Aunty!" Roland came backstage looking for his Eva.

"Yeah, Roland?"

Roland stopped dead, as he looked at his aunty getting ready to perform. He had never seen her dressed that way. She was beautiful. And suddenly Roland realized that his aunty had never had a boyfriend, or anyone. Just Matsuoka's. Always Matsuoka's.

"Yeah, Roland?" she asked again.

"Oh—uh—Aunty—people stay lining up for our food already. No going have enough!"

"Going have enough."

"Maybe I should go back the restaurant and—"

"Roland! Trust me. Going have enough. Now go take care the booth!"

"O-okay, Aunty."

Eva turned to Violet. She thought about the kitchen and all those ladies coming in for help her. And trying to get Nona's recipe, then meeting Noelani, to whom the hula was the world, just like plate lunches were for her.

Eva winked. "Sometimes you have to believe, yeah?"

Violet nodded, thinking for the first time how different Eva was from her mother.

And everyone was ready. Nervous, but ready. Except for one person.

"Where Nona?" Frances asked.

"No worry about her," Noelani said, "Nona going be here."

"I just hope she stay wearing the right muʻu-muʻu," sighed Violet.

*   *   *

"H-HARRRYYY!! COME OVER QUICK!"

"What, Nona?!"

Sounded like something real bad was happening. He hung up the phone, and jumped in his car. *No! Not on the day of the performance!* What could possibly go wrong?

He shouldn't have asked.

He pulled up to Nona's driveway, but no more Nona outside. "Hey, Nona? You stay there?" He opened the door— was unlocked.

"Nona?" No answer.

"Nona!"

"H-harry?" A voice came from the bathroom door. But as Harry opened the door, Nona slammed it shut.

"HARRY, STOP!"

"What?"

"Before you come in, promise you no going laugh."

"Laugh? Laugh? What you mean laugh? Come on, Nona..."

Then Harry opened the door.

"Holy shit! What happened to you?"

"HARRRRYYY! WHAT I GOING DO?"

Nona Watanabe was as orange as a pumpkin.

*　　*　　*

"Nona, what the—hell went happen?" Harry felt a little faint, because he had never seen Nona orange before. He honestly thought Nona might be sick—that maybe was jaundice or something. "You like I call the doctor?"

"No!" Nona wailed. "I–I—"

"What-what?"

"I went use the stuff Darin went give me."

"Darin? What kine stuff?"

"Da kine bodybuilding kine stuff. From da tube! For make my skin more dark li'dat." Nona started sobbing again.

"What?! No worry Nona, I going find that Darin! Then I going kick his ass!"

"Harry, wait!" But Harry had gone.

"Harry..."

Nona started sobbing again. It wasn't Darin's fault... Was her! Nona Watanabe! The stupid one! The stupid orange one!

"Oh, child."

Suddenly she felt a hand on her shoulder. Was warm and calm.

Nona looked up and saw an old Hawaiian lady, no—THE Hawaiian lady—the same one she saw at the Hilo Hawaiian performance. She was in one bright red mu'u-mu'u, and was far more beautiful than any old woman had a right to be.

The old woman looked at Nona, and her orange skin,

and smiled. Not one mocking smile—okay—maybe a little mocking, 'cuz was funny, yeah?

"Tell me. Why you went make yourself orange?"

"I wanted to be more Hawaiian," Nona sobbed.

"Silly girl. No more orange Hawaiians."

Nona sobbed some more.

"Oh, maybe now get one orange Hawaiian now. You."

Nona stopped and looked up. "Me?"

"Yes you—silly girl. You Hawaiian, what."

"No—I Japanese... I cannot be."

"What you mean cannot be? Of course you Hawaiian. You stay born here an'den. Child. When you stay bon dance around and around li'dat, you go back Japan?"

"N-no—I go Pa'auilo."

"There, you see?" She rubbed Nona's back. "You one island girl. Now... Why one local girl like you stay orange?"

"Huh?"

"You like stay orange, or what?"

"N-no."

"Okay. No stay orange then."

And Nona looked and she was never happier to see her white sharkbait skin then at that moment.

acceptance

"You get one big show tonight, yeah?"

Nona nodded.

"Oh, you going have such fun!" The old woman laughed as she helped Nona up and out of the bathroom. "Now put on your muʻu-muʻu...there you go... Oh, how beautiful you look!

"Now, child, make this old lady happy and let me dance for you."

Nona watched, as the old woman began her chant, lifted her arms and eyes, and started to move...

It seemed like an eternity and an instant all at the same time. Laughter and crying, mountain and ocean—felt to

Nona like her soul was being pushed and pulled to grow, to expand, to fill an almost impossible embrace, an almost incomprehensible love.

And then this old woman in red motioned to Nona. "Come, child, now you follow me. Lift your hands, just like this. Let aloha fill your heart.

"Now, *step*."

*   *   *

Harry pounded the steering wheel. Dammit! Nona, why she never listen? The big big day, her biggest day *and now she stay orange?* How da hell she going dance like that?

No way he was going ask Steve for help—this was stupid kine problem, even if was one big big deal.

Harry found Darin right away. He was at the gym, talking to some girl.

"Hey—I'm with a client, Uncle."

"I don't care. It's your Aunty Nona's big day, and now she is orange," Harry stated. "You going help her, then I going kick your ass."

Harry grabbed his arm, dragged Darin out of the gym and threw him in his car. Darin was praying *please god sorry god please god sorry god* the entire way, not just because Uncle Harry was going kick his ass, but because he never know how for help his Aunty not be orange.

They rushed over to Nona's house. Harry threw opened the door and found...

Nona waiting for them, with a quiet smile.

"Everything okay. Let's go now."

As they left, Darin was so relieved he went fut, and Nona slapped him. Their car rattled, coughed, and zoomed down the road.

Chapter 17

He Mele a Hilo

A song of a place that most people thought was sleepy and slow, and maybe it was, but up on the mountain, there was smoke and it wasn't a volcano. Was a recently returning artist up before sunset firing pots in an earthen kiln made exactly like the ones in 15th-century Japan. Firing takes all day, and all day is what the island gives. So meantime, she washed up and went for go watch the dancing.

Was people inexplicably fishing in the bay, though no one ever caught much there, except a few good stories, and talk that tonight the water just wasn't right. Ah, never mind, we go watch the dancing.

Was that Noelani had friends and Nona had friends and Violet and Frances and Ervin had friends. Yeah, even Ervin, whose parents decided oh whatever, we go watch our boy dance.

Noelani's dancers, they all had friends. Jonny-Boy and Carl and Saul—they all had friends. And Kam, remarkably had some of his neighbors from Pahoa come down because it sounded, like such a cool, authentic happening.

And not only did they have friends, but their friends had friends, and oh it sounds like such a wonderful thing to go see and stay free, so we go.

And they did.

From backstage, Noelani looked at the crowd and said to Kam. "My goodness! Do you know how many people stay out there?"

"And that's not counting the webcast," said Steve Yates, who just happened to be walking by.

Because when Steve Yates suggests watching something, people do. People who had dreamed of Hawai'i, or hula, or a place where they could relax and hear wonderful music. All across the world, a state of mind triggered a search and magically the site appeared.

Free Will?

No one knows how the show started. Steve Yates must have announced it, or maybe Lois Cabral from the radio. There must have been a national anthem, something, because suddenly, everyone was in a seat with one fruit punch and plate lunch as the stage lights hallowed the night.

For those of you not familiar with hula, get two main divisions. Kahiko is traditional, ancient kine stuff. People stay dress up in leaves and ferns and plenty plenty maile. Get da kine dog teeth anklets (nowadays shells) and the kumu stay beating on one ipu and chanting something in Hawaiian usually about Pele or how beautiful the Waipio Valley is or King Kamehameha's sexual prowess.

Hula auana is the contemporary dance where get full band with bass, guitar and lap steel, maybe drum, but not usually. Instead of chanting, get singing—stuff like "Hi'ilawe" or even more contemporary kine like "Opihi Man." The women wear mu'u-mu'us with plenty beautiful kine leis, and the men often dress up like the Brothers Cazimero.

Halau o' Waiakea went up first. From the time Noelani went leave Ignacio went tell everyone at the community center now they going finally do the kine stuff one good halau was supposed to do, that they going be known as one top flight halau and all da kine competitions they were going win.

Ignacio looked out at the crowd—completely full up with people—and shouted to his halau, "Okay now we going show 'em what we about!"

Which was, to win hula contests. For everyone to look at his group and see not a hair or flower or step out of place.

And that was exactly what the audience saw. Ignacio with his ipu and banging on 'em and chanting one tribute to King Kalaka'ua that he had researched back and forth with his friends at UH Manoa and the Bishop Museum. His chants projected into the crowd, on a night where it was supposed to rain, but somehow, the rain was almost but not quite there, so the air was thick with the rainy smell of the forest, but not actually wet.

The stage was filled with 30 dancers, all in the green and red of leaves and historically accurate flowers. In their malos, his male dancers were, as Darin might say, ripped, thanks to creatine and a stack of aspirin, caffeine and mahuang. The women each were beautiful, with their long wavy hair and skin lustrous like polished koa and kukui.

Noelani looked at them and part of her couldn't help but feel pride at how hard Ignacio must have worked. And yet, most of the faces she saw were not from her original halau, but were dancers from other halau, even other islands. And, although it said that no halau has all knowledge, and it was good that Ignacio was able to attract so many fine dancers, what about those who had stayed with him that night at the community center?

Noelani looked into the audience where Ignacio's non-participants were sitting. And there was Betty Manibog, trying not to be noticed. And Arlene Aragaki. Spectators. Maybe some of them were hoping to dance for Ignacio one day, but Noelani knew better. And, deep inside, so did they.

Ignacio's band came out to do a few songs while the dancers changed into costumes for the auana number. And his band had just finished their rendition of "Opihi Man" when he signaled they were ready.

Ignacio's auana was one pretty song about a pikake lei. Ignacio had dressed his entire halau in white, with the pikake and yellow ginger leis. With the flowers in their hair and the lights shining on them, they seemed simply luminous, and a sigh went through the crowd like a gentle wind.

The song began and they all moved just like one unit. Gesturing, swaying, moving, all with the same smile, and same intensity. Ignacio's work and vision laid out there for everyone to see.

And watching them was sort of like watching one flower arrangement, or one waterfall. Precious. Waves of pikake scent came through the whole place, and if you've never smelled pikake, ask someone who has, and they will tell you, because it stays with them, delicate and far away, forever.

And I suppose for most people in the crowd it was all they wanted, and if they hadn't seen Halau o' Kahakunoe, they would have thought it was one of the best hulas they had ever seen.

And that's what the remaining crowd was saying at intermission, how it was one of the best hulas they had ever seen, *like that other one, remember? Oh yeah, just like that other one?*

But most people were already in the lines to the food, which was all catered by Matsuoka's. Roland and Yates's serving staff were moving sooo much food that day, 'cuz was all free—Yates had picked up the entire bill.

*   *   *

In Da Beginning

[handwritten: Millicent]

The crowd grew silent as Halau o' Kahakunoe entered the stage. After their set, Ignacio had given Millicent Ponui a *let's see if you can top that* look.

Of course that wasn't why Millicent Kapolinahe Ponui had even come, but if you wanted to rumble...

[handwritten: Indigenous]

The dancers of Halau o' Kahakunoe *were* the reigning Merrie Monarch champions. Millicent stared at Ignacio and winked. After all Ponui was, after Noelani, Aunty Kapolinahe's most accomplished student and had even taken her name.

Kahakunoe had done the whole pikake and awapuhi and songs to Pele thing. But after a while, you realize that there has to be something more than pikake and awapuhi and songs to Pele.

The kahiko started, not with each one moving as one unit, but with each dancer chanting as the entered, emoting in their own individual ways. But the music of their chants were perfectly harmonious, each one's tones and intonations combining with the others the way all the smells of the

[handwritten: Harmony]

flowers and fruits and earth combine to bring life to the land.

Millicent's chanting went over the PA, and there was more than correctness to it—in fact, some might say it was a little bit imprecise, but the delivery was so full of soul that it the imprecision seemed even more perfect. Steve Yates had a big smile on his face, like a teacher whose student had finally got the lesson right.

As they went into the dance, each dancer seemed to catch his or her own special fire, yet their voices melded in perfect harmony. Lisa watched, entranced by the ebb and flow of the dancers breaking formation, then coming together. And she wasn't alone—the audience hung there in silence, forgetting themselves, until the last beat of the drum, when the entire stadium came to their feet in spontaneous applause.

As she exited, Millicent blew Ignacio a kiss.

Rushing offstage to change costumes, Millicent saw Noelani, face radiant and wet with tears. But backstage, everything wasn't as harmonious. Ignacio kept his halau away from the others, and when Ku'uipo went for say hi to Kahala, they said, "Excuse us, boys, we're very busy right now," and went on with their business.

Kahala played two numbers while Halau o' Kahakunoe changed costumes. As they played Carlos listened thoughtfully.

"They haven't been hungry in a long time," he finally said.

And when they were pau, he shrugged. "That style of music always gets gigs."

And Kam looked at Saul and Saul looked at Jonny-Boy, and they understood. That was good for Kahala, but it was not what Ku'uipo wanted. And Ku'uipo would never be intimidated by Kahala, or bands like them, again.

When Millicent's halau came for their auana number, it seemed to give the audience everything it wanted— luxurious mu'u-mu'us of crushed velvet, the scent of plumeria emerging like the sunrise over Haleakala. The dance was gorgeous, almost painfully beautiful. And the song, of love lost, but never forgotten, reminded Kam of the theme from "Titanic."

Saul winked. "Of course it's the Titanic theme. They went translate 'em."

Kam grimaced.

Ignacio, too, was grimacing. But he was holding his camera thinking, *Damn why couldn't I have thought of that?* But of course he'd have something like that ready next year...

As the number went pau, and Halau o' Kahakunoe left the stage, Noelani nudged Kam and gestured at the audience. Some of them were stretching and getting ready to leave. Especially the Japanese, who always liked to go home for watch the news.

Kam shook his head. "I knew this was going to happen! People always leave when you play last."

In the audience, Harry elbowed Steve and whispered, "Eh—I thought you went plan this better!"

"Harry, it's only 9:30. And it's Friday!"

And Harry yawned. "*Of course it's Friday!* After dealing with work all week everyone stay getting tired! Besides—try look! Get old people in da audience! And look how many Japanese—they getting ready for go home!"

Suddenly, there was a crack of thunder, and Harry said, "Oh, and now it's going rain!"

And Steve said, "It's lucky I installed—"

"Retractable screens?" Harry rolled his eyes.

"Why, yes, now that you mention it. But I heard the weather report and it wasn't supposed to rain."

"Wait." Kam stopped him. "You mean you never do this?"

"Uh, no. I don't do that flood thing anymore."

But the rains did come, and they came down hard, the way they can only come in Hilo. People took a look outside, then smelled the ono kaukau coming from the Matsuoka booth and said, "Shoots, let's stick around." And somehow, the rain was refreshing, even to the oldest of the spectators, as a mother nourishes her young. And it was true, right? For when compared to the island, the wind, the smell of rain, who *wasn't* young?

The stage went black, and to the sound of the storm, Saul thought he heard the laughter of a little girl as old as time skipping upon the rain. And he smiled, as he thought of her, all in green...

He started his oli, and that was all he could think about, as he chanted a traditional tale about Hi'iaka and Lohiau, two doomed lovers of Hawaiian legend. It was more than a story, wasn't it? *Wasn't it?*

And, as the lights slowly faded on, to Saul, dressed in his best T-Shirt and shorts and rubber slippers with his trademark hat. Around his neck, a the twisted ti-leaf lei— the lei of Hilo. At first, people were going, *What, no more costume?* But as the chant continued, the most peculiar thing happened. Fishermen saw night fishing by torchlight, carpenters heard trees being hollowed into canoes, mothers smelled taro being pounded into poi. Ervin's father swore he heard machetes and smelled burning cane.

"Hey, not bad this kanaka," he said to his wife.

Then, the chant was over, and Noelani's halau made their entrance.

This should be interesting, said Ignacio to himself.

The little halau spread itself out on stage. Violet and Frances and Ervin and Eva and Nona. And rather than stepping proudly or powerfully, they seemed to glide, as if they were floating, pulling silence from the night. Each of their costumes was unique, unlike any of the others, but somehow they all worked together, like one of those mix-and-match sets of Japanese dishes. And their silence. Most people couldn't understand what was happening, but even those who could, such as Millicent Ponui, asked, "How could silence be so powerful?"

Then from the distance, it seemed like one angel was singing. But was Noelani. But you knew that.

And everyone was expecting Noelani to come out, but she didn't. Everyone was expecting Ku'uipo to play.

But no. It was chanting.

And, instead of Noelani, another of the dancers walked to the end of the stage and began.

Violet's smile was the smile of belonging, to a choir, or a family, like a middle child or one plate lumpia next to the mac potato salad on the picnic table, wanted, wanting to be wanted, easy, like when the nighttime comes and time for sleep and you no question 'cuz you tired anyway and had one full day and you already get everyone's lunch all ready and packed. And oh, it feels so good to have someone next to you and know the rascal kids finally asleep 'cuz you can hear 'em breathing soft and quiet, and you husband already sleeping and tomorrow going be just like that, too.

Even now, when her husband no longer there, to visit the grave, to say *how much I miss you* and *the kids are all doing fine, all grown up and they just sent Christmas cards, and the new neighbors get one dog that digs up all the vegetables, but they going keep 'em on one rope.*

And now I stay performing with Noelani at one place, oh I wish you could see how beautiful it stay. But then again, I know you watching from Heaven, yeah? Here, then, I going smile for you!

Then Saul lilted a melody over the ipu, Kam and Jonny-Boy kicked in the guitar, and all of a sudden, it was music.

The next section was actually wordless, as Kam had composed a guitar piece that he originally thought to be part of a song about the warrior kings David and Kamehameha I, but when that whole Bible thing fell out

Merging traditions

the window, Noelani said let's keep the music and just go with it.

This was Ervin's favorite piece. He thought of all the times he had so much inside himself but never had the words to say 'em. And he always thought was his problem, that he was too slow or too stupid and yeah his friends who went take all his money never do anything for discourage his from feeling li'dat.

But, when he went do this hula, when he heard this music, he didn't feel weak or stupid at all. He didn't know why, but maybe get stuff too big, or too much for words?

And instead of feeling shame, he started feeling one love for the music and that's why he kept coming back, even when he was scared. Even after he went be one stupid idiot and let the money get wasted. Even Steve Yates went talk to him...and he finally replied.

Or when he came home night after fricking night to one house that was so cold, you couldn't even believe it was Hawai'i.

Of all the halau, Ervin alone was dressed in kahiko costume.

Noelani had him in some maile, dog teeth, and one malo, and when he came to the front of the stage, his father and mother cringed, and Ervin's so-called friends who had come by anyway, mostly to eat free food and check out the girls snickered and whispered, "Look that loser in da diaper, yeah?" And they were laughing until the big Hawaiian guy in front of them gave them stink eye, but that didn't keep them from making fun more quietly.

But Ervin wasn't thinking of them. He thought of his afternoon with Steve Yates. If everybody seeing him thought he was a nobody, then, that's what they thought. Not his problem. People walked past Steve Yates, thinking he was

*Truth independent of thoughts, feeling, beliefs

one haole. Or no one special. Never bother him. Never change one thing who he was.

He thought of Steve Yates. Then of Steve Yates and the music. Then, only the music.

Ervin opened his arms wide, and stared straight into the crowd. Suddenly Ervin let out with a war cry. High pitched and fierce, he had been working on it in secret with Saul for months. The big Hawaiians and Samoans in the audience cried back automatically, and their applause for a while drowned out the music.

Jonny-Boy nudged Saul, and Saul winked and kept playing.

Then Ervin's arms flexed, his legs tightened, and in the distance, as if on cue, the thunder struck.

I felt everything you did to me, he seemed to say. *Heard everything, felt the shame, the loss, the closed fist, the open hand. And you know what?*

It never broke me. I'm still here. I'm too strong.

And then he remembered what Steve Yates said about truth.

"Two questions. One you can answer. One you can't."

In that moment, Ervin finally understood what Yates had meant. Some truth he could answer. And what he could not? It wasn't that he didn't know. It was because he *was*.

And as he danced, he *was*, for his parents, for all those days they never spoke to him. His friends, who had betrayed him. And what they wanted to see—no, what they *had* to see—changed. Ervin's parents, Ervin's so-called friends, they all had stopped breathing, for reasons they didn't know, as Ervin stomped his dog-tooth anklets and glared, it seemed, directly at them.

The music stopped, and Ervin walked to the front of the stage, pointed at the crowd, then shouted at the heavens. In the light, his fingers even seemed dangerous and powerful. Some of the girls (and some guys, too) began shrieking and catcalling, with whispers of "he *sooo* ono, that one."

And then the singing resumed—and Noelani came onstage.

*   *   *

Dressed for now completely in one black muʻu-muʻu, not often a color used in hula, Noelani staggered and fell to the stage. *My god, she's really gone nuts,* thought Millicent, and even Ignacio, and the crowd hushed. But they didn't catch that she stumbled right next to a strand of maile.

She effortlessly picked it up in one gentle motion, held it to the heavens, and draped it around her neck. And Millicent knew right them that this was Noelani's tribute to her lost kumu.

Kam had put down his electric guitar for an acoustic, tuned to an open-G Wahine slack key tuning. Slack key style, so easy on the ears, so familiar...*just pull the strings and set them free.*

Noelani sang along with her dance, and was so gentle, so *nahenahe* that you could hear the last mist of rain veil upon the forest outside. It was as soft as Ervin's part was loud, but in its own way, even more powerful, as Noelani wove innocence with misunderstanding...her doubts with her faith, and everything, all of it, with hula.

This was a master at work, and the genius that Kahakunoe saw—not that she knew every nuance of the dances, not that she knew the history, the ancestry, but that with or without those details, she had a connection with the viewer, reaching through her dance into their souls. And in this song of mourning and birth, it was as if waves upon waves of remorse and contemplation overtook the crowd. And love.

A hand moves and the rain begins. A foot moves, and an ocean is crossed. Noelani's dance wept like the storm-tossed seabird that had finally reached these shores, only to find itself alone.

* * *

"Excuse me," Steve Yates coughed as he got up to leave. He didn't return right away, so Lisa excused herself, too, where she found him, Steve Yates, sobbing behind the seats.

"How did you find me?"

"I can always find you, dear."

"Lisa—what am I going to do without you?"

Lisa looked at him, shocked. "What do you mean? What you've always done." And Lisa looked at Steve, and for the first time felt strong. More than healthy. Strong. "Everything will be all right, love."

Roland Matsuoka ran past them with a bucket of boiled macaroni. "Kayla!" Roland shouted to his helper, "Kayla, we need more mac potato salad, so go mix this!"

"But I stay grilling the kalbi ribs!"

Lisa looked at Steve, and then winked. "Harry must be worried. Go find him. I've got to do something now." As she left, she wondered if this is what Steve felt when he left her, leaving the one he loved behind, yet knowing what must be done.

Roland was in full panic. They were overloaded. Yates's staff could help with plating and serving, but none of them were local cooks. Roland looked at the crowd, all waiting for food. "Shoots, Aunty said was going have enough! How we going make more mac salad now?"

"I'll do that."

And Roland looked and there was Lisa Yates. "Frances showed me how to make mac potato salad that night in your kitchen. And I'd love to help."

"Oh no—not you..." Roland sputtered. "You the hostess an'den!"

"Give me the macaroni, dammit!" Lisa took the large mixing bowl from his hand.

"Okay, okay, but put on one hair net! Kayla! Go get her one hair net! *Kayla!*"

Steve watched her go and tried (and almost succeeded) to stop crying.

As he got back to his seat, Noelani finished, and people began throwing flowers onto the stage...

And the flowers seemed to multiply as they came down, covering the stage with a fragrant cloud of multicolored petals.

And then the music opened up with the first chords of "In Da Beginning" and the crowd erupted, recognizing the song that elevated Ku'uipo to the top of the Island charts.

And there was no time to clean up anything, since the music was still playing, so the halau came out and right on top the petals.

The little halau began to dance. Frances Silva and Eva Matsuoka moved to the front, and Frances Silva marveled that in all her years and all those generations she had tried to dance, this was the first time she was ever in the front row. Usually, she was just in the back watching the dancer in front of her intently, trying not to forget the next move.

The dancing was nothing fancy. In fact, the crowd never

even notice anything special, but for Frances, for the first time in her long, long life, she felt like something other than a beginner. As she danced, she felt the stage lights on her face and found that it was real hard to look at the audience—she never noticed that before.

But she didn't care, because the first time her body knew the moves, her heart was open. She even smiled at the crowd—for the first time sure enough of herself to do so.

And reflected in their eyes she saw a dancer—a real dancer—free.

As Saul began "In Da Beginning," Kam tilted his head at the sound guy, who shrugged back. Something was different with Saul's voice. Like a chorus effect of many voices, many lives—the sound was ancient, immediate, eternal, and it felt like there were searing icicles being jabbed in his soul.

And the listeners nodded, as if they were all feeling this—that to each of them a voice was speaking truth.

Because after all these years, Saul finally knew who he was. And who she was, all in green. He knew. The times they had held each other. The times they were apart. The times he had died and come back for their love. Legendary times. And he took his hat off, to the lush, black curls, like time-polished coral, or the monk seal's endless eye. And, with all the passion of the ages, he sang, not in Hawaiian, or English, or Japanese or anything else—but in the purest language of the heart.

In Da Beginning
When everything was without form,
without time
even then, I loved you.
Even when day and night were made
the stars, the sun and moon...

Even when day and night were made
even then, I loved you.

When the islands were first made,
the first wave broke upon their shores,
when the first plant took root,
the first bird landed,
even then, I loved you.

When the first rains came
and the clouds obscured the sky
when the first rains parted,
and the first rainbow
reached out across the land,
even then, I loved you.

Even then, I loved you.
Even then, as I love you
even now.
Aloha... aloha au ia 'oe.

And his song to Hi'iaka called her home, in the middle of the night, when was all dark like that, to those who looked, it seemed that a wash of green hands and hair stretched over the sky to embrace him. It was a song so beautiful, that even Pele was glad.

It was the sort of thing Lisa would have cried over, had she not been elbow-deep in macaroni.

"Lisa! Hurry up, we stay almost out the mac salad!" Roland was busy shoveling another scoop rice on one 'nother plate. Lisa ran over to him with the next batch.

"Good good," Roland said. "Now try help Kayla with the takuan."

Lisa went over to Kayla, who was trying to slice picked

...ushes. "No, no!" Lisa said, "you have to hold the knife like this—sheesh—doesn't anyone ever take Home Economics anymore?"

*   *   *

Roland, scooped out the mac potato salad Lisa made and dropped it on one paper plate. The salad held its shape perfectly—right out of the scoop—no cling, no splash, no nothing.

Then he watched her working, working...and thought wow, that girl get potential, that one.

He was going continue that thought, but the whole place suddenly stopped. Noelani and her halau paused, and from inside them drew up that silence that they had worked on from those first days. And with all the families watching, all the people even on the Internet—it seemed like they were all held in the quiet, loving arms of God.

Nona Watanabe stepped onto the stage, as if across lava, in her purple and orange and green—sharkbait skin and all.

Something in her quiet halted the world. Folks stopped fidgeting, talking. They actually stopped eating, mid-bite, as she paused for a second, looking, it seemed, within each one of them. And then she smiled, and was like one pure hit of aloha.

And on her finger? A ring made of two interlocking fish, one silver, one gold. There was a center diamond, surrounded by one emerald, one amethyst, and one bright orange fire opal.

"Just be yourself, Nona," said the old lady in red. "That's all you ever had to be."

Tears streamed down Noelani's face, and she didn't care. As she watched her dancers working together, Nona

Watanabe in the front, she felt all her work, all her time finally being realized.

Millicent watched the hula, and knew, after all this time, why Aunty Kahakunoe wanted Noelani Choi to dance with them, to lead them. And deeper than that, she understood why Noelani had to leave, to a new place, a birthplace.

Forgive me for not seeing, 'Lani.

These *are* the ancient times—and these are modern times as well. In the sphere of eternity, distinctions between one time and another are arbitrary. Even now, Lo'ihi reaches skyward from beneath the sea—who will sit upon the shores of Kilauea and write the ancient chants for her?

Who will dance the dances that will be remembered only in part, scraps handed down from generation to generation, revered almost as much for what is lost as what is retained?

Are the ships and airplanes now any different from the outriggers in days past? Are the stars not the same, the sunsets the same colors? Don't the rains make the same sounds as they fall onto the forest canopy?

And as for Nona, she finally understood what it meant to simply be. That in her purples were all the colors of the sky and ocean at night. In her oranges and reds, the color of the sun, setting and rising. In her shimmering greens, the color of the forest, and sugarcane, and yes, even more ocean, and in her smile, the radiance of the sun itself.

The water, the fire, the wind, the day, the night. The clamorous green of the Kulani forests. The rocky serenity of the Ka'u desert.

Incongruous elements meet, blend, do battle. The fire meets the water. The fire cools, the water parts, and the land emerges from the sea.

The words, the music, the hands, the feet. Only when incongruous elements meet, blend, do battle, and resolve, can they become, like magic, the hula.

And then it was over. And for a few seconds, the audience was silent, as if it was waking from a dream.

And then someone stood up and clapped. Then everyone did, and as they cheered and thundered, a rainbow of fragrant flowers rained upon the stage. Noelani looked at Nona Watanabe and couldn't move. She had never seen anyone so beautiful in her life.

Finally, Noelani recovered enough to wave at Millicent and Ignacio. The kumu brought their halau back onstage to a final wave upon wave of applause.

In the commotion, Eva found her way to the microphone. "Okay everybody! Get plenty more food, and plenty more music, so eat up and enjoy!"

And the show became a party, and dancers mingled with audience, with the members of the various bands taking turns at the stage. Eva went back to join Roland and Lisa at the table, marveling at how much food everyone was eating.

"What stay moving, Roland? Nona's chicken?"

"Shoots, Aunty—your pork adobo! People coming back for seconds and..."

Roland trailed off as he saw his Aunty Eva— gently rocking, eyes closed, lips whispering syllables he was never meant to hear.

People were acting funny kine around Nona, wanting her to look at them but shying away as soon as she smiled. It was as if her dance had created an aura about her, amazing, but lonely, almost like she wanted to say "I the same person as before!" But no one would listen...

Then she saw Harry and Harry looked down, and she thought *Oh Harry—please no be like that, too!* But then she breathed a huge sigh of relief as she realized it was the same old Harry fumbling with a Tupperware, "I knew you must be hungry—so I made you musubi and eggs!"

The party went on deep into the night, but the next day, no matter how late everyone go in, even the Hawaiians, everyone felt magically as if they had gotten their 8 hours—maybe even a little more!

* * *

Throughout the performance, Gozo Shimabukuro had been looking for his friend Ciles Molina. He was nowhere to be found. Finally, he found another of his work friends from the old times, but when he asked him about Ciles, the other man turned pale and shook his head. "Cannot be, Gozo."

"What you mean, cannot be?"

"Gozo. Ciles Molina *make*. Was three years ago. I went his funeral myself."

* * *

In the days and weeks after the show, it became obvious that Steve Yates, as usual, was right. For every person at the show, a thousand more watched the webcast, forwarded it, and passed it to their friends and loved ones. In fact, for quite some time afterward, Steve found himself on being asked more about his concert than about his business.

Noelani and Kuʻuipo were swamped with invitations. This concert, that concert. Honolulu. Fiji. The State of Hawaiʻi wanted to know if they could use Nona Watanabe's image for one of its official tourist guides.

Lois Cabral was arranging a Kona tour with Kuʻuipo at the Hilo Bowl when her phone rang. "Yes, *yes?*" Was hard to hear above all the bowling. "Oh my God, that would be wonderful? Really? Of course! Yes! Thank you! No—thank *you!*"

Lois put her phone down. "That was Ellen Degeneres. She wants you on her show."

Fame?...

*   *   *

why
Not far away, Harry and Steve were having beer and pulling nut grass.

"Long time, yeah we never go fishing?" Harry said.

"Yeah." Steve looked out from where they were sitting and gasped. "Did you know you could see the ocean from your yard?"

Harry shook his head and smiled. "You mean, took you this long for notice? So, when we going fishing? He squinted at the horizon. Water going be good tonight."

Steve smiled, "We go, then!"

*   *   *

On Sunday, at the crack of dawn, Lisa Yates came into Matsuoka's. Eva looked at her and smiled at the eager popolo girl.

"Okay, first let me show you how we make the pork nishime." Eva paused, and a twinkle came into her eyes. "You going like this—came from a good family, this recipe."

*   *   *

Noelani used her Sunday morning to go back to church. First time in long time she went back, and when she walked inside, everyone went hug her and everything. Jonny-Boy hadn't been to church since small kid time, and he kept looking around for what to do, but Noelani told him relax, God not peeking over your shoulder...

And when the pastor began speaking, something inside Noelani changed, let go, as the form of Steve Yates appeared from behind what was behind the pulpit. She gasped, started to fall to her knees, but Yates caught her and held her up.

Blah

"Noelani. It's okay. It's okay."

"Where have you been?" she asked.

"I was always here," Yates said. "And always, always listening."

"And so were we," a voice said from behind her, and Noelani turned around and saw Aunty Kahakunoe and her kumu, and her kumu before that. It seemed the entire church had transformed into a vision of kumu going back through time.

"Yes, child. And we're so proud of you," Kahakunoe said, and the whole congregation nodded.

Another voice, farther away, yet just as immediate said "We've all been where you are right now—wondering about the meaning of the dance."

Yet another voice. "And each of us discovered, just as you, that the meaning of the dance is the wonder."

Then Noelani blinked and everything returned to what it was, and she smiled at Jonny-Boy, to the preacher, and the rain, and the silence in between.

*   *   *

Saul   Kam

Lohiau and Mele were at Blane's eating chicken, thinking about being on TV and their first Mainland tour.

They saw Nona drive by and waved.

"You know," Mele said, "I think I finally got it."

"What?"

"It. You know, that thing I was looking for when I came here."

"What, that you stay happy?" Lohiau sipped his beer. One day, he would go into the rain and never return. And Hi'iaka would be waiting with memories and brand new song.

"Yeah. My songs. Me."

"Well, of course. That's your name. Except for the Schulnam part."

"Schulman."

"Whatever."

"So, now what? On to tour, to fame, fortune and happily ever after?"

"Oh, I don't know." Saul laughed at Kam and adjusted his hat. "Things seem pretty good right about now."

* * *

Nona drove as far as she could, then walked out to where the lava was even then steaming into the ocean below.

"Is there anything I can do for you?" Nona had asked.

"Well—I always wanted to taste that chicken I keep hearing about..."

Nona brought out a Tupperware and leaned over the edge of the earth.

"What the hell?" A young park ranger nudged his partner as he saw the Japanese lady. "She shouldn't be out there— she's past the warning signs..."

"No, no—leave her alone. For Hawaiians this sacred place."

"What you mean Hawaiian? She's not Hawaiian."

"Stupid, you!" said the older, more perceptive man. "Try open your eyes."

The younger man looked again. He blinked and shook his head.

"Oh yeah, what was I thinking?"

And he waved and she waved back before she turned

back to the ocean and flung the chicken into the molten sea.

Epilogue

Lisa, the old lady, and a jar of red ohelo jam were sitting on what used to be jet-black lava. Now, it was cool, earthy brown, and plants had started to take root in the crevices. Life was beginning. And more.

"Look!" I pointed to where the ocean had been boiling. Just then, a fiery plume of lava erupted to the surface with the hungry wail of an infant child.

The two of us watched silently as the new island appeared for the first time.

"That going be my new home," I said.

"It will be a good place," Lisa replied.

"Yes, I think so. And you? How things?"

"Steve's busy as usual, but we are enjoying ourselves."

"Good, good. And Nona them?"

"Steve says they're still dancing."

And we sat there, the two of us, as the sky seemed to fill with music, and the island before us even in that short time grew large enough to catch the sun.

THE END

A Hilo Glossary

Note to mainlanders: This glossary will help you read like one local, but remember—reading pidgin and speaking pidgin stay two different things. So listen, take your time, and when you try talk, no worry if we stay laughing at you. We not trying for be mean! ;)

adobo – A yummy Filipino dish made with meat, garlic, vinegar, soy sauce, bay leaves, and sugar.

aholehole – Flagtail fish. Really tasty when breaded and fried!

aina – The land, and/or the spirit of the land.

alas – Testicles, as well as all the sensitivity and fortitude they imply.

aloha – Love, spirit, hello, goodbye, take care, see you soon... Think of "aloha" as Pidgin English MSG. It seems to make everything better, but when it's overused it gives some people a headache.

aloha au ia 'oe – I love you. And I do.

auana – Hula competition category based upon contemporary music. As opposed to kahiko.

Aunty – English word for tutu.

auwe – An expression of surprise or distress.

'awa – Hawaiian word for kava. Supposed to be good for help you relax. Back in the day, was prepared by having girls chew the root and spit in a cup. Then you drank the spit. Sheesh, why would you need to drink someone else's spit to relax when you stay in Hawai'i?

bonsan – Japanese Buddhist priest.

brah – A local surfer expression of familiarity that evolved from "brother."

buggah – Guy. Boy. Son-of-a-bitch. "That buggah, how he can afford go Vegas all the time?"

bumbye – Next time. Sooner or later. One day. From "by-and-by." "When we going movies?" "Bumbye." "You said 'bumbye" last week!" "I know, same bumbye." "Waste time, you! I going find another boyfriend."

broke da mouth – Delicious. Tasty.

chop suey – This is NOT the American-Chinese food. In Hawai'i, "chop suey" means "mixed up," which is closer to its original meaning, anyway.

choke – A lot. Plenty.

da kine – The most important phrase in all of Hawai'i. What's for dinner? Da kine. Who you went vote for? Da kine. Where you like go fishing? Da kine.

daikon – A long, fat, white Japanese radish. In the summer when you put on shorts and Grandma says you get daikon legs, sure you get mad, but you cannot do nothing because she stay your grandma.

duck soup – Simple. Easy. No problem.

furo – Japanese word for bath. Originally, it meant bathing in a wood-fired outdoor tub, but now, any bath will do. So listen to Grandma and go furo right now!

fut – Fart. "Fart" sounds strange to pidgin speakers because the Hawaiian okole doesn't usually make an "r" sound.

goza – A thin rollable mat made of woven straw. Always

have one in your car in case you decide at the last minute to have a picnic.

garans – guaranteed. A sure thing.

garans ballbarans – A really sure thing.

gutfunnit – Magical swear word of unknown origin. Why is it magical? Okay, just say "gutfunnit!" right now. Come on, do it! Now, don't you feel better already?

halau – A group dedicated to learning and developing hula.

haole – Caucasian. Can be neutral or pejorative, depending on context, or the haole.

high mukka-mukka – Very rich. Mukka-mukka evolved from the Mainland slang term "mucky-muck."

Hi'iaka – Pele's sister, Goddess of the Hula and the rain.

Hoku – Kind of like a Hawaiian Grammy.

holo-holo – To go out, exploring for whatevahs.

ho'olaule'a – A music festival/gathering.

ika – Squid.

i'o – The Hawaiian hawk.

ipu – A dried and hollowed gourd used as a percussive instrument in Hawaiian mele, especially in hula kahiko.

kahiko – Hula competition category based upon ancient chant. As opposed to auana.

kahuna – Priest, seer, healer. Kanaka odaisan.

kakimochi – Rice crackers, often flavored with seaweed or wasabi, or some other salty spicy flavor. Goes well with beer.

kalua – Slow cooking, traditionally done underground in one pit, or imu. Nowadays, one oven on low heat works fine. Usually associated with kalua pig.

kamaboko – Japanese fish cake, a little rubbery, but good in saimin and the occasional omelet. Or omelette, if you like be more classy.

kanaka – Ethnic Hawaiian.

kaukau – "Food" as a noun and "eat" as a verb. Yes, you can kaukau kaukau. Hopefully the kaukau you kaukau stay ono.

keiki – Child.

kine – Type. Variety. "What kine fish that?" "Papio."

kokua – Help. "Thank you for buying our kulolo! Your kokua going help our team get new uniforms!"

kolohe – Rascal. Mischievous.

kukae – Excrement. One reason why you never wear slippers in da house.

kulolo – One dessert made with coconut and taro. Kids groups like soccer teams, canoe clubs, or hula halau set tables up outside supermarkets and sell kulolo for fundraisers. Ono, but rich and gives some people the runs.

kumu – Teacher. Also, foundation or base.

ku'uipo – Sweetheart. A ubiquitous word on Hawaiian jewelry.

li'dat – Like that.

li hing – Li hing started with li hing mui, salted and spiced dried plums. The spices started showing up on everything, and suddenly we had li hing shaved ice, gummy bears, popcorn and tequila. One of the weirder food developments in the islands.

Lohiau – Hi'iaka's true love.

lolo – Stupid.

lomi salmon – Get salted salmon (make sure add plenty or people going talk stink), get onions, get tomato. Chop and mix in one bowl. Add ice. Serve cold on top hot rice or poi!

lumpia – Filipino egg rolls, only tastier. If you are in college, and your roommate's mother brings lumpia all the time, you will gain weight, garans balbarans.

mahalo – "Thank you." An unfortunate misunderstanding sometimes occurs because Hawaiian businesses (such as the local McDonald's) often put "Mahalo" on their trash bins. Tourists, however, sometimes assume "mahalo" means "trash," which has led some poor souls to feel insulted when all that was meant was "Here's your Happy Meal, please come back again."

malo – A type of loincloth reminiscent of Hawaiian warrior garb and often used in kahiko performances. You wear one malo, you better have one nice okole.

makai – Down toward the ocean, away from the mountain. Opposite of "mauka." Where high mukka-mukka haoles like build hotels.

make – Dead. Deceased. Any time in this book that "make" makes no sense, try read 'em instead as make.

make A – Make an ass.

make-die-dead – Really, really dead.

malasada – Fried dough balls with sugar on top. Originally from Portugal, they are made in both airy and doughy styles. Tex Drive-In in Honokaa make the best, although the O'ahu people like Leonard's malasadas. Oh, those O'ahu people!

manang – Filipina.

manong – Filipino.

mauka – Up toward the mountain, away from the ocean. Opposite of "makai."

mele – Song, tune, or musical story, as in a chant.

monku – To complain, bitch, give the silent treatment, or otherwise act hurt. Everyone has his or her own monku style.

mukka-mukka – Rich. "Mukka-mukka" evolved from the Mainland slang term "mucky-muck."

musubi – Rice balls, which are not balls, but are triangles. The rice is usually salted to prevent spoilage and wrapped in seaweed. Often, the musubi are stuffed with ume.

mu'u-mu'u – A long flowing dress made with Hawaiian print fabric. Worn by aunties to weddings and hula dancers during auana performances.

nahenahe – Gentle as the softest island breeze.

natto – Fermented soybeans. Most people no like. That's okay; get more for me.

nene – The Hawaiian goose, adapted to life on the lava plains. The state bird of Hawai'i.

ni'ele – Nosey. Always want to get in your business. Waste time ni'ele neighbors! Urusai!

nishime – Japanese stew made with meat, seaweed, lotus root, shiitake mushrooms and other various vegetables. Traditional New Year's dish and comfort food throughout the year.

odaisan – Priest, seer, healer. Japanese kahuna.

ohana – Family, in all senses of the word. Very important concept when you stay on an island.

ohelo – A bright red berry that grows at higher elevations in the Volcano area in Kilauea. Tart and sweet, it makes the most ono jelly. Sacred to Pele.

ohi'a – Sacred trees to Hi'iaka. Ohia trees produce Lehua flowers.

okazu – Food. Usually associated with plate lunches.

okole – Butt. Rear-end. Strange to have "okole" right next to "okazu."

oli – Hula monologue or chant. Always in Hawaiian.

ono – Tasty, delicious. Broke da mouth.

opae – Small kine shrimp the keikis catch with nets. Good for bait, or you can dry or salt them for eat on top rice.

opihi – Hawaiian limpet. Getta pry 'em off da rock, but some ono!

pake – Chinese. Get reputation for having plenty money. But not for you.

pau – Finished. Completed.

papio – The juvenile, schooling form of the Giant Trevally. Despite being juveniles they can be over a foot long, and are a major local food fish.

Pele – The Volcano Goddess. Appears in a variety of forms and temperaments, including the narrator of this book.

pikake – Hawaiian jasmine. One of the most beautiful scents in the world.

pilau – Filthy. Dirty. Dishonest.

pilikia – Danger. Trouble. Stay away kine stuff.

poke – A local dish made of chunks of raw fish (like ahi or aku), squid, or octopus, mixed with seaweed and kukui nut paste. Onions and tomatoes are often included, too. Sort of like tartare or ceviche, but the fish is not denatured by lime.

popolo – Person of African descent.

porogee – Portuguese. Also a slang for talkative. Because they often are.

pupule – Crazy.

saimin – The official soup noodle dish of Hawai'i. Made with egg noodles and (usually) fish stock, it is topped with a variety of ingredients, including Spam kamaboko, eggs, onions, and char siu (Chinese pork). Saimin is an iconic Hawaiian food, perhaps the single most popular and universal dish in all of the islands. NEVER tell a Hawai'i person that ramen is better than saimin.

shishi – Urinate.

slack key – A fingerstyle guitar technique in one of a group of open tunings. Developed by Hawaiians and visiting cowboys, traditional Hawaiian guitar music is almost always played in slack key.

stay – Often used in place of "is" or "am" in a sentence. If you just broke up with your boyfriend, but you no like people worry, you say, "No worry. I stay fine."

stink eye – Giving someone a dirty look. "Stink eye" has evolved into a high art form among certain of Hawaii's people.

talk story – Chat, share, hang out with a friend for no reason only you like just hang out and talk. Not for any reason, just for talk story.

tako – Octopus.

Tupperware – Nothing says "picnic" in Hawai'i like Tupperware. Then again, nothing says "the pickled eggplant Aunty Mavis keeps making that you hate, but don't have the heart to throw away" like Tupperware, either.

tutu – Could be your actual aunty, or some random old lady whom you need to be polite to for one reason or another (like a friend of your mother's).

ulu – Breadfruit, and a popular quilting pattern inspired by breadfruit.

'uli 'uli – Feathered gourd rattles used in traditional Hawaiian hula.

ume / umeboshi – A Japanese salted plum, often put in the center of a musubi. Often removed by fussy keikis who just like plain rice.

urusai – Annoying, like Jehovah's Witnesses knocking on your door Sunday morning when you were trying for sleep in.

wahine – Woman.

weke – Goatfish. No laugh! Ono, you know!

ABOUT THE AUTHOR

RYKA AOKI

RYKA AOKI has been honored by the California State Senate for her "extraordinary commitment to free speech and artistic expression, as well as the visibility and well-being of Transgender people." Ryka earned an MFA in Creative Writing from Cornell University and is the recipient of a University Award from the Academy of American Poets. She is a professor of English at Santa Monica College. Find out more on her web site www.rykaryka.com.

CPSIA information can be obtained
at www.ICGtesting.com
Printed in the USA
LVHW08s1331280818
588389LV00020B/863/P

9 781627 290074